THE GIRL
IN THE
DARK

BOOKS BY ZOË SHARP

ZOË SHARP

THE GIRL IN THE DARK

bookouture

Published by Bookouture in 2024

An imprint of Storyfire Ltd.
Carmelite House
50 Victoria Embankment
London EC4Y 0DZ

www.bookouture.com

ISBN: 978-1-80019-905-7
eBook ISBN: 978-1-80019-904-0

For Ayo Onatade
One of crime fiction's greatest friends

ONE

If I'm late, he'll kill me.

The thought dominates Tess's mind as she scurries between the stalls of the crowded market. She clutches her bag to her chest, desperate for a cigarette to calm her tattered nerves.

Smoking is something else he disapproves of. Every time Tess lapses, he can tell as soon as he walks in. Once, she tried to explain how his expectation made it harder to resist the craving. Only once.

It took days for the bruises to fade.

There's a young Ukrainian woman who works as a carer in the flats across the street. She and Tess bump into each other coming and going, often enough that the woman noticed the marks. Tess told her she'd tripped on the stairs, knowing – maybe even hoping – that she'd see straight through the lie.

He makes sure Tess avoids the neighbours now.

Still, at least she gets to shop on her own – if she doesn't dawdle. She fumbles in her pocket for her phone and checks the countdown timer. She has to send him a picture every fifteen minutes, just to prove where she's got to. It's almost time. She should be at the dry cleaners by now, to pick up his shirts, but there was a queue in the chemist's...

She picks up her pace. Distracted by the rolls of pretty fabric on one of the stalls, she isn't prepared when someone cannons into her shoulder, knocking her off balance and spinning her round. Tess almost drops her bag.

'Sorry,' she mutters, a reflex now. 'I'm so sorry.'

The stranger lurches on without speaking. A woman, Tess sees. She is relieved because if anybody sees her talking to another man – however innocent it might be – and *he* checks up on her...

But as Tess watches, her relief turns to anxiety. The woman staggers, tripping over her own feet. She collides with the side of a big wheelie bin, hard enough to make Tess wince, and folds over the railing next to it like falling cloth. Halfway down, she grabs for the top rail and clings to it.

Tess hesitates, torn. She's unwilling to simply walk away, equally reluctant to get involved – to provoke scrutiny on her world.

She's probably drunk...

But the woman looks at her then – right into her eyes. And where Tess expects to see glassy oblivion, instead a terrified awareness stares back. As if the woman is trapped inside her body as it fails her, and neither of them have any idea how to make it stop.

Tess glances across at the dry cleaner's shop on the far side of the stalls. She bites her lip. Then she turns her back on it and leans over the woman, reaching out.

'Are you all right?'

An inane question. From the way she's wrapped one arm around her head, the woman is in agony. Maybe a migraine – they can make people sick and dizzy, Tess knows. She is close enough to see the mist of sweat on the woman's upper lip, the waxy tint to her skin.

The woman says something Tess doesn't quite catch. She frowns, tilts her ear closer. The woman speaks again, louder this time, and Tess realises it's not her hearing that's at fault.

The words are scribble – a meaningless jumble of sounds.

The woman blinks in surprise, as if she can't understand it either. She tries again, with the same result.

'I'm sorry,' Tess says again, feeling helpless. 'I don't...'

The woman tries to take a step closer, but as soon as she lets go of the railing, she can't keep her feet. Her right leg buckles. Her right arm now dangles useless by her side. If she were older, Tess would think she was having a stroke, but the woman looks to be maybe in her forties. Not young, but not old either.

Tess casts about her, hoping someone else will take over. For once, she would welcome being taken charge of, being told what to do. *Even by him.* The market is busy, but suddenly no one is looking. Not long enough to count, anyway. Just hurried glances – their disapproval diluted by distance and indifference.

Each gaze melts away when Tess tries to catch hold of it. She can tell they think her a fool for stepping in, and they have no wish to add their foolishness to hers.

From Tess's pocket comes a warning buzz. She grabs her phone to silence the timer, aware of a momentary spike of fear that it's sounded when she is not yet where she should be. Only then does she remember what is in her hand – what else it does.

'I'll get you some help, OK?' she tells the woman, hitting the first of the three nines. 'They'll send someone.'

The woman paws at Tess's arm and speaks again, making a colossal effort to produce two slurred, but almost recognisable, words.

Tess freezes.

Did she just say 'No, please'? Or was it 'No police'?

The woman drops to her knees, slumps onto one side. She is still gripping one stanchion of the railings with her left hand. Her body begins to shake and twitch, her limbs to thrash. Tess is horrified by the hollow clunk of the woman's skull bouncing against the paving slabs, by the way her eyes have rolled back in their sockets so only the whites show. Vomit spurts from the woman's mouth, and Tess jerks back.

Around them, everyone keeps walking. In a burst of shameful selfishness, Tess wishes she had, too.

Then the phone connects and the operator says, 'Emergency services, which service do you require?'

'Ambulance!' Tess hears the squawk in her voice, swallows. 'You need to send an ambulance. Watney Market. This woman... she just collapsed in front of me. I think she's dying!'

On the line, the operator is asking if the casualty is breathing and conscious. On the ground, the woman quietens to a shiver. Tess can see her eyes again. They swivel upwards, lock with hers, showing a mix of panic and resignation.

'No,' Tess whispers. 'Come on. Don't do this...'

But the woman takes a deep, hitching breath, and says one word with calm precision: 'Blake.' Then her eyes drift closed, and she goes still.

Tess murmurs, 'Who in the world is Blake?'

The taste of failure is sour on her tongue.

She doesn't wait for the ambulance.

She runs.

TWO

MILE END ROAD, BOW

Six weeks later

The address Blake had been given was a stone's throw from Mile End Underground Station. Derelict flats above a row of shops, fire-damaged at one end from the third floor up to the charred rafters. Late eighteenth century, the building had stood through the London Blitz, only to be laid low by rat-chewed wiring. Now held in stasis by disputed insurance claims, unpaid contractors, and planning limbo.

It was perfect.

Blake arrived after dark. As dark as it ever got in London, where there was only light and its absence, and that contrast created pockets of utter black.

In the shadows lurked those who'd fallen through the cracks

.

Those without home, without help, without hope.

Blake had enough experience of those things that she approached the building with care. She circled the exterior, and saw the figure loitering beneath the rusting metal staircase at the rear, long before he saw her. The glow from the screen of his mobile phone stood out like a beacon. She recognised him from soup kitchens and church halls, round and about.

Blake got within touching distance before she murmured a quiet greeting that had him jumping out of his skin. He tried to cover a yelp of surprise with a cough that turned real as he almost swallowed his dog-eared roll-up.

'Alwyn, isn't it?' she said, eyeing his hacking with concern. She made no moves to touch him. When you had no private space, crossing that last boundary was like walking into a stranger's house, unannounced and uninvited.

'Ace. I go by Ace,' he managed at last, wheezing. 'I know you. New, aren't you?'

'Uh-huh. How many inside?'

He shrugged. 'Dunno. Quite a few, I think. Cold tonight. Room up top.'

'You on sentry duty?'

'Nah, just... y'know, having a smoke.'

He gave a dismissive wave, continuing to cough more like a man in his eighties than not far past eighteen. Blake didn't ask him about the mobile phone she'd seen him checking. He would have denied having it anyway. Nobody admitted to owning anything that might be valuable. Not if they wanted to keep it.

The chipboard covering one of the doorways had been levered open. She squeezed through, pausing to let the feel of the building settle around her.

As she moved through the lower floors, Blake found most of the prime spots already taken. Word spread quickly when there was still the prospect of night frost, even snow. It was almost the end of March, but it had been a long, hard winter.

She followed the man's advice and found space on the top floor of the end-terrace flat. Servants' quarters, originally, with lower ceilings and meaner windows, tucked up under the mansard roof. Unpopular now because no insulation let the cold leach in.

Still, the women had staked a claim there. The men took the lower floors and would police each other to see those under the eaves were not disturbed.

Even on the fringes of society, among the outcasts, there were unwritten rules.

And she was glad of them.

Blake edged around the sleeping bodies, inured now to the stink of necessity. Hardened, too, to the rasping, the coughing and mumbling – even those who ranted in their sleep.

It was the ones who wept in the night who still got to her, every time.

She rolled into her sleeping bag, fully dressed down to her boots, and slid the small backpack under her head. Partly as a pillow, partly as a precaution. She threaded one arm through the straps. Just because there were rules, of a sort, didn't mean no one would break them.

As she lay, eyes open in the dark, Blake wondered about her fellow travellers, where they'd come from and where they were going. She could make out nothing of the other women except vague humps in the gloom, like piled earth on new graves. Maybe she'd ask.

Tomorrow will be soon enough.

But tomorrow never came.

Blake hardly seemed to close her eyes before they snapped open again. She was sitting bolt upright, still zipped into her sleeping bag, heart punching in her chest. She had no idea how much time had passed, but it was pitch dark.

She sensed restless movement from maybe half the others. Those who were still new to living rough and slept like prey animals – shallow and scared. The others were cushioned by drink, or drugs – or a mix of both – not to wake even if the building fell around them.

'What is it?' a voice whispered from alongside her. Young, scared.

Blake froze. 'I don't know. I thought I heard—'

From far below came a crash. Shouted voices, breaking glass, boots heavy on the stairs, and the clatter of gear. Then a bellow from one of the men sleeping downstairs.

'Raid!'

Blake tore open the zip on the sleeping bag and staggered upright, kicking free of it. The pack was small enough not to slow her down. She hesitated a moment, then swung it onto her back. It contained everything of current value to her, and she would leave it behind only as a last resort.

Someone shoved past her, bolting for the doorway. Others followed, jostling as they stumbled towards the stairs.

Blake held back. Before coming inside last night, she'd thoroughly checked out the building. She had learned a long time ago never to get herself into somewhere she didn't know the way out of. Or preferably several ways out.

So, she slipped into the corridor and moved away from the main staircase. Already, she could see beams of torches jolting up from below as the cops cleared the building. She'd barely taken two steps before she felt a hand on her sleeve.

Instinct kicked in. Blake twisted loose, heard a startled gasp. She glanced back, but against the fractured light from below she could make out no features.

'Sorry, I'm sorry,' a voice mumbled. Blake recognised it – the girl who'd been sleeping alongside her. 'It's just... Where are you going?'

'I saw another way out.' She jerked her head towards the fire-damaged part of the building.

'But... is it safe?'

'Dunno. You want to trust the cops instead, then follow the others.' Without waiting for a reply, Blake hurried on. She paused at the end of the corridor, letting her eyes readjust to the darkness. Part of her worried the girl might want to tag along. And part of her was afraid she might not.

After a moment, Blake knew she was alone. She sighed, pushing through the heavy polythene sheeting hung by the builders. It was ink black on the other side. She risked firing up her phone to shed some light, used its dimmest torch setting to avoid the missing sections of flooring and charred stud-work.

The place stank of burned timber and plastic, an acrid stench that quickly drove out the more human smells filling her nostrils. The girl's fears for the safety of the structure proved unfounded. The builders had laid scaffolding planks across any sections of floor they didn't like the look of. Blake reasoned that if this was enough to take the weight of an average brickie or plasterer, she would be fine.

Even so, she didn't linger.

A minute or two later, she reached a door leading out onto a metal fire escape at the side of the building. The last section of ladder let down into a narrow alleyway running front to rear. Blake suspected the rusted mechanism would make a god-awful noise in operation – if it worked at all – so she climbed over the railing and dangled herself as close to the ground as she could, then let go.

The cold concrete leapt up to meet her, slapping hard at the soles of her boots as she dropped and rolled. She came to her feet again, crouched low in the shadows. The rear of the building was lit up like a Christmas storefront. She could see the reflected bright white of torches and headlights, and strobing blue from the collection of vehicles crammed into the yard.

'So, two-point-five crimes committed in London every minute,' she muttered under her breath, 'and *this* is what you do with yourselves, eh?'

Blake knew she should go – get out of there before the police spread their net any wider – but that would mean abandoning the others to their fate.

Whoever they might be.

With a quiet sigh, she edged forwards until she could peer around the corner of the building.

There were four police vans as well as half a dozen squad cars in the yard or the service road leading into it. Blake read the name of a twenty-four-hour security firm on the side of another van, further back. A couple of blokes in the firm's livery carried steel security grilles towards the entrance to the flats.

Blake felt the anger in the tensing of her shoulders. OK, so having homeless people squatting in the building left the place in a bit of a mess, but it wasn't as if they stole anything. Or wrecked anything beyond forcing loose a few boards or locks to get in. What did it say for society that adequate shelter stood empty while human beings slept out in all weathers? That property was worth more than people?

The cops started bringing them out. Some came under their own steam. Some had to be marched out, wrestled, or dragged. It was two thirty in the morning. They had been asleep in a safe haven. In the harsh lights, most looked groggy and bewildered, but a few were more belligerent. Blake saw one young man putting up a struggle, winced at the thwack of a baton against his elbow, making him howl.

After that, there was little resistance. Men and women alike were herded together in the middle of the yard, no allowances made for state of health or mind. A couple of the uniforms began demanding ID, asking questions.

Meanwhile, Blake saw more cops emerge from the building. They were carrying the sleeping bags, rucksacks, clothing that had been left behind. For a moment, Blake thought they were going to leave them for the owners to collect. But, as she watched, they carried it all past the waiting homeless and threw it into the open back of a police van. One of the officers made a comment about getting the vehicle fumigated later. The others laughed.

'Hey, that's *mine*. You can't just take it. You got no right!'

A black girl pushed her way through to the front. She was barely in her teens, small, thin, her cornrowed hair gathered in a loose ponytail. Blake recognised her immediately and swore under her breath.

She swore again when the girl shoved past one of the cops forming a loose ring around them, tried to reach the van holding her gear. Two cops – a man and a woman – went to grab her. The man was easily twice her size, and smiling. Clearly, he took in the girl's small stature... and underestimated her.

The girl kicked him in the shins and dodged past the woman. She made it halfway across the yard before they recovered enough to go after her. The male copper's baton to the side of the girl's knee sent her sprawling onto the concrete with a cry of pain. The cry was repeated as they wrenched one arm up behind her in a vicious lock.

Blake's breath hissed out. She rounded the corner of the building and charged towards them.

'Oy, leave her alone!'

She knew she couldn't go in hard enough to cause them any real damage – that wasn't her intention. Her only aim was to distract them from hurting the girl any further. So she pretended not to see the male copper's obvious counter to her attack, and let him take her down.

The cops patted her pockets, taking her phone. Then they bundled the pair of them into the cage in one of the larger vans and slammed the doors.

Blake tilted her head back against the steel side panel and let out a long breath.

Not quite how I saw this evening ending.

She glanced across, saw the raw scrape across the girl's chin where she'd hit the ground, the way she was gripping her knee. 'You all right?'

'Had worse.' The girl shrugged, hesitated a moment, then asked, 'You?'

'Just about.' She gave a wry smile. 'I'm Blake, by the way.'

'Kensy.'

I know...

Blake leaned forwards. 'Listen—'

But the van doors swung open again and a shrieking wildcat was thrust inside. The coppers let go, and the cage door slammed behind the spitting fury who kicked the bars, yelling abuse.

The woman was scrawny, even bulked by layers of torn clothing, her skin bad and straw-coloured hair lank.

Blake recognised her at once.

'Hey, Caz! Calm down. It's not like they're going to let you out, is it?'

After another few expletives, the thin woman threw herself onto the bench near Kensy and scowled at them both. One leg jittered.

'Don't need you to tell me that! Not stupid, am I? Just wanna ride with Tris.' She kicked the cage door again.

Kensy flinched.

Old Tristram had been on the streets for years. Caz, barely out of her teens, latched onto him not long after she appeared. When Blake first saw them together, she'd been suspicious of the woman's motives for hanging around with the old man. The possibility that Tristram took some kind of anti-psychotic medication, with a street value, was not one she ignored.

'You'll have to be patient,' a female PC said, bringing the next woman shuffling to the cage door. 'You know I can't put you in with the blokes.'

'That's against me human rights, that is!'

'Oh aye?' The copper snorted. 'Get your barrister to take it up with the European Court.'

The new arrival took a seat on Blake's side, as far from Caz as she could get. Kensy, too, tried to edge further away.

Caz glared. 'What's your problem?'

'Nothing,' Kensy muttered, head down.

Caz half rose, loomed over the youngster and prodded her in the chest with one bony finger. 'You got a problem with me, you tell me to my face, yeah? Or I'll—'

'Sit down,' Blake said, voice stony. 'Shut up. And leave her alone.'

Caz turned on her, eyes flared so the whites gleamed. Blake kept her face expressionless. Caz must have seen something nevertheless. She subsided, threw herself back onto the bench.

Kensy used Caz's distraction to swap over, sidling close to Blake's shoulder.

It wasn't until they were fully loaded and on the move that Kensy spoke again, low enough for only Blake to hear.

'Thanks... But why did you do it?'

'Do what?'

'Stand up for me? Before... and at the squat.'

Blake kept her face blank.

'I didn't do it for you,' she said.

Which was the truth.

Just not all of it.

THREE

LIMEHOUSE POLICE STATION

'Wakey, wakey. Rise and shine.'

The uniformed copper banged open the hatch in Kensy's cell door with more gusto than he needed to, in her opinion. If he'd hoped to jolt her awake, though, he was bound for disappointment. By the time she and the others had been taken back to the cop shop at Limehouse, searched, processed, and dumped in the cells, it was almost morning anyway.

No time to sleep.

Besides, in here, Kensy was scared of every loud noise, every shout and cry, in a way she'd never been scared out on the streets, or even kipping in some grotty squat. That and the constant ache from her knee.

They know exactly where to hit you.

And she hated being watched – by the coppers who flipped open the spyhole in the door, or those monitoring the camera mounted high in one corner. Growing up as a black kid, in the system, had taught her that anyone in authority was to be trusted about as far as she could throw them.

Also, she wished they'd put her in with Blake.

Like they were ever going to do that...

There was something reassuring about the young woman who'd come to her defence, back there in the yard. It happened so rarely, especially now. Somehow, she knew Blake had been there, done that, and could handle anything that came her way. It would have been good to have someone she could trust again.

But she was alone.

She was still sitting propped in a corner of her bunk when the cell door swung open.

'All right, Kensy, let's have you.'

For a moment, she thought they'd come to take her back to the care home. The fear sucked all the moisture from her tongue.

'What's going on?'

'You're being released. No charges – this time. You just watch yourself in future, though, eh?'

She scrambled up, followed the copper out of the cell, limping stiffly. 'What about my stuff?'

'Gone to the incinerator,' the man said, offhand. 'Infested with fleas and lice, wasn't it? Health hazard.'

'No way! That's a load of—'

He sniffed, pointedly, and her face flamed.

'Well, you try stayin' clean when you don't have no regular shower or nothin', and no hot water.'

He didn't respond to that, just jerked his head. She edged past him, out into the corridor. Most of the doors to the other cells stood open and empty.

'What about Blake?'

'Who?' The copper barely paused. 'What about 'em?'

'Is she still here, or you let her go already?'

'Oh, *her*.' The man grunted. 'No, we've been told to hang on to her.'

'Why? What's she done?'

Again, he ignored her, handing her over to the custody sergeant at the front desk. Kensy reclaimed her phone with relief, clutching the pink sparkly cover, dotted with unicorns. It was silly – childish, even – but at least nobody tried to steal it. And if they ever did, she'd know it anywhere.

Before she could persist about Blake, the outer door opened and a smallish man in a three-quarter-length dark overcoat strode in. He had olive skin that would hold a tan, dark hair brushing his collar, and he walked in as if he owned the place.

Her eyes flicked over him. The overcoat was wool, tailored and expensive. His shoes were polished to a high shine, and he wore soft black leather gloves Kensy would have killed for.

She'd learned to make snap judgements of people – whether to approach or avoid. The new arrival looked like he might have an ego to match his bank balance. Somebody's high-priced brief?

'I've been notified that you're holding Blake Claremont,' he said at the desk. 'My name is John Byron.'

His voice surprised Kensy. Oh, it was posh enough, but quieter than she'd expected, without that entitled edge. The custody sergeant eyed him with weary disdain – until the man passed over his ID.

'Yes, sir! Right this way.'

That reaction triggered sirens inside Kensy's head.

Not a brief, and not quite a copper, so who is he? Someone high up the food chain, for sure – important enough to make the rest of 'em jump. So, what does he want with Blake?

Taking advantage of the distraction, Kensy slipped out of the front entrance with her head down. Bitter disappointment coated her tongue. Just when she thought she'd found someone who'd help her – who might watch her back – it seemed Blake needed to watch her own.

A small, ragged group had gathered on the pavement outside, huddled together against the spray thrown up by six lanes of traffic on West India Dock Road. They tensed as Kensy appeared, relaxing only slightly when they recognised one of their own.

She nodded to those she knew. Spider, who'd been on the receiving end of a police baton last night, too. He was still cradling the arm they'd hit.

Old Tristram, muffled with wild grey beard and wilder hair sticking out in all directions. He was a northerner, who sometimes used long words Kensy didn't understand. He'd been around longer than most could remember and, way back, he'd had some serious schooling. It just went to show that anyone could end up on the streets. Some days he seemed almost sane.

His usual sidekick was the Glaswegian teenager, Caz. On the surface, they were chalk and cheese. But Caz had latched onto him as her protector. Or maybe she was his – it was hard to tell.

Nobody liked admitting they were scared of Caz, who could kick off good style if she was in the mood. Kensy knew she'd been about to go ballistic in the cop van last night – didn't like to think what might have happened if Blake hadn't been there to face her down.

Kensy perched on the low wall by the noticeboards outside the main door and gingerly stretched her leg. Spider perched next to her. They both powered up their phones. He'd decorated his with a cool image of Spider-Man, for the same reason she had unicorns.

'How is it?' Kensy asked him, nodding to his arm.

'Sore. Bastards,' he mumbled, grimacing, flexing his fingers so the web tattoo across his hand rippled. 'What about you?'

'Oh, I'll be all right in a couple of days,' Kensy lied with a cheerfulness she didn't feel.

Never let weakness show.

'I tell you – they have it in for all of us,' Tristram said, sounding calm for once. Kensy caught a few rolled eyes at his words. 'Orders from on high, take it from me. They've been told to "reduce the negative impact of rough sleepers on the public by removing tents and bedding from inappropriate locations", so that's what they're doing. Clearing us out, moving us on.'

'What's so "inappropriate" about us kipping in some old wreck of a building – one nobody's using, eh?' Caz demanded. 'Not like we was camped out in the middle of Mayfair, was it?'

Tristram shook his head. 'They try to tell you, if you're a victim of crime, go to the cops,' he said, gesturing at the building behind them. 'But it's no use doing that when *the police themselves are the thieves!*' His voice rose, as if he was *trying* to get himself nicked again.

Feet were shuffled and nervous glances cast towards the station entrance.

Caz took Tristram's arm. 'How about we go find a nice cuppa?' she suggested, her voice over bright. 'St Anne's ain't far. We could try there, hey?'

As they began to move, two mid-size vans pulled into the spaces reserved for cop cars directly outside the station. Both bore the logo of a charity Kensy had only vaguely heard of – Kinfolk.

'Ah, there's good timing,' Spider said. He sounded relieved.

Tristram paused, threw him a dark look. 'Don't be a fool, son. You know the cost of their so-called kindness just as well as anyone.'

'Yeah, well, some of us aren't in no position to be fussy.'

'What does that mean?' Kensy struggled to her feet, tried and failed to catch Tristram's eye. She tried to keep her weight on her good leg. 'Spider? Why did he say that?'

Spider didn't answer.

One of the Kinfolk drivers, a big Asian guy, stayed behind the wheel. Two women got out. An old saying flashed into Kensy's head – something about speaking softly but carrying a big stick. Maybe the women were the soft-spoken part. The guy, he was the stick. He looked the part, anyway – glowering from the cab. Sometime in the past, his nose had been broken and he still looked mad about it.

The women smiled a welcome. One was tall, with long pale hair in dreadlocks. She wore a loose, coarse-knit sweater and patchwork jeans. The other woman was smaller, Asian – a little plump but no less attractive for that – in a long turquoise tunic over matching close-fit trousers. There was something familiar about her. One or two people even called out to her by name.

'"Adhiti"?' Kensy repeated under her breath. '*Oh*. Oh, I've seen her on the telly! She does those cooking shows. Adhiti...?'

'Chatterjee,' Spider said. 'Yeah, that's her.'

'But what's *she* doing here?' Kensy blinked as the first splatters of rain blew into her eyes. 'And what's Kinfolk?'

'Kinfolk?' Spider paused. 'Well, if you wanna listen to Old Tris, they're all part of this big conspiracy, yeah?' he said, just as Tristram, Caz, and a couple of others hurried away, heads down into the weather. 'But if you was to ask me, they're who's gonna offer you a decent meal, a hot shower, and a crib – out of the rain with no preaching. So, I'll let *you* decide.'

FOUR

LIMEHOUSE POLICE STATION

John Byron had no doubt that his former status as a detective superintendent with the Met's much-whispered-about Special Projects Investigation Unit was responsible for the sudden change in attitude after his arrival.

The sergeant had him quickly shown to a soft interview suite – a room normally used for victims rather than suspects. It had two sofas arranged around a low table, rather than the usual bolted-down hard furniture. They even offered refreshment, which he declined.

It was stuffy inside the station, the heating cranked high. He shrugged out of his gloves and overcoat, folding the latter on the cushions next to him. Out of habit, he clasped his hands in his lap.

Sitting there, waiting, he tried to keep his impatience in check. The fact he had to try was out of character – something he shied away from analysing too closely. Blake had that effect. She disturbed his equilibrium.

His mind skimmed back six months to the last time he'd seen her. He'd attempted to get in touch with her since, but eventually came to the conclusion that she was avoiding him.

He'd be the first to admit that he had allowed himself to be given the brush-off. If she was not interested in continuing their... friendship, well, he wasn't going to force the issue.

He had his own qualms, in any case.

Losing his wife two years previously in a sudden, violent attack, had left Byron filled with grief and guilt in equal measure. She had been in her early thirties, as was he. They should have had decades ahead of them. He hadn't had the chance to say goodbye to Isobel then, nor to make his peace with it since. In many ways, he still felt married, albeit to a ghost. Any thoughts of another woman brought on feelings of intense disloyalty.

But that had not prevented him from thinking about Blake.

Perhaps that was why, a month ago, he'd decided on the spur of the moment to drive north to the small Derbyshire village where they'd first met. And where he'd assumed she was living. Instead, he found a caretaker in residence, overseeing renovations. The woman initially denied all knowledge of Blake. Only when Byron produced his official ID did she grudgingly impart that she'd been hired by 'the family', who had temporarily moved out until the work was done.

Byron cut short his trip. Heading south again, he'd called in favours with old colleagues. By the time he hit the M25 London orbital, he was confident that if Blake showed up on police radar anywhere in the country, he would be notified.

And he was.

But he hadn't expected it to be in these circumstances.

She had lived rough before – that much he knew. When she was fifteen and had found herself alone in London with no other options. That she'd survived at all – never mind more or less unscathed – said much for her resilience. He'd never considered for a moment, though, that she would be forced back onto the streets. The fact that she had been picked up in a raid

on a homeless squat in an empty building on the Mile End
Road defied his expectations.

They'd met the previous autumn. He'd initially suspected
the young woman was attempting some kind of con on the
family of a former MP who'd just died in a car accident. Why
else would she turn up on the day of the man's funeral, and
break into his family home? The truth turned out to be rather
more complicated. In uncovering it, Byron solved a murder
from a decade earlier. One most people were not aware had
even happened.

And as for Blake... he assumed she'd pursued a claim to the
Derbyshire estate, Claremont. Even if that had failed, surely
she had enough friends who would have given her a place to
stay?

*Hell, I would have given her a place to stay. She only had
to ask...*

Maybe that was the problem. Blake's independence was
hard-won. Such people hated having to ask for anything.

He was making a mental note to look into one friend of
Blake's in particular, when the door opened and she was shown
inside.

'Thank you, Constable,' Byron said to the uniform who'd
accompanied her. 'You may leave us.'

The man looked about to protest, but he took in Byron's
face and tone and thought better of it. The interview-suite door
clicked shut behind him.

For a moment, the pair eyed one another. Byron noted the
dullness of the white-blonde hair, the way the dirty,
mismatched clothes hung baggy on her frame. There was barely
ten years between them, but she could have passed for a
teenager.

Then Blake swore under her breath and slumped onto the
sofa opposite. 'I might have *known* it would be you.'

He raised an eyebrow, determined to let neither surprise nor disquiet show. 'Oh?'

'Admit it, Byron. You've got me on some kind of watch list, haven't you?'

She was unnervingly close to the truth, but he kept his voice even. 'What makes you think that?'

'The fact you're here, for a start.' She gave a bitter laugh. 'I'm clean. So, there's no reason for everyone else they lifted last night to be released – all except me – unless they were given an order to hold me by somebody with clout. A detective superintendent, for instance.'

'*Former* detective superintendent,' he said automatically. He realised he had no idea where to start. For someone who'd spent much of his professional career interrogating suspects, it was unsettling. 'Look, Blake... what on earth is going on?'

'Not here. Come on.' She got to her feet and headed for the door, glancing back as she reached it.

He regarded her without moving.

She sighed. 'OK, you've just blown in minutes something I've been working on for weeks. The very least you can do is give me breakfast.'

FIVE

LIMEHOUSE TO PRIMROSE HILL

They had been heading west along the Commercial Road for a mile or so before Byron asked, 'So, are you going to tell me what this is all about?' He glanced across from behind the wheel of the Mercedes. 'Quite apart from anything else, are you really... homeless?'

Was that disbelief she heard in his voice?

They were approaching Watney Market on their left. Maybe that was the reason there was more bite in Blake's tone than she intended.

'A little late for you to be taking an interest now, don't you think? How long has it been? Six months?'

She was tired, and hungry, and dirty, and still strung tight from the night before. And she had enough self-awareness to admit, albeit privately, that she was half hoping he'd take issue so she had something to rail against.

Instead, he completely took her legs out from under her when he said, gently, and without apparent ego, 'Blake, when you didn't return my calls or respond to messages, what other conclusion could I draw, except that you didn't welcome any interest on my part?'

Blake slumped back in the leather seat, trying not to luxuriate in the heating element warming her back and thighs. His correctness of speech made him seem older, she remembered this from the last time they met. At first, she'd thought him aloof, uptight, and far too clever for her peace of mind. As she'd learned more, she'd realised he wore manners as a shield. Even now, there was a spark of humour lurking beneath the surface, as if his own formality amused him.

'Dammit, Byron. Do you have to be so unutterably *reasonable*, all the time?'

'I know,' he said in a dry voice. 'I'm told it's one of my less appealing traits.' His eyes flicked away from the road just long enough to send her a look of quiet reproach. 'But, if I'd realised your situation sooner...'

'Look, I'm fine. I'm where I need to be.'

He was silent for a moment.

'Where you need to be in order to do what, exactly?'

Blake took her time answering. She was struggling to kick-start her brain. Weeks living rough had left her weary to her bones, she realised. Not just the cold, and hunger, but the constant vigilance.

Perhaps that explained why she'd allowed him to bundle her out of the police station and into his car without protest. Now, the calm safety of Byron's presence, allied with the drone of the big Merc's engine, the warmth and comfort of the interior, proved hypnotic. She gave herself a mental shake.

'Where are you taking me, by the way?'

'North London – somewhere private. Don't worry, you're free to leave at any time. Even if you *are* avoiding the question.'

Blake rubbed her hands across her face, feeling the grittiness of her eyes.

'A woman collapsed and died,' she said at last in flat capitulation. 'Her name was Shannon. She was someone I... used to know. A friend.' It sounded so commonplace, put like that. It told only a fraction of the story. 'I needed – *need* – to find out why.'

'Something that can only be done from the streets?' Byron's tone was neutral. Only the upward quirk of an eyebrow made it a question.

'Something like that, yes.'

'Blake, please tell me you *do* have somewhere to live?'

'Yes... of course. But Kensy was living rough, and I knew if I was going to find her with any speed, I needed to be in the same situation.'

'Kensy?' He frowned. 'I think you better start at the beginning.'

She felt her lips twist, almost in spite of herself. 'Why, how far are we going?'

'Far enough,' he said. 'So, who's Kensy?'

'The young black kid who was also arrested last night. They turned her loose just as you arrived.' Blake stilled. 'She didn't hear you asking for me, did she?'

'Ah, she... may have done, I'm afraid.'

She swore under her breath. 'I've been searching for Kensy for weeks. Finally, yesterday, I got word that maybe there was someone who might turn up at that squat on the Mile End Road, who maybe knew where I might find her.'

'That's a lot of mights and maybes.'

She gave a derisive snort. 'Yeah, welcome to my world.'

The traffic slowed. He braked smoothly. Ahead, the skyscrapers of the City loomed like a far country, misted by rain.

'Did you find the person you were after?'

'Well, it was better or worse than that, depending on your point of view. Turned out, unbeknownst to me, I bunked down right alongside Kensy herself last night.'

'You didn't recognise her?'

She threw him a sour glance. 'Not exactly well lit, those

places, are they? All I had to go on was a name and an out-of-date photo. It wasn't until they hustled everyone outside and she was busted that I got a good look at her. As soon as I realised who she was, I had to, ah, improvise.'

'Yes, so I gathered from your arrest sheet.'

She shrugged. 'It worked, didn't it?'

'You still haven't told me what the connection is between this Kensy and the woman you mentioned – Shannon?'

'Kensy is... me,' Blake said simply. 'The new me,' she added, knowing he would query that. 'When I first... ran away to London – back when I was fifteen, I mean – I was woefully naïve.' *God, was that only ten years ago?* 'I doubt I would have lasted a week if Shannon hadn't taken me under her wing.'

'You do yourself an injustice,' he said at once.

But Blake shook her head. 'Shannon was big sister and surrogate mother, all rolled into one. She looked after me for no other reason than because I needed it, without expecting any kind of payment in return.'

'I thought you said it was Lex Vaganov who... took care of you.'

She flashed him a quick grin. 'Jealous, Byron?'

'I have neither right nor reason to be.'

She gave a short laugh, hoping to cover the fact his answer disappointed her – something she didn't wish to explore too closely. Instead, she said, 'Lex might have saved me *from* the streets. But Shannon saved me while I was on them.'

In Whitechapel, Byron had swung northwards, skirting the City, the grey sky reflected in the glass towers. Between buildings, bracketed by cranes, Blake caught glimpses of the Gherkin – the landmark building shaped like the pickle that inspired its name.

'I don't know if Shannon had a premonition of sorts, or if she knew she was in some kind of trouble, but I got a letter from her, after she died. Somebody found it when they were clearing out her stuff. They posted it, together with a note telling me what happened.'

'How long after?'

'A few weeks. I hadn't heard from her for years before that. I tried to keep in touch, but she... pushed me away.' Blake swallowed, kept her voice light. 'It was as though, once I didn't need her anymore...'

'Perhaps she just didn't want to give you an easy way back to living on the streets.'

The smoothness in his voice roughened her own. 'You don't *live* on the streets – you exist. You survive. And it's never *easy*.'

'But, it seems to me, the route there often is.'

'Maybe.'

He cast her a quick glance, but didn't call her on it.

'So, what did it say – this letter from Shannon?'

'It asked, if anything happened to her, to look after Kensy. Shannon took her in, kept her straight, kept her clean. Only, by the time the letter reached me, Kensy was gone.'

'Gone, as in...?'

'As in, she'd been kicked out of Shannon's flat. It was housing association – Kensy's name wasn't on the lease, and she wasn't old enough to rent in her own right. Social services tried to take her back into the system, apparently, and that's when she disappeared onto the streets.'

They drove on in silence, through Spitalfields and Shoreditch, around the edge of Clerkenwell, heading towards King's Cross.

Then Byron asked, 'What do you hope to do for this girl – when you find her again?'

'Well, I... To help her, however I can. Whatever she will accept...'

'Do I hear a "but"?'

Blake shook her head. Her vision danced. She needed to eat something, and soon.

'No "buts". Although, if Kensy knows anything more about what happened to Shannon, then I need her to tell me. Not just how she died, but the events leading up to it.'

'You haven't said what *did* actually happen to her,' Byron said, almost diffident.

She considered for a moment, but couldn't see a reason to keep the remaining details to herself.

'Shannon had sorted her life out, last I heard. Working, off the booze, staying out of trouble. It was all looking good for her.'

'Life can be cruel that way,' he said quietly.

'Yeah, well. She was picked up for being drunk and disorderly and resisting arrest at some retail park just the other side of the Isle of Dogs. She had a flat, like I said, but she'd clearly been living rough, and gave No Fixed Abode as her address. They stuck her in the cells overnight, supposedly to sleep it off.'

'I thought you said she was sober?'

'She was,' Blake muttered. 'At least, that's what I was told.'

'Reliable source?'

'Lex.' The single-word answer needed no other explanation. 'Something must have happened – something that made her fall off the wagon.'

'Does anyone know what?'

'I don't think anyone tried very hard to find out.'

'And you owe her that,' he said. A statement not a question.

'It's the least I can do.' She propped one elbow on the door, resting her forehead against her hand. 'If she cared about Kensy – and the letter made it sound as though she did – then she must have known she risked the kid being taken away from her. Unless it was something Kensy herself did that caused it...'

'Sadly, it's not an unfamiliar story when you're dealing with an addict, regardless of what substance they're addicted to. Something happens, however minor, that person's ability to deal with it is compromised, and before you know it...'

'Oh, really? Is it also a "not unfamiliar story" for her to be dead twelve hours later?'

'Of?'

Blake swallowed. She ought to be angry, but strangely found Byron's detached tone easier to square. 'A bleed on the brain, caused by a significant blow to the head – hard enough to fracture her skull, even if it didn't break the skin. A blow from a police baton, for example.'

'Blake—'

He took a hand from the wheel to reach for her. She shook him off.

'She made it a couple of miles – as far as Watney Market back there. Apparently, she tried to ask for help, but people couldn't understand what she was saying.'

'Why was she released in such a state?'

'They thought she was still drunk, so they reckon. And she'd made such a nuisance of herself – being loud, crying out in the night, disturbing everyone – that your lot couldn't be bothered getting a doctor to look her over.' Her mouth twisted. 'I'm paraphrasing there, of course.'

'They're not "my lot",' Byron said, and she heard the grim in his voice. 'Not any longer.'

Maybe it was the burn of tears behind her eyelids that made her seize on the change of topic.

'You didn't go back to the Met?'

He shook his head. 'I took an investigator's role with the IOPC.'

That took her aback. 'Aren't they the people who check out complaints against the police? That's a bit of a... sideways move, isn't it?'

'I report directly to the Home Office. Some might see it as a promotion,' he said mildly. 'And it's the Independent Office for Police *Conduct*, actually.'

'Same difference.' She shrugged. 'I didn't think they allowed coppers – even ex-coppers – to go after other coppers. Divided loyalties, and all that.'

He flicked her a brief glance. 'It's a new initiative. I'm something of a scouting party, sent ahead to get a... feel for things before any investigation proper begins.'

She found herself surprised – and disappointed. 'So you're in charge of the official cover-up?'

'Hardly. It's more like damage limitation. If there are bent coppers to be found, I'll find them, don't you worry. But washing dirty linen in public rarely does any good.'

'Apart from restoring public confidence in the integrity of the police, you mean?'

'That's one perspective. I prefer to think of it as avoiding further deterioration of morale across an already underfunded and overstretched service.'

Something had hardened in his voice. She was poking a tiger with a stick, she realised. Just because he hadn't bitten her yet, that didn't mean he wasn't going to.

'Shall we agree to differ on that one?' She took a breath. 'Still, it's good that you felt... ready to get back to work, I guess. I know that must have been hard.'

He gave a stiff nod and said nothing. When they'd first met, he'd been on long-term sick leave and it had looked as though he would be medically retired before he was out of his mid-thirties. She had learned enough about him to know that would have been harder to bear.

They left Euston's drab exterior behind them and entered gentrified Camden. The buildings were lower, with more open sky and greenery.

As they were skirting Regent's Park, Byron asked suddenly, 'Where did they take her?'

Blake had been almost dozing.

'Who?'

'Shannon – which police station?'

'Limehouse.'

'Should I read anything into the fact that you contrived to get yourself locked up in the same place as your friend?'

'I didn't set out to get locked up at all. But once I realised where they were taking us, I was interested to see how we were treated, I must admit.'

'And?'

'Nothing to get excited about, one way or the other.' She shrugged. 'And my skull is still intact, so...'

His fingers clenched momentarily around the rim of the steering wheel, but all he asked was, 'What do *you* think happened to Shannon?'

She turned, still unable to read him. 'I don't know. Was she drunk when she was arrested? Maybe. I still think it's unlikely – but, if so, I still don't know *why*. Was she still drunk when she was released, or was she already dying? That's another question altogether.'

'You believe the police killed her?'

'It's a possibility. Anyway, I thought there was supposed to be some kind of investigation when someone died within twenty-four hours of being in police custody, so isn't it now *your* job to find out?'

SIX

Kensy raised her hand to knock on the office door but, at the last moment, she hesitated.

Taking a deep breath, she flexed her fingers and then knocked quickly, before she lost her nerve altogether.

The Kinfolk shelter, in the shadow of the huge white church of St George-in-the-East in Shadwell, was a noisy place. They were clearing away breakfast in the dining hall just along the corridor; the rattle of empty plates and cutlery going into big plastic tubs, the clatter of metal-leg chairs being stacked, the voices – even a radio playing from the kitchen. It all had Kensy leaning close to the door, afraid she'd miss the command to enter.

They never liked having to call out twice. It was always her fault if she missed it the first time.

So, the last thing she expected was the door to open briskly from the inside. She ducked back, flushing as if caught listening at the keyhole.

'Sorry, I—'

'Ah, now, it's Kensy, is it not?' said the man. His smooth,

crooning Irish accent sounded like someone pouring syrup over hot pudding.

She recognised him now, of course – off the telly. At one time Diarmuid Mackie had been a fixture of one of those breakfast TV programmes. Kensy vaguely recalled him from daytime talk shows and quizzes playing in the background in one group home or another. But, still, he was a celebrity. That alone was enough to send her mute. She gave a nod, flustered.

'What a terrible night you've had. At least now you've got some hot food inside you. Come in, me darling, and sit yourself down.' He waved her into the office. His suit fit him like a glove and he wore it easily. Like someone who dressed that way for real, not just court appearances.

As she limped inside, Kensy realised they were not alone. Adhiti Chatterjee looked slim and regal, in chef's black rather than white. Her signature and the Kinfolk charity logo were embroidered in gold on the breast pocket. She wore no obvious make-up, and no jewellery except a wedding ring and small gold studs in both ears, but she made the work uniform seem expensive.

'You remember my wife from earlier?' Mackie asked. 'I hope you've been enjoying her expertise in the kitchen.' He gave a conspiratorial smile. 'I'm not allowed in there myself. A terrible cook, I am.'

'Hello again, Kensy,' Adhiti said, her voice low and musical. 'Welcome to Kinfolk.'

Kensy's eyes lifted. The woman was smiling, with her hand outstretched. Kensy shook it briefly and mumbled something in reply. It was only then she remembered that the two were married. In fact, Adhiti had got her big break doing a cookery slot on one of Diarmuid's chat shows. Now she was better known than he was.

Being in a room with two famous people at once completely frazzled her brain.

'And how's that leg doing this morning?' Diarmuid asked, leading her towards the cluttered desk. It was squeezed into one corner of the room, below a noticeboard and shelves of ring binders.

Kensy sank onto the edge of the visitor chair with hands shoved under her thighs, supporting her knee. 'Bit sore,' she admitted.

'Well, we could get you some ice for it, perhaps?' Diarmuid said. The raised eyebrow in his wife's direction made it a request.

'Er, no, it's OK. I don't want to put you to any bother.'

'Nonsense. It's no bother.'

'Really, I—'

'Don't bully the poor child, Diarmuid,' Adhiti broke in, gently. 'If she doesn't want—'

His face darkened as he cut her off with a brusque, 'It'll do her knee the world of good. And she'll need to be up on her feet again quickly, hey?'

Adhiti blinked, then she said, 'I'll bring some from the kitchen.' And she went out, closing the office door behind her.

Diarmuid took his seat as if nothing had happened. Kensy let out a slow breath.

'So, I saw you having a bite to eat with young Spider. A pal of yours, is he?'

'Not really,' she said. 'I mean, I've seen him around and everything, so... yeah, I guess.'

Diarmuid smiled at her, as if she'd given the best answer he'd heard all day. That smile was starting to unnerve her.

'Did he tell you he's already signed up for our bed-and-board programme to start getting his life back on track? No? Ah, no matter.' He leaned forwards, looked her right in the eyes until she could hardly breathe. When he spoke, his voice was gentle. 'I want you to know, Kensy, that you're safe with us. We make no judgements on people here. What's past is past. It's human to make mistakes – it's the only way we learn – and you should know that we'll always fight your corner. You understand what I'm saying?'

She didn't quite, but she nodded anyway.

'Grand,' he said again. He gave yet another brilliant smile that faded into seriousness. 'But, for us to do that, you have to be completely honest now. Will you be?'

Another nod, more fervent this time.

'In that case, me darling, tell me this – is anybody out there who might be looking for you?'

SEVEN

JUST OFF AINGER ROAD, PRIMROSE HILL

In Primrose Hill, Byron turned onto a residential street lined with trees that had been heavily pollarded. Most had not yet started to put on leaf, and the bare, cut stumps of branches were fists shaken against the sky.

Blake kept her eyes moving, checking road signs and landmarks. More habit than necessity. Even so, as they swung into a side street, she wasn't expecting Byron to almost immediately nudge over the lowered kerb into a garage.

There was nothing inside. Not even cobwebs or leaf litter. Instead, the space was spartan, the walls stark white and the floor pale grey, gleaming under the overhead lights. By the time he'd switched off the Mercedes's engine, the roller-shutter door was already clanking shut behind them.

She said, 'I'm guessing this is not some Met police safe house.'

'Considering I'm no longer with the Met, you'd be correct.'

'So... where are we?'

He regarded her for a moment, as if trying to pre-judge her reaction. Then: 'My place.'

Blake blinked and said nothing.

He circled round to open her door. Looking down, he sighed. 'I'm demonstrating a certain amount of faith by bringing you here, Blake. Is it too much to ask that you reciprocate?'

After another moment's silent hesitation, she climbed out.

In the corner was a heavy-duty door with an adjacent keypad. He entered a six-digit code. The locks disengaged. Blake was careful not to let the quickening interest show on her face. She was familiar with all manner of locks – enough to recognise the sophistication of these.

It occurred to her that, during their first encounter the previous year, she had never really asked about the consequences of the terrorist incident that finished his active police career. Not the incident itself, but what came after.

She remembered it on the news at the time. The latest in a spate of extremist attacks. The security services released only the barest facts. Two perpetrators, with knives taped to their hands and explosives strapped to their bodies. They'd chosen St James's Park as their killing ground, for its proximity to the heart of government. Afterwards, the authorities had found a manifesto of sorts, together with the components used to put together the fake suicide vests.

Nineteen people were wounded, including the off-duty detective who pursued and subdued one of the men, at considerable personal harm. The other attacker was shot dead by armed police, arriving within minutes of the first panicked call.

By then, six people lay dead or dying, including a young probationary constable, and a surgeon, who managed to prevent the total becoming seven before succumbing to her injuries. And when it emerged that the detective and the surgeon had been married – in the park by tragedy of coincidence – the media went into a feeding frenzy.

For days, it led every bulletin. Until the next horror pushed it from the headlines.

Blake didn't know any of the victims. Didn't know anyone

else who knew them, either. She was ashamed to have almost forgotten the incident.

Until she met Byron.

Then, she'd seen the physical scars on his hands and arms. She could only guess at the emotional ones, not to mention the psychological damage she knew he'd suffered. Less from what was said – more from words left unspoken.

And the loss.

One thing she had not truly appreciated was that the danger hadn't ended when the attack was over. To most, Byron was a hero for his actions that day. But to others, he became a target.

She gave an involuntary shiver as she stepped through into a slate-tiled hallway. Byron slid back a frosted-glass door and disposed of his gloves, overcoat, and outdoor shoes in the cupboard behind it.

Blake looked down at her own dirty, scuffed boots and toed them off. Underneath, her socks had holes in them, so she took those off, too. The tiles were surprisingly warm against her bare feet.

'Underfloor heating?' she asked, flexing her toes.

He nodded.

'Hm, all mod cons.'

He made no response. They climbed three flights of stairs. At the top was a landing, another security door. Blake pointedly turned away slightly while Byron entered the code, but she caught the pattern of numbers out of the corner of her eye, nevertheless.

They were on the top floor, she realised. What had been a three-storey Victorian corner property at the front had been extended up and out at the back. The entire floor was now an open-plan living, dining and kitchen area. There was even a baby grand piano tucked into a book-lined corner.

One wall was glass – bi-fold doors leading out onto a roof

terrace with views across the chimney pots and TV aerials of Chalk Farm and Belsize Park. The furniture was, to her eye, expensive but well-worn, suggesting lived-in comfort rather than shabbiness. It was also generous – the dining table had eight chairs. The sofa would have seated a family, including a dog.

It made Byron's widower status seem somehow more painful.

'I imagine you'll be hungry,' he said.

She turned and realised he had been watching her appraisal of his home. She hid the urge to apologise with a nod.

'I'll show you to a bathroom, then you can shower, if you wish, while I rustle up some food.'

'You can cook?'

For the first time, he almost smiled. 'I like to eat, and a diet of nothing but takeaway meals gets old rather quickly, I'm told.'

An internal staircase led to a lower floor. All muted greys and greens, carefully lit. Byron pushed open the door to a bedroom that was neat and luxurious, but impersonal as a hotel. The inbuilt wardrobe contained racks of clothing.

'Something in here should fit, if you'd care to help yourself.'

Blake hesitated. 'I can't just...'

'Of course you can. I should have taken it all to a charity shop ages ago anyway.'

'You mean...?' She gestured to the wardrobe. 'Byron, did these belong to... to your wife?'

'Yes,' he said, without expression.

She eyed him in flat silence until finally he said, 'If you prefer, I can run the stuff you have on through the washer and dryer while we eat?'

'I think that would be best – thank you.'

He reached into the wardrobe and pulled out a long silky garment in dark green and black, held it out to her. 'It's just a robe, Blake. Something to wear until your clothes are dry,' he said. And when still she didn't move to take it, he added, 'Unless you'd prefer to sit around in a towel?'

Despite herself, she felt the flush of colour in her cheeks. 'All right. I mean, thank you very much.'

Again, that ghost of a smile. 'Come upstairs when you're ready. No rush.'

After he'd gone, Blake stripped, leaving her dirty clothes on the bedroom floor. She locked the bathroom door behind her, although the only thing she didn't trust about Byron was her own response.

The en-suite bathroom was slate grey and gloss white. The walk-in shower cubicle was big enough for two, with a rainfall head. She lathered her hair twice, trying to ignore the colour of the water on the first pass. When she finally emerged, the room was filled with steam, despite the extractor fan, but she felt close to human again.

Her discarded clothes had disappeared from the guest room – no doubt to the laundry, as promised. She pulled on the robe and knotted the sash. It felt cool against her skin. She lifted the sleeve to her nose briefly, wondering if there would be any lingering trace of the original owner. All she could smell was fabric conditioner. She wasn't sure if that brought disappointment or relief.

Blake headed towards the stairs, then paused. There were several other doors leading off the corridor, and she told herself it would be foolish to miss the opportunity; that she was gathering intelligence, not simply being nosy.

Opening each door in turn revealed another guest room, a linen cupboard, a family bathroom, and – at the end of the hall – the master bedroom. She glanced over her shoulder but could hear nothing from the staircase beyond the distant clattering of pans. She slipped inside.

Two tall windows looked out over back gardens and mature trees. There was a small walk-in wardrobe, neatly racked, and an en-suite that held a slipper bath and a shower. It was bigger than the one attached to the guest room, but almost as impersonal. In fact, the only signs of occupation in the bedroom were two books and what looked like a bound typescript, stacked on the bedside table, and a collection of framed photographs on the wall opposite the bed.

Blake couldn't help but be drawn to the photos. They were mostly candid shots, taken in a variety of locations, and the same woman featured in all. Sometimes alone, sometimes with other people Blake didn't recognise. In two, Byron was also pictured.

In the first he was sitting in the cockpit of a modern yacht, barefoot, one hand on the huge brushed stainless-steel wheel. His other arm was draped around the shoulders of the woman, who reclined with her back against him. Byron was looking ahead, eyes no doubt on the horizon, but the woman was gazing directly into the lens, pushing her wind-blown hair out of her eyes. She was smiling, as though she and the camera were in on some private joke. Byron's left hand rested at her waist, fingers splayed so that his wedding ring was visible.

Blake moved closer, inspecting his face with its serious expression. He looked different, somehow. He looked... content.

The other photograph had been taken at the couple's wedding. They were leaving the church, running through a shower of confetti with heads slightly ducked. Their hands were tightly clasped, and they were laughing.

Unbidden, a lump rose in her throat.

A noise from above made her freeze. She recognised a washing machine moving into spin cycle, and was grateful for the reminder. The rest of the room revealed nothing she hadn't expected. The wardrobe held mainly bespoke suits and shirts bearing the labels of individual tailors, polished shoes, an anti-ballistic helmet and a full set of body armour.

Everything for the well-dressed man about town.

The books, when she tilted her head to read the titles, turned out to be an explanation of the body's immune system, and the latest edition of Jane's guide to handguns. The typescript was a copy of Baroness Casey's 'independent review into the standards of behaviour and internal culture of the Metropolitan Police Service'.

Her lips twitched. *Bedtime reading for everyday folk.*

She slipped back out into the corridor having learned little except that Byron's marriage seemed to have been happy. Apart from the photos, she had no clearer understanding of his psyche. Disappointed, she padded upstairs, tightening the sash of her robe.

Byron stood at the kitchen centre island. He had dispensed with his jacket and tie, and rolled back his shirtsleeves. He cooked as he did everything, with an economic grace.

Blake found her gaze drawn to him. He wasn't a hairy man, which served to highlight the play of muscles along his bare forearms as he worked. His tan emphasised the pale criss-cross of scars between elbow and wrist.

Hurriedly, she flicked her eyes up to his face, but his attention was on the stove. He was stirring something in a skillet. The smell of it made her stomach rumble.

He glanced up and stilled momentarily. His expression as he regarded her was sombre, almost forbidding. She had never seen him look any other way. Except, perhaps, in those photographs on the wall of his bedroom.

'So, did you find everything you wanted?'

EIGHT

Byron couldn't deny it was a shock, seeing her standing there wearing Isobel's robe. He wondered if offering it to her was a mistake. If bringing her here at all was a mistake.

Too late for regrets now.

'Yes, thank you,' she said, in answer to his question. She drifted over towards the bookcase, head on one side to peruse the titles, and remarked over her shoulder, 'Nice place. Been here long?'

'About ten years. My great aunt left us the house, and we had the conversion work done.'

Blake nodded without asking for an explanation of 'we', so he did not elaborate.

'The ground floor is completely separate?'

'The first two floors, actually. And the garden.'

They hadn't wanted the responsibility of a garden when neither he nor Isobel possessed green fingers. The roof terrace, with its planters of herbs, night-scented stock, honeysuckle and lavender, had provided more than enough outdoor space for summer evenings. On the occasions when one or the other wasn't summoned to some urgent case, anyway. The responsibilities of doctor and policeman were sometimes remarkably similar.

'Did you sell off the lower portion to pay for the work?'

'No. Renting it out seemed a good way to ensure agreeable neighbours.' He paused, hovering between annoyance and amusement. 'Satisfied by my prospects, are you?'

She turned away from the books, flashing him a quick grin. 'If, by that, you mean am I satisfied you're not an easy target for bribery because you're living beyond your means, then yes, I suppose so.'

'You thought I might be open to inducement?'

'Most people are.'

He raised an eyebrow – more at her weary tone than the words. Before he could comment, she'd moved on, running her finger lightly over the corner of the piano lid.

'Do you play?'

'No.'

For that to be entirely true, he ought to have added, 'any longer' but that would have led to questions he wasn't ready to answer. Most people who knew his situation would have let that one lie. Byron knew she would not. Instead, he moved back to the hob, slid the bulging folded omelette onto a plate and sliced it in two to serve. 'Eat, before it goes cold.'

They sat at the breakfast bar at one end of the centre island. She forced herself to eat slowly, despite her obvious hunger. She chewed and savoured, doing justice to the flavours. Someone for whom eating was a pleasure, not simply a refuelling operation.

'I went up to Claremont, did they tell you?' he said as she put down her knife and fork.

The news seemed to come as a genuine surprise.

'No, why? Why did you go, I mean?'

'I wanted to see you.' And, just as she was processing that statement: 'I wanted to check that you were all right.'

'When?'

'A month ago, probably.'

'Ah, well, I was here in London by then, so I'm sorry if I wasn't picking up my messages.'

He sighed, resting his elbows on the countertop and folding his hands together under his chin.

'Who owns the estate, Blake? The woman who answered the door wouldn't say.'

'Checking on *my* prospects now, are you?'

He huffed out a short breath, stared her down.

'I'm OK. You don't have to worry about me,' she said then. 'I came to an... arrangement, of sorts, with my late father's second wife.'

'Which was?'

'Satisfactory to both sides, thank you, so—'

'Blake.' He cut across her without raising his voice. 'What I'm trying to ascertain is whether there is any element of... necessity to your current situation.'

Something shifted in her expression, closer to a scowl. She sat up straight, rigid. The robe slipped open at the front. He kept his eyes locked on hers.

'Oh, there's *necessity*, all right,' she said tightly. 'I need to find Kensy, so I can learn what she knows about Shannon's letter. I need to find out what led Shannon to risk losing her by getting herself arrested. And then, I *need* to find out if that arrest had anything to do with her death. So, yeah, I'll say there was necessity involved!'

Byron heard the catch in her voice, and without thinking he dropped his hands towards her, palms upwards.

'Blake—'

Her eyes flicked down to his hands, across the patchwork of scars that injury and surgery had left on them. And he caught the shudder she failed to hide.

Sympathy or revulsion?

He closed his fingers and drew his hands back until they dropped off the edge of the countertop into his lap.

How could I ever have let myself think...?

'If Shannon's death was related to her arrest, then I will get to the bottom of it,' he said, aware of the stiffness in his tone. 'I would strongly advise you to leave any investigation to me. That *is* now my job. If it helps, I'll make it an order.'

'No, it doesn't,' she said stonily. 'It doesn't help at all.'

NINE

CLEMENCE STREET, LIMEHOUSE

Tess flinched as, beyond the kitchen, the back door slammed behind him. The silence left behind in the house made noise all its own.

Crumpled where he'd left her, on the rug in the front room, she let her eyes slip closed. Tried to breathe softly around the graunching ache. Ribs again.

'Get up,' she mumbled to herself. Her mouth was swollen, half her teeth loose. 'C'mon, girl, get *up*.'

With a groan of effort, she got one arm underneath her. The rush of dizziness almost took her down again. She rode it, eyes closed tight, gripping the leg of the shattered coffee table.

He'll blame me for that, too – for the damage I made him do.

The thought of him returning, of finding her still where he left her, provided the extra impetus. She made it to her knees, clinging to furniture. Finally, she was upright – swaying, but on her feet.

A major triumph.

In the mirror above the fireplace, she caught a glimpse of her face. Normally, he didn't mark her where it showed. But since the day the woman collapsed and died in her arms, something changed.

For both of them.

He hated that she'd used her phone to call for help, as if doing it once might encourage a repeat offence – she was only allowed a mobile at all so he could keep tabs on her. He'd raged at her for being stupid enough to dial 999, even if she'd fled right after.

The phone was a cheap Pay As You Go, so it wasn't like the cops could get her name and address from the number. Even so, he wouldn't let her shop at Watney Market again, just in case. And she'd jumped at every unexpected knock on the door.

But the image of the dying woman wouldn't let go. Tess scoured the local free papers for news reports. This way, she discovered the woman's name – Shannon. She'd had a history of homelessness, of drug and alcohol abuse that kept her in and out of rehab. It made the reports brief and unsympathetic.

Like she had it coming.

Shannon had died from a blow to the head. Not immediately fatal, but fatal nonetheless. One of the free newspapers carried an appeal for witnesses – anyone who'd been at the market that day.

She'd made the mistake of keeping a clipping.

He'd found it, of course.

After that it was almost a week before she could manage stairs unaided.

And it finally dawned on Tess that sooner or later, if she didn't get out, she would end up like Shannon.

It was the ultimate wake-up call.

As was the feeling that not getting out would somehow be a betrayal of the woman. That it would make her death meaningless. A lesson unlearned.

So, Tess began making preparations, looking for times when his guard was down.

She still wasn't sure how he worked it out – a predator's instinct perhaps, that recognised when his prey was about to take flight.

This morning, he'd confronted her. She'd denied it, of course.

It didn't make any difference.

He beat her anyway.

Only, this time he didn't seem to care if the marks left on her body couldn't be masked by high collars, or long sleeves, or makeup.

Like it didn't matter anymore.

She shuffled gingerly down the hall into the kitchen, went into the pantry squeezed beneath the stairs.

Inside, behind the small chest freezer, she groped until her fingers touched the nylon strap of her go-bag. A small backpack she'd bought for a few pounds in a charity shop. Filled with the barest essentials, one change of clothes.

She'd had a bit put by when they first met, but somehow he'd always had a good reason why any expense came out of her account. Now there was nothing left.

He'd driven away her friends, and she'd become distant from what little family she had. Her parents were long dead. He'd never liked her younger stepsister, managed to convince Tess that she didn't much care for her, either.

Shannon had no family, Tess learned. She'd dropped off the bottom rung of society's ladder, with nothing left to stop her falling. She'd been living rough on the streets, reduced to drowning her sorrow in drink and drugs.

But then she'd somehow managed to turn her life around. Tess wished she'd had a chance to ask her how.

And to ask her what had made the woman leave the housing association flat she'd leased, down near West Ham Station. Tess knew the area, and it wasn't good – crime rates had really shot up over the past few years. But surely anything was better than sleeping in shop doorways and shelters?

Tess thought of *him* again, and realised that no, some things might actually be plenty worse.

She was pretty sure the first piece of advice Shannon might have given her would be to get out from her life before it killed her.

Finally, she was heeding the warning bells ringing in her head for months. Unless that was just concussion.

She tottered along the hallway, pausing by the side table where she'd already placed her keys. She dug her mobile phone out of her pocket, gripping it tightly for a moment longer. She still wasn't sure if he could use it somehow to track her. Her only option was to go. To take a leap of faith, and hope that somebody would be there to catch her.

TEN

KINFOLK, CABLE STREET, SHADWELL

'Where is he?' Kensy demanded. 'What have you done with Spider?'

'Hey, calm down. We haven't done anything to him,' the woman with the dreadlocks said, sounding defensive. Her name was River.

'So, where is he?'

'How should I know? Do I look like his mother? He'll do as he likes.'

The fight went out of Kensy. She slumped into her chair, eyes fixed on the melting bag of ice, wrapped in a tea towel, that was draped across her knee. It had been two days since she and Spider had arrived at Kinfolk, and they'd stuck to each other like glue.

Until now.

'I know, but we only just got here.' She swallowed. 'An' I didn't think he'd just... *go*. Not without...'

'Aw, hon. Didn't he say goodbye?' River put her hand on Kensy's shoulder. 'I'm sorry.'

Kensy shrugged out from under her touch, scowling. 'He

wouldn't *do* that to me.' She aimed for angry and missed. 'He just *wouldn't*.'

'Men, huh?' River's laugh had a bitter edge. 'Only thing you can rely on 'em to do is let you down.'

Kensy opened her mouth, then shut it again, aware she was making too much of a show. They were in the dining hall at Kinfolk, late morning. Breakfast over and a long way from dinner. Not much else going on. There were a dozen people at the tables, drinking tea from the urn, chatting, or reading, or just sitting. All of them listening in.

'Come on, hon,' River said, voice gentle, but face tight. 'Maybe you misunderstood—'

'Don't!' Kensy jerked to her feet. 'Don't treat me like I'm too young to get it. They was always doin' that, at the home. I know what's goin' on.'

River gave a loud sigh, flicked back her dreads. 'Look, I didn't want to tell you, but Spider did say something before he left.'

'What?'

'That he thought you were getting a bit too... attached.' She bit her lip. 'Said he needed his space, y'know?'

Kensy shook her head. 'No way.'

And if she had doubts, it was only because those didn't sound like Spider's words.

No other reason.

'I'm sorry, hon,' River said again, turning away as she added, 'blokes don't like it when you get clingy.'

That stung. Kensy's vision blurred – tears or temper, she wasn't sure which.

'They warned us about this place,' she threw at River's retreating back. 'Warned me what you was like! So, Spider kicks off because you make him work all night, like slave labour, and now suddenly he's just upped and gone, huh? Yeah, right!'

River stopped, turned back, staring. Her mouth opened and closed again.

Kensy became aware of the silence. It rippled around the room as conversations dropped away. She felt her face flame. Shame, embarrassment, or just fighting the urge to flee, take your pick. 'I—'

'Wait there,' River said, and stalked out through the double doors leading towards the office.

Restless shuffling began, whispers started up. Nobody would meet her eyes. Her gaze darted about, desperate for an escape route. She grabbed the soggy bundle of ice and cloth and hurried towards the kitchen, trying to seem like she wasn't running away.

The kitchen was empty, the overhead lights reflecting from scrubbed stainless-steel prep areas and cold gas burners. Kensy hesitated, then dumped the bundle into the nearest sink, shaking the water from her hands.

The door opening from the walk-in freezer made her jump. She spun with a gasp.

'Oh! I'm sorry, I know I'm not supposed to be in here, but—'

'Do not worry.' Adhiti Chatterjee smiled as she came forwards, handed her a towel. 'Here.'

She was wearing the same black chef's outfit as yesterday, creases sharp. Either she washed it overnight, or she had a stack of them.

Kensy dried her hands. When she looked up, Adhiti had moved close enough to whisper, 'Please, you must come with me.'

'What?' Kensy saw the woman flinch and lowered her voice. 'I mean, why?'

Adhiti glanced over her shoulder. 'Please! We have little time. We must not let him find you here.'

'Who? I'm sorry, I don't understand...'

She was bewildered enough to let Adhiti shepherd her into

the empty staff room, just off the kitchen, where the volunteers left their belongings. There were coat hooks and small lockers along one wall. Adhiti pushed the door to behind her.

'We need to get you away from here, and quickly,' she said, speaking fast and low. 'Before he comes to get you.'

'Who?' Kensy tugged her arm free. 'Please, Adhiti, you're scaring me. What's going on? What's happened to Spider?'

'He is gone. It is you they are after.'

'What? Where? And why would anyone...?'

But she knew why. Social services had her flagged as a runaway. The cops might have missed it – or simply not bothered to check – but she'd foolishly given her details to Mr Mackie when she arrived. No idea what she'd been thinking. He'd kind of charmed it out of her.

'I do not know,' Adhiti admitted. 'But I fear the worst, which is why—'

But she didn't get to finish. The door was thrust open, hard enough to bounce off the lockers behind it with a hollow clang.

With the bright lights from the kitchen behind them, it was impossible to see a face, but Kensy had been on the streets long enough to read intent in the man who owned the doorway.

'You,' he said, 'are coming with me.'

ELEVEN

BECKTON

Paarth Sharma liked animals. In truth, he liked them better than people.

As a child, growing up in the northern Indian state of Uttar Pradesh, he had been compelled to work with the beasts. He'd had no choice.

After his father died, and their small patch of land was appropriated by his uncle, Paarth and his mother and siblings had become indentured labour. His uncle might claim to have taken in his dead brother's family in a charitable spirit. In reality, they were little more than slaves.

While Paarth's mother and sister worked the fields, scratching in the dirt that was permanently parched or flooded, Paarth and his two younger brothers saw to the livestock. The animals lived in better conditions than those who tended them, but he had gazed into their eyes and knew that they understood their place only too well.

Paarth had sympathy for the tall Jamnapari goats, with their long ears and placid faces. He could recognise every individual in the herd, knew when they were about to deliver the kids that kept them producing milk. And he wept in private when they were sent to slaughter.

He had learned young to hide his feelings or risk ridicule, if not a beating.

Those days were far behind him – in time and distance, if not in memory. Who would have believed he'd come so far?

But still, he stood in the barn, collar pulled up around his ears, watching the two adult pigs on the other side of the bars. They chomped their food with powerful jaws, snapping up each mouthful.

The pigs were Durocs, fully grown, thickset animals in shades of copper and bronze. Broad of chest and deeply muscled. The sow was only slightly smaller than the boar, and both were almost two metres long. The male tipped the scales at over 360kg – four times Paarth's weight.

He never ventured inside the pen alone, and always checked the fencing. Heavy-duty steel railings, panelled in on the lower half. The upright stanchions were buried over a metre into the concrete base. They had to be. When the animals became restless, they could easily punch through anything less substantial.

They were restless now, the sow banging against the barrier, making it clatter and jump. The boar stood with his front feet up on the second railing, meeting Paarth eye to eye.

'Go on. Get down.'

He gave the boar a nudge with his knuckles, making sure to pull away as the massive head swung round. The flesh was unyielding, packed with muscle. It was like trying to push back a truck.

Slowly, reluctantly, the boar shifted, dropping back onto all fours. Paarth gave his back a quick scratch and dropped another lump of meat into the trough. The sow, realising she was missing out, started a barking noise, like a dog.

Both animals had been fasted to guarantee their appetite.

Paarth listened to their grunts and snorts and squeals as they tore in, crunching through bone as readily as flesh and fat. They reminded him of the more desperate souls who came to the shelter, shovelling whatever they were offered into their mouths without tasting it, scared of losing out.

The boar finished its last chunk of meat and pushed the trough roughly with its snout, making it clang against the railings. Then it looked up, lop ears slipping back so the small eyes came into view. Paarth understood it was his imagination that the notoriously short-sighted animal was staring at him. Even so, he knew the pig recognised him; knew he controlled the food supply.

'Still hungry, huh?' he said, and the boar jerked his head as if in agreement. A mix of blood and saliva flicked from its working jaws. Paarth wiped a small drop off the sleeve of his jacket, and warned, 'Hey, you be more careful, old man.'

He reached into the wheelbarrow with gloved hands and picked out the last two chunks. He held them up, one in each hand.

Both pigs stilled, nostrils flaring as the smell reached them. While their eyesight was poor, pigs could distinguish flavours – sweet, sour, bitter, or salty. They had a sweet tooth, but what they savoured above all was meat and blood.

He threw both pieces into the troughs at the same time. The pigs darted forwards in sync.

Paarth watched them eat. Watched as the skin on those last pieces was torn and swallowed. It had been covered in a fine network of lines. Viewed as a whole, they connected up into a distinctive spider-web tattoo.

But Paarth knew that, when the pigs had finished, there would be nothing left at all.

TWELVE

Byron sat on a bench in Victoria Tower Gardens, looking out over the Thames. On the opposite side of the river, he could see the offices of the International Maritime Organisation. The front façade would have been nondescript, were it not for the verdigris'd bow of a ship, complete with anchors, that had crashed out of the ground floor to lie across the pavement. He wondered, idly, if the sculpture had been part of the original design, or added as an afterthought in an attempt to supply some architectural élan.

Behind him, the sliver of green space was separated from the traffic along Millbank by a set of spike-tipped iron railings and a line of naked trees. In front, the river flowed sluggishly under Lambeth Bridge. The Thames was supposed to be much cleaner these days, but the water resembled the caffè latte he sipped from an insulated mug. It was a bright but bitter day, and he was glad of the warmth.

Part of him wondered where Blake was right now. It had been two days since she'd walked out, refusing his offer of the guest room. Just as she had refused to assure him she would not continue her investigation into Shannon and Kensy.

He could admit – privately, at least – that he had probably not handled the situation well. But the prospect of another person he cared for putting themselves in danger had brought him near to quiet panic. He needed to keep an eye on her – keep her safe. Because the last time he'd lost that focus, the woman he loved had died.

He still recalled, with aching clarity, his wife on her knees in the bloodied grass, keeping pressure on a teenager's pumping chest wound. He should have seen the way her body curled around her pain. Should have ignored the airy lie: 'I'm fine, Byron. It's barely a scratch.' And when still he hesitated, flinching at the next scream: 'Trust me, I'm a doctor. Now, go!'

It was the last time he'd seen her alive.

Women had visited the flat since then, but not like her. Not like Blake. Having her there had affected him in ways he had not anticipated, and was not altogether sure he welcomed.

Nor had he expected the sudden emptiness when she reclaimed her clothes from the dryer and departed.

And, he realised, he still hadn't got to the bottom of the situation regarding the Derbyshire manor house. Had she succeeded in her bid to inherit the place or not?

Another knot to unravel.

He sighed. 'One problem at a time…'

Eyes hidden behind dark glasses, Byron caught movement at the far end of the gardens without turning his head. A tall black woman was striding towards him. She wore a long overcoat in pale-lemon yellow, over a black suit and high-heeled boots. The way she moved radiated confidence and authority. A passing jogger couldn't help doing a double-take, stumbling as his toe caught on the path. The woman strode on regardless. Only the quirk of her lips told Byron she was well aware of the jogger's misstep, and the reason for it.

As she neared his bench, Byron rose. 'You wanted to see me, ma'am?'

The woman paused. 'You don't report to me any longer, Byron, and there's nobody around to make more of this meeting than it is, so if you don't stop calling me "ma'am", I'll throw you in the bloody river. Understood?'

'Yes, ma'am.' Byron held his face straight a moment longer, then allowed a wry smile. 'Sorry. Old habits.'

'Break them.'

'Ah, if only it were so easy...'

'Make the effort.' She sat, tucking the coat around her legs, and gestured for him to join her.

Her parents, Somali immigrants, had been doctors in their country. Unable to practice in the UK, her mother had used her surgeon's hand and eye to alter clothing. Her father got a job on the underground. On the occasions Byron had met them, they'd seemed baffled both by their daughter and her career choice. She had been raised in the rough-and-tumble of London's East End, and was cut from very different cloth.

Commander Shamshi Daud had once been Byron's immediate boss in the Metropolitan Police, until she'd climbed further up the career ladder. He was never sure if she regretted having to swap chasing villains for more mundane, divisional concerns. But she certainly excelled at the combination of threats and diplomacy her job entailed. In Byron's experience, Daud was good at just about everything.

Except, perhaps, feigning nonchalance, he thought, as she crossed her legs and let her foot swing. 'So, how're you keeping, Byron? How do you like the new job?'

'Small talk? Really? Things must be worse than I thought.'

She uncrossed her legs, almost slamming her boot back down onto the concrete. 'Since when is showing concern – *genuine* concern, I might add – for an old friend just making small talk, hm?' she demanded. Her voice softened. 'What you've been through, I can hardly imagine what that must be like. Just because I try not to ask, doesn't mean I don't care.'

Byron removed his dark glasses and pushed them into the top pocket of his overcoat. 'I know. Don't worry, I'm... fine. Thank you for recommending me for the post.'

She cast a glum eye. 'Only "fine"?'

'I admit it's taking a little while to... settle in. I was a copper, don't forget. I spent years on the other side of the fence, thinking of the IOPC as wannabes with no real investigative experience, who would make our lives hell for six months, then reach exactly the same conclusions as the internal review.'

'Hmm.'

He twisted to face her. 'What does that mean?'

'You've already requested to start your first investigation,' she said, as if he hadn't spoken. 'The death of Shannon Clifford.'

'News travels fast considering – as you yourself pointed out – I no longer work for you.' Byron's eyes narrowed. 'Who's pulling your strings, Commander?'

'Don't take it that way. I was asked to have a quiet word, that's all. I've been... *reminded* that your job is to investigate major breaches of the police code of conduct on an institutional level. Not to look into the death of one alcoholic junkie who was drunk as a skunk when she went into the cells, and probably hit the bottle again as soon as she got out.'

'From what I can gather, it was more a case of the bottle hitting her,' Byron said. 'Besides, a life is a life. With one or two notable exceptions, I don't place a lesser value on one than another.'

'Which is all very commendable—'

'But?'

'*But*, is it the best use of your time and resources?'

'I thought the whole point of the Home Secretary and the IOPC creating my role was that I had a free hand to stick my nose in – quietly if possible, loudly if not – to any damn thing I deem worthy?'

Daud laughed. 'Did you honestly expect the politicos to be happy about their newest attack dog slipping the leash so soon, and fearing he won't come to heel?'

Byron stared out over the Thames, his gaze following one of the ferries heading towards the Millennium Pier further along Millbank. How appropriate, he thought, to be having such a cloak-and-dagger meeting outside the headquarters of MI5. He recalled Blake's words about a cover-up.

'I have to admire their promptness, if nothing else. I only put the request in yesterday.'

'That point did not escape me, either,' Daud said. 'In fact, it rang bloody great alarm bells, if you must know.'

'Hm. So, what else is at play here?'

'That, I don't know. And I dislike being kept in the dark. There are no senior officers implicated, as far as I'm aware, and the two arresting officers have no high-ranking connections...'

'So, that leaves the station itself,' Byron concluded. 'Is there anything going on at Limehouse I ought to know about?'

'If there is, they're keeping it to themselves.'

'Does this mean you're telling me to watch my step?'

'Hell no,' Daud said. 'But if you're determined to follow this up, be prepared to go stamping about in hobnailed, steel-toe-capped boots, and see what scurries out from under the floorboards.'

He saluted her briefly with his coffee. 'Message received and understood, ma'am.'

She cocked her head to one side and regarded him. 'How did you hear about this case, anyway? Someone in the job?'

Byron thought about being evasive, just for a second. 'From Blake.'

'Ah.' Daud nodded. 'I wondered why you had her flagged in the system. Regretting not making a move on her when you had the chance, are you?'

Byron said nothing.

A smile crept across the corner of Daud's mouth. 'I thought so,' she murmured, earning her a sharp glance. 'Friend of hers, was she, this Shannon?'

'Something like that.'

'Well, just make sure you're doing this for the right reasons – meaning that you're not opening up a can of worms solely in order to impress a woman.'

'Lecture over, is it?'

'It is.' Daud got to her feet, buttoned the lemon coat, then paused. 'Although, if you *are* going to take a closer look at Lime-house, I did notice that their inspector, Huw Lloyd, hits a surprising number of their targets for rough sleepers.'

'Creating them?'

'Removing them. The raid the other night, which scooped up your girlfriend, was the latest in a series of such operations. He seems to have uncanny luck when it comes to discovering the unauthorised places those poor devils congregate.'

'I'll bear that in mind.'

She nodded, jerked her head toward the road behind them. 'I have a meeting at the Home Office. It's only five minutes from here. Walk with me?'

Byron gestured vaguely with his cup. 'I think I'll stay and finish this, if you don't mind.' He cleared his throat. 'We used to sit here, in the summer, when Isobel was working over at St Thomas'. We'd have lunch, when one or other of us wasn't on call.'

Daud put her hand on his shoulder, squeezed. With uncharacteristic hesitance, she asked, 'Do you... still have the nightmares?'

He gave a fractional nod. 'Less frequently now, I think.'

It was a comment on the strength of their friendship, he considered, that she did not call him on the lie.

THIRTEEN

KING'S CROSS, ST PANCRAS

The area surrounding King's Cross brought back memories for Blake. Many of them bad.

It was the place she'd set down in London after her flight from the north, more than a decade ago. She'd been fifteen years old – frightened, bewildered, and most likely suffering from some kind of post-traumatic shock.

By that time, of course, the area had lost its utterly seedy red-light reputation, although there were still any number of run-down hotels around Argyle Square, just to the south, where the rooms were cheap enough that, in dribs and drabs over the course of the day, she might beg enough to cover one.

And on the days when she didn't manage that, there was always the station itself. Between King's Cross, St Pancras, and nearby Euston, she could pretend to wait for a train and doze in snatches before being moved on. Enough to keep her just this side of desperation.

She quickly learned to recognise the sharks that circled. The men who tried to entice girls like her – young, lost, maybe a little naïve – and those who tried to threaten. There were others, too, who viewed her purely as a marketable commodity.

Something they could acquire, mark up, and sell to the highest bidder.

Over and over again.

More by luck than judgement, Blake avoided the clutches of all of them. Her upbringing had led her to regard any sign of affection with deep suspicion, and any hint of controlling behaviour with knee-jerk alarm.

Then a security alert had closed down all three stations, leaving no safe place to go. Just before dawn the next morning, she was burrowed down behind a couple of wheelie bins on Argyle Street when they grabbed her. She was off the ground with her arms pinned, being swung towards the open side door of a van by the kerb before she came to her senses enough to struggle and kick out.

The cold had made her sluggish. It was almost too late.

The man who had hold of her cursed in a language she didn't speak back then. He threw her towards the vehicle, but at the last moment Blake had managed to brace her boots against the bodywork, landing with a boom like a bass drum.

A second man appeared in the doorway of the van, a roll of duct tape in his hand. He tried to knock her feet loose. She lashed out, caught him in the throat. Hard enough to make him stagger back.

The man holding her let go of her arms long enough to hit her in the face. An awkward angle for him – the blow stung rather than stunned. She let out a roar and reached over her shoulder, clawing for his eyes. He jerked his head away instinctively, off balance. Blake thrust off the side of the van with her legs and the pair of them tumbled backwards onto the pavement, with her on top.

She realised her mistake almost at once. He hooked his legs around hers, grabbed her arms again, and tucked in his chin so she had no purchase anywhere. She could feel his hot breath panting against her neck as she struggled uselessly.

The other man climbed out of the van with blood in his eyes.

'The feisty ones are always worth the trouble, yes?' he said in thickly accented English.

'Oh yeah?' said a woman's voice, Liverpool roots coming through strong. 'Well in that case you're gonna *love* me!'

Blake didn't see where she'd come from. Neither did the guy with the duct tape. A split-second later, one of the giant wheelie bins came crashing into him, knocking him sideways. His head made a similar sound to Blake's boots as it rebounded off the panel-work of the van.

She didn't see what the unknown woman did to the man who had her pinned, either. But she felt the jerk of his reaction, and his grip loosened enough for her to writhe free. A hand clasped hers, hauling her to her feet.

'Run!'

Blake didn't need telling twice.

They darted through the maze of back streets, didn't stop running until they reached the edge of Bloomsbury. The woman led her into a café on Marchmont Street. They sat right at the back, next to the fire exit, away from the windows and with a good view of the entrance. The woman went to the counter, returning with brimming mugs of tea.

Blake eyed one of them longingly. 'I... don't have any money.'

'Don't worry about it, queen. This one's on me.' The woman shrugged. 'I'm Shannon, by the way.'

'Blake. And it should be me buying you a cuppa.' She bit her lip. 'If it wasn't for you... well, I—'

'Don't, OK?' Shannon said. 'One day, you'll get your chance to pay it forwards.'

'I... OK. And thank you.' Blake wrapped her hands tight around the mug. It helped stop them shaking. She stared into the steaming brew and muttered, 'If *ever* I can do anything for you, you only have to ask, and I'm there. I swear it.'

'Yeah,' the woman said easily, then she stilled. 'Eh, you mean it, an' all, don't you?'

Blake looked up, took in the woman's features properly for the first time. A little worn, a little hard, a little stunned, if she was honest. 'Of course I mean it. Why wouldn't I, after what you did?'

And just like that, a friendship was born.

Ten years later, what drove Blake on was the memory of that friendship, and that promise.

She'd been hanging around King's Cross for most of the morning – watching, waiting – perched on the stone seating in the open plaza between the underground station and King's Cross itself. Sipping a takeaway coffee, she scanned the crowd, spotting a gang of pickpockets slipping between marks, a dealer palming off baggies amid apparently friendly handshakes and casual chat.

It was the dealer she watched. She didn't recognise him, but there was always a shifting cycle of names and faces.

It was an hour before she saw the guy she was after. He cut across the plaza from Euston Road, making a poor show of hiding the urgency.

The dealer did not look pleased. His need was too obvious – he drew too much attention.

Even so, the exchange was over in a second and the man hurried away with head down and shoulders hunched.

Unnoticed, Blake followed.

She caught up on York Way, which ran along the east side of the station, rounding the corner as the man crossed onto the far side of the street. Blake slipped between the cars, making the opposite pavement just as he passed one of the gated service yards between a chain restaurant and a tanning salon.

One of the steel gates was ajar. She hit the man with her

shoulder, pushing him off balance and into the gate. It swung open. In a moment, she had the front of his jacket bunched in her fists as the gate clanged shut behind them.

'Hello, Ace,' she said. 'Remember me?'

'What the—? No, get off me, you freak!'

Blake twisted her hands, tightening the jacket at his throat.

The fear leapt in his eyes. 'Take it! Just don't—'

'I'm not interested in that, Ace.'

His struggles subsided.

She leaned in. 'Let me remind you – Mile End Road squat. You were hanging around outside, but amazingly, you didn't get scooped up with the rest of us. So, how did you get to be so lucky?'

FOURTEEN

LIMEHOUSE POLICE STATION

As the police van came to a final stop in front of Limehouse Police Station, Jemma Weeks leaned back in the passenger seat and closed her eyes.

Thank God that's *over*.

For as long as she'd been with the Met, Weeks had always hated night shifts. Being out on patrol from eleven until seven clashed with her natural rhythms for sleeping and eating. Plus, it covered the hours people were on their worst possible behaviour.

She pulled off her standard-issue bowler and rubbed at her scalp where her dark hair had been flattened down during the shift. The band inside her headgear seemed to tighten around her head like a boa constrictor. She could still feel its imprint.

Her partner, Greg McCoubrey, glanced over at her and grinned. He was one of those annoying blokes who always looked put together, even at the end of a long night. And no doubt he would go straight from the station to the gym before he finally went home for some kip. She might almost admire him for it, if he wasn't already so impressed with himself.

Weeks didn't know where he found the energy. Wearing

seven kilos of gear – around fifteen pounds – didn't sound too bad, until you had to do it. During last night's shift, she'd had to chase after a bunch of teenage gazelles who'd broken into one of the buildings on a derelict industrial estate. As she ran, she'd felt every one of those extra seven kilos.

And while she was in pursuit, McConceited had driven to the far side of the estate and waited there for them to emerge – probably admiring his reflection in the rear-view mirror – and then claimed the collar.

'It's all about working smarter, Jem, not harder.'

If she hadn't been wrestling to get cuffs on the second teenager at the time, she would have cheerfully thumped her shift-mate for the smug-factor alone. And he *knew* she hated being called 'Jem'.

Now, she watched him gathering his gear, taking his time.

He caught her gaze and grinned. 'Not a bad week, eh?'

'You think?' She managed to keep the contempt out of her voice – barely. 'The biggest thing we did was harass a bunch of homeless people, chuck them out of somewhere that's probably going to be demolished anyway, and confiscate all their gear. What's good about that?'

McCoubrey glanced behind him, as if checking the cage in the rear of the van, used for transporting prisoners, was empty. For the first time during their current shift, it was.

'I know what you mean, Jem,' he said. But just when she thought he might be showing a trace of humanity, he added, ''Cause some of 'em don't half stink.'

Weeks gritted her teeth. 'You would, too, if you had no money, nowhere to live, nowhere to clean yourself up, or wash your clothes, and people like us kept moving you on every five minutes!' She shoved open the passenger door and jumped down, ignoring him when he called her name. As she marched towards the door into the station, she heard his booted footsteps hurrying to catch up.

'Hey, hold on a minute!' He grabbed her arm, spun her to face him. 'Just because you're feeling hormonal, or it's that time of the month, don't take it out on me, right?'

Weeks shrugged her arm free and said sweetly, 'Wow, if that's your reasoning for the reaction you cause, you must wonder why every woman you meet is on her period.'

That, at least, raised a scowl. 'We're told to do a job and we do it. End of,' he muttered, punching in the outer door code and shouldering through.

As she followed, Weeks murmured under her breath, 'Yeah, we do. But you don't have to enjoy it quite so much.'

She recalled him laying into one of the rough sleepers during a raid a few nights ago. The man had made a grab for his filthy rucksack. The sound of McCoubrey's baton cracking against the man's arm still echoed in her head.

She hated being paired with McCoubrey. Somehow, they always managed to find out the *last* person you'd ever want to work a graveyard shift with, and put you together. Still, at least the shift was finally over, so it wasn't all bad. A hot bath beckoned, as well as the less scintillating tasks of doing the laundry and restocking her empty fridge. At least the latter activity would also involve buying a large bottle of Lambrusco with a very short life expectancy.

'Ah, PCs Weeks and McCoubrey – just the dynamic duo I was looking for.' The voice of the custody sergeant broke ominously into her thoughts as they reached the front desk.

The mental image of a wine glass big enough to dive into vanished with a pop.

Weeks forced a smile and turned towards him. The custody sergeant was a big black man with a melancholy air and a deep resonant voice that could make a shoplifting charge sound like a hanging offence. He was noted for reducing those arrested to quivering jellyfish.

From his usual position behind the high counter, the

sergeant shifted the phone receiver from ear to shoulder and regarded the pair of them with mournful intensity.

'Inspector Lloyd wants a word with you two,' he reported. 'The very moment you got in, he said.'

'What for?' Weeks blurted out. A hollow feeling unfurled in the pit of her stomach. The idea of fizzy red wine now provoked heartburn.

McCoubrey pointedly checked the wall clock above the desk. 'Officially, we're off duty, Sarge.' He frowned. 'Is there overtime for this? I was heading for the gym.'

The sergeant stared him into silence. 'Mine is not to reason why, PC McCoubrey. Mine is simply to pass on the message and to make sure you and PC Weeks get your arses upstairs – sharpish.'

Grumbling, the two uniforms keyed through the security door and began climbing the main staircase. At the first half landing, Weeks tapped McCoubrey's arm, pausing until one of the civilian support staff had trotted past and disappeared up the next flight.

'What d'you reckon this is all about?' she asked.

McCoubrey favoured her with a nasty smirk. 'Mind reader now, am I?'

Weeks rolled her eyes and pushed past him. But two steps later she faltered, turned back.

'It's got to be something to do with that Clifford woman, hasn't it?'

'Who?'

'Oh, come off it, Greg!'

He shrugged, not quite pulling off complete nonchalance. 'That druggie who died, yeah? Well, statistically speaking, that's what happens to druggies – sooner or later. I wouldn't worry about it if I were you.' He set off up the stairs again.

A moment later, Weeks followed him, muttering, 'It's all very well to say "that's what happens to druggies", but it's a different matter when we were the ones who had her in the cells less than twenty-four hours before...'

The woman dying wasn't the issue – it was the timing that stank.

Why couldn't she have waited another day or two?

Weeks felt an immediate pang of shame for that thought. After all, the woman was still dead.

Exactly. So, she's beyond suffering or help. I need to think about my own skin.

For once, Inspector Lloyd didn't keep them waiting in the upstairs corridor. Instead, he summoned them straight into his office and firmly closed the door behind them. A big, barrel-chested Welshman, Huw Lloyd had a reputation for being blunt and to the point, which was probably why he had yet to rise further up the career ladder.

He sauntered back to his desk. The surface was cluttered with framed photos of his wife and family, which he was using as paperweights for the piles of reports.

'What's up, boss?' McCoubrey asked.

'Shannon Clifford,' Lloyd confirmed flatly. Over his reading glasses, his eyes darted between them. He nodded. 'I see the name rings a bell. Anything further you want to tell me about what happened...?'

'No, sir,' they both said in unison.

'Hm,' was his response. 'You're quite sure? If there *is* anything, you'd best speak up now.'

'What's changed, boss?' McCoubrey asked. 'I mean, I thought this one was all done and dusted. No case to answer.'

The inspector sighed. 'So did I, Greg. But it appears the IOPC aren't quite as satisfied as we were led to believe. They've sent a "special investigator", if you please – some daft new initiative from the Home Office. He wants a word with the pair of you and is waiting in the conference room, so you better have your story straight.'

It did not escape Weeks's notice that Lloyd was on first-name terms with McCoubrey. She wasn't sure if that was a good thing for both of them, or a bad thing for her.

'Why wait until now? What kind of special investigator?' Weeks heard the note of strain in her voice. So did the inspector, if his sharp glance was anything to go by.

And what's he doing on our doorstep at this time in the morning?

'Well, the good news is that he's an ex-copper, so he may even have half a brain. They're trying the softly, softly approach before they bring out the thumbscrews.' His attempt at humour fell on stony ground. 'Anyway, once they start an *official* investigation, they're obliged to report the findings. I assume this chap knows when to dig, and when to—'

'Cover up?' McCoubrey suggested.

'I was about to say, and when to *stop* digging, if you don't mind. Because there is nothing to "cover up", is there, Constable McCoubrey?'

'No, sir.'

'Still, be careful. He's been here already, unannounced, a couple of days ago – sneaky bugger. Wanted to see one of the people we brought in after we raided that property on the Mile End Road, so heaven knows what she had to say. And now he's demanding hours of CCTV footage, going back weeks, like we've nothing better to do!' He huffed out a breath.

'Are we *obliged* to talk to him?'

Lloyd paused, eyeing McCoubrey over his glasses again. 'Unofficial or not, he's still an investigator for the IOPC. So, I would strongly advise a *certain* amount of co-operation, all right? Now, off you go, the pair of you!'

As she pulled the inspector's office door shut behind them, Weeks looked at her partner. 'When he said "a certain amount of co-operation" what does that mean, exactly?'

McCoubrey's lips twisted. 'It means make sure you cover your arse, Jem.'

As they reached the conference room, her feet slowed. She didn't feel ready to face this. She needed more time to think about what to say.

The door to the room stood open. McCoubrey rapped his knuckles on the frame and leaned through the gap, as if he had no intention of lingering.

'You wanted to see us... sir?'

The man sitting at the far side of the conference table looked up from his iPad. He was small and dark, wearing a suit that fitted too well to be off the peg. And he was younger than she'd expected. For some reason, that annoyed her. If they were going to be investigated, the bloke doing it should at least look as if he'd been around the block a bit.

'Constables Weeks and McCoubrey?'

They both gave a murmured, 'Sir.'

'Good,' the man said.

He had a quiet voice. Authority without arrogance, leaving nothing to object to. Somehow, that made it worse.

'I think you know what this is about, so I won't waste time. Jemma, isn't it? I'd like to speak with you first, if you don't mind?'

Weeks did, but could hardly admit it. She flashed a quick sideways look at McCoubrey. He'd taken a breath to argue, but something about the man's utter calm shook the belligerence out of him.

The man nodded, taking their silence as acquiescence. He looked straight at her without blinking. 'My name is Byron,' he said. 'Please, come in. And close the door behind you.'

FIFTEEN

LIMEHOUSE POLICE STATION

An hour later, Byron walked out of Limehouse Police Station, buttoning his overcoat. It wasn't the first time he'd interviewed serving police officers. But it *was* the first time he'd done so for the IOPC.

He'd anticipated that it would change things, of course. In the past, the IOPC had made a point never to employ ex-police. Byron's background made him unique when it came to misconduct investigations. He'd hoped this new approach might make those under scrutiny more inclined to co-operate. He'd even wondered if Lloyd might try to trade on the fact that Byron was likely to have been in the same situation at some point in his career. Might try to claim that even the best of coppers bent the rules every now and again. And, mostly, they got away with it.

But he hadn't expected such immediate resentment from Lloyd. If the inspector realised that Byron's intervention might be the only way to avoid a formal enquiry, he didn't let it show. He'd gleaned from Lloyd's record that the man would probably not progress further than inspector. The fact he'd greeted Byron by his former rank when they were introduced rang alarm bells immediately.

Ah, so it's like that, is it?

So, he had no illusions they'd prioritise getting him the CCTV footage he'd requested of the area between Limehouse Police Station and Watney Market on the day of Shannon's demise. And Lloyd had clearly briefed his officers to give out the bare minimum, keeping just shy of obstruction.

Their statements bothered him, too. Not the differences – there weren't any. That was the point. They were very well rehearsed.

He sighed as he walked to his car. He had deliberately not used the official car park behind the station. Instead, he'd snagged one of the spaces reserved for police vehicles by the kerb in front. They stretched along West India Dock Road in both directions.

As soon as he left the station, Byron noticed the loitering figure. He recognised the bulk of PC McCoubrey, even in his civvies, and resisted the urge to quicken his pace. His parking space was beyond the reach of the security cameras outside the station. No doubt McCoubrey was well aware of that.

As he approached, McCoubrey drew up to his full height and stared down at Byron. He was probably just over six foot, and clearly enjoyed the advantage he felt that gave him.

In Byron's experience, being smaller, faster, and meaner, usually won the day. It was, quite possibly, the reason he was still alive. His eyes flicked over the Mercedes, half-expecting sabotage. Nothing seemed amiss.

'PC McCoubrey.' Byron stopped a couple of metres away. 'Did you wish to add to your statement?'

McCoubrey hesitated, hands stuffed into the pockets of his bomber jacket.

'Look, sir, we've been told to say as little as possible – stick to the bare facts.'

'I gathered.'

'Yeah, but... if the ship's sinking, I don't want to go down with it, you know? I mean, if the IOPC have sent someone like you to dig around, they must think there's something to find...'

'Not necessarily. My job is to ascertain if the situation demands an official investigation. If not, then it all goes away quietly and the IOPC proper were never here.'

McCoubrey nodded, frowning.

'Why don't you tell me what's troubling you, and I'll see if I can put your mind at rest?'

'Yes... thank you. Well, sir, it's Jem – PC Weeks. During the arrest she did end up losing her temper a bit. Clifford was wild when we got on scene, you see – staggering about, shouting nonsense. She caught Jem a belter. Unlucky, really, but Jem kind've walked onto the punch. That's when she drew her baton.'

'Where did she strike Ms Clifford?'

'Well, I *thought* it was across the shoulders, but the way that woman was thrashing about, it was hard to tell. And afterwards, when she died, like... Well, you wonder, don't you?'

'Are you saying that PC Weeks's baton did indeed connect with the back of Ms Clifford's head?'

'Well, yeah, I suppose that is what I'm saying.' He frowned again, adding hurriedly, 'But, if it did, it was completely accidental, I'm dead sure about that.'

SIXTEEN

HENRIETTA PLACE, MARYLEBONE

The art gallery was just off Henrietta Place, north of Oxford Street. There was no name above the glossy windows, and very little displayed within, but a discreet brass plaque on the door read:

Dalchetta & Child
Valuers and Purveyors of Fine Art, Est 1891
Commissions undertaken

Blake didn't bother trying to get in that way. There was no point, dressed as she was. The staff had a keen eye for money, and Blake knew her appearance came up way short of affording anything the gallery had to offer – officially, or unofficially. She doubted they would bother releasing the door, even to shoo her away.

Instead, she took the narrow service alley alongside the building. A large wheelie bin put her close to the top of a high wall, then onto a sloping roof and up to a convenient sash window. It was closed, but she knew the alarm would not be set during business hours. In a few moments, she had finessed the window lock. She dropped inside, landing lightly on the balls of her feet.

Blake remained there, immobile, for another five seconds, but heard nothing. Satisfied at the lack of response, she slipped down the staircase to the shop floor, timing her descent of the next flight, to the basement, when the staff had their backs turned.

Below street level, there were no windows. The space had been turned into storage at the rear, a waiting area and tiny kitchen at the bottom of the stairs, and a lavish office directly under the sales floor. As she neared the closed office door, Blake heard two distinct male voices, speaking Ukrainian.

It took a second to register the voices were getting louder. She dived for the kitchen, just making it inside before the office door opened and the two emerged, still in discussion. She listened to their feet on the stairs, then the buzz of the outer door as the client departed.

By the time the other man returned, she was leaning back in the leather chair in his office, with her boots up on the desktop, feet crossed at the ankles.

The man paused in the doorway, eyeing her with no expression on his cruelly handsome face. Staring back, she could understand why some people sweated at the mere mention of Lex Vaganov's name.

The first time she had encountered him, Blake feared she might not survive the experience. She was still living rough, doing whatever she had to. Shannon had drilled street smarts into her, taught her to look out for the easy marks and the ones to run a mile from.

Vaganov fell firmly into the latter category.

And maybe, if she'd been less desperate, she would have steered clear, as her instincts demanded. But she *was* desperate. And cold. And hungry.

So she bumped him as he crossed the pavement between

limo and high-end Knightsbridge store. In the time it took her to mutter an apology, head down, her fingers had dipped inside his jacket.

She didn't pause. Kept moving. Thought she'd pulled it off until a hand grabbed the back of her hoodie and yanked her to a standstill.

Instantly, she twisted like a hooked fish, hands and feet flailing. For all the effect it had, she might as well have been hitting a statue.

She tried to squirm out of the hoodie, but he'd got a fistful of hair as well, and held tight.

Before she knew it, she was sent sprawling onto the jump seat of the limo. Her captor climbed in behind her. The door slammed, the locks engaged, and the big car launched into traffic.

For a second, Blake lay where she'd landed, sore, frozen, her mind in turmoil.

When she'd caught her breath, she levered to a sitting position.

Her captor lounged in the opposite corner of the rear seat, legs crossed, regarding her with cold eyes and a half smile that did not reach them. Blake took in the cigarette-paper-thin veneer of civilisation – bespoke suit, handmade shoes, manicured nails – and silently berated her lousy judgement.

She mustered her dignity, dug up the private-school accent she thought she'd left far behind, and said, 'I suppose you know that kidnapping is a crime?'

One eyebrow lifted fractionally. 'So is theft.'

His accent was Eastern European – Russian, if her luck was bad.

She hid a tremor, spreading empty hands. 'Theft of what, exactly?'

His eyes narrowed. Frowning, he reached inside his jacket, stilling as his fingers encountered the 'missing' wallet. He brought it out, fat with cash, and tossed it carelessly onto the seat alongside him. As if it was of no value.

Blake allowed herself one brief look, hid the longing. Her turn to raise an eyebrow.

'You stole it,' the man said, almost to himself. 'And then you put it back.'

'A fascinating theory. I think you may have trouble proving it in a court of law.'

'Who said anything about court?' He let that one settle. 'And I have my own law.'

Which she had just broken, no doubt. Big time.

She swallowed, but said lightly, 'So, what's it to be – fed through a wood chipper, or fitted for a concrete overcoat and sent to sleep with the fishes?'

For the first time, something flickered in his face that might have been amusement in a weaker man.

'Both time-consuming and overly elaborate. You are homeless, clearly. A needle in your arm and dumped in a derelict building might be more appropriate, perhaps?'

'Except I'm clean.' She pushed the sleeves of her hoodie back to the elbows. 'No track marks. Some bright copper might smell a rat.'

He flicked his fingers, dismissive. 'Such things can always be... overcome.'

'I'm sure they can. But you might encounter the Met's only honest copper. Think of the hassle.'

He grunted, the spark of humour dying away as he regarded her in unnerving silence. Then: 'You do not seem to be afraid of me.'

Hard to know if that was question or statement.

For a split second, Blake hesitated, then decided on truth. 'Of course I am. I'm not a complete fool.'

'And yet, you attempted to rob me,' he said, as if that proved otherwise.

'A sign of desperation trumping common sense.'

'How desperate?'

'Not *that* desperate,' she said quickly.

He pursed his lips. 'What is your name?'

Again, she thought about lying.

Again, she did not.

'Blake. Blake Claremont.'

He gave a fractional nod. 'I think I could use someone like you. And I know you could certainly use someone like me – if you want to get off the streets.'

'Really? I don't know anything about you, or what you do.'

Or what you might expect me to do.

He leaned forwards, held out his hand. 'Lex Vaganov.'

After a beat, she took it. They shook.

'Now we have been introduced, and you know who I am. Here's my card. My offer expires in twenty-four hours.' He glanced at his expensive watch. 'No extensions.'

The driver glided to a stop at the kerb without being asked, ignoring both bus lane and double red lines. They were outside a Turkish café on Brompton Road. The door locks clunked open.

Vaganov peeled several twenties out of the wallet and proffered them. 'I recommend the food here,' he said. His lip curled. 'Or, there is a McDonald's just across the street.'

Blake took the money. 'I'm not *that* desperate.'

* * *

As he regarded her now – in his office, behind his desk – she caught an echo of that first meeting.

'I will not ask you how you got in, because I think they probably heard you crashing about up there all the way out at Watford Gap,' he said at last, coming fully inside and closing the door behind him. 'You're losing your touch.'

'Liar.' Blake flashed him a quick grin. 'New cameras?'

'That is for me to know.' He rounded the desk, nudging her feet off the desktop with his hip as he perched on the edge, looming over her. 'What are you doing here, Blake? Aren't you supposed to be keeping a low profile?'

'Lowering the tone, am I? I might have just wanted to see the new place. Far more upmarket than the old Chiswick gaff, but not *quite* in Mayfair, is it?'

'It's close enough that my clientele do not have to step too far outside their comfort zone,' he returned easily.

His accent, when he wasn't putting on his Russian heavy act, was pure cut glass. Or perhaps that was the act, she'd never been sure. There was an air of an ageing Hugh Grant about him – after the actor had started playing heavies and stopped playing fops.

She indicated the closed door with a nod of her head, and by dint of that, the man who'd just left. 'Another satisfied customer?'

The silence lay between them for a beat, then Vaganov said blandly, 'The gentleman has just paid pleasingly over the odds for a Diasec-mounted Giclée on Aluminium piece by Damien Hirst, as a matter of fact.'

'Oh, such a fancy way of describing an inkjet printout glued under a layer of plastic.'

'It's a patented process of joining together transparent acrylic onto prints. Gives a permanent mount, a flat finish, and more brilliant colours, if you don't mind. And it's a limited edition – signed and numbered.'

'I'm impressed. You sound almost as though you know what you're talking about.' She paused, smiling. 'And what *else* did he pay for?'

'Let's just say he is more than happy with his purchase, even allowing for my... fees, and leave it at that, shall we? Another eighteen months and the piece will have recouped his additional expenses in any case.'

Blake shook her head. 'There's nothing like hiding in plain sight, is there?'

'No,' he said bluntly. 'I'll ask you again. Why are you here?'

'I'm just checking in, Lex – as instructed, I might add.'

'I had in mind that you would do so maybe every couple of days.' He flicked his eyes up towards the ceiling, as if asking a higher power for strength, or patience. Then he glanced pointedly at his watch. Today, he wore an Omega, she noticed. No doubt the James Bond influence. 'This is the first time you've been in touch in a month.'

She shrugged. 'There was nothing to report.'

'And now there is?'

'Maybe.'

'OK, so sit down and report.'

She smiled again. 'I am sitting.'

'Somewhere *else*, Blake.'

She waited another beat, then rose, sliding around him when he didn't give her an inch, and slouching into the visitor chair opposite the desk.

Lex undid the button on his suit jacket and took the chair she'd just vacated. He leaned back, steepling his fingers while she gave him a brief run-through of her recent history. When she was done, he looked at her for a long moment before his face softened.

'That smart mouth of yours aside, it's good to see you, kiddo.'

'Worried about me, huh?'

'When you go off the grid like that? Yes.'

'Aw. I can take care of myself – you of all people should know that.'

'Yeah, but it's been a long time since you were last on the streets.'

'Trust me, I know that. And I know it hasn't got any easier in the meantime.'

'But you're OK? Nobody has given you any trouble?'

'Apart from the cops, no.'

He gave a snort, murmured, 'So, nothing changes.'

She got up, suddenly restless, circled the office as if trapped there.

'And... Byron has stuck his nose in again.'

'Has he now? The last I heard of John Byron, he is with the IOPC. A policeman investigating policemen. What could possibly go wrong?'

It should not have surprised Blake that Lex knew all about Byron's new role. But she was a little put out that he hadn't passed on that information. Information was, after all, his primary business.

'Well, he turned up at Limehouse, asking for me. And last time I checked, I was not a policeman.'

Vaganov swore under his breath. 'I told him to leave you alone. The damn man doesn't listen.'

Blake stilled.

'When?' she demanded. 'When did you tell him to leave me alone?'

'He came looking for you.' Vaganov leaned back in his chair. The leather creaked under him. 'About a month ago. I told him if you had wanted to get in touch with him, you would have done so by now.'

'But you didn't think to tell *me* any of this?'

'If you had checked in, as you were supposed to, I would have mentioned it.'

Blake rubbed her hands across her face. 'Yeah, well, I'm checking in now, aren't I?'

'You are. Better late than never.'

Blake glared at him, gleaning nothing. Lex's poker face was impervious to the assault.

'He even went up to Claremont looking for me,' she said.

'Did he indeed?'

'They told him zilch.'

'I should hope not, after all you've done for them.' Lex pursed his lips, considering. For a moment, she thought he might say more, but when he looked up it was merely to ask, 'Was there anything else?'

'Possibly.' She hesitated. 'What have you heard about an app for the homeless?'

'It's not something that's come up on my radar.' He raised an eyebrow. 'Designed with what purpose in mind?'

'That's a good question. In theory, it allows good Samaritans to report sightings of homeless people. It's supposed to trigger a quick response from local authorities to go out offering shelter, food, meds, whatever.'

He threw her a cynical glance. 'Seriously?'

'I did say "in theory".'

'Oh, of course! Because we all know how much cash local authorities have to spare, simply burning a hole in their pocket,' he scoffed. 'Whose hare-brained scheme was this?'

Blake shrugged. 'I was rather hoping you might be able to tell me that.'

She gave him the name of the app, which he typed in to his laptop, preparing to do a search. Then he paused, studying her intently.

'Why do I get the feeling there's more to this than idle curiosity?'

She let out a long breath. 'It would seem that someone is also using the app for... other purposes.'

'Such as?'

'That squat I was in on the Mile End Road the other night?'

'The one that was raided. Ah, you think someone reported it using this app?'

She nodded.

'That might be coincidence. It would only have taken one nosy neighbour to call their local cop shop.'

'It might,' she agreed sedately.

When she didn't continue, he fixed her with a glare. He had very deep blue eyes in a classically handsome face, at odds with a haircut that looked as if he'd just come from boot camp or prison. 'But?'

'When I got there, I did a quick recce, as always. I spotted a guy who I've come across occasionally – he calls himself Ace, would you believe? Anyway, he was hanging around outside. He hid his phone, and there was just something slightly off about him.'

'And still you went in?' Vaganov swore under his breath. 'Dammit, Blake, I taught you better than that.'

She didn't quaver. 'I'd got a lead on Kensy, so it's not like I had a choice.'

He scowled but said nothing.

'Anyway, afterwards, it occurred to me that I didn't see Ace picked up with the others, so when the cops let me go, I tracked him down and... asked him a few questions.'

Vaganov showed his teeth. 'Politely, of course.'

'Of course.' She grinned in return. 'He confirmed that he reported our location and scarpered.'

'Reported it to whom?'

She shrugged. 'Just keyed it into the app, so he reckons.'

'And what was in it for him?'

'He said that he picked up a bounty the next day. They pay in packs of cigarettes, although I think he'd prefer something stronger.'

'And he's no idea who "they" are?'

'He reckoned not, and I pushed him as hard as I considered wise, given the circumstances.'

'I'm sure. Where does he collect from?'

'Different places – usually ones where you'd expect to find the homeless – churches, shelters, soup kitchens and the like.'

He tapped his forefingers against his lips, pensive. 'Leave it with me for a day or so. I'll see what I can find out.' He rose, buttoned his suit jacket again and gave her a grim smile. 'At least it might mean you won't disappear for so long this time.'

Blake got to her feet, also, and headed for the door. But there she hesitated. 'There is something else.'

'Oh?'

'Byron.' She forced herself to turn back, to meet his eyes. 'I asked him to look into Shannon's death – in his IOPC capacity. After all, if the cops killed her—'

Vaganov went still. Blake tensed in automatic response.

'That's... unfortunate,' he said at last.

'I know, but he kind of goaded me into it.'

'Really? How?'

'By being so damned reasonable.'

That earned her a brief flash of a smile. 'As I say, that is unfortunate. Because, when we find out what happened to Shannon, I hardly think he will approve of our ideas on justice delivered, do you?'

'We could leave that part of it in his hands,' she offered. 'He claims he'll get to the truth, no matter whose toes he treads on.'

Vaganov shook his head. 'The police have already swept her death under the carpet when we both know they're responsible. And once a cop, always a cop. I don't expect Mr Byron to do anything other than whitewash the whole thing and try to push the blame onto somebody else.'

SEVENTEEN

Following his interview with the two constables, Byron found himself at the location of Shannon Clifford's arrest. A complex that was part industrial estate, part retail park, on the edge of Canning Town, where the Lea coiled sluggishly towards the Thames.

A large chain supermarket, nestling between the warehouses like a well-kept secret, incorporated a truck filling station. The in-store café was frequented as much by truck drivers as by shoppers.

It was the café manager who'd called the police after Shannon caused a disturbance, refusing to leave. Byron spoke to a couple of the counter staff who'd been working that day. The only thing they could add to the officers' statements was that one of the regular drivers, Big Frankie, had bought Shannon a hot drink.

Outside, Byron turned up his collar against the slanting rain as he surveyed the cluster of trucks near the fuel station. Big Frankie reportedly drove a DAF XF. He headed over, skirting the deeper puddles forming on the apron.

Close to, the truck was huge, hauling a standard forty-foot

shipping container. Byron knocked on the driver's door and stepped back. After a moment the window buzzed down and a woman with spiky dark-grey hair peered down at him. Her jaw rolled, working gum.

'Ah, you wouldn't be Big Frankie, by any chance?'

'Aye, what of it?' the woman demanded in a thick Glaswegian accent. It was hard to tell if she was being unfriendly, or merely cautious.

'My name is Byron. I'm investigating the circumstances surrounding the death of Shannon Clifford.'

'Is that the wee lassie that was here? 'Cause that's an awful long-winded way of putting it. You polis?'

'Not exactly.'

Byron started to reach for his ID, but the woman stopped him with a jerk of her chin.

'Not out here, bampot. Come around the other side and step into my parlour. And no funny stuff, eh?' she added. 'Or I'll batter yer – pretty boy or no.'

Byron was smiling as he followed her instructions, opening the passenger door of the cab and hauling himself up. He settled into the armchair seat before handing over his IOPC credentials.

Big Frankie was a stocky woman, but by no means large – Byron judged her height at maybe five foot one or two. She was dressed in loose yoga pants and a sweatshirt with the trucking firm's logo across the front. Putting aside a thick paperback, she studied his official ID with pursed lips. Eventually she sighed, folded the wallet closed and passed it back, regarding him glumly.

'Polis Conduct? Well, there's another of my illusions shattered.'

'Oh?'

'Just as I was thinking you were a step up from the usual rough trade we get working the truck parks, eh?'

Byron masked another smile. 'Sorry to disappoint you.'

She laughed, picking the paperback off her knee and sliding in a bookmark before setting it down on the wide centre console, next to a Thermos flask. She was reading Dostoevsky's *Crime and Punishment*, he noted.

'Enjoying your book?'

She shrugged. 'It's no my favourite, to be honest.'

'Oh?'

'Aye, I think *Demons* is a more satisfying tragedy for today's world. Really gets into the nitty-gritty of morality an' all that. Although, I've always had a soft spot for *The Idiot*. That story structure should'nae work, but somehow it just *does*, yer know?'

'I understand it was Dostoevsky's personal favourite.'

'Aye, well, there yer go. But I'm guessing youse didn't come out here to discuss Russian literature?'

'No – more's the pity,' Byron said. 'Tell me about your inter-action with Shannon Clifford.'

She made a harrumph of sound. 'Better late than never, eh?'

'Do I take it that no one has spoken with you before now?'

Big Frankie fixed him with a stern eye. 'If youse official, you'll know full well they've not. So what's yer game?'

'To collect the raw facts, and attempt not to throw whatever preconceptions I may have into the mix.' Byron matched her stare, raised and returned it. 'And then I look at where those pieces don't quite fit together.'

Big Frankie remained silent for a moment. Then she nodded. 'Aye, fair enough. Ask away, pal.'

'The staff at the cafeteria said you came in after Shannon, and that you bought her a hot drink. Why?'

'What kinda question is that? She was freezing and not right. I woulda called her an ambulance if she'da let me.' As if prompted by the memory, Big Frankie unscrewed the lid of her Thermos, poured steaming black coffee into a travel mug. She waved the flask in Byron's direction.

He shook his head.

'Do you make a habit of looking after strangers?'

'Trust me, she was no stranger. Oh, I don't mean we'd ever met before,' she went on before Byron could speak. 'But no woman down on her luck is ever gonna be a stranger to me, not when I lived with a pure pig of a man for ten year or more. I survived and I got out. There's plenty who're no so lucky. If I can lend a hand, I will, right enough.'

Byron inclined his head in acknowledgement. 'Where was Shannon when you first noticed her?'

'Coming from o'er that way.' The woman gestured with her mug. 'She was weaving about so much, she looked blootered.'

'"Blootered"?'

'Drunk, y'know? At first, I thought maybe she was one of the working girls they drop off here to "entertain" the truckers. Every now and again, one of the newbies will give a tap on my door. If it's cruel cold weather, I'll let 'em sit in the cab a wee while – just to warm up, eh?'

'Did you see where Shannon came from?'

'It was quiet – no so much parked over there. But there was this white van, from some charity. I kinda got the impression she mighta come from that.'

'Do you recall which charity? And what made you think it was that particular vehicle?'

'I cannae remember the name of it.' She flicked her hand towards the dashcam mounted near the top of the truck's huge windscreen. 'I'd check the video, but the SD card overwrites every three weeks, so it's long gone by now. And it was the lassie I kept my eye on. At first, I thought she was maybe high.'

'What changed your mind?'

'Well, she did'nae have the look. And... there was nobody dealing that day.'

Byron raised an eyebrow. 'You know this because...?'

Big Frankie scowled. 'I make it my business to know.'

'Ah.'

'No like that! Here.' She pulled her keys from the truck's ignition and tossed them at Byron with more force than was necessary. He caught the bunch in his gloved hands – thankfully without fumbling. The keys were attached to a black leather fob that bore a logo familiar to any copper.

'Narcotics Anonymous,' he murmured, meeting her gaze. 'You were an addict.'

'Still am – same as youse never stop being an alky. I just happen to have gone fifteen years now, "clean and serene", as they say.'

'Congratulations. That's quite an achievement.'

'For a wee jakey lass from Govan, yer mean?'

Byron was beginning to wish he had a translator, but she took pity on him. 'A jakey is a druggie, Mr Byron. And trust me, I can spot one a mile off.' She shook her head. 'I don't know what was ailing your lassie. Just 'cause I didn't smell booze on her, that doesn't mean she hadn't touched a drop. But I'd lay a wager she was'nae high.'

Byron paused a moment, considering his options and obligations, then said, 'She had a bleed on the brain.'

Big Frankie muttered a curse. 'That what killed her, was it?'

He nodded. 'Eventually, yes. There would have been some kind of a blow to the head initially. The question is when that occurred. Did you see what happened after you left her in the café?'

'Nah, but I didn't hang around – had to get back on the road, y'know? And with a slug of hot choccie inside her, she seemed to perk up a bit. Dammit... If I'd thought otherwise, I would'nae left her.'

'I'm told you're through here frequently. Had you ever seen Shannon before?'

'Nah,' she said again. 'If she'd been a regular, I woulda recognised her. I stop here twice a week – youse can set yer watch by me, right enough. Forty-five minutes minimum, every time.'

'That's very precise. Your mandated driving hours, I presume?'

Her eyes widened a fraction. 'Aye. Since they brought in these fancy digital tachos, you go a few seconds over yer four-and-a-half hours, or set off a few seconds before youse due, and they'll have yer for it. It's all black and white.' She paused, gave him a smile so dry it was almost arid. 'It's no like the law, eh? If your face fits, well, you seem to have a tad more leeway.'

Byron did not return her smile. 'As far as I'm concerned, the law is the law, and the fit of your face has nothing to do with it.'

EIGHTEEN

Blake sat people-watching in Trafalgar Square, the National Gallery looming in the background.

Alongside her was old Tristram. Blake had been told he'd once had a normal life, with a wife and a home somewhere up north. What happened then, he never spoke of. She guessed he'd had some kind of breakdown, and fallen through the cracks like so many others.

It was impossible to judge his age, under the mass of tangled grey hair and beard. Some people wore their bodies hard. He might have been anywhere from forty-five to seventy. On the far side of Tristram was Caz, as ever. After their previous run-ins, Blake wasn't sure of her reception. Caz went no further than a few daggered looks, which Blake let ride. Besides, the woman seemed genuinely fond of Tristram, making Blake second-guess her cynical take on the relationship. For now, she treated Caz with a kind of careful neutrality.

Out of habit, the three of them chose the end bench of a line set against the wall of the North Terrace, facing down Whitehall. The fountains were in front, with the empty Fourth Plinth just above them, and steps leading up to the terrace. Owning almost nothing did not prevent anyone with even less from trying to steal it. At least, this way, Blake would see them coming.

Vigilance was one of the first things Shannon had taught her about surviving on the streets.

Always be aware of who's around you – especially who's behind you.

Never walk with your head down and your eyes on your phone. If you gotta look, stop and stand with your back to a wall.

Walk close to the buildings if there's parked cars to hide between. Close to the kerb if there's alleyways.

Keep what you have close, zipped shut, and in sight.

Most of all, don't trust anybody. Especially the ones offering something for nothing.

There were a few exceptions, of course. She'd also taught Blake where to go for shelter, food, or the barest essentials. Lessons she had not forgotten in the decade or more since.

So, after her gear was confiscated by the cops, Blake had found a replacement backpack at a church on Spanish Place. A sleeping bag at the Salvation Army. She'd just picked up a knitted hat and gloves from St Martin-in-the-Fields, a stone's throw away. If she leaned forwards, she could still see the church spire from where she sat.

Caz noticed the replacements as soon as she and Tristram arrived. Blake saw her gaze turn calculating, and guilelessly chattered about where she'd obtained each of her new treasures.

'I was lucky,' she added. 'They said there'd been a run on this kind of stuff.'

'It's as I've been telling you.' Tristram stroked nicotine-stained fingers through his beard. 'The police and local councils have been told to crack down on us – "clearing away" our belongings.' He gave a rasp of laughter. 'Such a tidy euphemism for "stealing", don't you think?'

Blake glanced at him. Some days, Tristram was more alert

and lucid than others, and it paid to take advantage of that fact. He might be a bit of a conspiracy theorist, but that didn't make him wrong.

'They've been told by who?'

'By whom,' he corrected absently. 'By their elders and betters – the apparatchiks, the government. They squeeze us out onto the streets without a qualm, but don't like actually having to look at us afterwards. They're getting rougher, too. There's no call for it. Made last winter worse than it needed to be for a good many of us, that's for sure.'

'You wasn't around then, was you?' Caz made it sound like an accusation.

'I was in Derbyshire,' Blake said blandly. 'Foston Hall.'

'Ooh, that some fancy country house?'

'No – women's prison.'

Blake hoped her spur-of-the-moment invention would shut down Caz's line of questioning. It had the desired effect.

She watched a straggle of tourists hurrying past. It was too cold to linger. They were speed-walking through the sights on their must-see list. A quick selfie for social media with Nelson's Column in the background, then on to the next.

She'd almost forgotten what it was like to be semi-invisible. People carefully didn't make eye contact, didn't smile or call a greeting, but were obviously aware of the trio by the space they left around them. Like an unofficial exclusion zone.

One or two, she noted, eyed the cloth cap Tristram had placed, upturned, a metre or so in front of the bench. He'd seeded it with a few coins, but no one added to their paltry total.

'Slow day,' Tristram grumbled. 'Nobody carries cash any more.'

'Think we're gonna waste it if they give it to us, more like,' Caz put in.

Maybe, Blake considered, that was where this new app

came in? A way for people to salve their conscience without actually having to put their hand in their pocket.

She tried not to think about the meagre info she'd dragged out of Ace outside King's Cross the day before. It was in Lex's hands now, and she would just have to be patient.

A bitter wind shimmied through the square. Blake huddled deeper into her thin jacket.

'Gonna be another cold one tonight,' she said. 'Any word on a good place?'

But Tristram's attention was no longer on Blake. He'd stiffened, sat up straighter, and unconsciously pulled his bags and bedroll closer in around his knees, as though circling the wagons.

'I wondered how long it would take them,' he muttered.

'Who? The cops?' Blake scanned the square. There were a couple of uniforms in sight, for the sake of the tourists. They'd been there for maybe half an hour – she'd been keeping an eye on them. So far, they'd showed no interest.

'Oh, no, worse than the police.' Tristram lifted his chin. 'Them.'

Blake followed his gaze. A van had pulled up at the bollards marking the pedestrianised zone near the statue of General Napier. The van was white, with a stylised logo on the side, and 'Kinfolk: registered charity' underneath.

Three people got out – an Asian couple, and a woman with long white dreadlocks surrounding a face so pale she looked Scandinavian. The Asian woman was a head smaller, dressed in a long kurta tunic over matching trousers, a silk scarf around her neck. The scarf slipped and she tossed it back over her shoulder. A trademark gesture.

Adhiti Chatterjee.

'Oh, isn't that the celebrity chef woman from the telly?' she asked with more enthusiasm than she felt. 'Who are Kinfolk? What's up with them?'

'Ah, they're no bother if you know how to treat 'em.' Caz smiled, got to her feet. 'Might see what goodies they've got.' She strolled towards the van.

'Just be sure you don't let them take you,' Tristram called after her.

She waved at him without looking back.

'Are they really so bad?' Blake asked. 'I mean, they're legit, aren't they?'

He shrugged, distracted, following Caz's progress with an anxious frown. 'Maybe they are. Won't stop them spiriting you away. All in league together...'

'Why would they spirit anyone away?'

'I told you – they want to clear us off the streets. By any means necessary. Oh, they might dress it up nicely as "rescuing" you, but it's kidnapping, plain and simple.' He grasped her arm, a sudden urgency to his voice. 'Don't let them take *you*, either.'

Almost absently, Blake twisted herself free, using technique rather than force. 'I won't *let* anyone do anything to me, don't you worry. Or to anyone else, if I can help it.'

'No, I don't think you would.' He regarded her through eyes turned sharp. 'You remind me of a girl I used to know. She was fierce, like you. She could take care of herself, too. And the others...'

'The others?'

But his gaze had drifted back to Caz, standing by the open side door of the Kinfolk van. She was chatting with the Asian woman, who laughed at something Caz said.

The Asian man who'd been driving was inside the back of the van. He was big enough to bend almost double to clear the roof. As Blake watched, he lifted the lid on a plastic storage bin, and Caz leaned to get a better look at the contents. Adhiti Chatterjee and the woman with the dreadlocks both seemed to take a step closer to her. Blake heard Tristram's sharply indrawn breath.

She had a sudden flashback to the van all those years ago near King's Cross. And Shannon, coming to her rescue.

But then Caz straightened, and the women stepped back. The memory faded.

Tristram let out a breath. He shook his head, as if to loosen old memories of his own. 'Young Kensy and Spider... Maybe if the police hadn't hurt them, they wouldn't have fallen prey to those people. Easy pickings, the injured...'

'Wait – that's where they went? With Kinfolk? Where would they have taken them?'

He shrugged. 'They have a shelter over near St George-in-the-East. After that? Who knows...?'

Blake grabbed her backpack and shot to her feet, just as Caz began to head back towards them.

'You're not thinking of going with them, are you?' Tristram demanded hoarsely. 'After all I've said?'

Blake glanced at him. 'Because of it.'

She walked away, crossing over with Caz, like an exchange of prisoners on a Cold War bridge in Berlin. Caz gave her a sideways look, but said nothing.

As Blake approached the van, the woman with the dread-locks had just got behind the wheel. The man was climbing out of the rear sliding door. He straightened, slamming it shut before he caught sight of Blake. He was a big guy, wearing a leather jacket over a Kinfolk sweatshirt. Something about the way he stared at her set all the hairs rising at the back of Blake's neck, but she forced her feet to keep moving.

It was Adhiti Chatterjee who smiled at her.

'Hello, sweetie, do you need some help?'

Blake pasted on a smile, injecting what she hoped was just the right amount of desperation into it. 'Yeah, I do...'

NINETEEN

NEASDEN LANE, NEASDEN

Tess knew something was wrong as soon as she opened the main door and heard the baby crying in the flat upstairs.

For a second, she froze in the tiled hallway. Her gaze was locked on the half-landing where the stairs turned above her. Nothing stirred up there. That frightened her more than screaming.

Carefully, she bent her knees until the two bags of shopping settled onto the floor at her feet. Not taking her eyes off the landing overhead, she groped her left hand into the top of one bag until she found a can of something. She didn't look to see what.

With the can clenched in her fist, arm straight by her side so it was mostly hidden, Tess began to climb. She put her feet down very deliberately, as if whoever lurked upstairs might hear the treads creaking, even over the bawling infant.

The baby cried on, great gulping, howling sobs, like her throat was tearing.

If he is here, that will have really set him off – made him so much worse...

As Tess reached the first floor, she saw the door to the flat was open. Not just a crack, but thrown wide. She hurried along the open landing, slowing only as she stepped inside. The can was still in her hand, knuckles white around the label.

'Viv?' Her voice came out wavering rather than strong. She cleared her throat. 'Viv? You in here?'

There was no response other than the baby's unrelenting cries. Every now and then they ebbed as she was forced to choose between screaming or dragging in breath. As she refilled her lungs, she began afresh – the note shrill and vicious.

Tess shuffled forwards, her feet unwilling to take her on. She glanced into the sitting room as she passed through. Books had been snatched from the shelves and stamped on. They lay splayed and scattered, spines broken like dead birds. Viv's few knick-knacks – plates and vases, that bit of china from her gran – lay in pieces. The TV had been kicked off its stand in the corner, the screen in fragments.

Tess ducked through the archway into the kitchenette – now liberally redecorated in flour and what she hoped was tomato pasta sauce.

'Viv!' she called again, more sharply this time.

'H-here.'

She found her friend in the bedroom, hunched down in the narrow space between the bed and the wall. Viv was clutching the screaming baby tight between knees and chest.

Tess crouched in front of her, only realising as she did so that she was still gripping the tin can. Light rice pudding, she noted vaguely. It would've still been heavy enough to do him damage, though, if he'd been there.

Or so she tried to tell herself.

A moot point, anyway. He was long gone, leaving only carnage behind.

It took Viv a while to register her arrival. Eventually, she raised bloodshot, tear-stained eyes to meet Tess's above the baby's empurpled face and wisp of hair. The infant screeched on, but her heart wasn't in it.

'Was it... *him*?' Tess wouldn't say his name. Never again.

Viv shook her head. 'How should I know? Had one of them ski mask things on, didn't he?'

Tess let out a long breath. 'I'll go, yeah? Give me a couple of days to—'

'No!' Viv's sudden vehemence shocked even the baby into momentary silence. She swallowed. 'Look, I'm sorry, Tess. If it were just me, that would be different, but—'

'It's OK, you don't have to say it.' Tess's shoulders slumped. 'I'll get my stuff and be out of your hair. Unless...?' She studied Viv's face, caught both relief and fear there. 'Do you want some help...? With the clearing up, I mean?'

Viv shook her head mutely. Tess didn't miss the slump of her shoulders.

Tess rose, stumbling as she left the bedroom. She gathered her few bits and pieces. By that time, Viv had recovered her nerve enough to hover in the bedroom doorway, the baby still in her arms. The little girl had quietened to mewling, her face a mess of snot and tears – both child and mother, for that matter.

'I'm sorry,' Viv repeated. 'But you didn't see him – how he was, I mean. Like some kind of *animal*. He just barged his way in here and... Well, you can see for yourself...'

Tess closed her eyes for a moment, hiding from the anguish in her friend's face, and the guilt in her own. 'Did you... um...?'

'Did I what? Call the cops?' Viv made a noise that was half snort, half sob. Her mouth twisted derisively. 'What do *you* think?'

TWENTY

KINFOLK, CABLE STREET, SHADWELL

When Blake knocked on the door marked 'Office' after breakfast, nobody answered. She tried the handle more in hope than expectation, was surprised to find it unlocked.

After only a momentary pause – and a quick glance up and down the deserted corridor – she cracked open the door and slipped inside, leaving it ajar behind her.

Doing so was a calculated risk. If she was caught, she could always claim the door had been open when she arrived. If she shut it behind her and anyone came in, it spoke of criminal intent. A place like Kinfolk dealt with addicts all the time. People who were prepared to sell their granny – and had probably done so, in many cases – for their next fix. The only thing she was looking to steal was information, but they didn't know that, and she wasn't about to tell.

Inside, the office was surprisingly ordered. A set of filing drawers filled one wall, with directories and lever arch files on shelving above. The wall opposite had a desk and cork-board, covered in leaflets, phone numbers and staff or volunteer rotas. The chair looked like its owner either spent little time typing or didn't care much for good posture, but it was quite new, as was the desk and guest chair. Even the carpet tiles were a step up from the usual type – ugly, but without that sticky top layer Blake had come to expect.

An expensive-looking laptop stood on the desk, lid closed. Blake hooked the tip of her finger under the corner and pried it open. Not surprisingly, the system demanded a password. She let the lid close again. There wasn't the time for guessing games.

There were twelve filing drawers in four cabinets. The filing system was alphabetical.

Blake had no idea of Spider's last name – or his real first name, come to that. She made a mental note to ask Lex to find out. But Kensy's was Young, so she started there.

She slid the bottom right-hand drawer open, pleased to note that when you went for quality, you also got near-silent operation. She began flicking through the personal files until she found one marked 'YOUNG, Kensy'.

Inside the manila folder, the paperwork didn't tell her much beyond Kensy's basic details – her date of birth, mother's name, and previous addresses. The space for National Insurance number was blank – a reminder, if Blake needed one, that Kensy was still a child. The second sheet, though, held information that gave her pause.

It gave a list of apparently random questions:

- 'What was your favourite food as a child?'
- 'What city were you born in?'
- 'What was the name of your first school?'
- 'What was your mother's maiden name?'
- 'What was the name of your first pet?'

Kensy's answers told Blake a good deal about her childhood. In a scrawling hand, she'd written 'Don't know' in answer to where she was born. Her mother's last name was also Young, so the woman was either a single mother or an independent non-traditionalist. Blake guessed the former.

Kensy's favourite food as a kid had been Pot Noodle. She'd never owned a pet.

But the thing that disturbed Blake most was that she recognised all these questions because she'd encountered them before. Back when she'd been forced into grifting to get by.

They were the kind of security questions you were likely to be asked in order to complete online forms and official documents. What she was holding was the means for anyone to steal Kensy's identity.

Kensy didn't even have to be there.

Hell, she doesn't even have to be alive...

Blake glanced over at the clock mounted above the desk. She tried to calculate how much longer they were likely to leave her unsupervised.

As if in response to her thoughts, she heard the squeak of the self-closing mechanism on the door at the end of the corridor outside the office, and the low murmur of voices.

She was almost out of time.

Quickly, she scanned the rest of the file, trying to do it fast, but the last two pages had stuck together. Suppressing a growl of annoyance, Blake flicked at the edges with her other hand – the one she'd been using to keep the file's space marked in the drawer. She glanced over her shoulder at the door as she did so. By the time she looked back, the other files had spread to fill the gap.

Dammit! Ah, well...

She just had time to take in that the final page held notes about an application to social services for whatever benefits Kensy was eligible for.

It was dated the previous day.

Blake felt her eyebrows climb. *Wow, you people don't hang around, do you?*

She jammed the folder back in approximately the right place and shoved the drawer shut, coughing loudly to muffle the noise.

By the time the office door opened fully, she was standing near the desk with her head tilted, apparently absorbed in reading the leaflets on the noticeboard on the wall above. As Diarmuid Mackie paused on the threshold, she glanced at him, contriving her face into guileless vacancy.

Just for a second, she thought he hadn't bought it.

Then he smiled – that practised, instant, celebrity smile. The kind he switched on and off like a light. The kind that mimics warmth, but somehow makes you feel colder.

'So – Blake, is it not?' He spread his arms, shepherding her into a chair, all friendly. But he leaned too close while he was doing it. Blake hardly had to feign her flinch. 'Now, then. Tell me all about yourself.'

She sat, throwing him a wary glance, mumbled, 'Not much to tell.'

'Oh, I don't believe that for a moment.' His face grew serious. 'You see, darling, I know why you're here.'

Blake's heart bounded in her chest. She had to unglue her tongue from the roof of her mouth before she could speak. 'What d'you mean?'

He sat forwards, never dropping eye contact, took one of her tightly curled fists between both his. Either Blake's hands were too cold, or his were too warm.

'Let's level with one another, shall we?'

'I... Um, OK...?'

'You're here because... you have nowhere else to go, am I right? This is the end of the line for you – living on the streets. I believe you said you'd no family to turn to?'

His tone of voice made that last one a question. Blake shook her head in reply. He gave her hand a squeeze. She did her best to mentally disconnect all nerve endings from the elbow down.

'We both know that you cannot get off the streets without a job. And these days, you cannot get a job without first having somewhere to live. You cannot even apply for help from the government, or get yourself onto a list to see a normal family doctor, or open a bank account, without a permanent address.'

Blake managed a shrug. 'Maybe.'

He shook his head with every appearance of sorrow. 'Ah, Blake, darling. I'm afraid there's no "maybe" about it. But don't you worry, because *now* you've got us – your new family – to help you fight for what you deserve. How does that sound?'

It didn't take much for her to stammer in amazement. 'But... how? What can *you* do?'

'We can provide you with that permanent address you need to get the ball rolling – right here. And we can take care of all the form filling and applications for all the benefits you should be claiming.'

'Wow,' Blake mumbled. 'That's unbelievable... I mean, why would someone – someone like you, I mean – do that for... someone like me?'

'Life's been good to me,' Mackie said, 'but my mother's family were tenant farmers in Ireland, living hand-to-mouth. Is it so surprising that, when Adhiti and I got the chance, we wanted to help people less fortunate than ourselves?'

Blake mumbled her agreement.

'But,' Mackie said. He waited a beat, giving the single word additional heft. '*But*, for us to help you, Blake, you have to be completely honest with me now. Can you do that?'

'Yeah, of course.' She pushed eagerness into her tone. 'What about?'

'About any kind of... trouble you might be in. We're not here to judge you,' he added quickly, 'but we can't help you if we don't know the whole of it. So, are there any arrest warrants outstanding? Any court orders? Is anybody – anybody at all – going to come looking for you?'

Blake hesitated. Every cue she could pick up told her that her answer to this question was a vital one. The only trouble was, she had no clue what answer he might be looking for.

She took a wild guess that what he was after was someone nobody would miss. So, shaking her head sadly, she said, 'No. Nothing like that.'

And just for a second, she caught a flash of something in his eyes that she could almost swear was disappointment.

TWENTY-ONE

KINFOLK, CABLE STREET, SHADWELL

When Byron arrived the following morning at the address registered to the Kinfolk charity, he found the main entrance to the premises firmly bolted. Pressing the intercom, he gave his name to the disembodied voice that answered, and waited. His eye skimmed across the security camera, tucked behind a wire screen high on the wall above the doorway.

He couldn't blame them for caution. He hadn't contacted anyone beforehand about his visit. Although Kinfolk was – according to his information – primarily a charity for the homeless, inevitably they would deal with those dispossessed by domestic violence. Under those circumstances, he would have been more disturbed had he been allowed to walk straight in.

Eventually, the door unlocked. It opened a crack, and a woman with bleached dreadlocks appeared in the gap, glaring out at him.

'Can I help you?'

'My name is Byron.' He unfolded his ID and held it out to her. She took the wallet, running her thumbnail across the edge of the laminated picture as if to confirm it hadn't been tampered with, and matching it twice with his face.

'What's this about?'

'I'm investigating the circumstances surrounding the death of Shannon Clifford.'

He was watching the woman's face as he spoke and didn't miss her jolt at the name. Was that recognition? Alarm?

She thrust the ID back at him and opened the door wider. 'You better come with me, then. I'll see if I can find someone who will speak with you.'

Byron nodded as he stepped past her into the lobby area. He had been prepared for institutional paintwork and machine-polished lino. In reality, it had the feel of an upmarket office building rather than a homeless shelter. Furniture that matched, and real potted plants, most of which were still alive. Even the carpet had plenty of pile. Byron had worked in police stations that were far more down at heel.

'I'm sorry – you are...?'

He caught the flicker of the woman's eyes as she weighed up whether refusing to give her name would cause more trouble than it was worth.

'River,' she said at last, then added grudgingly, 'I'm staff here.'

'River?' he repeated.

She raised an eyebrow, as if daring him to mock. 'My parents were hippies.'

'Of course,' he said politely. 'What do you do here, River?'

'Whatever needs doing. We all pitch in.'

'Does that include driving any of the vans registered to the charity?'

He caught the way her spine stiffened, just a fraction. 'They're all fully insured, if that's what you're worried about.'

'Oh, I don't doubt it.' He pulled out his notebook, flipped it open and unclipped his pen. The action seemed to increase her discomfort. 'The same van each time, or different ones?'

'Depends. Usually, we stick to the same one – if you swap

about all the time, you never quite know what's on board. Why? What's this got to do with... with anything?'

Byron ignored that, thumbed through his notebook to the page he was looking for. 'And which van is it that *you* usually drive?'

River's mouth tightened. 'It's not as simple as that. As a rule, nobody goes out solo – especially not the late-night runs.'

'During the day, then, which one would you regard as yours?'

He waited until it finally dawned on her that he wasn't going to take no answer for an answer. She bit out a registration number.

'Thank you, River.' He offered a small smile.

That seemed to ruffle her all the more.

'Anything *else*?'

'I'm sure there will be,' he said pleasantly.

It was not designed to be a reassuring response.

They pushed through a pair of fire doors and skirted a large room divided up by a curtain-and-railing system like an old-fashioned hospital ward. Byron glimpsed sets of bunk beds.

'This is just temporary sleeping quarters,' River said quickly, following his gaze. 'The demand shot up recently, and we don't turn anyone away if we can help it – not at this time of year. Do you have any idea how many homeless people die on the streets every winter? We're moving people out into better accommodation as fast as we can.'

Byron said nothing.

She ushered him along a corridor, and paused in front of a door marked Office. 'If you wait in here, I'll find Mr Mackie – see if he'll come and have a word.'

As she pulled out her keys and searched for the correct one, two women entered the corridor from the far end, moving towards them. It was narrow enough to prevent them being able to walk side by side. Byron saw the bruises on the first woman's face, and could understand her wary expression at the sight of him.

It wasn't until they drew level that he saw the second woman clearly. He knew her at once.

He would have known her anywhere.

TWENTY-TWO

KINFOLK, CABLE STREET, SHADWELL

What on earth is he *doing here?*

As the thought leapt into Blake's mind, the woman with the bruised face grabbed her arm and almost dragged her into the makeshift dormitory, glancing back to check for pursuit.

The action took her by surprise. They hadn't been introduced – just happened to finish breakfast at the same time and walk out of the dining hall together.

'Who the hell is that?' the woman demanded in a frightened whisper. 'Is he a copper? He looks like a copper.'

Blake hesitated, swallowing back her first response, which was to ask how she recognised Byron's profession when he was in plain clothes. True, there was something watchful about the man, something measured and slightly unnerving – she'd experienced exactly the same feeling of disquiet the first time she'd laid eyes on him.

But that was different. Blake had spent years skirting the borders of legality. She'd learned – better late than never – to avoid attracting the wrong kind of attention from the wrong people. She could tell from the woman's clothes – still decent, and her own – her skin, the shell-shocked air, that she had not been long on the streets. So where had she learned that skill?

Blake slowed her face, as her thoughts raced ahead. If she went for the knee-jerk reaction to the question, which was to claim ignorance, that might hold – for now. But they'd made brief eye contact. Enough for recognition. What if Byron wanted to see her – asked for her by name?

Would he? He knew she was trying to stay under the radar. Just as he knew he'd almost blown it for her once already, back at Limehouse nick. So, what was he up to? Was he keeping tabs on her? Or was his visit some kind of subtle warning to get out while she still could?

It might be coincidence, but it might not. Byron knew Blake was looking into Shannon's death. Had he actually taken her impulsive challenge seriously – that it was the IOPC's job to investigate? And, having been here once, would he come back again? If so, and if Kensy was around, would she recognise him as the same guy who'd asked for Blake, the morning after they were both arrested?

Blake frowned. 'I dunno – you could be right,' she said at last. She didn't have to improvise the reluctance in her voice. It came naturally.

The woman reacted with a jerk, eyes widening. Too late, Blake realised that all she'd been hoping for was reassuring denial.

Damn.

'I could go see if I can find anything out for you, if you like?' she offered.

'No!' She grabbed Blake's arm again, fear making her grip hard enough to hurt. 'No, please don't. I don't want any trouble.'

'OK. Only, I—'

Adhiti Chatterjee hurried through the entrance to the dormitory.

'Ah, there you are, sweetie,' she said, voice low. 'Come, we need to get you out of here.'

She was in her signature chef's outfit, in black not white, as Blake had seen her on countless TV shows. It was out of place here, but enough of a uniform to lend authority.

'What? Why?' Blake asked in genuine confusion.

Adhiti smiled and patted her arm. 'Not you.' Her gaze was on the woman with the bruised face. 'The man who just arrived, he is with the police,' she went on, speaking low. 'It's not safe for you here.'

The woman backed up a step, shaking her head. She trembled as her body began to fold in on itself. 'No, *no*. What am I going to do?'

It was on the tip of Blake's tongue to correct their misunderstanding about Byron. But there was no way she should know that, so she said nothing, just kept her eyes wide.

'Don't worry, sweetie. We won't let him anywhere near you,' Adhiti said fiercely. 'Grab your gear and we'll get you out of here – right now.'

'But... where else can I go?'

'Don't worry about that for now, hey?' Adhiti squeezed her arm, then paused, as if coming to a decision. 'Look. I know my husband probably mentioned the possibility of a job to you when you arrived. Have you thought any more about it?'

'Have I what?' The woman's tone was sharp, but tears welled in her eyes. 'No, of course I haven't! What does—?'

'It's live-in – a shared house, so you wouldn't be on your *own*. In a quiet area. Safe.'

Blake's eyes swivelled between the two women. She was beginning to get a tightness in her chest and didn't like the feeling. Something was off here – either Byron's appearance, or this apparent overreaction. At the moment, she struggled to know which.

But she trusted her instincts. So she clutched the woman's

arm and forced a wail into her voice. 'Please, don't go! I know we just met, like, but everybody always *leaves*.'

'*Sweetie*,' Adhiti spoke the endearment as a warning, ducking to make eye contact and hold it firmly. 'If you do not come with me right away, we cannot guarantee your safety. Once it gets into the police system where you are, you know it's only a matter of time...'

Blake bounced on her toes. 'But—'

'Be *quiet*,' Adhiti snapped. She must have realised how that sounded and flashed a brief smile. She looped an arm around Blake's shoulders, giving her a little shake that was rougher than it looked. 'I'm sorry, but you don't really understand what's going on here. This is serious. Look what someone has already done to Tess's face. You don't want anyone to hurt her again, do you?'

'No, but—'

'Well then. Let us get her somewhere out of harm's way and, later, when everything is sorted out, you can see her again, can't you? Trying to get her to stay here just because you want her to, when she might be in danger, is being just a tiny bit self-ish, don't you think?'

Recognising defeat, Blake fell silent, trying not to grind her teeth at the slow careful way Adhiti spoke to her.

My own fault for cultivating this persona.

But at least the interaction seemed to have given the woman pause for thought. She frowned at Adhiti. 'You sure you can't wait a few days? See what happens?'

By way of a reply, Adhiti reached up and ran gentle fingers across the bruising on her face. 'Are you *sure* you want to do that?'

The woman flushed, ducked out from under her touch and turned away, muttering, 'I'll get my stuff.'

Blake would have followed, but Adhiti's hand closed around her wrist. Blake had to force herself not to jerk free.

'Her safety is at stake. This is not a game,' Adhiti said. 'Don't ever do that again, Blake.'

'Blake?' The woman had stepped back into view, clutching her backpack. *'You're* Blake?'

Blake blinked at the mix of emotions in the woman's voice. Shock, anguish, maybe even a little fear.

'That's me. Why?'

'Look, I need to—'

'What we *need* to do is leave,' Adhiti cut in. She was already starting to move. 'Right now!'

The woman hesitated for a second longer, then she threw Blake an apologetic glance as she hurried after Adhiti. The outer door slammed behind them.

Blake was left standing alone in the mouth of the dormitory.

'What the hell,' she murmured, 'was *that* all about?'

TWENTY-THREE

KINFOLK, CABLE STREET, SHADWELL

The first thing Byron noticed about Diarmuid Mackie as the man strode into the office, was his utter self-confidence. He expected to own any room he entered, and that expectation naturally fulfilled itself.

He headed for Byron without a pause, all smiles as he reached for hand and forearm. The kind of double-handed greeting so beloved of American politicians on the campaign trail, oozing insincerity.

Byron acted entirely on instinct, stepping back and swiftly withdrawing his arm. He covered the snub by dipping into his inside jacket pocket for ID, as if that had been his intention all along.

Mackie didn't like it. Byron noted the hardening around his eyes as they went through the formalities. But he recovered enough to wave Byron into a chair, taking the high-backed swivel in front of the desk for himself. Mackie settled, rocking gently, and crossed his legs. He might have been a picture of ease, were it not for the nervous flip of his swung foot.

'So, you're not actually with the police, then, Mr Byron?'

Mackie said with reproach. 'I'm afraid you rather gave River the impression that you were.'

'Oh? And yet she examined my credentials more thoroughly than most.'

'Ah, well.' That famous smile came and went. 'You will excuse me if I just...' He indicated the phone on the desk and, without waiting for agreement, picked it up and hit speed-dial.

'Ah, hello. It's Diarmuid Mackie here. Yes, hello, darling. Listen, I know I'm being awful cheeky, but could I just have a very quick word with the Deputy Commissioner, if he's available...? Ah, Philip, how are you...? Yes, yes, well, I have a feller here by the name of Byron...'

Byron tuned out the power play. Or, rather, he tuned out the smarmy tone. It went with the expensive suit, the silk tie, and hair that was styled rather than cut.

He'd never been much of a television viewer, other than the news channels. Certainly not the inane breakfast shows. Even so, he was aware that Diarmuid Mackie had once been their undisputed face. At one point, it had seemed hard to escape the man on screen – or his wife.

Byron knew their story well enough. Mackie had invited Adhiti Chatterjee, rising star of Indian cuisine, onto his breakfast show. She'd come across so well that a one-off appearance had become a regular slot, not to mention a romance largely played out in the media. On the rare occasions he'd caught their double-act, Byron had always thought Adhiti came across rather better than Mackie himself.

So, it transpired, did the TV execs. Gradually, his appearances gave way to hers. Mackie bore this decline with apparent equanimity. He was probably making more from after-dinner speaking engagements and his many and lucrative advertising contracts in any case. These days, he played the philanthropist card, concentrating his efforts on the homeless charity they'd founded.

And, less publicly, in furthering his political ambitions.

It occurred to Byron that Isobel had come out with a perfect assessment of Mackie's character some years previously. They had been enjoying a rare Sunday at home, off the clock for once, when some chat show came on the TV. Sprawled on the sofa, surrounded by the wreckage of the weekend papers, they were both slothful from a late lunch and an early glass or two of wine. Neither stirred to change the channel when Mackie began his slick spiel, but he recalled Isobel's forehead creasing in bemusement.

'Now there is a man who will never suffer from spots,' she'd announced firmly, reaching for her wine glass.

He'd frowned, he remembered, as he glanced at her. 'Oh? Is that a professional opinion, Doctor?'

'It is,' she'd agreed dispassionately. 'He's so thoroughly oleaginous they would simply slide off.'

There were times when he missed her so acutely it caused an actual, physical pain.

Mackie put down the phone, snapping Byron's attention back to the present.

'I'm sorry about that,' Mackie said. 'Can't be too careful, running this place, about who we let in and what we tell them, you know?'

'Quite.'

'So, what is it I can help you with?'

'Shannon Clifford.' Byron said nothing but the name – putting it out there and letting it dangle. He wasn't quite sure what he expected.

After a moment sitting with eyebrows raised, Mackie said easily, 'Sure, she volunteered here sometimes. I was very sad to lose her – especially in such circumstances.'

'Circumstances?'

'Well, of course I'm not privy to the same details as your good self, but it was no secret that when poor Shannon was arrested, she was not quite herself, and didn't go quietly,' Mackie said with pursed lips. 'And then – from what I read in the papers – not long after she's released, she goes and dies from an earlier blow to the head that could well have been dealt when she was still in *your* care.' He tilted his head back, flashed a wry smile. 'I do understand the real reason behind your visit, Mr Byron.'

Byron took a breath, but didn't get to argue the case one way or another. There was a brief rap on the door, and it opened without invitation. A big Asian guy in black jeans, T-shirt, and leather jacket came in. He nodded to Mackie then fixed his gaze on Byron. The contrast between the two men was stark.

'Ah, the very feller,' Mackie said smoothly. 'Mr Byron, this is Paarth Sharma – my right-hand man here.'

'River said you were asking her about the vans we use,' Paarth launched straight in without preamble, not offering to shake hands. 'That's my department.'

'Actually, I was enquiring about Shannon Clifford – one of your volunteers,' Byron said, as if he hadn't only just discovered that information. 'Did she ever drive any of the vans?'

'No,' Paarth said, 'but she did a lot of the regular runs with other people driving.'

'I understand she'd had problems with alcohol addiction,' Byron said. 'Was that why you didn't let her drive?'

Mackie frowned. 'She was sober while she was here, I can promise you that. We wouldn't have allowed her to work with us if she wasn't. How could she help others with a similar problem unless she had a grip on her own?'

'Nevertheless, she appeared to be drunk when she was arrested.'

'She didn't have a driving licence,' Paarth said. 'That was the only reason she didn't drive for us. Not because she was back on the drink.'

Byron switched tack. 'She was arrested at a retail park over

by Canning Town. A strange place for someone to be if they
didn't drive, don't you think?'

'I've been known to visit airports.' Paarth shrugged. 'Doesn't
mean I can fly a plane.'

'But you don't know what she might have been doing there
on the day of her arrest?'

'No idea. It's not like she worked for us full time. She could
go where she wanted.'

'True.' Byron nodded. 'But, one of your vans, from Kinfolk,
was seen on the services at the same time as Shannon that day.'

'Seen by who?'

It was Mackie who asked the question. To Byron's mild
surprise, it was Paarth who answered.

'Yeah, that would have been me – with the van.'

'What?' Mackie asked faintly. 'But—'

'We had a fundraising display there, Diarmuid, remember?
I used to call in and check if they needed more leaflets, or to
pick up donations. I could have been there that day.' His gaze
shifted to Byron again. 'Don't recall seeing Shannon, though.'

'Really? I thought River said nobody took a van out on their
own?'

'She meant none of the female staff,' Paarth said, his tone
dismissive. 'It's not safe.'

Byron raised an eyebrow but let that one pass. 'My witness
seemed to think Shannon came from your vehicle.'

'Oh yeah?' Paarth scowled. 'My van, or just any white
Transit driven by some Asian guy? You know what people are
like – we all look the same to them.'

'Surely, now, Mr Byron, that's—'

But Paarth was not about to let his boss intervene. 'It's OK,
Diarmuid. I've had years of prejudice – especially from cops.
Not surprising you come calling on me, huh?'

'I'm with the IOPC.' Byron regarded him calmly. 'We're
independent of the police. And my witness didn't see a driver –

just Shannon and the van. CCTV confirms the registration as one of yours.'

Paarth gave a dismissive shrug. 'Tenuous. Look, independent or not, you still don't want it to be the cops' fault she died. So here you are – looking for a scapegoat.'

'At the moment, all I'm doing is gathering information. Following the evidence – wherever that takes me.'

'Ah, well,' Paarth said, his mouth twisting. 'Isn't there some quote about knowledge being sorrow, and those that know the most, fare the worst? Strikes me *you* ought to know.'

It wasn't the first time Byron had the words of his namesake quoted at him, but it was one of the more unexpected, he had to admit. And one of the more apt. All too often, as a detective with the Met, Byron had come away from an investigation having seen, or heard, or learned, things that he would far rather forget.

But sometimes he'd come away with things he wanted to cling to, however much he knew he ought to let them go.

'That's the other feller,' Byron said. 'But he had it right, more often than not.'

Mackie rose, making it clear the interview was over. Paarth hovered, looking as if nothing would delight him more than being given the order to forcibly eject Byron.

Or try to, at least.

As they stepped out into the corridor, Byron made a show of looking around him and said, 'Just one last thing. I'd appreciate a word with a couple of the homeless people staying here. There were two women passing when I came in, for instance. Perhaps they wouldn't mind speaking with me? No doubt River would be able to identify them.'

Paarth glared at him. 'River's not here. She's out on one of the regular runs.'

'Ah. And when will she be back?'

He shrugged. 'It takes as long as it takes.'

The doors at the end of the corridor pushed open and the three men all turned. Their combined attention caused the figure who emerged, a teenage girl in chef's clothing, to falter.

'What is it, darling?' Mackie asked.

'Er, somebody said the cops was here,' she said. 'Only... somebody's nicked me moped.'

TWENTY-FOUR

Blake knew there was little chance the stolen moped would go unnoticed for long. But the urge to find out more about the woman with the bruised face – and her reaction to Blake's name – overrode caution.

Mopeds were everywhere in London. They were used by couriers, by trainee taxi drivers learning the knowledge, to ferry takeaways. One looked very much like another – particularly in the rear-view mirror. They were practically invisible and were nimble enough in traffic to keep pace with anything. Even the most powerful supercar had no speed advantage on Wandsworth Bridge Road in the rush hour.

As it was, she caught up with the van before it cleared the lights onto Cannon Street, then tracked it eastwards on The Highway. Eventually, the van turned onto a grubby industrial estate down near the river where Silvertown met Woolwich. She bumped the moped up the kerb and parked up near a set of rusted iron gates, venturing the rest of the way on foot.

Blake wasn't sure what she'd been expecting – some kind of grotty temporary accommodation, maybe? But she quickly realised that this was something different. Not the safe housing Adhiti had promised, but a dark kitchen.

Blake recognised the set-up – it was not the first time she'd seen one. They were sometimes called ghost or cloud kitchens. Mostly, they were perfectly legit – a fully-equipped commercial kitchen, rented by different operators, who cooked food for delivery only. With no customer seating, there was no need for a costly high street location. But the temporary nature of this set-up led her to suspect the worst.

The van had stopped. As the occupants got out, Blake saw it was not Adhiti behind the wheel, but the Scandinavian-looking woman with the dreadlocks. Blake had been told her name was River. Ten minutes later, River drove out alone.

The shipping containers that made up the dark kitchen were a hive of activity, although Blake was too far away to see much. She had no opportunity to get closer. People came and went all the time, and were watchful. It would be better returning after dark, if she got the chance.

Hanging around outside an industrial unit was not as easy as blending into a city street. It wasn't long before a couple of the guys from a nearby auto-body shop began to cast her suspicious glances. And when she caught sight of a cop car turning into the approach road, Blake decided it was time to move. It might have been a routine patrol, but technically she was in possession of stolen property.

All she'd intended was to find out where they were going, and make sure the woman was safe. As she fired up the moped and headed back into Central London, Blake's mind raced ahead through the logistics of getting her out.

The real problems would start if she didn't want to go.

TWENTY-FIVE

ARNOLD ROAD AND SILVERTOWN

By the time Kensy had been working for Kinfolk for three days, she could hardly remember how things were before.

Had it really been *only* three days?

Every morning, she and the others were led from the rooming house in Bow to the waiting van. It wasn't always the same man driving – the big Asian guy – just as it wasn't always the same people in the back. But the routine never varied. The van would drop them off in groups, at the site of one dark kitchen or another, dotted around London. Then, late in the evening, they were scooped up and taken back again.

Kensy had been there a few days before she realised that, if things carried on the way they were, she'd be working an eighty-hour week. By the time they locked her into her tiny room at night, she was too exhausted to do more than crawl into bed and sleep. And, if she was honest, she yawned and dozed through most of the ride back to the shipping containers the next day.

If the containers themselves were always the same, the locations were not. Initially, she'd thought they *were* the same containers, moved around, but she soon realised they were just laid out the same, every time.

Yesterday they were stacked under a flyover in Blackwall, two deep, with a rickety staircase of scaffolding poles and boards. Today they were sandwiched between City Airport and the river. Across the water to the south-west was the O2 Dome, surrounded by high-rise housing developments whose view of the river added another zero or two to the price tag. But here, hidden among the building sites, scrap metal dealers and transport yards, tucked away in one corner behind a shabby industrial estate, they were beyond the developers' reach.

When Kensy climbed out of the van, she had to be careful where she put her feet, to avoid tripping over splintered shards of old pallets, rusted banding tape, and discarded tyres. Cables snaked between the containers and the generators providing electrical power. The gaps between were filled by tall gas bottles, pallets loaded with bulk supplies in plastic wrap, and giant wheelie bins overflowing with the rotting cast-off from their trade.

The containers had been shoved over to one side of the car park, up against a fence made from concrete panels and topped with razor wire. Rags of plastic flapped from it like bunting she'd once seen at a street party Shannon had taken her to. It troubled her that she couldn't remember now what the celebration had been all about. Kensy slipped into her allotted container, blinking in the harsh light from fluorescent tubes strung along each wall. It was no warmer inside than out, and she shivered.

There were four other people already at work. She recognised a nasty-tempered chef called Christopher, who wanted to believe he was better than this, and was resentful that he was not. Other than that, she knew no one. The staff changed as often as the locations.

The interior of the container smelled of blood and old flesh. She wrinkled her nose. The smell was always worse when she first walked in. By the end of her shift, she'd got used to it.

Nodding to Christopher in the hope that he wasn't already in a bad mood, Kensy moved sluggishly to her station and looked at the note clipped above the stainless-steel work surface. Her list of tasks seemed unending. As the morning wore on, tiredness dragged at her shoulders. Her feet grew numb from standing on the cold steel floor, and her legs ached – especially the knee the cops had belted.

Kensy found it hard to remind herself that she had never heard of dark kitchens before she started working in one. They were pop-up units in old warehouses, industrial units, or – like this one – converted shipping containers. Quick to set up and tear down again, and could be shifted to almost any location according to demand. Plenty of catering outfits used them for convenience. But, in this case, she suspected they were more interested in the corners they could cut. No planning permission. No permits or licences or inspections. No food hygiene certificates, or health and safety regulations to throw a spanner in the way of more profit and lower costs.

And, to top it all, they used people like her as cheap labour. She wasn't even making a fraction of minimum wage. OK, so she knew this industry didn't pay well. She'd had casual summer jobs waiting tables, had heard the staff grumbling often enough, but that had been in real, permanent kitchens – in restaurants and cafés.

This was a very different experience.

The actual work was much the same – peeling potatoes, prepping endless veg and salad, chopping onions until her eyes ran so bloodshot she could hardly see. If she'd been earning decent money, the conditions here might almost have been worth it. But the 'allowance' as they termed it, was pitiful to begin with. Then they took away for food, shelter, transport and clothing. And by the time they'd finished, there was almost nothing left.

The thing was, she was pretty sure, when she'd first spoken

to Diarmuid Mackie, he'd said she was owed benefits from the government. She'd asked about that, but it turned out she wasn't due anything after all. Worse, applying in her name had alerted social services to her location. They'd already been to Kinfolk, she'd been told, looking to drag her back into the system.

And she wasn't going back there. Never again. Even this was better. Working her arse off, seven days a week, or being packed off back to one of the care or foster homes she'd suffered in the past – at least until she turned sixteen. Or going back on the streets. Running and hiding.

And it was amazing how easily you got used to sleeping in a bed every night. Of not being afraid of getting rolled for what little you had. And there were always worse things that could happen to you.

There was a homeless guy she'd heard about, down in Hackney, who'd been done over by half a dozen tanked-up youths. When they'd finished punching and kicking him half to death, they'd thrown acid in his face and set him alight.

Alongside her, flames suddenly shot a foot into the air and she flinched, catching the side of her forefinger with the knife.

'Watch it,' Christopher muttered. He was flash-frying spices over a gas burner, tossing the contents into the air with a practised flick of his wrist.

Eyes stinging from the smoke and the chilli oil as well as the onions, Kensy shifted as far away as she could in the confined space. It wasn't far enough. She began to cough, hardly noticing that her finger was dripping blood onto her work surface.

'Hey. Not in here!' Christopher snapped. 'Take it outside.'

Stuffing a rag around her finger, Kensy stumbled out of the container. The wind up from the river cut straight through her thin sweatshirt and she tucked into herself.

'You OK?' asked a woman's voice.

That made her jump again. She turned to see a dark-haired woman, not much taller than she was and pale as fog, standing outside the neighbouring container. Like Kensy, she wore a stained apron. A cigarette was cupped inside her hand against the wind.

'Yeah... no... Well, not really.'

'Want me to take a look?'

The woman pinched out the remains of her cigarette and shoved it back into the pack, stepped towards her. Still, Kensy hesitated, trying to weigh up her angle.

'I'm no expert, but I've had quite a bit of experience at patching up,' the woman said, gesturing to her face. 'I'm Tess, by the way.'

Kensy saw the bruises and relaxed, uncurling her hand.

'Yeah, OK. Thanks. I'm Kensy.'

'Ooh, that's a deep one,' Tess said. 'Let me see if they've got a first-aid kit in there.' She grimaced at the state of the rag. 'And a tube of antiseptic.'

While she was gone, Kensy squeezed the base of her finger, re-opening the cut and letting it bleed. If nothing else, it would clean out any bugs.

Tess reappeared with a plastic box and dug through the contents for scissors and micropore tape. She cut the tape into strips to close the edges of the wound, then stuck a couple of plasters over the top.

'That looks really pro,' Kensy said.

Tess flashed her a smile. 'Well, the friend I've just been staying with over in Neasden, Viv, she was a paramedic before she had her kid. We used to share a flat, so I guess some of it must've rubbed off on me.'

Kensy flexed her finger a few times. The dressing felt firm without making her finger throb. 'That's great. Not sure how I'm going to keep it dry, though.'

'Cut the finger off a washing-up glove and tape that over the top,' Tess said. 'You better hang on to the tape and scissors.'

'Yeah, OK. Thanks again.' Kensy shoved them into her pocket. 'You a chef? I haven't seen you before.'

The woman grimaced. 'Yeah, I'm new. And I don't know about being a chef – commis chef, maybe. I did an associate degree at an online culinary school, but it's not quite the same thing. I must admit, though, this wasn't what I envisaged when they offered me a job with the famous Adhiti Chatterjee.'

Kensy looked at her blankly. 'What d'you mean? What's this place got to do with her?'

Tess gave a low laugh. 'You don't think, if you live in the posh part of Docklands and order a takeaway from her snooty place in Knightsbridge, that it's actually cooked there, do you? I know for a fact that one of the entrées they've got me prepping sells for over a hundred quid a plate.' She raised her eyebrows and glanced around, murmuring, 'If they could see where it *really* comes from... Anyway, if you're OK, I better get back to—'

Suddenly, she stilled, eyes fixed on the far side of the industrial estate, where a high, wire-topped gate separated the yard from the access road.

'Hey, did you see that?'

Kensy twisted to follow her gaze. 'See what?'

'I don't know... I thought I saw someone – watching us.' She shivered, clutching the plastic first-aid box to her chest, and gave Kensy a wan smile. 'I don't really want anyone to find out where I am.'

As Tess hurried back into her container, Kensy scanned the area. She saw nothing.

I don't want anyone to find out where I am, either.

TWENTY-SIX

KINFOLK, CABLE STREET, SHADWELL

The narrow parking area to the side of Kinfolk sloped downwards slightly away from the road. Blake switched off the moped's engine and coasted silently back into the space it had previously occupied.

Before she'd nicked it.

She snuck back into the dining hall. The keys she'd taken from the staff break room were in her pocket. The helmet she'd also 'borrowed' was tucked under her arm, partly hidden beneath her jacket.

There were a few people still sitting around the tables, reading newspapers, books, or one of the leaflets provided. Two older guys were hunched over a chess set, faces stony with concentration. Blake slipped past them towards the break room door, near the kitchen, holding her breath until she was inside.

'Wondered if you'd be back.' Paarth's voice made her jump, almost losing her grip on the helmet. She spun, and there he was, looming, shoulder against the wall and arms crossed. The stance seemed to emphasise the muscle in her upper arms and chest.

Perhaps that's why he chose it.

'Wow, you scared me,' she said, letting her surprise show. There was nothing to be gained trying to hide it. Without taking her eyes off him, she felt for the table behind her and slid the helmet onto it.

Paarth twitched away from the wall and stalked towards her. She forced herself to stand her ground, to resume her almost-vacant guise.

When he was looming over her, he demanded quietly, 'Did you really think we wouldn't find out?'

That had her heart catapulting into her throat again. 'What?'

'Oh, come on, kid, don't play dumb.'

Just for a second, Blake worried that he really *had* seen through her whole act. She eyed his stance, trying to gauge how fast he might be, how versed in violence. Just because a guy was his size, that didn't necessarily mean he could fight.

Blake had learned to take care of herself on the street, where the only rule was survival, and the penalties for losing might cost you everything you had and more.

Paarth shifted his weight and she tensed instinctively, but all he did was hold out his hand.

'Keys. Now.'

With a show of reluctance, Blake fished in her pocket and held out the keys to the moped.

'I only borrowed it,' she muttered, turning her expression sheepish.

There was a tic in the side of his jaw, then he snatched the keys out of her hand and jerked his head. 'Get your stuff. You're out of here.'

'W-what?' Her voice wavered. She'd been expecting worse, couldn't believe it was going to be that easy. She raised her chin, tried to push a hint of sulk into her voice. 'Don't worry. I'm going!'

But even as she turned for the door, it opened again and Diarmuid Mackie stood in the gap.

'Ah, there you are, darling. Where have you been?'

Paarth gave a grunt. 'Joyriding.'

Mackie's eyebrows climbed. 'Is that so?'

'I've told her to get out,' Paarth said, his voice brusque. He spoke, it seemed, as much to her as to Mackie, when he added, 'You put a lot of trust in the residents when you invite them in – you and Adhiti. And this is how they repay you? If there's no trust, there's no more to say, is there?'

Blake shrugged. She edged nearer the door, aware that Mackie blocked her escape route, one hand still at the handle, and the other on the frame. She forced herself not to look at him directly, but all the time she was willing him to stand clear.

Move, move, move!

'Ah, now, I think you're being a little hasty there, Paarth,' Mackie said. He spoke gently, but Blake suppressed a shiver. 'Everybody deserves a second chance.'

'Diarmuid—'

Mackie held up his hand. 'Girls like Blake are exactly the sort we need to try harder with, do you not think?'

'I'll go,' Blake muttered. 'Best way all round.'

'No, no. You're going nowhere.'

Mackie was still smiling. He moved faster than she would have given him credit for. Faster than he *seemed* to be moving. Before she knew it, he had his arm around her shoulder and was steering her out of the break room and propelling her across the dining hall, hugging her close to his side. And all the time, he kept talking in that deceptively mild, soothing voice.

'You know your trouble, Blake? I think you've grown used to people giving up on you, that's what it is. They look at the surface of you, when they should be looking deeper. People may have let you go too easily in the past, darling, but I promise you, I'm not one of them.'

TWENTY-SEVEN

SILVERTOWN

Kensy's finger had begun to throb by the time the early evening rush started. However well Tess had dressed it up, Kensy couldn't keep it dry and cope with the workload. She hadn't even had time to modify a pair of rubber gloves.

Eventually, Christopher, the chef, noticed the blood leaking through the dressing and the layers of paper towel wrapped around her hand, despite the strips of tape holding it all together.

Or mostly together. Every time she chopped, or sliced, or rinsed, that seemed to open it up and set the bleeding off again.

'You clean?' Christopher demanded curtly, stopping her as she headed to the cold store.

'What d'you mean? You watch me scrub before I do anythin'!'

'Not like that.' He gestured towards her hand. 'Hepatitis? HIV? Anything else I should know about?'

She shook her head.

'All right then, just try not to drip everywhere. And for heaven's sake, keep up!'

Kensy swallowed a snappy response and heaved another

sack of carrots over to her station. Her waste bucket was full of peelings from the last batch. She winced as she lugged it outside.

Heading for the nearest wheelie bin in the gathering gloom, she heard the rats scuttling from almost under her feet. It never took them long to turn up. Kensy tried not to think about that too much. It wasn't the first time she'd had to share space with the rats. That didn't mean she had to like it.

It was that weird time of the evening when the sky was a mass of pink and turquoise, but at ground level it was almost dark. Across on the South Bank, the flats built overlooking the river near the Royal Arsenal had begun to light up, sparking reflections off the water like crystal.

Behind her, the car park buzzed with delivery vans, mopeds, and taxis. Even a handful of electric bicycles – less noise for the neighbours to complain about.

Kensy carried her empty bucket back inside and grabbed a new liner. They were thin polythene that stuck together, and she ended up with two, stuffing the spare into her pocket. She was careful to clean her hands again before she went back to work. Which, of course, reopened the cut on her finger. Maybe she really *did* need to get it stitched...

She wondered how Paarth would react to that – or even if he'd allow it. She hadn't pushed the boundaries to find out for sure if she was being looked after or locked up. In some ways, she didn't want to know. But this might bring things to a head, and then she'd have to face the reality of the mess she'd got herself into.

If only Shannon was here. She'd sort it...

Kensy tried to dismiss that sense of longing. It only led to tears, and she was fed up feeling sorry for herself. She thought again of the young woman she'd met in the Mile End Road squat. There had been something about Blake – something that reminded her of Shannon. That same inner strength.

Maybe I should have waited for her.

She tried to let go of that regret as well.

With a sigh, she picked up a knife and bent to cut through the binding at the top of the carrot sack.

As she did so, all the lights inside the container went out.

Alongside her, Christopher swore at the generators. Kensy caught a brief glimpse of his face in the flare from the gas burner he was working over. She saw him begin to whirl towards the open doorway, his face tight with anger. The sleeve of his whites caught the handle of the pan on the hob. It jerked and tilted. Hot oil slopped over the side, hitting the burner.

It ignited instantly.

Then all Kensy could see was yellow fire and black smoke.

She shut her eyes, flinched away.

But not fast enough.

Then all she could feel was scalding pain.

She screamed and threw herself backwards, crashing into a hard-edged object in the dark. Part of the storage racking? She dropped, landed heavily.

A second later, it seemed, the rest of the world landed on top of her.

TWENTY-EIGHT

SILVERTOWN

'Oh my God. Kensy!'

Tess rushed forwards. One of the chefs and another kitchen worker had dragged the girl out of the container and laid her on the wet concrete. In the glare of a security light, she lay broken and unmoving. Her clothes still smouldered.

'Is she...?'

'No.' The chef barely gave Tess a glance. He lit a cigarette with hands that weren't quite steady. 'Might as well be, though. Poor cow.'

Tess scowled at him, kneeling alongside Kensy. The girl's shirt was burnt to tatters, gaping down one seam from underarm to waist. Beneath what was left of the material, her skin showed raw and blistered. The smell of charred flesh turned Tess's stomach. She'd never be able to sear another steak.

But it was the state of the girl's leg that had a faint moan escaping Tess's lips. She'd heard of compound fractures, but never seen one for real. Kensy's left leg lay twisted at a strange angle. Her shin was swollen and lumpy. Halfway between knee and ankle, the jagged end of bone stuck out through her blood-soaked sweatpants. Someone had tied a towel around the top of her leg. She continued to bleed steadily, regardless.

'What happened?' Tess asked faintly.

The chef, pulling fixedly on his cigarette, stared into the darkness.

'Pan of oil on the hob went up when the lecky went off. She panicked, fell trying to run, and brought half the steel racking down on herself.'

Tess heard the defensive note in his voice and knew that wasn't the whole story. Tentatively, she felt for a pulse in the side of Kensy's neck. It took a while to find it. When she did, it was little more than a flutter under the skin.

'She should be in hospital! How long 'til the ambulance gets here?'

The chef shrugged. He would not meet her eyes.

'Please tell me you *have* called an ambulance...?'

'I'll take care of it.'

She turned towards the voice. The big Asian guy from the shelter, Paarth. He emerged from the container, carrying an empty fire extinguisher. In the confusion, she hadn't seen him arrive.

'"It"?'

'Her.' He didn't sound concerned. His eyes, when they moved over Tess's face, held no emotion. 'Get back to work.'

'You can't be serious.' She glanced at the chef.

He shrugged again, threw down his cigarette and ground it under his toe. As if he was just finishing a normal smoke break.

Tess went cold. Her eyes flicked to the girl again. Still she hadn't moved, or made a sound.

'You're not going to take her to hospital, are you?'

Paarth put down the fire extinguisher and took a step towards her. 'I thought I told you to get back to work.'

That was all the answer Tess needed.

She turned and ran.

The steel gates with the coiled razor wire on top stood open. She sprinted through them, ignoring the shouts behind her. Instinct made her swerve left, towards the nearest corner. The area was dilapidated, halfway through being redeveloped. Building sites on either side of the road were edged with high boards to keep the scavengers out, offering no escape.

Tess ran on.

She'd been a cross country champion in her teens. Although she was long out of condition, some faint muscle memory remained. The echo of footsteps pounding after her was enough to spur her on.

Tess wished she still had her phone – that she hadn't been so fearful of being tracked she'd left it behind. River had promised to get her another, but so far there'd been nothing but excuses. Her eyes stung with tears. Somehow, she expected men to play her for a fool. Having a woman do so made the betrayal doubly bitter.

She turned another corner, saw a long straight road in front of her. To her right was another high barrier marking yet more construction. To her left were old industrial units, a mix of brick and steel buildings. She risked a backward glance. She'd pulled out a small lead, but it wasn't enough.

She veered off towards the nearest building. It had a loading dock facing the road, lined with roller-shutter doors. To one side were a dozen or so pallets holding bricks or tiles wrapped in clear plastic. They made bulky blocks about a metre square.

Tess wasn't sure what cover they might offer. She just knew she couldn't keep running and hope to stay ahead. The instinct to hide was overwhelming.

She scrambled over the front rows of pallets and dropped down at the back. If she kept low and she was lucky, he wouldn't want to waste time searching.

As she crouched there, heart punching beneath her ribs, she

heard footsteps. Moving fast to begin with, then slowing. She held her breath.

'Tess! Come on, you can't stay out here all night.' He huffed out a breath. 'Look, all I want to do is talk, OK?' Paarth's voice was tight with anger, though he was trying hard to keep it concealed.

She'd heard that voice – that same controlled tone – too many times before. Knew what it meant was in store for her, if she was daft enough to believe him.

She stayed down.

Eventually, the footsteps faded. Tess waited another few minutes, then emerged from cover on legs that wobbled alarmingly. The road was deserted in both directions. She headed away from the river, looking back over her shoulder frequently, just in case. There was nobody following.

Lights appeared at a junction ahead, slowing for the turn. She tensed, uncertain if this meant possible danger or potential rescue. The desire for rescue won out, particularly when the vehicle turned into the road, heading towards her.

Tess moved to the edge of the pavement and waved her arms. The driver braked.

She smiled in relief as she stepped off the kerb and hurried towards it, risking another glance behind her.

'Thank you, thank you,' she began. 'Please, you have to help me—'

By the time she looked back, the driver was out of the car and too close for her to run. He grabbed her arm while the shock still froze her.

'Hello, Tess. Don't worry, I'll take care of you all right...'

TWENTY-NINE

LYLE PARK, SILVERTOWN

At first light the next morning, Jemma Weeks shivered in the icy breeze whipping up from the Thames. She ducked down into the neck of her jacket, tucking her hands inside the armholes of her stab vest. Loitering just outside the crime-scene tape, she was tasked with guarding the approach path and keeping the log of comings and goings.

Her eyes strayed out onto the mud exposed by the low tide, to the tread plates dotted like stepping stones towards the white tent that shielded the body from view. Part of Weeks's job was to keep gawpers at bay, but there weren't any. The short section of shoreline, bordering Lyle Park, was tucked away between the new developments on Royal Wharf, and the industrial waste-land of Sunshine Wharf. Way off the usual tourist track.

If it hadn't been for the bloke who raised the alarm, they might not have found the victim at all.

The tide had already turned, and if the Tyvek-suited crime-scene techs didn't get a move on, they'd shortly be paddling.

She stamped her feet a couple of times, trying to kick-start her circulation. It didn't much help.

'Forget your woolly vest this morning, Jem?'

She looked up to see Greg McCoubrey ambling towards her across the grass. It was only the takeaway cup he carried in each hand that silenced her snappy response.

Instead, she said, 'It's my woolly socks I should have remembered. My feet are flippin' freezing.'

He handed over her brew. She didn't know how far he'd come, but there was enough warmth still in the cup to take the chill off her fingers. She prised off the plastic lid and took a welcome sip of strong hot coffee. It almost made her sigh. For a moment, the two of them stood side by side, watching the activity down on the tideline.

'So,' McCoubrey said then, 'what have we got?'

'Dead female. Too early to put an age on her, although I daresay the doc will have given them a better idea. He's not been here long.'

He raised his eyebrows without comment. 'Do we have an ID yet?'

She shook her head.

'Who called it in?'

Weeks gestured with her cup in the direction of the high-rise construction work going on next to the park.

'Crane driver, would you believe? He likes to birdwatch when he's on a break – so he reckons – and he spotted something down there. He wasn't sure it was anything out of the ordinary, so we're lucky he bothered to dial three nines at all.'

'Yeah,' McCoubrey murmured. 'You'd have thought the tide would have taken the body by now.'

Weeks glanced at him. 'Not necessarily. Yesterday was neaps.'

'You what?'

'It was a neap tide. Low water and high water were both lower than normal.' Weeks felt the unaccustomed satisfaction of knowing something he didn't, for once. 'As opposed to a spring tide, when they're both higher than normal. Something to do with the position of the sun and moon in relation to the earth. The extra gravity either pulls the water up or pushes it down.'

He scowled momentarily, then shook his head. 'You've been watching too much *University Challenge*.'

She took another sip of coffee to hide the smile, despite his sarcasm. 'I had an uncle used to keep a sailing dinghy out at Canvey Island. He took me out on it sometimes when I was a kid – made me learn about that kind of thing.'

'Amazing,' he said, although his tone was grudging.

'That's a point. Do you think I should say anything to the investigative team? If whoever dumped her didn't know about the tides, they might have expected her to be washed away.'

McCoubrey did not look enthusiastic. 'The body might not have been dumped necessarily. She could have jumped off a bridge somewhere upstream. Have they definitely ruled out accidental death, or suicide?'

'I was first on scene.' Weeks shivered, not altogether from the cold. 'Either she went into the water from a great height and hit plenty on the way down, or she was bludgeoned to death.' She nodded towards the forensic tents. 'And seeing as they've already assigned an SIO, I'm betting on option two.'

A Senior Investigating officer was designated once a death was upgraded from suspicious or violent to the result of a suspected crime.

McCoubrey shrugged. 'Who've they sent?'

Weeks pulled a face. 'DI Goodwin arrived about twenty minutes ago.'

Iain Goodwin was a relatively new arrival at Limehouse. He'd stepped up to detective inspector rank after serving with the drug squad, and was rumoured to have his eye on bigger and better things. Most of the blokes who worked with him, as far as Weeks could tell, considered him solid. Most of the women found his tendency towards mansplaining a pain in the arse.

'Not a fan, then?'

She shrugged, suddenly wary of saying much more. To her mind, Goodwin and McCoubrey were cut from very similar cloth.

But, to her surprise, McCoubrey's expression mirrored hers. 'Take my advice, Jem – if you're going to try to tell God's Gift Goodwin anything, best of luck to you,' he said sourly. 'If it were me, I'd say nothing and let him sort that one out for himself.'

THIRTY

'Again?' Inspector Lloyd's voice held annoyed disbelief. 'With respect, Mr Byron, you can't just turn up here expecting to speak to my officers whenever you fancy. McCoubrey and Weeks have better things to do than be at your beck and call. You've already interviewed the pair of them once. Surely—?'

'I appreciate that you feel my request is inconvenient, Inspector, but better we get to the bottom of this now, don't you think, rather than launch an official inquiry?'

Byron had always preferred to speak softly and keep a big stick hidden about him, just in case. As it was, he caught the flash of resentment in the uniformed inspector's eyes, but knew the argument held weight.

Lloyd sighed heavily. 'All right, but I hope you'll keep this brief. We're in the first twenty-four hours of a murder investigation and it's every man to the pumps. I'm sure I don't need to remind you how vital these early stages are.'

'Of course.'

Lloyd eyed him as if suspecting mockery, but said nothing.

'I'm sure you'll be exploring every avenue to find out what

happened to your victim,' Byron went on. 'Including looking at CCTV footage, perhaps?'

He saw the realisation dawn of where this was heading. 'Now, wait a moment—'

'So perhaps you will be able to dig out the footage of Shannon Clifford's final route, while you're at it?'

'We haven't got the manpower for non-priority tasks, boyo!'

'I realise that, which is why I have not chased you in the seven days since I made my request.'

Lloyd had the grace to look shamefaced. 'I'll see what I can do,' he said, grudgingly.

'I'd be grateful for anything that allows me to report your co-operation.' Byron stood, buttoned his jacket. 'Now, where will I find Weeks and McCoubrey?'

Lloyd huffed and got to his feet. 'I'll take you up there myself.'

'*So you don't stick your nose in where it isn't wanted.*' Byron heard the words, even if the inspector didn't utter them out loud.

Walking along the corridor, Byron asked, 'Who's your victim?'

Lloyd glanced at him sharply, but seemed to accept that Byron's question stemmed from the copper in him, nothing more.

'A young woman found by the edge of the river down near Royal Wharf,' he said at last. 'No ID on her, and not much we can use to *get* an ID, either.'

Byron heard the grim tone. 'Ah. A bad one?'

'Whoever did this seems to have gone out of his way to make sure her own mother wouldn't recognise her – not even with dental records. It's too early for DNA. We're doing house-to-house near where she was found, but I'm afraid we may have to hope for some kind of hit via MisPer.'

Missing Persons, Byron knew, was always going to be a long

shot, with more than thirty-five thousand people reported missing every year in London alone.

'I don't envy you that one,' he said as they climbed the stairs to the next floor.

Lloyd said nothing, but he nodded, and his shoulders lost something of their stiffness.

This lasted until they reached a turn in the stairs and a voice from the upper landing called, 'Mr Byron, sir? I thought that was you!'

Both men paused, glancing upwards. Byron recognised the face immediately. He rarely forgot an officer who'd served under him – not the good ones, at least.

'DC Desai?'

The young Asian man grinned at him over the railing and came galloping down the staircase like an over-eager puppy. He had designer stubble around his sharp chin, and unusual pale-green eyes that were alight with pleasure.

'It's Detective *Sergeant* Desai now, sir.'

Byron smiled. It was hard not to in the face of such enthusiasm. 'Congratulations. Although I can't say I'm surprised. You were destined for great things.'

Desai beamed at him. 'Thank you, sir. Are you here about our floater? I think we could do with your expertise on this one.'

Byron said nothing, flicking his eyes in the direction of Lloyd's glowering countenance.

Desai's expression faltered. 'Ah, well, I won't keep you from... whatever it is. Good to see you again, though, sir.'

'You, too, Hari,' Byron said. Impulsively, he reached out his hand, still wearing the leather outdoor gloves he'd arrived in.

He could tell Desai knew of his injuries by the slight hesitation before the young detective sergeant gingerly clasped Byron's hand, keeping the shake brief.

Lloyd waited until Desai had bounded back up the stairs,

taking them two at a time without apparent effort, before he said heavily, 'Get about a bit, don't you?'

Again, Byron said nothing.

Lloyd scowled.

As they reached the next landing and walked through a fire door into the corridor beyond, a uniformed female officer emerged from a doorway up ahead. Their eyes met simultaneously and Byron caught the flare of alarm as she quickly moved away.

'PC Weeks!' Lloyd called. 'Just a moment, if you don't mind.'

Weeks turned back with obvious reluctance. 'Sir?'

'Mr Byron would like another word. Now,' he added, when she looked about to argue.

'Yes, sir.'

Lloyd ushered them into an empty conference room further along the same corridor. He glanced at Weeks. 'Need me to stay?'

'No – thank you, sir.'

'All right, then.' The inspector glared in Byron's direction. 'Don't keep her all day.' He shut the door on his way out.

Weeks lifted her chin, tucked her dark hair behind her ear. 'May I ask what this is about, sir?'

'Shannon Clifford.'

'Again? I thought we'd answered all your questions...'

'You did. And now I have more,' Byron said evenly. 'You know how an investigation works, Jemma.'

Weeks said nothing.

'Or perhaps you don't.'

Her head jerked up. 'Sir?'

'Perhaps you and PC McCoubrey *don't* know how an investigation works. Perhaps that's why you did such a sloppy job after Ms Clifford's death.'

She flushed. 'Sir, that's not—'

'You didn't go back and talk to anyone at the retail park about where Ms Clifford might have come from that day, did you? Or how she might have got there, or what her state of mind might have been at the time of her arrest. Never mind her state of health.'

'We... OK, no, we didn't. We're stretched thin here as it is. And anyway – what was the point? Do you know how many thousands of people pass through a place like that every day? We'd still be there now.'

Weeks's tone was defensive, but the mottled colour in her face told Byron she was also ashamed. Or maybe that was guilt showing through?

'And yet, I made one visit and found a witness – someone who calls in to the fuel station and the café every week,' Byron said. 'Someone who saw Ms Clifford coming from the direction of a parked white van.'

'With respect, sir, that hardly narrows it down. Do you know how many white vans there are inside the M25 on any given day?'

Byron ignored the question, ploughed on. 'A white van bearing the logo of a particular charity, the registration number of which was captured by CCTV?'

'Oh! Well—'

'The truth of it is, you wrote her off as a junkie and didn't take the trouble to look any further, even though you thought *you* might have killed her.'

'Look, she was causing a disturbance and we handled her with the minimum of force necessary to ensure the safety of the public and ourselves,' Weeks said primly.

'Did you consider for a moment that she might be ill? Already dying?'

'We thought she was high! You didn't see her – the way she was acting. Like a woman possessed. Lashing out at the pair of us. Spouting utter nonsense.'

Byron stilled. 'What nonsense?'

'Oh, that we were spying on her and the entire homeless population of London. That we were in league with "them" – whoever "they" were. That it was all some big conspiracy.' Weeks huffed out a breath. 'Like I said – paranoid nonsense.'

'Why didn't you mention this in our earlier interview?'

She almost rolled her eyes. 'It didn't seem relevant. I know, I know,' she added quickly, holding up her hands. 'That's the kind of thing witnesses say to us all the time, and it's infuriating. But if I had to take verbatim notes of every drunk or druggie's ramblings, I'd fill a notebook a week.' She gave a tentative smile that lit up an otherwise ordinary pale face.

Byron almost felt bad at extinguishing it.

'Something else you neglected to mention... I understand that you may have landed several blows with your baton that were close to – or directly connecting with – Ms Clifford's head and neck. Any comment?'

Her mouth opened and closed several times, then she slumped onto the edge of the conference table and said glumly, 'I don't need to ask who told you *that*, do I?'

Byron raised an eyebrow and said nothing.

'I thought not,' she muttered. 'However far you think you've come, at the end of the day it's still a boys' club around here, isn't it?'

'Are you saying that my information is... incorrect?'

Weeks bit her lip. 'Not necessarily...' she said at last. 'I mean, I was going for the side of her legs. When that didn't slow her down, I aimed for her upper arms. Anywhere I could land a blow that I thought might slow her down a bit, to be honest. But nowhere that might do her permanent damage.'

'And you're quite sure no blows landed on Ms Clifford's head or neck?'

'I don't think so, no.'

'You "don't think so"? Or you know they didn't?'

Her shoulders drooped a fraction. 'I don't *think* so,' she repeated, meeting his eyes. 'But I can't swear to it a hundred percent.'

'OK, Jemma. Thank you. I'd like to speak with PC McCoubrey now. Where would I find him?'

'He's manning the phones, sir. In the incident room. I should get back there myself.'

'After you, Constable.'

She headed for the door.

He let her open it before adding, 'And, for the record, anyone who thinks he can rely on the old boy network to get an easier ride from me will be gravely disappointed.'

That almost raised a smile. 'Good to know, sir.'

Inside the incident room was a cluster of mismatched desks, at which sat plain clothes and uniformed officers, their attention tuned to computer screens and telephones. Byron noted Hari Desai sitting with a phone receiver wedged in the crook of his shoulder as he jabbed furiously at the keyboard in front of him.

PC McCoubrey was across the far side of the room, next to the murder board. He, too, had a phone pressed to his ear. Weeks caught his eye and jerked her head in Byron's direction. Something flitted through his eyes, then he gave a tight smile and held up a finger to indicate he'd be another minute.

Byron's gaze fell automatically on the murder board. Even in a digital age, detectives still clung to this form of old-fashioned display. Everything pertaining to the crime scene, the victim, or the potential suspects, went up on the board, where everyone involved in the investigation could see it and take stock.

In this case, the board exhibited notes on the sparse timeline in erasable marker pen, and photographs of the evidence from the crime scene. At the top were photographs of the victim as she'd been found, plus others of her clothing, including a single shoe.

Not much to go on.

Byron's eyes were drawn to the victim. Almost without realising it, he registered the colour of her hair – about the only recognisable feature.

It's not Blake. Her hair's not brown...

Even as the thought formed, it detonated a chain reaction inside his head. Images, memories, fragments of conversations. It was all just out of reach, just out of recall. If only he could...

His view was cut off abruptly as a man stepped in front of him, blocking the board.

'Hey, I asked who are you, sunshine? And what the hell are you doing in my incident room? PC Weeks, if you've allowed some damned reporter in here...'

Byron vaguely registered Weeks mutter something, and Desai putting a hand on the man's arm. Whatever the two of them said, it had an effect. The man shifted sideways, and Byron saw the photos again.

This time, prepared, it slotted into place like a key in a lock, and turned.

'I'm sorry, sir,' the man said stiffly. 'I didn't realise... DI Goodwin. I'm in charge of this investigation.'

Byron ignored the hint of territorial claim-staking. He stalked forwards, eyes fixed on the photos. When he was close enough to be sure, he stopped, turned back. Just about every eye in the room was on him. He ignored that, too.

'You haven't identified her yet?'

Goodwin cleared his throat. 'Well, no, not yet. As you can see, we've not much to work with.'

It was Desai who spoke up. He was watching Byron intently.

'You know who she is, don't you, sir?'

'No.' Byron shook his head. 'But I know where she was yesterday.'

THIRTY-ONE

LOCATION UNKNOWN

Kensy woke to pain.

The first time, it was stark, vicious. Consciousness lasted only moments, then her brain shorted out and she was swallowed into oblivion again.

The next few times were just as bad.

After that, she stopped counting.

Finally, she opened her eyes and they stayed open.

At once, she wished they hadn't. The pain from her leg was unlike anything she'd ever known. It came in pulsing waves, each more intense than the last, until she didn't think it could get any worse.

And then it notched up another level to prove her wrong.

Over. And over. Again.

She grabbed the top of her thigh with both hands and gripped tight, as if by doing so she could somehow stop the agony spreading into the rest of her body. It didn't work, but she held on anyway.

She tried to keep very still, hyperventilating in shallow pants until her head spun and her vision tunnelled. Only then, when there was nothing else left to her, did she risk raising her head to look.

She was in an outbuilding of some kind. Bare concrete floor, scattered with bird droppings. The ceiling above was a corrugated tin roof on wooden rafters furred with cobwebs and mould. The interior of the building was dull but not dark, and she could see pinpricks of daylight showing through the rust holes above. The walls were bare blocks. In one corner was a heavy wooden door, in two halves like a stable, that was firmly shut. A strip of light shone in underneath.

She heard a shuffling noise behind her, tried to turn and was brought up short by a fresh wave of pain from her left leg. She cried out, the tears blossoming at once. When she could form thought again, she raised her head, very slowly, and looked down at her leg.

What she saw there made her gasp.

At first, she couldn't quite understand it. Below the knee, her lower leg was twisted so her foot pointed to the right. It rested against the concrete, limp as an under-stuffed rag doll. Something deep in the back of her mind told her it shouldn't bend that far, not without the rest of her leg turned inwards to match. Her shin wasn't supposed to have a joint halfway down. And she certainly shouldn't be able to see bloodied ends of bone sticking out through her skin.

She tried to straighten her foot. Nothing happened except spikes of pain that made her sob through clenched teeth and clutch again at her thigh. Bile rose in her throat. She swallowed it down. Vomiting would hurt too much to even think about it, however bad she might feel.

Moving slowly, Kensy lifted her body enough to get her elbows underneath her. As she did so, it felt like the skin along her ribcage torso tore away. Gasping, she managed to get a hand to her side, exploring gently. Her shirt was in shreds, her flesh exposed. As she pressed, the skin had a spongey feel that burst wetly over her fingertips.

She lifted her hand to the light, peering closely. But if she expected to see the darkness of blood, this liquid was clear.

Fire.

Burn.

Blister.

Fall.

The memories came tumbling in, one after another. A small part of her brain whispered that her body should be hurting as much as her leg. She could only wonder why it wasn't, and be thankful.

For now, at least.

Dazed, her eyes slid over her surroundings, over the dirt and the dust. The smells of the river and the kitchen were gone, replaced by something earthier, overlaid by the sharp, acrid tang of urine. And the scent of her own blood.

Where the hell am I?

'H-hello?' she called, swallowed and tried again. 'Help. Please... I need help.'

Her voice sounded pathetic.

She tried to remember how she'd got there, but that part was a blank. She took a breath to shout again when the shuffling noise came again from behind her head. A grunt that did not sound human.

All the hairs stood bolt upright at the back of Kensy's neck.

Taking enormous care, she slowly turned her head as far as it would go, stretching her neck so that her lower body remained still.

The room she was in led into a barn or big shed; the opening to it blocked by a couple of metal gates. Where they overlapped, they had been tied together with orange string. Normally, she could have untied the string, or simply hopped over the top rail without thinking about it. Down onto the deep packed straw on the other side, and away across the shed to the open air visible on the far side, and freedom.

But things were far from normal.

And the shed wasn't empty.

Through the bars of the gate, a pair of bright copper-coloured eyes stared back at her. They were deep set in a wrinkled face, covered in short, spiky hair in shades of black and tan.

Kensy swore.

The animal snorted, as if in reply, ducking its massive head and clanging against the gate, making her flinch and swear again.

The closest Kensy had ever come to a pig was walking past packs of bacon in the meat aisle of a supermarket. Now she was looking at one of the largest pigs she'd ever seen in her life, and it was looking right back as though *she* was the one on the menu.

THIRTY-TWO

Byron lay sprawled on his sofa with his face tilted up to the ceiling, staring at nothing. As was his habit, he'd removed his shoes and socks when he returned home. Now, he sat with bare feet propped on the coffee table, ankles crossed.

Officially, his new post came with a desk in the IOPC's Canary Wharf offices, but Byron had declined to work there. When the Home Secretary had persuaded him to take the job, she had stressed the need for him to be totally independent of a system that had lost public trust, so he preferred to work from his study.

When he was still with the Met, he'd inevitably brought work home with him. Although, as he rose in rank, that work had been less and less about the business of catching villains. One of the attractions of this job was a chance to get back to that, however much it grieved him that some of those villains might be in uniform.

He had spent much of the day reviewing his notes, waiting for the promised CCTV footage from Limehouse of Shannon Clifford's last journey.

It never arrived.

THE GIRL IN THE DARK

He let his thoughts swirl and coalesce, allowing the tracks to play at random. Under the cover of music, shadows crept across the room and lengthened into twilight.

It was only when his mobile lit up and began to buzz that he registered time passing. He sat up, glanced at the incoming call – Daud.

'Good afternoon, ma'am.'

'Closer to evening. Where are you?'

'At home. Wait a moment. I'll turn this off.'

'What is that dreadful wailing you're listening to?'

'Verdi's requiem.' He cleared his throat. 'Not one of *my* favourite pieces, but...'

It was *one of Isobel's.*

'Ah,' Daud said in understanding. 'I'm sorry... to be disturbing you.'

'Don't be. To what do I owe the pleasure?'

She gave a snort. 'Not quite how I would have put it. Have you been poking the proverbial hornets' nest at Limehouse?'

'That *is* my job,' he pointed out mildly.

'And you must be doing something right – their station inspector's complaining already. So, how *is* it going?'

'Is this a professional enquiry, ma'am?'

'Oh, for goodness' sake! No, it's one old friend to another. Stop being pompous. It doesn't suit you.'

Byron ran through his day, from interviewing Big Frankie the trucker, to Weeks's defensiveness over the poor follow-up.

'Well, she's not wrong about staffing levels,' Daud said. 'If we're asked to do any more with any less, the miracle with the fishes and the loaves will be a piece of cake.'

'Quite. But I would have expected a more world-weary attitude from a beat copper – that's the way things are, and what can you do about it? Instead, she seemed... embarrassed by the lack of action.'

There was something else. Something he couldn't quite put his finger on.

'Well, speaking of action, the warrant has come through for Kinfolk's records. Quite a surprise, from what I hear.'

'In what respect?'

'It seems that our Mr Mackie has political ambitions. He's been sucking up to his chums in the Cabinet and waiting for a by-election in a rock-solid safe constituency.'

'And until that happens, I'm guessing he has a personal guardian angel?'

'You got it. He's the original Teflon man – nothing will stick to him.'

'When is Goodwin serving the warrant?'

'First thing tomorrow morning – before anyone further up the food chain gets wind and nixes it.'

'I'd like to be there, if I may?'

She paused. 'Well, your remit is still in the developmental stage, so do as you see fit until someone tells you otherwise.'

'I'd hoped Goodwin would call me himself, though,' Byron mused. 'I saw the dead woman. Unless Diarmuid Mackie has become remarkably co-operative, all of a sudden, they'll need me to identify her.'

'Put it down to pride, I think. It's his first major investigation. He wants to prove he doesn't need his hand holding.'

Byron's jaw tightened. 'Then he's a fool.'

'That remains to be seen,' said Daud.

He thought of the tense interaction between the DI and his team. 'What's his story, anyway?'

'Goodwin? He was with CID, drug squad, in one of the boroughs, but wanted to move into a more specialised role, I understand. Limehouse had a DI slot they needed to fill.'

Byron paused. 'You seem to know a lot about him.'

'He had some notes on his file that caught my eye. I've kept track of him.'

'Oh?'

'Yeah. You know what it's like – some people are praised by their colleagues because they genuinely deserve it, and some in the hopes it will move them on quicker.'

'And which is Goodwin?'

'That remains to be seen, too.' He heard the smile in her voice. It quickly faded. 'If he digs his heels in, though, I'm not sure we can insist. Strictly speaking, this isn't your case. Are you sure it isn't old habits on your part?'

'Sticking my nose in where it isn't wanted, you mean?'

'Maybe.'

'If I were a civilian witness, he'd use me in a heartbeat.'

'Without doubt. But he wouldn't take a civilian along with him to serve the warrant. Even you can't have it all ways, Byron.'

'I'm aware of that,' he allowed. 'But I have already pointed out to DI Goodwin that if a woman from the same shelter where Shannon Clifford volunteered has also died, in suspicious circumstances, it may well be connected. He should be encouraging me to think along those lines, not shutting me out. *If* he's interested in clearing his colleagues, that is.'

'And is that what you think – that the two deaths are connected?'

'I don't know. Both women were hit over the head, but there the similarities end. Goodwin's victim was beaten to the point of being unrecognisable. Shannon was hit once, as far as we can tell.'

'Or she was quick, or clever, and she got away, and it was plain bad luck that blow ultimately proved fatal,' Daud said. 'Not all women have "victim" tattooed across their foreheads, you know.'

'You're right, of course,' he said, immediately contrite. 'And it would be useful to know if that was indeed the case. I'd like someone to take another look at her post-mortem results, if that's within my remit, also?'

'I would have thought the same answer applies,' Daud said. 'Have at it until told otherwise.' She paused. 'Who did you have in mind?'

'Doctor Onatade.'

'I thought she'd moved way up north somewhere? Don't you have anyone closer to hand?'

'Not anyone whose opinion I'd trust as much.'

'Hmm. But, speaking of someone who's quick and clever... have you heard anything from Blake?'

'No... No, I haven't. She seems to have gone very quiet.'

'That must be making you nervous. You've heard nothing from her at all?'

'No. And considering the last time I saw her she was in the company of the woman I suspect has now turned up dead, that makes me *very* nervous.'

THIRTY-THREE

ARNOLD ROAD, BOW

Blake lay on the top bunk in a tiny room on the uppermost floor of a Victorian terraced house in Bow. The walls either side were thin enough to hear every cough and moan.

The bunk beds were cheap and wobbly, the mattress so thin she could feel each slat of the frame underneath. The only concession to privacy was a curtain hanging from a plastic track on the ceiling, which she could draw along the side of the bed. As if it wasn't claustrophobic enough already.

By her reckoning, the house had started out with five good-size bedrooms. From what she'd seen on her way in, these were each divided into two or three narrow rooms, more like cells, with a set of bunks in each. Although the smallest bedroom on the top floor had been sacrificed to a second bathroom, turning the downstairs front room and the cellar into sleeping accommodation more than made up for that. If you weren't too fussy about damp. Or natural light.

In this house alone, by Blake's calculation, they were hiding away more than thirty people. Thirty bodies who were being rented out as cheap casual labour all over London. There was a variety of different trades involved. But the majority, from what she could gather, were being put to work in dark kitchens, or the supply or delivery side of that business.

She occupied her mind working out the profit margin. Not only were these people being paid a fraction of the legal minimum wage, with no tax or other deductions, but clearly Kinfolk were also claiming whatever benefits were available for them. No doubt, that also included a substantial sum for putting a roof over their heads.

She wondered how many similar properties Kinfolk owned around the city, and how long Diarmuid Mackie had been working this gigantic fiddle. A part of her was amazed he'd got away with it for as long as he had.

Why has nobody turned him in?

Even if – as she suspected – he was disappearing only those who either would not be missed, or who had a good reason for wanting to stay under the radar, you couldn't keep working people into the ground forever, could you? Sooner or later, everyone had their breaking point. What happened when they said *enough?*

And, when that happened, why had no word of the scam they were running leaked out anywhere? Blake knew from experience that while the homeless were on the fringes of society, they habitually supported each other. They left warnings of places that were dangerous, or where they weren't welcome. Just as good places to bunk down, or get a hot meal, or an extra blanket, were noted and passed on.

But as far as Blake knew, the only person she'd encountered with a bad word to say about Kinfolk was Tristram. And if her theory was right, why hadn't anything been done to silence him? Perhaps his eccentricity, his possible cognitive decline, was his saving grace, and Kinfolk thought nobody would take him seriously.

Caz would know better than most – if she could be persuaded to say.

And if either of them could be found.

That brought her back to Kensy, who hadn't been seen since Kinfolk extended their hospitality.

But if she's being kept somewhere like this, no wonder.

Blake's gaze went to the ceiling again, to the door, firmly bolted on the outside. The only window was a small opening casement, split in half by the new dividing wall so it was shared with the neighbouring room. One of the first things she'd done was to check out that window to see if it still opened. It did, but not more than an inch or so. Enough for fresh air, but nowhere near enough to allow anyone to escape.

Which is fine, as long as there isn't a fire...

So, the door was the only way in or out – apart from the loft hatch overhead. And even on the top bunk, the hatch was high above her. But if she stood on the mattress, she could just reach the inset board. She pushed at it, carefully. The hatch refused to budge. When she looked more closely, she could see the opening had been painted shut.

Blake unbuckled her belt and ran the tapered end of the prong on the buckle around the edge of the hatch, breaking the paint seal. Then she gave the board a thump with the side of her fist in each corner. She waited a moment to see if the noise, however muffled, had attracted attention. It had not. Next time she braced both hands against it, the hatch broke free and lifted.

Getting up into the loft itself was not easy. Blake used the small amount of bounce afforded by the mattress as a springboard to launch herself up, a foot on the wall to keep going, and the strength in her upper arms and shoulders to haul her the rest of the way.

Once up, she sat on the edge of the frame until she got her breath back, staring into the recesses of the loft space. It was entirely empty – no old boxes or packing trunks. Nothing useful. Just a dusty space, criss-crossed with roof trusses and beams. It wasn't even boarded out, and there was no sign of a light switch or bulb.

But it wasn't completely dark. Twisting, she spotted a small skylight in the tiles above her. She pulled herself up and, balancing carefully on the joists, picked her way across.

The glass was too encrusted with dirt and moss for Blake to see anything through the skylight. She unhooked the latch and lifted it slightly, peering out through the gap. The roof sloped away sharply. It might be possible to get out that way, she considered, but that would still leave her far above the ground.

Last resort only, then.

She made her way back to the loft hatch, treading lightly. At the opening, she slipped through, lowering herself onto the top bunk and lifting the hatch itself back across the void. It dropped into place with only a small clunk.

As long as she didn't get a roommate who was a light sleeper, she'd be fine.

She had barely dusted off her hands when the lock on the door rattled. She dropped back onto the bunk, aware of her elevated heart rate, and glanced back at the ceiling. From that angle, the tampering to the loft hatch suddenly seemed very obvious.

The outside bolt clanged back, the lock turned, and the door swung inwards, hitting the bunk bed frame. Blake was expecting the woman who ran the house, a large, sullen figure who spoke rarely and smiled less.

Instead, it was River who filled the gap. Her expression was sombre.

'Blake, I have some bad news for you. Your friend is dead.'

THIRTY-FOUR

PALACE OF WESTMINSTER

When Byron accepted the newly created position with the IOPC, there was one aspect of the job he had not fully appreciated. It was made very clear that he was answerable to the Home Secretary, but he didn't realise this also meant he was at the woman's beck and call.

Right now – had he been given a choice – he would rather be at home in Primrose Hill, listening to Verdi, instead of nursing a glass of flat champagne on the terrace of the Palace of Westminster, overlooking the night-black waters of the Thames.

He stood facing outwards, watching the scene before him. Over on the far embankment, the giant Ferris wheel, the London Eye, was outlined against the darkness in pink neon. The gaudy glitter skimmed across the surface of the river, lighting the arches of Westminster Bridge with an unearthly glow.

Behind him, the outdoor pavilion was filled with chatter as attendees of this pointless function did their best to drown out a rather talented cellist from the Royal College of Music. Byron gave up trying to listen to the Bach suites she was playing in the face of inane questions. Instead, he took his chances outside.

It was a bitter evening, the wind more inclined to go through than around. The white plastic sides of the pavilion slapped and rattled in the breeze and, despite the patio heaters at full blast, he regretted surrendering his overcoat and scarf on arrival.

He wondered where Blake would be spending the night. He hoped she was somewhere warm. *Somewhere safe.*

A sudden swirl of wind gusted up from the water, knifing through Byron's suit jacket as if it were cheesecloth. He edged slightly closer to one of the wooden planters that lined the terrace. The motley rhododendron it contained did not provide much by way of shelter. He wished particularly that he had not surrendered his gloves. His hands ached more in cold weather.

In theory, his presence had been 'requested' at this evening's soirée to help convince dissenting MPs that the Home Sec was serious about tackling corruption in the Met. In practice, people were more interested in his experience and his injuries, rather than his operational brief. Byron read a fearful fascination in their greedy faces.

There was only so much of that he could stand. So here he was, skulking outside until his ultimate boss finally noticed his absence. Whereupon she would, no doubt, send some flunkey to retrieve him. In fact, when Byron heard one of the doors to the pavilion open behind him, and footsteps on the paving, he thought that moment had come. Wishing to put it off as long as possible, he did not turn.

The footsteps approached, and his peripheral vision caught a taller man who moved to stand alongside him. For a long moment, neither of them spoke, then with an inward sigh, Byron glanced at the newcomer.

And every nerve inside him froze.

He recognised the man, all right, although he could honestly say it was the last person he'd expected to bump into at such a time, in such a place.

Lex Vaganov.

Nobody's flunkey, that's for sure.

After only a momentary pause, he said with admirable calm, 'Good evening, Mr Vaganov.'

He heard the other's low chuckle. 'Remind me never to play poker with you, Detective Superintendent. With that face you would be a formidable opponent, I think.'

'I no longer hold any official rank. It's just Byron. And I never gamble.'

'As much as we may *try* not to take risks, sometimes we are left with no other option, are we?'

The comment might have seemed a generalisation, but its point was not lost on Byron. He met the cold gaze without flinching. Vaganov was a man of contrasts and contradictions, such as the handsome brutality of his face. The few millimetres of stubble covering his head was at odds with the bespoke Brioni tuxedo that made Byron's own tailored suit appear ill-fitting by comparison.

Everyone else in attendance was in lounge suits, having come straight from office or chamber. But he knew that Vaganov's garb would make every other man present feel they were the ones under-dressed. He was making a deliberate statement.

The only question is, to what end?

On the few occasions their paths had crossed in the past, Byron had found Lex Vaganov a difficult man to read. Ostensibly an art and antiques dealer, his real forte was information, which he bought and sold at the highest levels. Perhaps, in that case, it was less of a surprise to see him at a Home Office reception than Byron had first thought.

Nevertheless, he asked, somewhat bluntly, 'What are you doing here?'

Vaganov appeared to take no offence. 'The same as you, I expect. Glad-handing with – or being glad-handed *by*, more to the point – the great and the good.' He inspected his glass. 'While drinking a very mediocre champagne.'

'Quite.' Byron couldn't help the smile as he tipped the contents of his glass into the planter alongside him. 'And, if you'll forgive me for asking... how did you...?'

Vaganov smiled, at his most wolfish. 'How did I get past security?' His hand dipped into his dinner jacket and partially revealed a piece of thick card with the parliamentary crest in embossed script. Byron had one exactly the same in his inside pocket. 'I used this handy little token.'

'Which, logically, leads me to my next question – why might you be on the guest list?'

'Be careful, Mr Byron, your prejudice is showing.'

'Not at all. Only my curiosity.'

'Officially, I am a supporter of various police charities, and I am also a very generous donor to the campaign funds of the majority party.'

Which, Byron surmised, meant that had the opposition been in government, Vaganov would have switched his allegiance without turning a hair.

'And unofficially?'

'Certain holders of high office occasionally find themselves in need of something only *I* can provide,' Vaganov said, without apparent arrogance.

Byron's eyebrow climbed. 'Really? When they have the entire security services at their disposal?'

Vaganov smiled again, and said nothing.

'Ah, no,' Byron murmured, more to himself. '*Because* of that fact...'

Vaganov's eyes drifted towards Westminster Bridge, with all its connections and connotations. 'You and I both know that the security services in this country, whilst admirable in many ways, are not always entirely... au fait with any given situation.'

As well as having a kernel of truth – the terror attack Byron found himself caught up in had not been on anyone's radar, as far as he could ascertain – the statement was delicately put. Almost as if Vaganov suspected those same security services might be listening in on their conversation.

Not beyond the bounds of possibility.

But Byron had been through enough debriefings that bordered on interrogation to make him disinclined to invite another. He took a step back, nodded briefly. 'If you'll excuse me, Mr Vaganov, I'm sure my presence is required—'

But the big man shifted sideways, blocking him. Before Byron could protest, he leaned in and said with quiet urgency, 'Blake. Have you heard from her?'

'Not since yesterday morning.' Byron's eyes narrowed. 'Why? Have you lost her?'

'She's hardly mine to lose.'

'Nor mine, so why ask?'

Vaganov regarded him for a moment with those cold eyes. He drew a hand out of his jacket pocket, opened a silver case and selected a dark cigarillo, flicked his lighter. 'I would offer, but you've never indulged, have you?' he said with a casual display of knowledge. He cupped his hand around the flame and curled smoke into his mouth. Then: 'Did she tell you about the app?'

'What app?' Byron demanded.

The corner of Vaganov's mouth twitched, as if he was keeping score. 'One being used to pinpoint the homeless for less than altruistic purposes, so it would seem.'

'What does that have to do with the death of Blake's friend?'

'Maybe nothing.' Vaganov shrugged. 'Maybe everything. She asked me to look into it for her, and I have. If you should see her before I do, tell her the app has a back door that anyone with a bit of know-how can access.' He paused. 'The police, for instance.'

Byron went to speak, but one of Daud's comments came

back to him – about Inspector Lloyd's success in reducing rough sleepers on his patch. So instead of a denial, he asked, 'Do you know who might be accessing that data?'

The answer caused Vaganov's eyebrow to lift. 'No, but I can probably find out.'

'I would be... grateful for that information.'

'Of course. And Blake – where did you see her yesterday?'

'At a homeless shelter just off Cable Street in Shadwell.'

'Ah, yes – Kinfolk. Did she tell you the rumours circulating about them?'

Byron quashed a sigh. 'What rumours?'

The corner of Vaganov's mouth twitched again – 2–0. 'That the charity is in some way exploiting the people they purport to help.'

'Again, what does that have to do with Shannon's death? Or with the girl Blake's searching for?'

'Kensy? Oh, Kinfolk picked her up outside Limehouse Police Station, and she hasn't been seen since. Although, strangely, applications for all kinds of government support payments have been made by them on Kensy's behalf.'

'When did Blake tell you any of this? Dammit, I told her I would look into things...'

Vaganov shrugged. 'I wouldn't take it personally. She has trust issues.' He picked a fleck of loose tobacco from his tongue. 'And did you really believe some vague promise of action on your part would be enough to make her stand down?'

'There was nothing "vague" about it. I'm in the middle of an investigation as we speak.'

'Of course you are.' Vaganov paused. 'And how is that working out for you?'

Byron sighed. 'Not... as well as I might have hoped,' he admitted. 'Let's just say I'm not experiencing the greatest co-operation from Limehouse. I've asked them twice for whatever

CCTV footage they have of the victim, and so far they've produced not a frame of it.'

'That might suggest they have something to hide.'

'In my experience, your average copper doesn't need much of an excuse to be obstructive towards the IOPC.'

Vaganov produced a business card out of nowhere. 'Call me with the exact search parameters. I can have what you need in twenty-four to forty-eight hours.'

Byron glanced at the card without expression, making a mental note to look into Dalchetta & Child – whoever they might be. 'In return for...?'

Vaganov shook his head. 'This is Blake we're talking about.'

Byron wondered why the implications of that brought his hackles rising, but he said calmly, 'If the inspector I'm dealing with has nothing for me by tomorrow morning, I'll be in touch.'

'Oh, you'll be in touch,' Vaganov said, and this time there was more than a hint of arrogance to his tone.

Behind them, the door to the pavilion opened. A well-dressed but rather bland young man stepped out and hurried over.

'I'm sorry to disturb you, sir, but the Home Secretary was wondering—?'

'All right,' Byron said tiredly. 'Please tell her I'll be with her directly.'

The bland young man faltered and stood blinking between them. 'Oh, um... That is...'

Vaganov sent the remains of his cigarillo spinning into the river below the terrace and smiled. 'Don't worry, Simon,' he said. 'It is just Mr Byron's... little joke. Lead on, if you please.'

He followed the young man inside without a backward glance, leaving Byron standing alone on the terrace in the bitter cold night air.

'Well played, Mr Vaganov,' he muttered under his breath. 'Well played.'

THIRTY-FIVE

JUST OFF WHITECHAPEL ROAD

'Mind out!'

Blake darted back as the flames roiled outwards. She could have sworn she felt her eyebrows singeing. The chilli-infused air she sucked down scorched her lungs, making her cough. The plastic apron she wore seemed suddenly clammy, as if starting to melt around her.

Alongside her workstation, the chef, Christopher – not Chris, if you don't mind – gave a bark of laughter. His eyes stayed on Blake as he tossed the contents of the sauté pan over a high heat with a practised flick of his wrist.

'Get you next time!'

It wasn't often Blake regretted the role she'd chosen to play. Not that it wasn't proving worthwhile to appear intellectually challenged. She found that people around her soon became less guarded about what they said within her earshot. But right now that didn't stop her wanting to take the paring knife she was using and jam it against his throat, so the tip of the blade just pierced his skin. Anything to wipe that superior, self-satisfied smirk off his face.

She'd come across enough bullies like Christopher in her time. If she'd been free to follow her instincts, they never made the mistake of picking on her twice. But not this time. This time, she ducked away from his mocking gaze and hefted her bucket of peelings without complaint. His laughter floated behind her as she hurried out of the container into the freezing darkness.

Being stuck here was frustrating. She had no freedom of movement – never mind working for a complete prat.

The wheelie bins were lined up in the shadows at the far side of the site. Blake fell into step with an Algerian teenager who was assisting one of the other chefs. His name was Ibrahim, and if he said little, at least he didn't mock her.

Blake held the lid while Ibrahim shook out his bucket and he returned the favour, letting it clang shut when they were done. Blake gave him a brief smile and turned away quickly, trying to ignore the scutter of rats around her feet.

As she started back, the chef Ibrahim was working with came out of the container opposite the one she and Christopher were assigned to. He leaned against the open steel door and lit a cigarette. She only realised he'd seen what Christopher had done, trying to frighten her, when the man called across to him.

'H'away, man, you shouldn't wind up the lackeys.' His accent was strongly Geordie. 'I mean, look what happened last time with that young black kid, eh?'

Blake's steps faltered and she edged sideways, merging into the gloom as Christopher laughed again.

'Working in this dump, you got to take your entertainment where you can find it, mate,' he replied. He emerged from his container, wiping his hands on the cloth hanging at his waist. 'Besides, she may be dumb as a brick, but at least Blake gets on with the work. Not like... I was glad to see the back of her, to be honest.'

The Geordie chef stared at him. 'That's a bit heartless, isn't it – considering, well, what happened?' He glanced around, lowered his voice slightly. 'Y'know – the fire n'all. And then look what came of that other lass who ran off. We only have Paarth's word for it that he never caught up with her, eh?'

The blood started to thump in Blake's ears as her system raced. The woman who'd run off – could that be Tess? And who was the 'young black kid' they mentioned? She'd clearly been injured in this fire. The way Christopher cooked, he was a Health & Safety infomercial waiting to happen. From what the two men were saying, it already had.

Could it be Kensy?

Regardless of who she was, what did *happen to her?*

'There's a lot of standing around yakking going on, and not much working!'

Paarth's voice rang out, making Blake jump. The man seemed to have the knack of turning up everywhere. He strode into view, the angles of his face thrown into stark relief by the high-wattage lamps. The light hit his black leather jacket and gleamed wetly.

'H'away,' the Geordie chef protested. 'I'm caught up on my orders and I'm just having a quick smoke break. Nothing wrong with that, eh?'

Paarth regarded him, unsmiling, for a long moment, then turned to Christopher. 'And are *you* up to date as well?'

'Almost,' Christopher said, bristling. 'Although, to be honest, mate, it would help if you didn't have me baby-sitting Florence Gump.'

After what Christopher had said about her only moments before, Blake waited – without expectation – for the Geordie chef to contradict him. He didn't.

'Well, you'll have someone else from tomorrow,' Paarth said. 'I'm putting Blake on deliveries.'

Christopher snorted. 'You sure she knows her left from her right well enough to follow directions?'

'Oh, I'm sure she'll follow instructions to the letter... if she knows what's good for her,' Paarth said. He turned, staring straight at Blake. She'd thought she was concealed by the darkness, but he was looking right at her. 'Won't you?'

THIRTY-SIX

LOCATION UNKNOWN

Kensy woke to the sound of gentle tapping. She jerked, the pain grabbing at her throat. As she slowly came back to herself, she swallowed down the bile. Her mouth was dry as dust, her teeth coated with grit.

The sound hardened into the drum of rain on the corrugated iron roof. It was either still light, or light again. She had no idea how much time had passed, only that she was lying on a freezing concrete floor, terrified and in agony.

Added to that, she was desperately thirsty. The noise of falling water – above her but out of reach – seemed a cruel taunt.

The rain had begun to dribble through the tiny holes in the roof. It fell in long drips onto the concrete floor. Kensy fantasised about lying with her mouth open underneath one, of the rain landing on her tongue and sliding down her throat.

She rolled her head side to side. The nearest drip was nearly two metres away to her right. It might as well have been two kilometres. She scraped her lips together, hoping to moisten them. It didn't.

Her back and hips were locked with cold. She tried easing

them. As she moved, she realised her right side was still wet. Gently, she touched the blistered skin over her ribcage. It was like touching somebody else's flesh. She felt nothing except the sticky fluid that soaked her fingers and what was left of her shirt.

Was no feeling good or bad?

Her leg made up for it, though.

It made up for it in spades.

Exhausted and shivering, Kensy lay back. She felt the sobs beginning to form in her throat. They welled up like a burst pipe, breaking loose in a quiet wail. Tears slid from between her closed eyelids.

'Hello!' she called, her voice rasping. 'Is there anybody there? Help. Please, help me...'

But nobody answered, and nobody came.

She would save her breath for when she heard someone, she decided.

She tried not to make that *if* she heard someone.

And she tried harder still not to imagine what would happen if nobody ever came.

Behind the rain there was no traffic, no sirens, no thunder of passing trains, no aircraft overhead. Wherever they'd brought her might not even be in London.

She hadn't felt this alone since the day her mum had taken them all – her, her younger brother and her baby sister – into social services, and walked out again without them.

Kensy had had no idea what she was planning, or she would have kicked off right from the start. She was only eight then, her little brother barely walking. Her mum left her in charge, bribed her into sitting quiet in a corridor with sweets instead of the usual threats.

I should have known something was up right then.

Kensy let her brother have most of the sweets, just to stop him crying. He was sick, and she cleaned him up as best she could with paper towels from the toilets. She knew her mum tipped a bit of gin into the baby's bottle with the formula. So, she was no trouble after that.

Just like mum, when she'd tipped enough gin down her own throat.

Kensy had never known her dad, could barely remember the other men who'd come and gone from her mum's life, fathering her two half-siblings, then disappearing when the reality hit home.

The three kids had waited all day in that corridor, before an irritated lady with an armful of folders came to collect them. Kensy initially refused to budge. She'd tried to explain that their mum wouldn't know where to find them, when she came back. And when they didn't listen, she screamed and shouted and kicked.

Their mum wasn't coming back, the lady told her. She couldn't cope with them any longer – and no surprise. She'd given them up, and now the local authority had to make room for them somewhere, and how inconvenient was that?

The lady was in a hurry, and cross, and she didn't make any attempt to soften the blows. Kensy was too shocked to make a fuss when they took the baby and her little brother away in a separate car. They were young enough to be adopted, the lady said. It was Kensy who'd be difficult to place.

They took her to a temporary foster carer, who already had a houseful of feral kids. They eyed her from the stairs and the landing when she was delivered, weeping, to the doorstep, sensing blood in the water.

Kensy had cried herself to sleep that first night. Then sworn she'd never trust anyone ever again.

And she hadn't.

Until Shannon.

'I gotta be patient,' she murmured aloud now, hating the feebleness in her voice. 'Someone will come.'

THIRTY-SEVEN

KINFOLK, CABLE STREET, SHADWELL

'I'm sure I don't need to remind you that you're here strictly as an observer, Mr Byron,' DI Goodwin said, as they walked from the cluster of squad cars towards the main entrance of Kinfolk.

'Naturally,' Byron agreed. He smiled politely. It confused people.

Goodwin did not look reassured. Out of the corner of his eye, Byron caught DS Hari Desai hastily quashing a grin.

Goodwin glared at them both, squared his shoulders. 'Well, let's get on with it, shall we?'

He jabbed at the buzzer by the door with more force and duration than was necessary, and was rewarded with a tart, '*Yes?*' through the speaker.

'Police. We have a warrant to search these premises.'

'All right, I'm coming, I'm coming. So don't you dare take the door off its hinges!'

Even Goodwin looked slightly chastened by the woman's thunderous tone. They waited in awkward silence until the door was wrenched open by the same blonde woman with the dreadlocks Byron had encountered on his last visit.

Goodwin handed over the warrant and began the usual spiel that accompanied it.

The woman – her name was River, Byron recalled – huffed out a breath. She snatched the papers out of Goodwin's hand without letting him get into his stride.

'Don't you think we've got enough on our plate today?' She scanned them briefly. 'Oh, come on then.'

Byron hung back. Goodwin had brought uniforms with him for backup. The one carrying the Big Red Key, as the Enforcer battering ram was known, trooped past looking disappointed to have been denied the use of it.

Deeper inside the shelter, Byron found the officers bunched around the door to the office where he'd met previously with Diarmuid Mackie and Paarth.

'What the—?'

When Byron was close enough to peer inside, he understood Goodwin's perplexity. The entire floor of the office, it seemed to him, was covered in a mass of spilled paperwork and torn file folders. The row of filing cabinets along one wall stood with drawers hanging drunkenly open.

'Don't you lot talk to each other at all?' River snapped. 'We had a break-in – last night.'

'How convenient,' Goodwin muttered.

River shot him a vicious look. 'I'd no idea you'd be landing us with this nonsense,' she said, waving the warrant under his nose. 'And these two were doing their Holmes and Watson impression long before you showed up.'

Byron recognised the pair River indicated as PCs McCoubrey and Weeks, who were standing up to their ankles in the sea of paper. Weeks flushed when she spotted him, her cheeks turning a blotchy pink.

'I arrived at oh-eight-twenty, sir,' she said quickly. 'Greg – PC McCoubrey – was already on scene.'

'You'd better talk me through it,' Goodwin said heavily. 'What happened here?'

River scowled at him, as if the answer should have been obvious. Byron couldn't help but think she had a point.

'It was like this when I came to open up this morning,' she said.

'What time was that?'

'I normally get in around seven, but I didn't come to the office right away. Mr Mackie and Ms Chatterjee were in already, setting up for breakfast. I gave them a hand, then came along here. So... around seven thirty?'

Byron eyed the office door, which was of sturdy construction, no doubt to meet fire regs. The same could not be said of the frame, which had splintered.

'Is the office normally kept locked?'

'Overnight, yes.'

'What about during the day, when it's unoccupied?'

'Not usually then, no.' A flash of irritation crossed River's face. 'Mr Mackie feels it's important to demonstrate trust towards our service users.'

An odd way of describing the wave of humanity that passed through the homeless shelter, Byron considered, but how else did one label them? They were hardly residents, by definition. Guest was too coy. Inmate too emotive.

'So, you mean anybody could be in and out of here during the day?' Goodwin asked.

'Yes, I suppose so... But that's why breaking in at night makes so little sense. We've people sleeping in the main hall. Why risk making noise and being discovered, when you could sneak in here in the daytime on any old excuse?'

Goodwin pursed his lips, looked about him. 'Is anything valuable kept in this room?'

'Not really. Just records and admin stuff. No petty cash or chequebooks or anything like that.'

It was DS Desai who nudged thoughtfully at the nearest bit of paper with the toe of his shoe. 'Well, looking at the state of the place, maybe the records were what they were after, sir?'

'Or just causing general mischief,' McCoubrey put in. He glanced at Goodwin and added a belated, 'sir.'

The detective inspector apparently ignored the suggestion. He kept his attention on River. 'Is there anyone you've pissed off lately?'

River stiffened, but whether at the choice of words or their implication, Byron wasn't sure.

'I wouldn't know about that. Perhaps you should be asking Mr Mackie or Ms Chatterjee.'

'And where would I find them?'

'I'll take you... If you'd like to follow me?' River pushed past Goodwin on her way out, hard enough to make him back up a step.

He scowled again but followed without a word.

Byron lingered. He glanced at the clock on the wall next to the barred window. It was only just after nine.

'You responded with admirable speed, PC McCoubrey,' he said mildly. 'Was there any suggestion that someone was still on the premises?'

'They seemed to think he – or she – was long gone.' McCoubrey shrugged. 'But I was passing, on my way in, so...'

Byron didn't miss the swift look Weeks threw in her partner's direction. He made a mental note to pick up on it – later – and nodded as if the answer satisfied him.

Perhaps it was the acoustics of the bare painted walls, but as Byron walked away along the corridor, he heard Weeks say, 'I thought you were working down in Bermondsey today?'

Byron slowed his steps.

McCoubrey grunted. 'S'posed to be. But, like I said, I was nearby when the shout came in. Made sense to take it.'

'But—?'

'Oh, give it a rest, Jem, eh? I'm here and I'm doing my job. Do you want me to leave you to sort this out by yourself? Because, be my guest!'

'I'm sorry,' she said quickly. 'Look, is everything OK with you at the moment? It's just... you've been a bit off with everyone, the last few days.'

'What did you expect—?' His voice chopped off, as though he'd thought better of whatever he'd been about to say. There was a long pause, then, 'Yeah... Yeah, you're right. I'm sorry. Just... personal stuff, you know? I'll try to leave it at home, where it belongs. Deal?'

'OK, yes. Deal.'

Even at that distance, Byron heard the surprise in her voice. McCoubrey, he surmised, was not a man who often apologised. And Byron found the fact he had done so now intriguing.

He filed the information away, and pushed open the doors into the main hall.

'So, you had a break-in, last night, and the only things disturbed were your records?' DI Goodwin said dryly. 'Doesn't that strike you as a little... coincidental?'

Adhiti Chatterjee flicked him a look of quiet reproof. 'Be that as it may, Detective Inspector, the facts remain.'

She poured tea from a large pot in the dining hall, and handed a cup to Goodwin. DS Desai accepted his with a nod that was almost a bow. Byron declined. He stood back and, for the moment, said nothing.

Adhiti had changed out of her usual chef's clothing into a long tunic top and wide trousers that draped expensively. A brightly coloured scarf was arranged with apparent carelessness around her neck. It, too, hung as if the fabric was heavy, although it had the look of silk. Byron had often watched Isobel dress, over the years they were married, to know the time and effort required to achieve so casual an appearance. He mentally tipped his hat to the woman's poise.

'How long do you think it will take to find the records we need?' Goodwin asked.

Adhiti smiled. 'However can I answer that question? You

have seen the state of the office for yourselves. It could be days – weeks, even – before we have it back in any kind of order.'

'We could always take everything away with us now,' Goodwin suggested. 'Just to be sure we don't miss anything.'

It was said as provocation, Byron knew. Goodwin didn't have the manpower to sort through the mess any faster than Kinfolk themselves.

If he had hoped to rattle the Indian woman, he was disappointed.

'I don't think that would be a very ethical solution, do you?' she said serenely. 'Quite apart from the Data Protection Act implications, I'm sure my husband has explained that we have a duty of care to the people who seek our aid.'

'Just as DI Goodwin has a duty to the dead woman,' Byron interjected quietly. 'Who, at the moment, doesn't have a name. Her family may not even be aware that she's missing. They certainly don't know she's dead, so they cannot begin to grieve for her.'

Goodwin shot him an annoyed glare, but Adhiti hesitated. Then she put down the teapot and straightened.

'Let me see what I can do.'

When she'd walked from the dining hall, Goodwin let out his breath in a hiss.

'Thanks, for that, Mr Byron. But, in future, please leave questioning witnesses to us, eh?'

'I wasn't aware that I asked a question.'

'Now you're just being pedantic.'

'To be fair, boss, what he said did seem to strike a chord—'

'Yes, thank you, Detective Sergeant. When I want your opinion, I'll give it to you,' Goodwin snapped. 'And what is it with you and this woman? I was expecting you to drop a curtsey at any moment.'

Desai's face closed up. 'Ms Chatterjee is doing a difficult job, and taking people off the streets that we would otherwise no doubt have to deal with... sir,' he said stiffly. 'She deserves our respect.'

Goodwin looked momentarily taken aback, but they were saved from any acidic retort by the return of Adhiti. She had a reluctant River in tow.

'Tell them,' Adhiti said to her, when they reached the three men. 'It's for the best.'

'But, Mr Mackie said—'

'Never mind what Diarmuid said. He's not here.' When still she hesitated, Adhiti added gently, 'And they do have a warrant, sweetie.'

River sighed. 'Her name is Tess. I don't know the rest of it. No doubt it's in the file, but...'

DS Desai put down his cup and reached for his notebook. 'Do you recall where she was from?'

'Neasden rings a bell. I can't remember exactly. Like I said – until we find the file...' River shrugged.

'Anything else you *can* remember?' Goodwin asked. 'Anything she mentioned, however trivial it might seem?'

River fidgeted. She glanced again at Adhiti, who gave her an encouraging smile.

'I do know she was in an abusive relationship, although she wouldn't say much about him. When she arrived here, she had bruises on her face.' She frowned. 'I got the impression that something had happened recently – not just the latest beating – but something that had given her that final push to get out, while she still could.'

'Did she say what in particular? Or anything about her partner? A name? A job?'

River shook her head. 'No... I mean, it was just an impression I got.'

Goodwin scowled and Desai took over before his boss could destroy the woman's confidence any further.

The detective sergeant's voice was coaxing. 'Had she reported any of this to us – the police?'

'No, I don't think so. In fact, she was pretty insistent that we didn't get you lot involved.'

'And she didn't tell you why that was?'

River gave a shrug, and when she spoke this time, a bitter note had crept into her voice. 'Some blokes are just very good at convincing you that you won't be taken seriously, or believed, and all it will do is make the situation worse.'

'And you're sure she didn't name this man?'

Another head shake.

Byron cleared his throat. 'When I saw her – Tess – here, she was with another young woman. I believe her name was Blake. Younger, long blonde hair. About five-seven, slim build. Is there any chance we could speak with her? Tess may have told her something that's relevant.'

River flushed, her eyes flicking towards her boss.

'I'm afraid she's gone,' Adhiti said.

Byron raised an eyebrow. 'Do you know where?'

'People who stay here are free to come and go as they wish. We don't keep tabs on them.' She sounded almost reproachful.

'Does that mean she's likely to be back, this Blake?' Goodwin asked.

'Sadly, in this case, that's doubtful.'

'Oh?'

'We don't have many rules here, Detective Inspector, but those we do have are... absolute. One of them is stealing. If you are in need, and we can help, we do so. But that does not mean you can simply take what you want without asking. There are... consequences.'

Byron kept his expression entirely neutral. 'Are you saying this young woman stole something?'

'Regrettably, she did. Paarth and my husband caught her, red-handed. She said she was sorry, of course – but sorrier to have been caught than about the theft itself, he thought. She was... asked to leave.'

From the corner of his eye, Byron saw River twitch, as if about to speak. But then she stilled, and said nothing.

Goodwin did not appear to notice. 'How did she take being thrown out?' he asked.

'I don't know – I wasn't here. But Paarth told me she reacted badly. That she was... violent.'

Goodwin pursed his lips, his gaze assessing now. 'How violent?'

THIRTY-NINE

KINFOLK, CABLE STREET, SHADWELL

'Excuse me, miss?'

Weeks looked up. She was kneeling on the floor of the office, sorting papers. She could almost see actual carpet. When the voice spoke, tentatively, from the open doorway, she was half-expecting some staff member or volunteer from Kinfolk, come to hover in the guise of offering yet another cuppa.

Being nosy, more like.

Still, she wasn't going to raise any objections. It wasn't often you ended up somewhere a warrant was served and were treated like a visitor rather than the enemy. But when she looked up, the words, 'milk and one, please' on her lips, she knew at once her mistake. The man looming in the corridor was no charity worker, not by any stretch. Not unless he was working deep undercover.

He had a long, tangled beard, the colour and consistency of steel wool. Layers of ragged clothing, and filthy boots, all wrapped in a thick cloak of body odour so acrid it made her sinuses burn.

Weeks got to her feet, suddenly aware that she was alone in the office. Other uniforms had been coming and going ever since they arrived, taking bags of papers to be sorted on tables in the main dining hall. She was just unlucky to have been caught here, by this man, when she was on her own. Either that, or he'd picked his moment with unusual care.

Weeks felt her heart kick down a gear, system starting to rev. She swallowed, tried to force a note of authority into her voice.

'What can I do for you, sir?'

He took that as invitation, shuffling forwards.

'Stop!'

The man froze, blinking, then snatched off the ratty cap he wore, as if that was at the root of her objection. But she saw the way he clutched it in fingers that were twisted both by arthritis and too many winters outside. The way the Adam's apple bobbed nervously in his scrawny throat.

With a sense of shame, she watched his fear outweigh her own, and the tension leached slowly out of her. She felt her shoulders unlock, her breathing steady.

'How can I help?' she asked more gently.

'I meant no harm,' he said. 'You must believe that, of all things.'

His voice surprised her, now she was better attuned to it. Somewhere beneath the jagged destruction of too many life-times lived, his accent might once have been... cultured. It had lost any hint of smooth refinement along the road, she reckoned. Whatever his origins, this man had clearly dropped through society like a plunging lift.

'Of course you didn't,' Weeks said carefully, hoping he'd get to the point. She'd resorted to breathing through her mouth, shallow gulps of air she could taste.

The old man nodded. His complexion was sallow under the compact fluorescents. A pall of sickness floated around him like smoke.

'Please... can you tell me what's wrong?'

'I never want to... never *wanted* to see her hurt,' he said, almost pleading now. 'But I had no choice.' He shook his head vigorously. 'No choice at all.'

'No choice about what?' Weeks asked. She was confused, but still not ready to commit. For all she knew, unprompted confession was this guy's personal tic. And she wouldn't put it past McCoubrey to have wound him up and pointed him in her direction, just to wind *her* up. 'Sir, who is it that you... that you think has been hurt?'

He winced, as if he knew she'd been about to ask him who *he'd* hurt.

'The woman,' he mumbled, dropping his gaze. 'I didn't want to, but somehow it just... happened.'

Something cold pooled at the base of Weeks's skull. 'Tess? Is that the woman you mean?'

But the old man shook his head again. He looked up, his eyes unnaturally rheumy.

It took her a moment to realise he was weeping.

'Shannon,' he whispered. 'Lovely Shannon. I have to... I killed her.'

FORTY

The address on the business card Lex Vaganov had given to Byron turned out to be a stone's throw from the Wigmore Hall. Dalchetta & Child was an art gallery – or so it appeared. The card claimed the premises was 'just off Mayfair'. In fact, it was Marylebone.

No doubt, Byron thought with a hint of cynicism, Vaganov spun this to his benefit. For the type of clientele he attracted – and the services he was rumoured to provide – the unlikelihood of bumping into members of one's social set whilst on or about his premises might be considered a distinct advantage.

Byron had come straight from Kinfolk, happy to have been asked to find his own way after the surprise confession and arrest of Tristram Shelseley.

'Not the case I thought we'd be on our way to solving today,' DI Goodwin remarked with satisfaction as they watched the old man shuffling towards one of the squad cars, in handcuffs. 'But hey, I'll take a win where I can get it.'

Byron had his doubts about that, but kept them to himself as he watched the bewildered old man taken away. The uniform driving him was scowling furiously, having drawn the short straw for the task. He'd dropped all the windows on the squad car, despite the drizzle beginning to fall and the constant traffic fumes.

But it was not the development in the Shannon Clifford case, however surprising, that brought Byron here now.

Mindful of the rain, he loitered outside the gallery only briefly, studying the two abstract canvasses arranged in the window. There were no prices attached. It gave an impression of the kind of place where, if one needed to ask, one definitely could not afford to buy.

The security system at the entrance meant the staff had to buzz him in. He waited while they inspected him via the camera not quite hidden in the door frame, and tried to make up their minds whether he fitted their customer profile.

Evidently, someone must have sized up his cashmere overcoat – a gift from his late wife – and decided he might just make the grade. The door mechanism released with a click.

A stick-thin, androgynous figure sashayed forwards to greet him as he entered. Hair, lips, and nails were a matching shade of electric blue.

'How may I help you?'

'I'm here to see Lex.' Byron spoke directly towards the lens of another camera, less obvious this time, which was mounted high in a corner behind the counter.

'I'm sorry, sir, I don't think Mr Vaganov is—'

The phone on the counter began to ring. A moment or two later, Byron was descending the stairs to the basement. There were a couple more paintings hung here, spotlighted against stark white walls, and what looked like the entrance to a vault.

Towards the front of the building was an office. Lex Vaganov filled the doorway, watching his approach. He wore a suit so black it seemed to suck in the surrounding light. Once again, Byron felt staid by comparison.

'Mr Byron. This is an... unexpected pleasure,' Vaganov said, without expression. 'Please, come through and take a seat. May I offer you coffee? Herbal tea? Mineral water, perhaps?'

Byron shook his head.

Inside, the office was minimalist in design and stark white everywhere, making Vaganov's suit take on an even darker hue. The desk was all sharp angles and glass, without a stray wire in sight.

Vaganov might pose as a dealer of artwork, or antiques, or whatever else the big man could make money out of, but his main line of business was the buying and selling of information. He seemed to delight – not so much in the money he made – but in being the spider at the centre of the web, with the data threads running silken through his fingers.

When Byron was still with the Met, Vaganov's name had been familiar for all the wrong reasons. He was suspected of any number of illegal activities, but no one had ever been able to make anything stick. Not even close.

'So, what can I do for the IOPC today?' Vaganov regained his place behind the sleek desk, leaned back in his chair, and straightened a cuff. 'Or is this to do with business of a more... personal nature?'

Byron took the chair opposite and regarded him in stony silence. Vaganov stared back, unintimidated.

Eventually, Byron said, 'Blake. Where is she?'

Now, Vaganov offered a thin smile. Byron didn't miss the touch of flint in his eye, as he answered in a drawl, 'She's a little young for you, isn't she?'

There were ten years between Byron's thirty-five and Blake's twenty-five. That he'd previously voiced the same concern himself did not make hearing it now any easier.

'A little young for *what*, exactly?'

'Well now, that's the question, isn't it? What did you have in mind?'

'At the moment, what I have "in mind" is calling up an old

friend, who is currently in charge of the Met's Art and Antiques Unit, and suggesting that he might care to go through your inventory with a fine-toothed comb.'

Vaganov's fractional stillness gave away his disquiet, even if his smile never wavered.

'By all means, go right ahead. My paperwork is impeccable, I assure you.'

'Oh, I don't doubt that for one moment. But how understanding will your customers be, when they see police vans on the pavement outside for the next few weeks?'

Vaganov inclined his head. 'Touché, Mr Byron. Now we've dispensed with the unpleasantries, shall we cut to the chase? What is it you want with Blake?'

'Firstly, to know that she's safe. I'm... concerned about her.'

'What an interesting way to show it. But you have no need to trouble yourself over Blake's... welfare. She is more than capable of looking after herself.'

It was the amusement as much as the complacent tone that irked Byron. He'd been taunted by murderers and child molesters without turning a hair. Now, it took effort to keep his hands relaxed in his lap, his expression neutral.

'Something for which you no doubt take credit?'

Vaganov's eyebrow lifted. 'Either you overestimate my abilities, or you underestimate hers,' he said, a little more coldly. 'There hasn't been anything that girl needed to learn from me since she was seventeen years old.'

As rebukes went, it carried a subtle double edge. Not only designed to reinforce how long Vaganov had been a part of Blake's life, but also his faith in her capabilities, when Byron's fell short.

Perhaps that was why he felt compelled to murmur, 'Oh, I don't doubt that.'

'But?'

'But...' Byron paused, poised on the edge of betraying a

principle. 'But this is different. A woman has been murdered, and the DI leading the investigation wants to interview Blake.'

'As a witness?'

'Mm, but possibly also as a suspect.'

'Oh?'

'Blake was one of the last people seen with the dead woman. Allegations have been made that she was acting... aggressively.'

Vaganov flicked his hand, dismissive. 'And you believe that?'

'It's not a matter of what *I* believe. As I indicated, it's not my case. But, if you know where she is, or how to contact her...?'

Vaganov's smile was mocking now. 'My, my, Detective Superintendent. You wouldn't be attempting to pervert the course of justice, by any chance? First you threaten my entirely legitimate business with unwarranted harassment, and in the next breath you're suggesting that I should interfere in an ongoing investigation. How quickly your integrity slips when your head is turned.'

It was on the tip of Byron's tongue to deny it, but instead he said, 'Since you've known Blake for so long, you must be well aware that she is not capable of murder.'

'Isn't she?' Vaganov's smile turned grim. 'Oh, I wouldn't be so sure, if I were you.'

'To defend, or protect, maybe. But this was vicious, and personal. Whoever killed this woman went to great lengths to ensure facial recognition would not be possible. So, yes, I *am* sure.'

Vaganov did not reply immediately. He leaned his head back and stared up at the ceiling for a moment, frowning.

'I assume we are not talking about the death of Shannon Clifford now?'

Byron shook his head. 'We – *they* – don't have a full ID on this victim, as yet. Just the name "Tess" and the fact she was trying to get away from an abusive relationship.'

'And yet they're looking for Blake, rather than this woman's partner?'

'Because she was last seen with Blake, at the Kinfolk shelter.'

'Then the charity has all the details of exactly who she is, where she lived, and, no doubt, the name of her abuser. Surely, *he* – whoever he is – would be a more logical suspect?'

'They had a break-in at the shelter last night. Someone ransacked the office and their records are in disarray.'

'How very convenient,' Vaganov remarked drily. 'Deliberate misdirection, I wonder? Or coincidence?'

'It's hard to say with certainty. I might have accepted it as Kinfolk safeguarding the privacy of their people, rather than obstruction – had they not then today suggested Blake had something to do with this woman's death.'

'They're looking for a scapegoat.'

'Quite possibly.' Byron rose, re-buttoned his coat. 'I don't expect it will take the investigation team long to uncover Tess's information, but until they do, you might like to advise Blake to keep a low profile.'

'I'll pass on your concerns – *if* I should happen to see her, of course.'

'Of course,' Byron echoed. 'And, please tell her to be... vigilant.'

'Anyone might be forgiven for thinking you cared, Detective Superintendent.'

Byron smiled. 'Oh, now *that* is something I've never tried to deny.'

Vaganov let him reach the door before he said, still in that drawling tone, 'I don't suppose, while you're here, you'd like to view that CCTV recording you were inquiring about? You may find it... interesting.'

FORTY-ONE

'Oy, Jem!'

The booming voice from the open doorway to the station startled Weeks. Not quite enough to make her straighten up into the boot lid of the squad car she was leaning into, but almost.

Knowing McCoubrey, that might have been his aim.

Carefully, she backed out with the armload of evidence bags she'd been retrieving, turned and scowled in his general direction.

'My name isn't "Jem",' she called back.

Jem is a name you give a dog. How many times do I have to say it, Greg?

He pulled a face – one that told her he'd taken no notice of her objection.

'So sorry, Police Constable Weeks,' he mocked. 'But, if your ladyship can spare a moment of your *most* valuable time, the boss wants to see you upstairs – sharpish.'

'What does—?'

But McCoubrey had already disappeared back inside. Weeks dithered for a moment, then huffed out a breath. She dumped the bags back into the boot and slammed the lid shut before hurrying to follow.

She might have caught up with him on the stairs, but another voice stopped her in her tracks.

'Hey, Weeks!'

She turned, saw DI Goodwin by the notoriously fickle drinks machine, prodding a stirrer into the contents of a plastic cup as if trying to work out what it might contain.

She paused.

He fixed her with his idea of an intense gaze. After experiencing the real thing from the IOPC guy, Byron, she wasn't impressed.

'Sir?'

He continued stirring for a moment, making her wait. Then he said, 'Nice work today.'

She shrugged, feeling compelled to protest. 'I didn't exactly do much, sir. He just wandered in and started spilling his guts. All I had to do was listen.'

Goodwin shook his head. 'Now you're just being modest. There's an art to listening, and lots of... people haven't got the skill. But you? You persuaded your common sense to override your sense of smell, which – let's be honest – was no mean feat as far as this guy Shelseley is concerned.'

She blinked in surprise. 'Thank you, sir. How's it going with him?'

'I'm letting him stew for half an hour or so, then we'll take another shot at him.'

'You're taking it seriously, then, sir – what he said?'

'Of course.' Goodwin took an experimental sip of the brown liquid and winced. 'He's got form. A few years back, he was arrested in a serial rape and murder case up north.'

'Arrested, but... not charged? Or convicted?'

'No.' Something twitched in Goodwin's jaw. 'But it's indicative, nonetheless. They considered him a viable enough suspect at the time to bring him in for it.'

'May I ask, sir... has he given you anything more about Shannon Clifford – since you got him into interview?'

Goodwin nodded. 'Me and Hari – DS Desai – have been going back and forth over the basics, just to see if we can trip him up anywhere, but he's adamant he's the one who killed her.'

'Has he said... why?'

'Claims he doesn't rightly know. Much as I hate to see anyone slide out of a murder charge, I can foresee the shrinks having a field day with that old guy. He's as mad as a box of frogs.'

'And where did—?'

'Weeks! Get yourself up here. I haven't got all day!' Lloyd's roar from above resounded through the stairwell like a summons from the gods.

'I was just on my way, sir!' Weeks called back quickly. She threw an apologetic glance in Goodwin's direction as she moved towards the stairs.

He followed, peering upwards at the uniformed inspector, who was leaning over the top railing. 'Keep your hair on, Huw,' he instructed. 'I needed to ask your girl about our suspect's behaviour.'

Girl? I'm twenty-seven...

Nevertheless, Weeks gave him a muttered thanks.

He winked, toasting her with his cup.

She hurried all the way up to the top landing, aware of Lloyd's scrutiny on the way.

'Sorry, sir,' she managed when she reached him, trying not to gasp for breath. 'Mr Goodwin sort-of waylaid me – to talk about Tristram Shelseley.'

'Really? Only, from here, it looked more like you were loitering, young lady, indulging in station gossip.'

Weeks thought it wiser not to argue that point. Instead, in a neutral voice, she said, 'Sorry, sir. You wanted to see me?'

He jerked his head for her to follow, as if not trusting himself to speak. As she trailed after him, Weeks ran through what she might have done to warrant his mood.

It wasn't until they were inside his office, with the door firmly shut behind them, that he spoke again.

'Bit of a cock-up this morning, eh?' he said heavily, taking the seat behind his desk.

'Sir?'

Her obvious confusion had him glowering.

'Oh, come on, Weeks, I always took you for a bright girl. You're the subject of an IOPC investigation – can't you see the difficulty here?'

She gritted her teeth at the 'girl' thing again and said woodenly, 'No, sir. Initially, I thought he was talking about the latest victim. But, regardless, if Tristram Shelseley has confessed to killing Shannon Clifford, then surely Greg – PC McCoubrey – and I are in the clear?'

He shook his head as if in despair and let out a long breath. 'Let me spell it out for you, Constable. You allow a semi-deranged and possibly highly suggestible old homeless man to seek *you* out, alone, and make a spontaneous, uncorroborated confession to the very crime you're under investigation for.' He slumped back in his chair, making it creak under him, and threw up his hands. 'What do you think our Mr Byron is going to make of *that*?'

FORTY-TWO

NEW SCOTLAND YARD HQ, VICTORIA EMBANKMENT

Byron stood outside the Met Police Headquarters on Victoria Embankment. He was watching the main entrance, but also the famous three-sided revolving sign, idly calculating its rate of spin. Both the sign, and the lettering running above the ground floor, read New Scotland Yard. Formerly the Curtis Green Building, and Whitehall Police Station before that, most people dropped the 'New' part and used 'Scotland Yard' to embody the Met as a whole – the way 'Wall Street' had become shorthand for all New York finance.

On the whole, Byron had enjoyed his time working in the building – and at the steel-clad 1960s tower block before it, just off Victoria Street at Broadway. That was long gone, of course – jettisoned in the name of progress, and a higher rate of return.

Memories of his time at Victoria Embankment were part of the reason for Byron's reluctance to enter the building now. For one thing, he had no desire to be greeted with the suspicion that would come with his new role. More than that, he couldn't bring himself to sign in like a stranger, and clip on a visitor's pass.

Instead, he leaned against the low wall outside, turning his back to the building. Across traffic, footpath, and river, he could admire the old County Hall with its elegant curved façade, and the London Eye.

He and Isobel had ridden the big Ferris wheel numerous times. It turned at a more leisurely pace than the New Scotland Yard sign, taking half an hour to complete a full rotation. Usually, it had been an outing reserved for when friends came to stay – before the observation deck of The Shard building opened, the Eye had offered the best view of the London skyline. Though it had been a rare occurrence. Their respective jobs meant neither he nor Isobel had enough predictable free time to play host.

'Byron! You got my message.' He turned to see Commander Daud striding towards him, tying the belt on her chic mac as she did so. 'Sorry to drag you down here, but I've been in policy meetings all morning – ten minutes is the most I can manage.'

'It's hardly an inconvenience. Besides, I'm meeting someone for lunch not far away.'

'Still... I hope I haven't kept you waiting?'

'Not at all. I just this moment arrived,' he lied.

'Really?' She regarded him blandly for a second, then jerked her head towards the embankment itself, across the other side of the road. On the wide paved area was a bench, next to the Battle of Britain Memorial. 'Shall we go and sit... as you're so reluctant to come inside?'

Byron opened his mouth to deny it, but there was little point. Daud had always been able to read him. 'Why not?'

They crossed the road and threaded between the parked police vehicles on the other side. When they were seated, overlooking the Thames and Westminster Bridge, Daud leaned back and regarded him with serious eyes.

'How goes your investigation into Limehouse nick?'

'It's... progressing.'

'Well, I'd progress it a little faster, if I were you.'

'Oh?'

'Now they've arrested some homeless guy who's admitted to killing this Clifford woman, Lloyd is claiming it clears his officers of any wrongdoing,' Daud said, 'and continuing to "dig for dirt" – his words, not mine – smacks of a witch hunt.'

'He's assuming this confession stands up to scrutiny. The man may simply be looking for a warm bed and three-square meals a day, and will say whatever he needs to in order to secure them.'

'Well, however flaky he appeared at first glance, apparently he hasn't deviated from his story so far.'

'Ah, then you are better informed than I.'

'Don't go all grammatically correct on me, Byron. It makes you sound pompous.'

'One considers oneself reprimanded,' he said gravely.

She gave a snort of laughter. 'Anyway, you should be sent copies of the interview files as a matter of course.'

'Well, I won't hold my breath. If I'd done so when Lloyd promised me CCTV of Shannon's route from Limehouse to Watney Market, I would have asphyxiated by now.'

'You're still waiting? Well, I wouldn't assume conspiracy where inefficiency and staffing shortages might be the answer. Between that and the latest round of budget cuts, there isn't the manpower to go through—'

'Actually, I no longer need his co-operation in that respect.'
'Oh?'

'Mm. I've managed to view the relevant footage through... other channels.'

Daud held up a peremptory hand. 'Officially, I don't want to know *anything* about how you did that,' she said firmly.

She paused.

Byron said nothing.

Daud sighed. 'Oh, Byron, don't be so literal. Go on then – how did you manage it?'

'But I thought—?'

'*Un*officially, I'm all ears. Just as long as you recognise the distinction.'

'Ah. Well, Lex Vaganov, of course.'

'Of course,' Daud muttered. 'I don't know whether to be grateful or terrified that the man seems to have the run of our entire surveillance network.'

'Both responses might seem appropriate.'

'Yes... so, what did Vaganov find?'

'That she walked out of Limehouse Police Station under her own steam – but barely. She certainly did not appear in any condition to be released, except into medical care.'

'Which would suggest she received the blow that killed her before then.'

'Something had happened to her by that point, yes.'

'But this guy Shelseley claims he had his run-in with Shannon *after* her release.'

Byron stilled. 'Has he said where?'

'St Anne's Church. It's not far from Limehouse nick, and might conceivably have been on the woman's route. They have a drop-in centre-cum-soup kitchen.' She glanced at him. 'What?'

'The only place we lose sight of Shannon is when she cuts through St Anne's churchyard. It picks her up again coming out of St Anne's Passage onto Newell Street, but she's off camera for a good eighteen minutes – far longer than it would have taken her to simply walk through the grounds.'

Daud sat back. Byron heard her let out a long breath.

'So, he could very well be telling the truth, and our officers could well be in the clear,' she murmured.

'"Our officers"?'

'They're *all* our officers,' she said sharply. 'And it's always a relief to find they didn't do whatever we fear they might have done. Not a disappointment.'

'I'm well aware of that. Just as I am also aware that coincidences do happen. If Shelseley is claiming he had some kind of argument with the victim at St Anne's that turned violent, then there's nothing to say he didn't deliver another blow that might have contributed to, or accelerated, her demise. It's a possibility I'll be discussing with Doctor Onatade when she reviews the PM results.'

'Do I hear a "but"?'

Byron cleared his throat. 'You know that distinction you mentioned?'

'Between official and unofficial, you mean?' She groaned. 'Oh, why do I get the feeling that I'm *so* going to regret saying that...'

'Vaganov showed me the CCTV right up to the point Shannon collapsed and died in Watney Market.'

'OK, yes – we knew that.'

'She wasn't alone when she died.'

Daud nodded. 'Someone dialled three nines, but it was a Pay As You Go mobile, so there were no records for the woman who called. We do have the voice recording, though, which we might be able to match, if you have anyone in mind?'

'Oh, I have someone in mind, but we won't be able to get a match. And this is where I get to the unofficial part.'

Daud scowled. 'Go on.'

'The woman who was with her, and apparently talked with her, was the same woman I saw at Kinfolk, with Blake – this Tess. The same woman—'

'Who was fished out of the river with her face beaten to a pulp,' she finished for him, and swore under her breath. 'You'll have to share this with Inspector Lloyd, of course.'

'Of course. But you see my difficulty. Whatever Tristram Shelseley says he did or didn't do, Shannon was probably dying well before she stepped out of Limehouse. And the one person we have documented proof she was in contact with is also dead.

My question is, whatever Shannon said to Tess that day, was it enough to get *her* killed as well?'

'If it was, then it's well outside your remit, Byron. You may have to rely on somebody else to get to the bottom of it.'

'Yes,' he agreed. 'I was afraid of that.'

Blake was woken by a scream.

Her eyes snapped open. Just for a second, she was disoriented by the sight of the cracked ceiling and scuffed loft hatch above her. Not to mention having been up working half the night, and then sleeping halfway through the next day.

The scream came again, accompanied this time by heavy thuds. It sounded very like someone doing their best to kick down a door.

Blake sat up and swung her legs over the side of the bunk bed. The reorientation allowed her ears to focus. The sound came from somewhere below, she judged. Probably the next floor down, rather than ground level. And not directly beneath her, maybe towards the back of the house...

She could hear two voices now. One higher pitched and filled with panic, the other deeper, less distinct. The thuds started up again, increasing in ferocity. The deeper voice rose almost to a shout.

Blake didn't need to make out words in order to understand the escalating threat. She jumped down from the bunk, landing lightly on bare feet, and pressed an ear to the gap between the door and frame. When that made little difference, she pulled back the scrappy rug to reveal the pine boards beneath, and dropped to the floor. Cool air sifted up through the cracks between the planks. Sound travelled with it.

The voices were still muffled, but she could make out a few words. The higher voice – young, female, inside the room – was demanding repeatedly to be let out. The deeper one – older, male, most likely on the landing – was telling her to calm down and shut up. Blake was too far away to identify either of them.

Suddenly, there came the rattle of handle and lock from below, then the crash of the door bouncing against the inner wall as it was shoved wide.

Blake heard the girl give a yelp of shock and fear. Silence followed. She held her breath, realising she could still hear the man's voice, low and controlled. Whatever he said must have had the desired effect. The door closed again – more quietly this time. Blake thought she heard the mechanical clatter of the locks engaging, or the bolt being thrown home.

She let herself sag against the boards, adrenaline pounding the blood in her ears.

From far below came a slam overlaid with a distinctive rattle. The front door was wood rather than plastic. It had swelled in its frame over the winter, and shutting it now made the brass letterbox bounce.

She moved to the window. The room they'd put her in over-looked the front of the house. She peered through the gap in the curtains, careful not to make them twitch.

A van was parked at the kerb a little further along the street. She could see the passenger side, where Paarth stood with his hand on the door. He paused, looking back up at the house as if watching for watchers.

Blake froze. His expression didn't alter. He climbed in. She didn't see who was behind the wheel. The engine fired, and the van pulled away.

Blake stepped back from the window, letting out a shaky breath. She straightened the rug, and glanced up at the loft hatch.

'Well, now's as good a time as any...'

It was quicker, this time, getting up into the attic space. Once again, she tiptoed across the joists to the skylight and pushed it open. It was small, likely an original feature, and getting up through it and out onto the roof itself was not the easiest thing Blake had ever attempted. But it wasn't the hardest, either.

The slope of the tiles was comparatively mild. Keeping to a crouch, she moved across onto the neighbouring property, which had been much enlarged. At the back was a double-height extension with a pitched roof, leading down onto a further flat-roofed addition to the ground floor – no doubt an open-plan dining kitchen with tri-fold glass doors leading out into the trendy garden.

For Blake, the design might as well have been intended as a giant climbing frame. She mentally traced the most feasible escape route. Down onto the apex of the extension first, then to the lowest of the side gutters, onto the flat roof, the garden wall, and away across the patch of concrete used for parking, accessible from the service alley running along the backs of the houses.

The rooming house itself was one of the few properties in the row that had not seen large-scale building work. There was nothing remarkable about the property at all. The house was nondescript, but reasonably well-maintained, the exterior pebbledash intact, the windows double-glazed with uniform white plastic frames. Even the back lawn was cut and the paved area weeded. Nothing for the neighbours to take note of, or complain about.

She made it down onto next door's pitched roof extension easily enough. Briefly, she glanced at her route to freedom, then back towards the house. As she watched, the window of one of the rooms was opened abruptly. It hit whatever device had been added to prevent it opening fully, hard enough to rattle the glass. Someone cursed, banging the casement in futile temper.

She didn't have to wonder which room the newcomer was in, after that. And whatever Paarth had said to them, it hadn't frightened them into complete submission.

By edging halfway down the slope of the extension, she could just reach the corner of the window. With only the smallest of hesitations, she reached up and rapped her knuckles on the glass.

Behind the thin curtain, it was impossible to see movement inside the room. Not in daylight, anyway. Blake paused a moment or two, then tapped again.

This time, the curtain was jerked aside at once, as if the occupant had been standing behind it, waiting.

'Caz?'

'Blake!' Caz leaned closer to the open gap, lowered her voice. 'What are you doing here? I mean, out there?'

'I could ask you the same question. What are you doing *in* there?'

Caz smacked the side of her fist against the frame. 'What does it look like?' she demanded, sullen now. 'Those Kinfolk sods just grabbed us, for no reason. You've got to get me out. *Please!*'

'"Us"?' Blake queried. 'Who else is in there?'

'No one's with me in here right now, but they grabbed me *and* Tris. Come on, Blake. Don't leave me—'

'Tell me what happened.'

'Seriously? You want to do this now?'

'Getting you out right away isn't that easy,' she hedged. 'The way I got out... well, it doesn't mean I can get back into the rest of the house.'

But she had already spotted the neat shed at the bottom of

the neighbouring garden – the most likely place to find tools she could use.

Caz groaned, but Blake knew she would be much less forthcoming once she was out. And that was only the first step. Kinfolk seemed to be very good at finding people on the streets.

'Don't worry – I'll think of something,' she said, 'Where *is* Tris?'

She saw rather than heard Caz huff out an impatient breath. It caused a small circular patch of condensation to form on the inside of the glass.

'I don't know! We were over in Limehouse – Tris and me. He's not been well. His chest, you know? And I heard they'd got room at one of the night shelters over that way, but he wouldn't go on his own. Stubborn old bugger.' She scowled, but spoke without heat.

Blake glanced around, aware of her exposure, and made a 'carry on' gesture that, she hoped, also conveyed, 'hurry up'.

'I'd left him outside the tube station while I... had a bit of business to take care of,' Caz said, by which Blake knew she meant a punter to service. 'When I came back, Paarth was just... *there,* bundling him into the back of a van.' She swore, punching the window again.

'Paarth and who else?'

'Dunno. I didn't see who was driving. When I started kicking up a fuss, Paarth threw me in there, an' all. Broad daylight, and nobody lifts a finger!'

'Did he tell you what they wanted?'

She shook her head. 'Tris starts giving Paarth what for – if he's got any ideas about... hurting me, or whatever. Bless 'im. But Paarth just says, "Maybe it won't come to that," all nasty. And next thing, we're here and he's shoving me up the stairs. I dunno where they've taken Tris.' And despite the hard face she put on, genuine tears formed in Caz's eyes. 'Gawd only knows what they're doing to him. He's an old man! His heart won't stand any rough stuff, and he's like family to me...'

'Caz, take a deep breath and calm down, OK? I'll get you out.' She put her hand through the open window, having to turn it sideways so it would fit through the narrow gap.

Caz grabbed her fingers and held on, not meeting her eyes. 'You promise?'

'Hey, look at me. Yes, I *promise,* Caz. Just give me a minute.'

She made her way carefully down into next door's garden, taking her time to check for signs of life inside the back of the property. She'd been right about the layout of the ground floor – an expanse of glass.

Nothing stirred.

She tiptoed across the patch of lawn to the shed, prepared to force the door if she needed to, but it wasn't locked. Shaking her head, she slipped inside. There wasn't much of value in there except a few dusty cans of weedkiller and lawn feed, and gardening tools in a neat row on hooks at one side.

When her eye landed on the pair of secateurs, Blake smiled.

It took her a little longer to get back up onto the roof, to where Caz was waiting at the window. She looked nonplussed when Blake slid the secateurs to her through the window gap.

'What am I supposed to do with these – prune the furniture?'

Blake sighed. 'You see the inside of the window frame? There's a flat section, and then a trim that fits between there and the glass.'

'Yeah. And?'

'Take the point of the blade and push it into the join between the trim and the frame. The trim should loosen and pop off.'

She waited, not patiently, while Caz fumbled with the first piece. But after it came away, a determined look came over the young woman's face, and she stripped away the remaining trims more quickly.

'That's the last one. What now?'

'Get ready to catch the glass.'

Blake gave the centre of the double-glazed pane a shove, and the whole thing dropped out of the frame into Caz's waiting hands.

'Sweet!' Caz exclaimed. Her gaze turned calculating. 'I *knew* you wasn't as dumb as you was making out.' She dumped the unit onto the floor at her feet and grabbed both sides of the frame, preparing to climb out.

'Wait,' Blake said.

'What?'

'Pass me the secateurs.' And when Caz stared at her, she added, 'So I can put them back.'

Caz shook her head, as if Blake was out of her mind, but did as she was asked without comment. Then, with some help, she was on the roof, the top of the wall, and down into the garden of the rooming house.

When Caz would have headed for the alley at the end of the garden, Blake caught her arm.

'What are you planning to do now?'

'Try and stay out of *their* way—' Caz jerked her head back towards the house '—while I find out what they've done with Tris.'

'I know someone who can help you with that,' Blake said, 'but you've got to trust us to do the job and stay out of sight. If we manage to rescue Tris, but they pick you up again, we're right back where we started.'

'But...' Caz took a deep breath to launch into an objection. Then she stilled. 'OK. Who is it – who can help?' Her face twisted. 'Not the cops?'

Blake thought briefly of Byron, then shook her head. 'No, not the cops,' she said. 'His name's Lex Vaganov. You'll find him at a gallery just off Oxford Street. I want you to go there and tell him what you've told me, about what happened. Tell him I said you'll be safe at Claremont – he'll know what that means – and he's to track down Tris. Lex will find him – you can trust me on that.'

'What d'you mean *I'm* to tell him? Where are you going?'

'I'm staying.'

'*What?* You gotta be off your trolley. Why would you want to do that?'

'Because you're not the only person who's gone missing off the streets, Caz,' she said, low and serious. 'I'm looking for Kensy.'

'That kid? What's she to you?'

Blake silenced her with a look. 'She is to me what Tris is to you,' she said then. 'As close to family as most of us are ever going to get.'

FORTY-FOUR

LOCATION UNKNOWN

'What're you lookin' at?' Kensy demanded, her voice raw. 'Come on – don't just stand there. Say somethin'! What the hell do you *want*?'

The pig said nothing.

There were now two pigs. At first, Kensy had thought she was just seeing double. Two pigs, one slightly larger than the other. Both stared at her through the rails of the gate with their small, penetrating dark eyes.

Every now and again they flapped an ear. The ears reminded Kensy of a Rottweiler's – folded over and slightly triangular in shape. Or they would have been, had they not been torn and ragged at the ends, as though something – or quite a few somethings – had taken chunks out of them on a regular basis.

The black and tan colouring, and the body shape, too, was similar to that of a big dog. Altogether, it was somehow very un-piglike – wide across the chest and flat-backed, with a square stance. All rippling muscle under the bristled skin. They watched her with an intensity that was thoroughly unnerving.

Kensy searched for anything to take her mind off the pigs.

She had the feeling they were waiting for something she wasn't going to like much when it arrived.

Either she was getting numbed to the constant pain, or simply numb. But her side was hot to the touch and still oozing fluid. That seemed to be attracting insects – tiny things that scuttled, or crawled, or flew. She grew exhausted trying to keep them away. She might not be able to feel them on her skin, but her mind could, only too well.

She knew it wasn't good to let creepie-crawlies feed off her and lay their eggs, although she vaguely recalled someone telling her maggots had been used to eat the dead flesh around wounds during the crusades, to prevent gangrene. There was a special word for it, but she couldn't remember what it was.

Outside, it continued to rain steadily, and the water continued to drip in through the holes in the corrugated iron. Where the water landed, it seeped into the dry concrete beneath. Several patches formed, gleaming darkly.

Kensy had stayed in a squat once where the roof leaked. They'd found buckets and pans and bowls to put underneath the holes to catch the water, and used it for brewing tea.

Shame I can't do that now.

She licked at her cracked lips. It took effort to unglue her tongue from the roof of her mouth.

She shifted on the unforgiving concrete, and for the first time heard something rustle in the pocket of her sweatpants.

The pigs heard it, too. They pushed their flat oval snouts further through the rails of the gate and sniffed loudly, as if smelling the sound.

'I don't know what you're gettin' so excited about,' Kensy muttered, reaching into the pocket very carefully, so the material didn't shift against her lower leg. 'It's not like I got anythin' interesting...' Her fingers met with crumpled plastic and she remembered, with disappointment, the spare bin liner. The bags were so thin it had been easy to pick up more than one at once.

It seemed like all that had happened days ago. Perhaps it had. She had no idea of time passing.

She pulled the liner bag from her pocket and straightened it out across her hips. It wafted the smell of dried blood up from her leg. Even over the farmyard stench, she got a brief gust of meat left too long out of the fridge.

Maybe the pigs smelled it, too. Maybe that was what provoked them to snap at each other and head-butt the gates, which rattled and crashed.

Kensy startled, cursing as the movement jarred through her shattered leg. She tried to distract herself by stretching the bag out fully. The waste bins in the container had been large, and the bags were sized to fit. She stared at the bag for a long moment, frowning. What a pity she didn't have…

She slid her hand into the other pocket, hoping they hadn't searched her before they dumped her here.

It seemed they had not.

She studied the small pair of scissors and the tape from the first-aid kit that Tess had given to her. She'd almost forgotten about her hand, and lifted it now, turning it to inspect the grubby dressing.

The least of my worries.

She laid the bag over her torso and estimated the size. Then, laboriously, she began snipping up the sides with the scissors. The blades had rounded ends and were not very sharp. It seemed to take a long time before she managed to separate both halves of the bag, but she struggled on doggedly. It gave her purpose. It stopped her thinking about the pulsing pain in her body, and the ever-present pigs. And at least she was doing *something*.

She trimmed the bag down further, and wrapped the cut piece around her ribcage, as much as she was able to. She tucked part of it underneath her back, and adding strips of tape to hold the front to her stomach.

The white plastic, almost see-through, stuck to the fluid leaching from the burns. It smeared across the inside surface, merging into one giant blister. She dared not think what it was going to be like removing it again, and comforted herself with the thought that either it would be done in a hospital, by professionals, or it wouldn't be done at all...

No! Don't even think about that option.

It was a bandage – of sorts. Better than nothing. At least it would keep the damn flies at bay.

One pig snorted, as if in contempt.

'Oh, yeah?' Her voice came out croaky. 'Who asked *you*, anyway?'

When she'd plastered herself with enough tape that the plastic seemed to be holding, fatigue made her limbs leaden and her hands shake. She pushed it aside, took a couple of breaths, gathered her courage, and sat up.

Her ribs split into shards – or that was how it felt.

She gave a moan that turned into a roar as the pain ripped through her. She shut her eyes, leaning back slightly, braced on hands curled into fists. Her nails dug viciously deep into her palms. But she didn't dare let herself drop back.

If she did, she'd never get up again.

Instead, she panted until it dropped from unbelievable to simply unbearable.

And she took her first proper look at her leg.

It wasn't pretty.

In fact, it made her feel thoroughly sick. She began to dry-heave, which set her ribs off again. It took several minutes of deep breaths and swearing at herself before she got the panic under control.

Then she took the other half of the bin liner and began easing it under her damaged calf. Every tiny movement hurt worse than anything she'd ever been through, but she refused to give up. Refused to give in.

In the back of her mind, she could hear Shannon's voice telling her not to be such a baby. Not to let them beat her. Telling her she was stronger than this.

Kensy held onto that thought as she wrapped her leg loosely in the plastic, and taped it around her knee. At least that meant she didn't have to look at it. But she couldn't ignore how hot the skin was around her calf and shin, how tight it felt, and swollen. Kensy was no medical expert, but she knew enough to realise that meant the wound was infected.

She'd thought herself lucky for not already being dead. Now, she knew, it was only a matter of time.

FORTY-FIVE

THE ROYAL SOCIETY OF MEDICINE, WIMPOLE STREET, MARYLEBONE

'Scallops, I think,' Dr Ayo Onatade said decisively. 'Followed by the steak – rare.' She closed the menu and smiled beatifically in Byron's direction. 'My guest will pay.'

'Of course, madam,' the waiter said, without a flicker. 'And for you, sir?'

'The soup to start, please. As to the choice of main course, I concur – the steak, also.'

'An excellent choice, sir. How would you like that cooked?'

'Medium,' Byron said. 'Still pink in the middle, but no blood.'

When the waiter had gone, Dr Onatade's smile morphed into a grin. '"No blood"?' she queried. 'I would never have taken you for squeamish, Byron. Not a man in your profession.'

'You might be surprised how many police officers I've worked with who are queasy at crime scenes,' he remarked. 'But then, we don't, on the whole, spend most of our day up to our elbows in a ripe cadaver.'

'Touché,' she said, toasting him with her glass. She leaned closer, eyes twinkling behind her glasses. 'Although I wouldn't say that too loudly around here, if I were you, or you'll get us thrown out.'

'Ah, I didn't realise a strong stomach was a condition of entry.'

She laughed aloud. 'If they hear you casting such aspersions on the food, they definitely *will* throw us out.'

They were lunching in the restaurant of The Royal Society of Medicine, a building of gravitas on the corner of Wimpole Street and Henrietta Place. The location had been chosen originally for its proximity to Harley Street, Byron knew, but the irony of being back in the vicinity of Lex Vaganov's gallery – while embroiled in the same case – did not escape his notice.

It was a little after two. The lunchtime rush was winding down, and few of the tables in the high, bright room were occupied. Byron hoped to receive Dr Onatade's opinion while there weren't many eavesdroppers who might take a professional interest in their conversation.

She dipped her nose into her glass, sipped and savoured. 'Wine at lunchtime. What a treat.'

Byron had known Dr Onatade for ten years, first as an occasionally combative colleague, then latterly as a friend. She had always shown the same zest for everything, be it food or a mutilated corpse. Now into her fifties and married to her career, she tended to treat him almost as a favoured godson. And she was forthright and outspoken as he would expect of someone who had risen to the top of her chosen profession in spite of bias against both gender and race. Byron considered her the finest forensic pathologist he'd ever encountered.

'So, no doubt you'd prefer business before pleasure?' she said now, raising her eyebrows.

'Always.'

She laughed, striking a pose with fingers to chest. 'Ah, a man after my own heart.' She reached into the bag resting against the side of her chair and pulled out a file folder.

Byron said, 'Thank you for taking a look at this, Ayo. It is much appreciated.'

She waved away his thanks with a languid flap of her hand. 'You've given me an excuse to venture south and visit the big city,' she said. 'And every time I stay at the Society, I remember why I like it so much. Tomorrow, I shall spend the morning here, in the library, and the afternoon on Bond Street.'

It was hard to know which prospect pleased her more. As well as the restaurant and a bar, the Society had a renowned library of medical texts, and a hotel, Domus Medica, all under the same roof.

'It's been a while since I've been here myself,' Byron murmured.

Dr Onatade's face fell. 'Oh, Byron, I'm so sorry. I didn't think about... Well, Isobel was a member, wasn't she?'

'She was.'

'You are an idiot. You should have said something when I first suggested meeting here. We could easily have gone somewhere less... evocative.'

'There was no need – and no need to apologise, either,' Byron said gently. 'Being back here actually feels... comforting, in some ways.'

And painful, in so many others.

She regarded him acutely for a moment, then said lightly, 'Also, the food is usually *very* good – the desserts especially.'

He managed to return her smile. 'There is that.'

She cleared her throat, opening the folder. 'Anyway, your victim died from blunt force trauma to the head,' she said, her voice turning brisk. 'That much was clear from the outset.'

'Was alcohol a factor?'

'It can be, certainly – if there's a fall involved. But in this case, regrettably, the blood-work was not carried out. Very sloppy. It's in the notes that she reeked of alcohol, so maybe they thought it wasn't worth the price.' She sighed. 'I do so *miss* the Forensic Science Service. Since privatisation it's all become a cost-benefit analysis.'

'She had a record of disorderly conduct. The officers involved claim they thought she was drunk when they arrested her. Perhaps it was considered a foregone conclusion.'

'Hm. As I said – *very* sloppy.'

'What about timing?'

'Looking at the extent of the sub-cranial bleeding, I'd estimate the killing blow was struck somewhere between eighteen and thirty-six hours before she finally succumbed.'

'Eighteen hours would put her arrest inside our window. Thirty-six and she could have been anywhere...' Byron frowned. 'I don't suppose you can narrow it down any further?'

Dr Onatade straightened, fixing him with a piercing gaze over the top of her glasses. 'Only if she happened to be wearing a wristwatch, which was conveniently smashed during the original assault,' she said with a touch of asperity. 'Or if she'd been using a fitness tracker, or carrying a smartphone. Sadly, she was remarkably inconsiderate in that regard.'

'My apologies. In my defence, I ought to point out that I was merely *hoping* for a more definitive result, rather than expecting it.'

'Hm, well, as to the weapon used, it was mostly thin and cylindrical but with a protuberance at the end—'

'Like a police baton?'

She paused, pointedly, at the interruption. 'Not *unlike* a police baton, certainly. That's the most I can say about it. I have only photographs and measurements to go on. Your chap also didn't feel it necessary to take a cast of the indentation in the skull.' She sniffed. 'The blow was wielded with moderate to firm force.'

'Meaning?'

'Meaning a glancing blow from a man, or a more aimed

blow from a woman, or a really determined blow from a teenager or even a child.'

'That opens up our suspect pool somewhat.'

'Yes, sorry about that,' Dr Onatade said without apparent remorse. 'Ah, scallops!'

The waiter smoothly delivered their starters, topped off their glasses – Dr Onatade's with wine, Byron's with mineral water – and blended into the background again. They talked of trivia while they grazed through the first course, and caught up on more personal history during the sirloin steaks that followed. Dr Onatade had taken a position up in the northwest of the country, lured away from the capital with the promise of more autonomy, and a less frenetic pace of life.

'Although, I can't say you get more property bang for your buck up there. House prices in the southern Lakes are almost as bad as London.' She pinned him with that forensic eye again. 'You haven't thought of moving?'

Byron rested his knife and fork on the lip of his plate while he considered. Like all the RSM crockery, it was plain white, stylish yet unfussy, and adorned with the Society's crest.

'No,' he said at last. 'Isobel and I converted the house together. She spent so much time and effort getting it just as we wanted, that to leave now seems... somehow disloyal.'

'As long as you aren't turning it into some kind of shrine. That would not be healthy – and not at all what Izzy would have wanted.'

Byron thought again of Blake's presence in his home. Apart from that one moment of disquiet, when she'd appeared at the top of the stairs in his dead wife's robe, in retrospect he found himself less disturbed than he might have expected. Having another woman there, not as a friend, exactly, but someone he was... drawn to.

It should have felt wrong.

But it hadn't.

'What's that smile?' Dr Onatade asked. She tilted her head slightly, lasering in with deadly accuracy. 'Byron! Have you met someone?'

'What? No. Well, perhaps.'

'Thank you, that's a very illuminating answer,' she said dryly. 'Come on, give. After all, as you pointed out, I'm doing you the most enormous favour. The very least you can do – besides treating me to lunch, of course – is satisfy my rampant curiosity. So, who is she?'

It was a very good question – one Byron had been asking himself from the moment he and Blake had first met.

'A former teenage runaway who's ten years my junior; quite possibly a con artist – she certainly consorts with some very dodgy people – and is currently living on the streets, against all advice, while looking for our victim's surrogate daughter.'

'Oh,' Dr Onatade said. She frowned, then brightened considerably. '*Oh.*'

'What does that mean?'

'You really do like her, don't you?' She turned her attention blithely to the last few bites of her steak.

'How do you glean that from the information I've just given you?'

'Because you're trying to talk *yourself* out of liking her, of course.' She placed her cutlery neatly together on her empty plate. 'If you were lukewarm about her, you would have felt compelled to tell me her good points, as much to convince yourself as me. As it is, you're worried about getting in too deep, so you've told me what you think are her bad points, hoping I will tell you to kick her to the kerb. Although, for what it's worth, she sounds utterly intriguing.'

'I'm just not sure if I'm ready for... anything,' he admitted.

Dr Onatade reached across the table and tapped a finger on the society crest on the rim of his plate. 'You may not be able to read the motto – I'm referring to its legibility, not your comprehension. It says, "*Non est vivere sed valere vita,*" which means, "It is not sufficient in life merely to exist, but rather to flourish." Something to bear in mind, don't you think?'

Byron was saved from finding an answer by the reappearance of the waiter, who cleared their plates and then asked if they would like anything else.

'The dessert menu, if you please,' Dr Onatade replied promptly, smiling. 'And a few minutes to digest.'

The waiter brought over the menus. When they were alone again, she went back to the folder without a pause, as if the intervening conversation had not taken place. Byron had always rather admired her ability to compartmentalise.

'Various swabs were taken from the victim's hands and clothing, revealing some trace evidence, although, again, no actual tests have been carried out to determine its nature. I've taken the liberty of sending a batch off to someone I work with in the north. She's good.' She skewered him again with a look. 'I trust this is coming out of the IOPC's pocket, rather than mine – or yours, come to that?'

'Of course.'

She nodded. 'Excellent. I shall ask her to be thorough. And as soon as I hear anything, I'll let you know.'

'I don't suppose you've had a chance to cast your eye over the notes on the second woman's murder?'

'This Tess whoever-she-is? Briefly. Why, what were you hoping I might find?'

'Either a connection, or something to rule one out.'

'Ah, well in that case, you may be disappointed.'

Byron said nothing, but his raised eyebrow spoke for him.

'The modus operandi was very different,' Dr Onatade said. 'Different weapon, different type of attack. And the excess of violence – the deliberate targeting of the face – speaks to it being a deeply personal crime. Your killer knew his victim and wanted to make sure nobody else would know her.'

'He should have stripped her, then. I recognised the clothing rather than the woman.'

'Maybe he didn't have the presence of mind? Or the time?'

'Maybe.'

Dr Onatade slipped the folders back into her bag and picked up the dessert menu. 'I can't say categorically that the same perpetrator wasn't responsible, just as I can't say he or she was. Although, the force used on victim two would suggest a strong man – and I use the word purely in its muscular sense – as the assailant, if that helps at all?'

'Not really, I have to be honest.'

'Well, I have faith in your instinct.' She smiled. 'Not as much as my science, but enough to know that if you think there is something that links these two deaths, you will find it.'

'I'm touched.'

'As you should be,' she agreed, opening the menu. 'And now *that's* out of the way, can I interest you in sharing a nice tart?'

FORTY-SIX

DORA STREET, LIMEHOUSE

As another front door slammed in her face, Jemma Weeks held back a sigh.

'Thanks for nothing,' she muttered.

House-to-house inquiries were all part and parcel of any investigation, but that didn't mean Weeks enjoyed them. Especially not when she'd been allocated this low-rise block of flats. The open landings allowed the prevailing wind to drill the rain down the back of her collar with unerring accuracy. And the few residents who answered her knock were not inclined to stand and chat.

None of them invited her in.

None of them seemed to know anything.

Or they weren't inclined to share that information.

Instead, she'd heard a dozen different variations on the theme of 'we keep ourselves to ourselves around here'.

Weeks recognised that the worry was beginning to get to her, a nagging ache she couldn't seem to ease. It was only after they'd arrested Tristram Shelseley, and she'd suddenly felt taller, lighter, that she realised how stressed she'd been – having this whole Shannon Clifford thing hanging over her.

And then her inspector had poured a whole bucketful of cold water on her parade.

Not that she'd heard from the IOPC guy, Byron, one way or another, damn him. So, she was left to fret about whether he believed the old bloke singling her out with his confession was as suspicious as Lloyd seemed to think.

In some ways, having a concrete task was a blessing. If she'd been on standard foot patrol – or stuck in a vehicle for a shift with the likes of McCoubrey – it might have been far worse. Or not, considering the rain. Funny how he'd managed to score himself a cushy number back at Limehouse today, though.

They were still sorting through the records from Kinfolk, although talking to some of the 'service users' – she still couldn't hear that term without the inverted commas – and the staff had proved fruitful. One of the chefs thought she'd heard Tess say her last name was Parkin. 'Like the cake, y'know?'

After that, council tax records brought up an address on Clemence Street, only a stone's throw from the station. And here they were, in teams, knocking on doors in the surrounding streets, asking questions, in the rain.

She glanced at the end flat on the top floor and almost gave it a miss. There were no immediate signs of occupation. But as she hesitated, the door was yanked open. A thin, dark-haired woman glared out at her, arms folded combatively across her chest.

'Yes?'

'Ah, yes... hello,' Weeks managed, fumbling for her wits. 'We're making inquiries about one of your neighbours in this area. Are you the householder at this address?'

'No. I am carer.'

The woman uncrossed her arms and Weeks saw a local authority lanyard around her neck, from which hung a plastic ID card. The photo – more of a mugshot – showed the woman with an identical scowl to the one she wore now. Weeks managed to catch the first name – Irina.

'Well, would it be possible to speak to the resident? Are they...?'

She'd been going to ask if they were in, but for someone to need an at-home carer, surely that meant they weren't able to just pop out to the shops, were they?

A muffled voice from further inside the flat shouted something. Without taking her eyes off Weeks, Irina shouted back over her shoulder, '*Zatknis, staryii tee liubopitni bluydok!*'

The only response from somewhere deeper in the flat was a bark of laughter followed by a bout of coughing that sounded as debilitating as it did painful.

Irina combined rolling her eyes with a jerk of her head. She stepped back, and Weeks followed her inside, wondering if she should have radioed in first, just in case.

The living room had the sour smell of long-term illness, overlaid with disinfectant and some kind of floral air freshener that emphasised the other odours rather than obscuring them. The decoration was bland, the room crammed with dark heavy furniture that seemed out of place in a London flat. Classical music played quietly in the background.

An old man sat in a wheelchair by the window, where a pair of binoculars rested on the sill. He was flanked by a tall fringed lamp on one side and an IV stand on the other, from which hung a bag of clear liquid. The tube from it snaked into the folds of the blanket he was swaddled in.

The lines in the old man's face were cut so deep they seemed carved into his skull rather than his skin. His cheekbones protruded sharply enough to slice paper. A few last remaining wisps of hair clung to his scalp. Startling pale-blue eyes regarded her from deep hollows in his gaunt face.

'Konstantin tires easily,' Irina said with a sniff. 'But do not worry. *You* will tire of *him* long before then.'

The old man made a noise in his throat that was almost a growl. Irina sniffed again and went out. Weeks took his nod towards a threadbare sofa as invitation to sit and did so, pulling out her notebook. It was so warm in the flat her uniform had begun to steam.

'You are here about the young woman on Clemence Street, yes?' Konstantin said, his voice slow and thick.

Weeks blinked. 'Yes, how do you know that, sir?'

He gave a gentle snort. 'Because God has chosen to punish me by leaving mind strong, even as body fails me. My eyes will no longer allow to read, so I sit by this window every day, punishing myself by watching others go about their lives.' He gestured to the binoculars. 'Always watching. What else have I to do with the time that is left to me?'

Weeks frowned, then stood up and edged around the furniture to the window, peering down. From this perspective, she had a decent outlook over a portion of Clemence Street, from the converted pub at the end to about halfway along the row of terraced houses. Only the occasional tree canopy obstructed the view. She took a picture on her phone, and sat down again.

'You think I would lie to you?' Konstantin scoffed.

'No,' Weeks said, truthfully. 'But my inspector will ask for more than my word on it.'

'Ah, yes. Trust, but verify. Always so.'

'Well, my job is evidence based.'

'Of course.'

'So, Mr...?'

'Please – just Konstantin.'

Weeks made a note to check with the council. It might be easier than fighting him for it.

'So – Konstantin – what can you tell me about the young woman you mentioned? When did you last see her?'

'On day she left.'

'Do you know which day that was?'

'Of course! I told you nothing is wrong with my mind. Were you not listening?'

She suppressed a sigh. 'So, which day was it?'

'It was day they feature Ben Crosland Quintet, *Songs of Solace and Reflection,* on Radio 3 jazz programme,' Konstantin said, his tone making it clear that she should, of course, know exactly when that was.

Weeks opened her mouth, then closed it again and made a note. Doing a quick search through the BBC Sounds schedule would be less hassle than making the old man work it out.

She nodded. 'OK, what do you mean by *leaving*, exactly? She might simply have been going shopping, to work, or to stay with a friend?'

'*Nyet.* No. I see the way she walk. Always, she walk fast, but that day she almost running. She carry a bag of possessions, not shopping. I saw the bruises, on her face, and I knew. She will not be coming back.'

'She'd been assaulted?'

'Many times,' he said, 'but always he hit her where it does not show. Not that time.'

'If he hit her where it wouldn't show,' Weeks said, underlining the word 'he' as one to return to, 'then how did you know she'd been assaulted before? Did she ever speak to you about it?'

Konstantin shook his head fractionally. 'There was no need for words. Pain changes the way persons move. And I have seen many persons try to escape the pain in their bodies, the fear in their minds.'

'Because of your... condition?'

He stared at her for a long moment. 'No. In Soviet Union. It was lifetime ago – many lifetimes. Trust me when I say this – I know well signs of pain in others.'

Weeks took longer than she needed to note that down, just so she could avoid the haunted distance in his eyes. She could hear the fatigue in his voice, too. It was taking more effort to get his mouth around the words. She knew he only had a few more questions left in him.

'Ms Parkin was the only person registered at her address,' she said then. 'But did you see anyone else going in and out of the place on a regular basis?'

'A few times, at front door. A man came – not like stranger.'

Weeks stilled. 'Can you describe him?'

'Big man – in mind as well as body.'

'I'm sorry, I don't...?'

Konstantin sighed heavily and closed his eyes. For a moment Weeks wondered if she'd been dismissed.

Irina slipped back into the room and hovered, clearly about to tell her to leave. Weeks cleared her throat in desperation.

Konstantin opened his eyes again.

'He is big man, for sure... but not as big as he is in own mind. Way he walk, way he act. He has...' The old man clenched his bony fists as if showing off imaginary muscles.

A rapid conversation followed between Konstantin and Irina. Much frowning and shrugging on her part.

'Swagger?' Weeks suggested.

'Yes! Yes, swagger. He is much *swagger*.' He sucked on the word, savoured it like a boiled sweet.

'Was he a regular visitor? When did you last see him?'

'Not often, but... regularly. Last time was few days before she leave.' He managed a faint smile. 'Maria João Pires – Chopin Piano Concerto No 1 in E minor, Opus 11.'

Weeks nodded and wrote, asking, 'And what did he look like? White, black? Hair colour?'

'White. No hair. Not like this?' He gestured to his own head. 'Younger. He choose... shave.'

Irina butted in again. It was hard to tell, but Weeks could have sworn she was trying to talk the old man out of saying more. He brushed aside her concerns.

'Enough,' Irina said tartly. 'You go now.'

Weeks got to her feet, taking her time. 'Thank you, sir,' she said to Konstantin, as Irina tried to herd her towards the door. 'We may want to have you work with a sketch artist, if that's OK.'

He gave a vague gesture that might have been yes or no. His eyes closed again, head tipping back.

At the doorway, she dug her heels in for one last try. 'Sir, is there *anything* else you can tell me about this man you saw?'

'*Mayekop.*'

'What? What does that—?'

But Irina had her in the hallway and bundled out through the front door before she could finish. Weeks jammed the toe of her boot into the gap before the other woman managed to slam the door.

'Irina! What did he say? "*Mayekop.*" What does that mean?'

Irina huffed out a breath, glanced over her shoulder, and said hurriedly, 'Word means "garbage" but it *means...* Konstantin thinks your man was cop.'

'But—'

'No! We come from place where saying such things one day means – poof – next day you are disappeared. Gone. He is old man, dying. Leave him to die in peace!'

And with that she managed to kick Weeks's toe over the threshold, and the last door of the day slammed shut in her face.

FORTY-SEVEN

CLEMENCE STREET, LIMEHOUSE

When Byron reached the house on Clemence Street, there was a uniformed officer guarding the front door. Byron showed his official ID and asked for DI Goodwin. The uniform seemed glad of the excuse to duck out of the rain. He stepped inside, reappearing a moment later to show Byron into the front room.

Byron paused on the threshold. Goodwin, together with his DS, Hari Desai, were inside the small sitting room. The presence of the two men made the space seem smaller still. Both detectives wore Tyvek crime-scene suits, but peeled to the waist and knotted.

'You're starting to take on the hallmarks of a bad penny, Mr Byron,' Goodwin said. He smiled as he said it, but his tone was less jovial, and again he put emphasis on Byron's semi-civilian status.

'They told me at Limehouse that I'd find you here if I needed to speak with you urgently.'

'Well, we have this wonderful invention called the mobile phone,' Goodwin said, heavy on the sarcasm. 'You might want to try it sometime.'

'I did,' Byron responded mildly. 'There was no reply.'

'Well, perhaps that's because I'm rather busy at the moment, at what might prove to be our primary crime scene.'

Byron did not miss the frown Desai flicked in the direction of his superior. Byron cast his professional gaze quickly around the room, including the smashed glass of the coffee table standing on the rug in front of the fake fireplace. Indicative of a fight, maybe, but not one violent or prolonged enough to have caused the injuries listed in Tess Parkin's post-mortem report. Not unless the scene had been seriously sanitised since.

'Really?' he murmured, expressionless.

Goodwin scowled. 'Well, seeing as you're here now, what do you want?'

'I understand you're still holding Tristram Shelseley over the death of Shannon Clifford.'

'What of it? He confessed, so it seems the IOPC can take its bat and its ball and go home.'

'Ah. I had assumed that by now you would have received Doctor Onatade's report on the timing of the fatal blow.'

'It's on my desk, but in case it's escaped your notice—'

'You have your primary crime scene to... confirm. Yes, I do understand.'

'So, you've come to give me the edited highlights, have you?'

Byron said nothing, just locked eyes with Goodwin and waited. After a few moments, the DI let his gaze drop away and made an impatient gesture for Byron to get on with it. Even then, Byron waited a beat longer before doing so.

'Doctor Onatade's professional opinion is that the victim was struck between eighteen and thirty-six hours before she died,' he said, leaving the implications unspoken. 'Shelseley's statement claims he had an altercation with her less than an hour before she collapsed in Watney Market.'

'He confessed—' Goodwin began. Then he stopped, and scowled again.

'Yes – initially to PC Weeks, wasn't it?' Byron kept his tone rigorously neutral.

Goodwin bristled. 'I hope you're not suggesting—'

'I'm not suggesting anything. I'm stating the facts, because any decent detective never loses sight of the facts of the case. That time window means it is perfectly feasible that Shannon Clifford was *technically* killed during her arrest.'

'Only just!'

'And how many times have you heard a perpetrator say, "I hardly touched him," or "I just put my hands around her throat to frighten her, or shut her up, and the next thing I knew, she wasn't breathing"? Sometimes "only just" is all it takes.'

Now it was Goodwin's turn to say nothing.

Desai's eyes had been following the conversation back and forth like a tennis grudge match. He cleared his throat. 'I hate to say this, boss, but he does have a point.'

The glare Goodwin launched in Desai's direction would have flayed a lesser man.

'All right, all right. When we're finished here, I'll go back to the station and take a look at that report you mentioned. Then we'll see. Good enough?'

'Thank you,' Byron said.

'But I'm sure you'll understand that this case has to be my immediate priority.'

Byron waited until the other man had almost turned his back before he added, 'Well, there may be a slight complication to be considered there.'

'Oh, for—' Goodwin spun back, hands fisted on hips. 'What now?'

'I have received information about the anonymous caller who dialled three nines when Shannon collapsed at the market.'

'What information? How?'

'I asked for CCTV footage from the location. Something

that should have been requested by whoever did the initial investigation into Shannon's death.'

'Well, some of us don't have an unlimited budget for that kind of thing,' Goodwin snapped. 'And it might have escaped your notice, Byron, but you're not actually a detective anymore.'

Byron heard Desai's quick intake of breath and agreed with him. Goodwin was in danger of seriously overstepping the mark.

'Perhaps not, but I am still an investigator, and in many ways my reach and remit far outstrips your own, Detective Inspector.'

Goodwin flushed, but he took a breath and seemed to get a grip on himself. 'I apologise,' he said shortly. 'I'm under pressure to get results – do more with less. You know how it is.'

'Yes, I do.'

'So, who *was* this anonymous caller?'

'We're apparently standing in her living room right now.'

Goodwin's face froze for a second. He spun away, took a couple of paces as if gripped by furious thought.

It was Desai who asked, 'Does that mean the two deaths are connected? How? I mean, do you think Shannon said something to Tess before she died? Could that be why the level of violence was so much worse? He was trying to beat that information out of her?'

Goodwin turned back to them. His face had cleared.

'Thank you very much for that, Mr Byron. And unless you're seriously suggesting that any serving police officer, having accidentally – possibly, *allegedly* – killed one woman, then decided to beat another to death to cover up the crime, then I go back to my earlier opinion.'

'Which is?'

'That your work here is done.'

FORTY-EIGHT

LOCATION UNKNOWN

'Kensy! Kensy, can you hear me? You need to wake up now.'

'Hm? W-what? Who...?'

'MacKensy Young, you get your arse into gear. No more of this lazing around. You need to get moving.'

'Sh-Shannon?'

'Who else would it be, huh?'

Kensy cracked open gritty eyes. For a few moments, she peered up at the corrugated ceiling with no idea where she was. Without thinking, she tried to roll sideways.

That's when it all came back to her.

She wished it hadn't.

When she'd got her breath back, she scanned the corners of her cell. She was alone.

'Oh, Shannon,' she moaned. 'Why did you leave me...?'

She tried to swallow – something she did countless times a day, without thinking about it. Now, her mouth was so dry, her throat wouldn't work. She couldn't even remember how it should.

'You need water, kid. Without it, you're finished.'

When Kensy turned her head, the hazy figure of Shannon

was leaning against the block-work next to the pair of gates. She was wearing the old green bomber jacket she used to favour, with her hands stuffed into the pockets.

'Shannon... But, you're...'

'Dead? Yeah, never mind about that. Focus! Think: survival. Nothing else matters besides that. I survived on the street, and so did you. You're not going to let it all end in a dump like this, are you?'

'Like I have a choice...?'

'You always have a choice. You choose to give up, or you choose to keep trying.' Shannon straightened up from the wall, head on one side as she stared down at her. 'So, what's it gonna be, our kid?'

Kensy blinked, though she didn't even seem to have enough moisture left for tears.

When she opened her eyes again, Shannon was gone.

Kensy swore. Heartfelt, bitter words, filled with rage.

Then she set her jaw until she thought her teeth would crack, and forced her head and shoulders off the ground. Her scream turned into a growl. She sat up, struggling to breathe around pain that was all consuming. She tried to convince herself that maybe her ribs didn't feel as bad. It was only partly successful. At least the plastic liner gave the illusion of binding everything together.

The water still dripped in from the roof in several places. The nearest was barely a dribble. It hadn't even formed a puddle – just a damp patch on the concrete. But there was another leak nearer to the gates into the pig shed. Beneath that, a little water had actually pooled in a slight hollow. It was about where Shannon had been standing. Or the image of Shannon, anyway. Kensy didn't believe Shannon's ghost had actually been there.

I'm not quite that far gone. Not yet...

Kensy felt warmer than she had in days. Perhaps it was that

plastic again, keeping some body heat in? Her fingers fumbled at her collar, trying to loosen it, let in a bit more air. The shirt was stuck to her chest with sweat. Maybe it was just the effort.

Or maybe not.

Water. Think about the water.

She pressed down with both fists, straightened her arms, and with a grunt of effort, pushed her arse off the floor, just enough so she could move it. It was only a centimetre or two, but it was movement. The only trouble was, her lower leg stayed where it was.

She had a sudden vision of her body turning into one of those coiled metal toys she'd played with as a kid – a Slinky. The idea of her body over by the wall and her foot still in the middle of the floor, with her skin stretched thin between the two, made her feel faint as well as sick. But if her leg did stretch a bit, might it also... straighten?

It took a long time to inch across the floor, little by little. Her leg didn't straighten much. It didn't stretch much, either. And it hurt like the demons of hell were jabbing her with their pitch-forks, all the way. Sweat dripped from her face. Her arms shook with the effort. She closed her mind to it, as far as that was possible. And cursed everyone and everything she could think of when it was not.

Finally, if she leaned sideways, she could reach a hand to the drips. She folded the last piece of the bin liner into a kind of cone and held it underneath. Tried to take her mind off the nausea, and the growing dizziness – and her desperate thirst – by counting the falling droplets.

After fifty, she'd enough for a mouthful. It was the best thing she'd ever tasted.

She held the makeshift cone out, and counted again.

Somewhere in the back of her mind, she thought she heard Shannon's voice again.

'Good girl.'

FORTY-NINE

SILWOOD STREET, BERMONDSEY

Weeks lurked in the shadows, watching two grown men beating hell out of each other.

One of them was Greg McCoubrey. He was the larger of the two, but wasn't getting it all his own way. His smaller opponent was quicker. He also had a wicked left hook that he employed to great effect.

Every time he took another one, McCoubrey grunted past his gumshield and redoubled his efforts. He didn't land many punches himself, Weeks noted, but what her colleague lacked in accuracy, he made up for in power.

She wouldn't have liked to bet on the outcome.

'OK, lads, that's enough for now.' The trainer had stayed outside the ring, leaning on the ropes. 'Footwork, Greg. I keep telling you. If you planted your feet any firmer on the canvas, you'd take root. You gotta keep moving.'

As the combatants touched gloves and ducked out of the ring, Weeks moved forwards. Her arrival caused a moment of stillness, akin to the piano player freezing mid-note in the old western saloon. She gathered the gym didn't see many women applying for membership. She wasn't surprised. Tucked under a couple of railway arches in Bermondsey, sandwiched by auto-body repair shops, it wasn't an area she was happy walking around in after dark.

But she didn't feel like she'd had a choice.

By the time she'd got back to Limehouse, she still hadn't worked out what to do with the information gleaned from Konstantin and his carer. Initially, she'd headed for the mobile incident unit, of course she had. But on the way there she caught sight of a now-familiar figure walking out past the uniform on the door to Tess Parkin's house.

Former DSI John Byron.

Goodwin and Desai had emerged shortly afterwards. What-ever Byron had said to the DI, she didn't have to be a mind reader to know he was in a foul mood. She remembered her inspector's warning – that the IOPC man might have plenty to say about her interaction with Tristram Shelseley. And somehow she couldn't quite face having Goodwin's earlier approval of her actions turn sour. So she kept her notes vague and said nothing

Instead, she'd ventured south of the river to catch McCoubrey in his natural habitat.

'Can I help you?' the trainer asked, doubt in his voice.

'No thanks. I just need to have a quick word with Greg.'

McCoubrey eyed her and said nothing while the trainer unlaced his gloves. He took his time getting out of his head-guard and gumshield, sharing a murmured joke with the other two guys that Weeks was pretty sure was at her expense.

The three of them laughed, the sound both raucous and intimidating. Weeks suppressed a shiver.

McCoubrey draped a towel around his neck. As he headed in her direction, she realised the old Russian had been quite right about the swagger.

He had it in spades.

'So, what brings you to my neck of the woods, Jem? D'you fancy going a few rounds in the ring?'

She straightened. 'Why? Like the idea of punching a woman in the face, do you?'

Whatever he'd been expecting, it wasn't that. He flinched, then motioned curtly towards the door.

When they were outside, he turned on her.

'What the hell's got into you? Where did that come from?'

Briefly, she ran through her interview with Konstantin.

'Could be anybody, that,' McCoubrey dismissed, but there was something hollow in his tone.

'So, if I was to go back tomorrow and ask him to pick your mugshot out of a line-up—'

'All right, all right.' He scowled. 'Who else have you told?'

Weeks was suddenly aware of the darkness outside the gym, of the nearby scrap cars, no doubt soon to be on their way to a crusher somewhere. She wished she'd done this at Limehouse after all.

She swallowed. 'Nobody – yet.'

'Why not?'

That threw her. 'Because... I wanted to hear what you had to say first.'

He nodded. She didn't need to explain. It had been clear enough, with the IOPC sniffing around the station, that no one wanted to be seen as a grass. The irony of that, among coppers, was not lost on her.

Besides, if she was wrong, and it got out... Well, they'd never let her forget her disloyalty. Not a position you wanted to be in if you ever needed backup in a dark alley.

'So... you and Tess?'

'There is no me and Tess. I didn't even know her name.' He wiped a hand over his scalp, wafting her with sweat and aggression. 'Look, I got myself into a bit of a hole – financially speaking.'

'How?'

'You don't need to know.'

'Oh, I think I do, Greg. If you're asking me not to take this further up the line, I definitely do.' She eyed his bulk. 'What was it – drugs? Steroids?'

'Give me a break, will you?' he snapped. 'If you must know, my dad was ill for a long time, before he died. Alzheimer's. Refused to go into a home, stubborn old bugger, and there's only so much the local authority would pay for.' He hunched his shoulders, defensive. 'My credit cards were maxed out. The bank didn't want to know me. I needed funds and I didn't have much choice where I got them.'

'Oh, Greg,' she groaned. 'Who did you go to?'

'Does it matter? They're all as bad as each other.'

'And what happened, when you didn't keep up the repayments?'

He bristled. 'What makes you think—?'

'Nobody ever does, mate. Not for long.'

'I thought they'd be after me with a baseball bat, but turns out a copper's marker has a value.' His lips twisted. 'The shark sold it on. And before you ask, no, I don't know who to. The compound interest stopped, but I still have to pay off the capital. In cash, every month. Dropped through a letterbox.'

'Of that house on Clemence Street,' Weeks said slowly. 'But you never went in, or saw who else was there besides Tess?'

He shook his head. 'Must be a nasty bastard, though – if what was done to her was anything to go by.'

She paused, running over it in her mind, looking for the holes and finding them.

'I can't believe that, if whoever now holds your marker has stopped charging you interest, they haven't asked for something else instead.' She glanced up, caught his hunted expression. 'Oh, Greg. What have you done?'

FIFTY

KINFOLK, CABLE STREET, SHADWELL

Blake picked up the tray loaded with fancy nibbles, careful to make sure none of the creations toppled over. Playing her part, she moved between the crowd gathered in the dining hall at Kinfolk. She smiled vacantly at them as she proffered her tray, occasionally fiddling with the white shirt River had found for her to wear, as if she wasn't comfortable in – or used to – such clothing.

Slipping deep into such a role was a skill she'd learned years ago, under the demanding eye of a master. Lex had trained her in the art of the long con, when she'd had to not just play the part of someone else, but to become that person, completely. She'd slipped up only once, when she'd thought nobody was watching. It was not a lesson she'd ever forget. From then on she knew it was better to take it for granted that you were under constant surveillance, twenty-four seven. After she'd helped Caz make her escape from the rooming house, Blake retraced her steps onto the roof, through the skylight, and dropped back onto the bunk in her room. Then she waited for the discovery to be made.

And the fireworks.

She was not disappointed.

After the stamping and the yelling, there was an intense but muted argument. Blake couldn't make out the details, even with her ear pressed to the floorboards. But she guessed it might be the apportioning of blame.

A few minutes later, she heard the bolt on the outside of her door rattle back. Her heart rate spiked instantly.

How did they know it was anything to do with me? I checked for cameras – I always do…

She sat up, blinking away pretend sleep as the door opened and River hurried in.

'Ah, Blake. I'm sorry to wake you. One of the other girls has… um, she's sick, and there's a fundraiser tonight at the shelter for potential donors. Have you ever waited tables…?'

So here she was, dressed in borrowed clothes, with her tray. River had plaited her hair while it was still wet from the hasty shower she'd been all but shoved into. Pinned back and tied this tight, it would still be damp in the morning.

A small price to pay for the intel she was collecting.

Wait-staff, she'd discovered previously, were almost invisible to those they waited upon. Her current persona only increased their complacency.

She deliberately offered her tray to the small group that included Diarmuid Mackie and his wife, standing together with someone she recognised from news reports as a political mover and shaker.

'Ah, sweetie, are you coping all right?' Adhiti asked, smiling at her.

'Yeah – I mean, yes, thank you,' Blake mumbled.

Adhiti was dressed in one of the beautiful silk dresses that had become her trademark, a modern, western take on a classic eastern design, with another of those long scarves draped artfully around her neck. Her husband was in a tuxedo that fitted him like a particularly flattering glove.

'And is this one of your... protégés, Diarmuid?' the politico asked.

Blake gave the man a timid smile and tried to ignore the way her skin crawled as his piggy eyes drifted over her.

'She is, bless her. And looking at her now, you wouldn't believe that this young lady was on the streets when we found her, isn't that right, darling?'

She gave a mute nod. She didn't have to force the flush that came to her cheeks, and hoped they'd mistake it for awkward embarrassment rather than anger.

'Really?' the man drawled. 'And how old is she, exactly?'

Blake muttered her excuses and scurried away, eyes on her tray as she manoeuvred through the unseeing crowd. When someone large stepped very deliberately into her way, she stopped abruptly, toppling one of the canapés. For a second, she thought it might be Paarth. Her body tensed and her gaze jerked upwards.

'*Lex!*' she hissed. 'What on earth are *you* doing here?'

To the casual observer it would have seemed that Lex Vaganov leaned closer only to peer at the contents of her tray, while he casually lifted his champagne glass to his lips to screen his mouth.

'We need to talk.'

Blake stared at him, balancing her tray in one hand while she pointed to one canapé and then another, as if explaining their ingredients.

'What is it? Did Caz find you? Is she OK?'

'Calm down. Yes, she's fine. I had someone take her up to Derbyshire, as you requested.'

'Will she stay put?'

Vaganov shrugged, disguising the movement of his shoulder by reaching for the toppled canapé. He solved the how-to-eat-it question by simply putting the whole thing into his mouth at once. When he'd chewed and swallowed, Blake neatly twisted the side of the tray that held paper napkins towards him. He plucked one from the pile and dabbed his mouth.

'Fifteen minutes,' he murmured from behind it. 'Outside.'

Then he nodded – a gesture that would, she hoped, be taken as a comment on the food. She beamed in apparent response and turned away.

Across the room, she caught sight of Paarth, standing by the doorway to the kitchen. He was in his usual leather jacket and vaguely military black cargo trousers, out of place amid the suits and designer dresses. Out of place by his motionless intent, too.

And he was watching her with a focused, suspicious gaze.

Blake kept her face placid as she worked the room. As soon as her tray was empty, she hurried towards the kitchen. Paarth, she noted, was no longer guarding the entrance.

'Grab another and take it out,' River said over her shoulder, jerking her head to the trays lined up on the side counter as she lifted another loaded baking sheet out of one of the ovens.

'I... I don't feel so good,' Blake managed, swaying. 'It's awful stuffy in there... I think I'm gonna—'

She brought her shoulders up and forwards convulsively, clapped a hand over her mouth.

'Oh no you don't – not in here!' River cried. 'Outside. *Now*. Get some fresh air, for heaven's sake! And don't come back in until you know you're not going to hurl all over the place.'

With a moan, Blake scuttled for the rear fire door, hand still over her mouth. She was out in the parking area a moment later.

She straightened, and waited until her eyes had adjusted to the dark. All the while, she was watching for the telltale glow of a cigarette end, or a shape to harden in the softness of the night.

There was nothing.

And then there was a hand on her upper arm.

She whirled to face the danger, fists coming up, thoughts zinging to Paarth and that distrustful stare.

'Blake,' Lex said, fast and low. 'Relax.' He squeezed her

shoulder, led her further away from the building, to a corner where the shadows were deeper, and – she knew he would have checked – not covered by cameras. He had even turned up the collar of his tuxedo so the lapels covered the revealing flash of gleaming white shirt beneath his bow tie.

'Very 007,' she teased, flipping it with her fingers. 'Seriously, though, Lex, what *are* you doing here?'

He shrugged. 'I'm a potential donor, naturally.'

'And the girl – she's really OK?'

'She is. Someone I trust is driving her north, so she'll be safe. Don't worry.'

Blake felt something of the tension in her neck uncoil. 'Good,' was all she said. 'And what about the old man?'

'Still in custody, although I understand your... admirer is doing his best to resolve *that* issue.'

It was habit, more than caution, that they avoided using any names.

'Really?'

'Mm. If I'm not careful, I may have to revise my opinion of the man. And you know how I hate that.'

A smile ghosted across her lips. 'He's not as bad as you think.'

'He's not as good as you seem to think, either.'

'We'll see.'

She caught his smile, but when he spoke his voice held an edge. 'What are you doing still on the inside?'

'I haven't... found what I was looking for. Although, I haven't searched the whole place.'

'Then we need to clear it, en masse – and sooner rather than later. They'll be wise to your window trick now. I doubt that will work again.'

'Good job they were cheap windows, or it wouldn't have worked this time,' she admitted.

'Do you have an address? The girl had no idea where she was being held.'

Blake shook her head. 'We travel to and from in the back of a panel van, and I don't exactly have GPS on me.'

He sighed. 'Perhaps I should have you chipped – like a dog or a cat.'

'Try it, and you'll lose a couple of fingers, and maybe an eye.'

He grunted, reached into his pocket and brought out the latest oversize iPhone – his own – offering it to her. 'Take this. I didn't realise you'd be here tonight, or I would have come better prepared.'

Blake stared at the phone. It was bigger than her hand. 'And just where do you expect me to hide *that* where they're not going to find it?'

He paused a moment, then let out an annoyed breath. 'Damn... Ah, wait.'

Another pocket produced the keys to his Bentley, with a small plastic disc swinging from the fob. He quickly detached the disc – about the size of a £2 coin – and dropped it into her palm.

'Tracker?' Blake guessed.

'Passive tracker. If you're near anyone with a Bluetooth-enabled phone, it will upload your location to the cloud. When they take you back tonight, I'll come and get you.'

'Clever.' She paused. 'All of us?'

'Yes, all of you. You have my word on that.'

FIFTY-ONE

Byron had just driven into his garage and climbed out of the Mercedes when a figure appeared in the open doorway behind him.

He tensed in automatic response. It took his brain a moment or two to recognise the man as Hari Desai.

'Sorry, sir,' Desai said quickly, not moving any closer. 'I didn't mean to... startle you. I know it's late, but could I have a word?'

Byron raised an eyebrow, waiting for his system to wind down. 'Officially, or unofficially?'

Desai gave a wry smile. 'With respect, sir, if it was official, I'd have done it at work.'

Byron acknowledged the point. 'Come on up.' He led them both up the stairs to the open living room and kitchen area, stopping only to empty the explo-safe post box by the front door.

'Impressive security, you have. I suppose it's understandable, though,' Desai said, looking around. He hesitated, then began awkwardly, 'Sir, I wanted to say how sorry—'

'What did you want to speak with me about, Hari?' Byron

interrupted, but more gently than he might otherwise have done.

'I'm... concerned, sir, about the way this investigation is being run.'

'Be more specific. Which investigation? And what exactly are your concerns?'

Desai took a deep breath, straightened unconsciously, as if about to step over a physical line.

'DI Goodwin still seems to be set on Tristram Shelseley for the Shannon Clifford case. I mean, I know the old guy confessed, but...'

'But you're not convinced.'

Desai shook his head, his expression glum. 'Well, after what you said about the timing of the blow. And then there's the two women meeting... I know it *could* just be a coincidence, but – come on, *what* a coincidence. I mean, what are the chances that one victim dies in the arms of the next?'

'Coincidences *do* happen – we both know that,' Byron said evenly, dropping the unopened mail onto the kitchen countertop. 'But it's possible they knew each other – even that they had friends in common. If Shannon's dying words named her killer, and it was someone Tess knew as well, maybe that was what made her run. As to why she also ended up at Kinfolk not long afterwards... we just don't know.'

'So, maybe the connection is the charity...?'

'Or something to do with the homeless – Shannon spent time on the streets herself, hadn't she? And, at the time she died, she was unofficially fostering a teenage girl called Kensy, who was supposed to go back into the system, but is also now missing.'

Desai stared. 'That's not in the notes. Where did you hear that?'

'We're still off the record, I assume?'

Desai paused only momentarily before he nodded. 'Of course, sir. In fact, I was never here.'

'No, you weren't,' Byron agreed. 'The information came from Blake – the young woman Kinfolk seemed very keen to imply had a hand in Tess Parkin's demise.'

'But you know differently?'

'I do,' Byron said, hoping he was as certain as he sounded. 'The only reason Blake is on the streets at all is because she's looking for Kensy. I think it's fairly safe to discount her having beaten another woman to death in a fit of pique.'

Desai grimaced. 'Every time I find out something new about this case, it makes it more complicated, not less.'

'Some of them are like that,' Byron allowed. He stepped into the kitchen area, flicked on the under-cabinet lighting. 'Can I offer you tea? Coffee? Something stronger?'

'I'm still on duty, sir, technically speaking, but I could murder a cup of tea, if you're brewing up?'

He perched on one of the stools at the breakfast bar while Byron made tea – decaf for Desai, jasmine for himself. While the tea was steeping, he spread out the envelopes that had arrived that day. Most were routine, but one caught his eye, not least because it appeared to have been hand-delivered.

He stilled.

'I've been back over the original PM reports on both women, looking for any other connections or similarities,' Desai was saying, oblivious. 'I'm struggling to find any, to be honest. The MO is so different – minimum to maximum force. Total opposites. I read your forensic pathologist's second opinion, too. And...'. His voice faded as Byron's sudden distraction became apparent. 'What is it, sir?'

'From Doctor Onatade. When I saw her earlier today, she mentioned getting additional tests done, but I wasn't expecting anything back so quickly.'

No doubt he would pay for that privilege.

Byron slit open the envelope. The contents comprised printed-out results, and a handwritten summary sheet. Byron's eyes flicked over the summary. As usual, Dr Onatade wasted no words coming to the point.

'There was no alcohol in Shannon Clifford's system, but her clothing was doused in it,' he murmured, almost to himself.

'Which means... what, exactly?' Desai asked. 'That someone tried to make her seem drunk when she died?'

'Perhaps that was what Paarth was up to, with her in the van at Canning Town,' Byron mused.

'He could have been on his way to dump her somewhere well away from Kinfolk, where her death might be put down to alcohol poisoning and not questioned.'

'Quite possibly. Doctor Onatade also had clothing samples from both Shannon and Tess fast-tracked via a forensic textile expert, although where she managed to find one, I've no idea – there aren't many left,' Byron said.

He realised, even as he spoke, that the good doctor had clearly sent off the samples they'd talked about well before requesting his authorisation to do so.

What's that old saying about it being better to ask for forgiveness than permission?

'What does that tell us?'

'Here. See for yourself.'

Desai leafed through the printouts. It took him only a few moments to recognise what he was looking at.

'Grease, animal fat, olive oil, vegetable starch...' Desai listed, half to himself. 'Oh, and rodent droppings – nice.' He pulled a face. 'So they were both working in a kitchen. But not a very hygienic one.'

'Look at the quantities,' Byron said. 'Not simply a dirty kitchen, but a dirty *commercial* kitchen.'

'So, they were working in poor quality restaurant or take-away kitchens. That's a link between the two women we can work on.' His mouth twisted as he added in a mutter, 'Whatever my boss has to say about it.'

'Look again,' Byron said as he poured their tea. 'The trace evidence isn't just similar, it's identical. These two women may well have been working at the same place.'

'I thought Shannon was supposed to be an outreach volunteer for Kinfolk, not kitchen staff?'

'Indeed,' Byron said. 'Perhaps that's a discrepancy you might like to ask Diarmuid Mackie to explain?'

FIFTY-TWO

ARNOLD ROAD, BOW

When Blake was taken back to the rooming house at the end of the night, River searched her. She wasn't nasty about it, but she was thorough.

Blake had pushed the small tracking disc Lex had given her into her sock, reasoning that would be the best place of conceal-ment. And although River asked for her shoes – and checked inside – Blake was able to slide the tracker under the arch of her foot while she was fiddling to remove them.

'I didn't steal anything – honest!' she protested, so wide-eyed that River flushed with shame.

'It's policy. Drugs – you know,' River said, not quite looking Blake in the eye. 'Just in case anybody slipped you anything. I mean, what if you overdosed? The boss would never forgive me.'

Yeah, because everything else you're doing is so easily forgiven.

Blake said nothing, just stripped out of the borrowed trousers and shirt. When she reached for the catch on her bra, though, River stopped her going any further. Blake suspected that her apparent willingness to strip all the way was enough to convince the other woman of her innocence.

That and the fact that River's mobile rang. Although she didn't accept the call, it was enough to distract her. Blake, pulling on her old sweatpants and T-shirt, noted that River carried an iPhone. It was an older model, a bit scratched and with a cracked screen, but she hoped it was connected to the cloud, nevertheless.

Only one way to find out.

She climbed onto her bunk and lay awake in the darkness, waiting.

An hour passed before she heard a heavy diesel engine in the street below. The hiss of air brakes had her scrambling out of bed and pressing against the window.

He'd brought transport for all of them, all right – in the form of a fifty-two-seater luxury coach.

'Oh, Lex,' she murmured. 'You absolute star...'

FIFTY-THREE

LOCATION UNKNOWN

Kensy woke from a fitful doze to the sound of a distant rumble. It was dark, but the moon was fat, shining through the plastic panels in the roof of the larger shed, and slinking through the cracks in her little cell.

Kensy lay sweating and shivering. It hurt to shiver, but she couldn't stop. How was it possible to burn so bad with cold?

She tried to remember what had woken her. Her brain seemed to be working at half speed. At least the rainwater had gone some small way to quenching the thirst that raged in her.

While she'd slept, another few millimetres had collected in the plastic sheet. Her hands trembled as she gathered it, threatening to spill what little there was. She slurped it clumsily, sucking the sheet dry.

When she looked up, the ghost of Shannon was there again, sitting on the top rail of the metal gate. On either side of her were the two huge black and tan pigs. They seemed to glare through the bars with glowing eyes. All three were watching her minutely.

'Nice to see you finally got your act together, eh?' Shannon said, nodding to her makeshift drinking cup.

'It hurts, Sh-Shan,' Kensy mumbled. 'It really, *really* h-hurts.'

Shannon's face softened. 'I know it does, but you gotta hang on in there, queen. I'm so sorry I'm putting you through this.'

Kensy frowned, her thoughts too sluggish to understand. 'You...? What?'

Shannon sighed. 'Well, if I hadn't gone sticking my nose in, none of this would have happened, would it? And you wouldn't be here now.' Almost absently, she reached over and scratched one of the pigs behind an ear. The pig leaned towards her, squeezing its eyes shut in pleasure.

Kensy swallowed back a sudden rush of bile, her throat raw. 'So, why did you?' she demanded, plaintive – almost the cry of a child.

'Because I saw what they were doing and I couldn't leave it, after that, could I, eh?' Her voice grew gentle. 'And how was I to know... what would happen? None of us expect to die, do we?'

Somewhere in the distance, outside, the rumble seemed to come again, then died away.

Shannon's ghost twisted round. Even the two pigs swung their mammoth heads as if to follow her stare.

Kensy heard footsteps, echoing on the concrete. She tried to find enough moisture in her mouth, enough air in her lungs, to call for help. It emerged as little more than a rasp, like a moan.

Then the bolts on the outside of the wooden door shot back and the door was dragged open, catching on the concrete along the bottom edge with a judder.

Kensy's heart leapt into her throat and bounced there, fearful.

Is this rescue, or the end of it?

Her eyes flew to the gate, but Shannon had gone, leaving only the two pigs behind. The larger of the two bashed against the railing, as if desperate to be through and at her.

A figure loomed in the open doorway. The outline of a man.

Familiarity brought with it dread. She lay frozen as he stalked forwards until he was only inches away from her. He stood, staring down.

'So, still not dead yet...' he said, more to himself than her. 'But not much longer, now, I think.'

As if in agreement, both pigs battered against the railing again.

'It better not be,' the man muttered. 'They're getting hungry.'

FIFTY-FOUR

INDUSTRIAL ESTATE OFF A40 WESTWAY, NORTH ACTON

Through a series of shell corporations, Lex Vaganov owned a warehouse on a small industrial estate not far from Wormwood Scrubs. He claimed it was for storing artwork or furniture, and so it was more weathertight and secure than the run-down exterior suggested.

Somehow – and Blake had long since given up asking him such questions – he had obtained a job lot of camp beds in the time between the Kinfolk fundraiser and the pre-dawn rescue mission. These were now laid out, with bedding and pillows, dotted around the warehouse. Lex had built the existing contents into walls and dividers to offer some privacy to his unexpected guests. The beds were clustered in groups of two or three. He had managed to source an assortment of old but clean clothing, too, piled onto a couple of trestle tables. He had even brought in a catering company, who set up near the roller shutter door. They had a hot meal well under way by the time the bus he'd also borrowed – or stolen, she wouldn't put it past him – pulled up outside.

Blake counted thirty people, including herself. They stumbled from the bus into the warehouse, blinking against the lights. Thirty people who had been crammed into a standard three-bedroom semi in Bow. She wondered how many other such properties Kinfolk owned or rented around the city. Something Lex was, no doubt, working to discover.

Since arriving at the warehouse, she'd noted the faces. They were mainly the younger people who'd come into Kinfolk's dubious care. The ones who'd taken to the streets in desperation, but weren't yet so ravaged by trauma, or drink, or drugs – or a combination of all three – that they couldn't be profitably put to work in the dark kitchens.

The younger ones were probably also easier to control.

She had yet to find either of the two chefs she'd encountered. She assumed, therefore, that Kinfolk actually had to pay them. Even with the current state of the hospitality industry, skilled chefs were always in demand.

Unless, of course, they had some kind of flag on their record. *For crimes of violence, maybe?*

She sat with the young man she'd met briefly at the dark kitchen just off Whitechapel Road. Ibrahim's family had come to the UK from Algeria when he was a child, he told her. Family problems after his mother died, and friction with his father about his further education, had ended with him moving out.

A housing association rental soon became sofa surfing, then a hostel.

From there, it was only a short step to living on the streets.

'At first, I was happy enough to work in their kitchens,' he said. 'OK, I know they're sort of off-the-books, like, but I still thought I'd get some training, maybe even get the right qualifications, you know? But all they wanted was a dogsbody who would work for scraps.'

'Why didn't you just leave?' Blake asked him.

He dipped his nose into his mug of tea, but his raised

eyebrows spoke volumes. 'Because I heard the rumours,' he said at last, almost in a whisper.

'Rumours?'

He nodded, perched on the side of a camp bed with shoulders hunched and both hands clasped around his mug. 'They had me working with a kid called Spider. He reckoned he'd got a bad arm – said some cop had belted him when they raided the squat he was in, you know?'

'Yeah,' Blake murmured faintly, 'actually, I do know.'

'Well, he was struggling to get the work done, and I guess Paarth thought he was putting it on – trying to get out of doing much.'

'He wasn't,' Blake said. 'I was there when we were raided. If it's the guy I'm thinking of, I'm amazed they didn't break any bones.'

'Really? Well, Paarth was giving him a hard time, asking what use he was if he couldn't – or wouldn't – work? Spider got a bit arsey with him. First off, he said he'd go to the cops.'

'How did Paarth take that?'

'He laughed and told him to go ahead, like he knew they weren't going to do nothing. But then Spider said he'd go to the newspapers, and suddenly Paarth weren't laughing no more. Paarth said he'd take Spider to the boss, and that was the last anybody saw of him.'

'The boss – you mean Mr Mackie?'

'Dunno.' He shrugged. 'Think so.'

'Spider could simply have left – gone back on the streets.'

'I asked around – anybody new coming in, you know? Nobody'd seen him. And he's not the first who's disappeared after a run-in with that lot, so I've heard.' He gave a dark laugh. 'I didn't fancy the idea of getting chopped up for pie filling or something, eh?'

'You don't remember seeing a girl working in any of the

kitchens, do you? A young black kid? I've been searching for her.'

'Oh.' Ibrahim's face sobered at once and he winced. 'You don't mean Kensy, do you?'

Blake's stomach dropped, leaving a sickly hollowness behind. With reluctance, she nodded. 'You'd better tell me what happened.'

FIFTY-FIVE

INDUSTRIAL ESTATE OFF A40 WESTWAY, NORTH ACTON

Byron stepped through the personnel door into the warehouse. He was greeted by the unexpected sight of a cross between a refugee camp and a field hospital. It made him pause. He could not help but note the reaction to his arrival, also. Apprehension shimmied through those clustered inside the building. Nervous glances flicked his way before eyes were quickly averted, backs turned.

He supposed, in many ways, he couldn't blame them.

Lex Vaganov's summons had been brief and cryptic enough to be irritating. Not only that, it had come at two in the morning. At that hour, the ten-mile drive from Primrose Hill to North Acton had taken Byron less than twenty-five minutes. He had not made his entrance in the best of tempers, even so. He did his best to maintain a neutral expression, but recognised that a haze of subdued anger probably hovered around his head like a swarm of bees.

Besides, there were times when he would be the first to admit that he still had the look of a copper about him. Especially to those who were all too familiar with coppers.

As if sensing the sudden disquiet, Vaganov appeared from a

side office, beckoning him over. Byron took a couple of strides, then paused again, thrusting his gloved hands into the pockets of his overcoat. People watched in silence.

'Don't worry,' he said, loud enough to be heard. 'You've nothing to fear from me.' Then he walked straight past Vaganov, into his office. By the time the man followed, closing the door, Byron had unbuttoned his coat and settled himself into a chair facing the desk.

'Do you intend to add people trafficking to the list of services offered by Dalchetta & Child?' Byron asked mildly.

'I don't know whether to be more insulted that you think I would stoop so low,' Vaganov said, 'or that you think those poor devils out there are the calibre of people I would traffic.'

Byron shrugged, straightened his shirt cuff. 'Supply and demand.'

Vaganov showed his teeth briefly as he sat down and leaned back in his chair as if to contemplate the ceiling. 'Do you think that one day, perhaps, we will greet each other with polite enquiries about our health?'

The corner of Byron's mouth lifted. 'One day,' he agreed. 'Perhaps.'

'To business, then?'

'First, where's Blake?'

'She *was* here.' It was Vaganov's turn to shrug. 'And now she is not.'

Byron was aware that something twitched in the side of his jaw. But, looking at the set of Vaganov's shoulders, the tension in his hands, Byron determined that the other man was no happier about this state of affairs.

'OK, let's hear it.'

He listened without interruption while Vaganov recounted the bare bones of the rescue mission. In truth, Byron admired both the alacrity in getting these people out, and the care the other man appeared to have taken of them since. Freedom alone meant nothing without shelter, food, clothing, and safety.

'It seems that people who get on the wrong side of Kinfolk have a habit of disappearing without trace,' Vaganov said. 'Blake talked to a couple of people out there who had heard such rumours. Perhaps that is what happened to your dead woman?'

'Which one?'

'Either – or both.'

'Well, they hardly disappeared without trace, did they? We fished one of them out of the Thames.'

'A mistake with the tides,' Vaganov dismissed. 'Easily done.'

'And the other was found wandering around a retail park in Canning Town.'

'Unfortunately, not all killers are equally proficient, I've found.'

Byron almost snorted at that, but stopped himself in time. It sounded rather as though Vaganov had personal experience. He contented himself with a neutral, 'Oh?'

'After all, if you are transporting what you assume is a body, you would hardly bother to secure it, would you? Hypothetically speaking, of course.'

'We're talking about Shannon Clifford now, I assume.'

Vaganov gave a fractional incline of his head. 'From what we have been able to discover, she was asking too many questions about a certain charity. And it would seem there have been others since, who became surplus to requirements. A boy who was arrested during the raid at Mile End Road – his name was Spider. Blake was told he made waves about being made to work for a pittance, and has now "disappeared" also. As has the girl Blake herself was in search of – Shannon's unofficial foster child, Kensy.'

'What kind of waves was she making?'

Vaganov shook his head, and didn't try to hide the sorrow in his eyes. 'These dark kitchens, where they make people work, they are not regulated, nor inspected for any kind of safety. Apparently, there was an accident – and a fire. Kensy was... badly hurt.'

'When was this?'

'The night before the body of Tess was found. She was working in the same place, so Blake was told. Perhaps she objected to... what happened.'

Byron calculated the timescale. 'That's two days ago. The chances of survival, without treatment...'

Vaganov nodded. He waved a hand towards his laptop, sitting open at one side of the desktop. 'I have been searching the hospitals and private clinics, looking for any sign that she was admitted, but so far, I have found nothing. The outcome does not look... promising.'

'But Blake doesn't think so,' Byron guessed. He spoke with a conviction that had no need to make it a question. 'There's no way she would have given up on the girl.'

'No, she has not,' Vaganov agreed. 'Why do you think she has gone back out there, fully intending to make herself into the kind of target that Kinfolk will not be able to ignore?'

Byron swore softly, under his breath.

'Yes,' Vaganov said, his voice tired. 'For once, you and I are in perfect agreement.'

FIFTY-SIX

TRAFALGAR SQUARE, WESTMINSTER

Blake huddled on a stone bench in Trafalgar Square. One in the north-eastern corner this time, near to the mounted statue of King George IV.

It had stopped raining, and weak morning sunshine glittered off the spray from the nearest fountain. Blake, clutching her thin sweatshirt around her body, gazed up at the life-size bronze sculpture, if only to take her mind off the cold.

There was some kind of urban myth, she recalled, that said equestrian statues revealed the fate of the rider by the number of hoofs the horse had off the ground. One whose mount had two feet lifted was supposed to have died in battle. King George IV's steed, she noted, had all four feet firmly planted. She dredged some history lesson – or possibly TV documentary – and recalled that his majesty had died in his bed, decrepit and obese.

So, maybe the poor horse's legs should be shown buckling a little, too...?

At the periphery of her vision, she saw the figure making a beeline for her across glistening pavestones. He wore his usual leather jacket, collar up against the wind knifing through the open square.

As she tracked his movements from the corner of her eye, she kept her head tilted up as though completely transfixed by the statue, albeit in a vacant kind of way. It wasn't until the man stopped in front of her that she allowed herself to look at him directly, blinking in surprise.

'*Oh,*' she said. 'What are you doing here?'

Paarth regarded her, unsmiling.

'Looking for you.'

'Me? Why? And... how did you find me?'

Paarth didn't respond to that, just stepped sideways and jerked his head. 'Let's go.'

'Why?' Blake asked again, blankly. 'Go where?'

Paarth let out his breath and looked straight at her. Not just at the surface image she was projecting, she noted, but through and deep.

He leaned in. 'Cut the crap. I know you're not half as dumb as you make out,' he said softly. 'So, be a good girl and let's the two of us just walk out of here, nice and friendly, hm?'

'Or...?'

'Or somebody you care about might suffer for it.'

Blake, already cold, turned icy. She didn't have to feign the shiver that went through her at the intent in his voice. She got stiffly to her feet. He moved alongside her, close enough to grab her arm if she thought about running.

'How...?'

She didn't need to say more than that. Paarth spoke without making eye contact.

'We have eyes and ears all over this city,' he said.

Blake shrugged. 'But... I still don't know why you'd go to the trouble.'

He stopped then, abruptly, and turned in towards her, those dark eyes skimming her face as if stripping away her skin.

'Because you are – trouble, that is,' he said tightly. 'We know it was you, Blake. The rooming house. Caz.'

'I—'

'Save your breath. The old man might be loyal to Caz, but that girl's loyalties lie with the highest bidder, and she couldn't *wait* to tell us all about you.'

FIFTY-SEVEN
LIMEHOUSE POLICE STATION

Jemma Weeks was walking past the front desk at Limehouse at the start of her shift, when a sudden thought occurred to her. She stopped and turned back.

''Scuse me, Sarge, but you know all there is to know about everything round here, don't you?'

The custody sergeant regarded her with a baleful eye. 'I hope you're not implying that I'm a repository for idle gossip, Constable?'

'Oh, no, not at all. I was thinking more like... the fount of all knowledge.'

He grunted. It was hard to tell from his expression if that displeased him any less.

'What is it you want to know?'

'Well, you know I've been working with Greg McCoubrey quite a bit lately...?'

He straightened up behind the desk, as if to distance himself. 'What about him?'

Weeks glanced over her shoulder, but reception was empty for once. 'I'd heard his dad was very ill, but I'm not sure what's

wrong with him, and I don't like to ask. Can you clue me in?'
She looked at him appealingly. 'Just so I don't put my foot in it.'

The big sergeant seemed to relax. 'Ah, you're behind the
times. PC McCoubrey's father passed away early last year, but
in truth he was gone long before then. Some form of dementia, I
believe. A long slow decline, poor man.'

The relieved smile she offered was entirely genuine.

'Ah, right. That explains a lot. Thanks.'

FIFTY-EIGHT

INDUSTRIAL ESTATE OFF A40 WESTWAY, NORTH ACTON

Byron woke to someone shaking him by the shoulder. His eyes snapped open at once. He sat up, swinging his stockinged feet off the camp bed where he'd been dozing, and pushing aside the blanket. Lex Vaganov was watching him closely, a thoughtful look on his face.

'What time is it?' Byron asked automatically, while his brain was still rebooting. 'What's happened?'

'No cause for alarm,' Vaganov said, putting a mug of black coffee down on the floor next to the bed. 'It is nine forty-five, and it would seem that Blake has just been picked up.'

Once he'd realised that Blake had deliberately – wilfully, even – put herself in danger, Byron had refused to leave the warehouse. At least until Vaganov received word that she was safe. By the time dawn came, he'd reasoned there was no point in being too exhausted to react, as and when the need arose. A camp bed had been squeezed into Vaganov's office – as much not to make the homeless uneasy as for his privacy.

Now, Byron rubbed his hands over his face. He could hear the rasp of stubble against his palms, but mostly could not feel it. The surgeons had told him the scar tissue would become more pliable, over time. Some of the nerve pathways might even grow back, but at a glacial pace. For now, it was both oversensitive and numb at the same time.

Aware of Vaganov's scrutiny, he let his hands drop, reached for the coffee instead with a nod.

Vaganov himself appeared to have changed his shirt, at least, and was clean-shaven. Byron resisted the urge to straighten the tie he'd loosened in the early hours, or to rebutton his collar.

'You do not sleep peacefully, my friend,' Vaganov said then.

Byron glanced at him sharply, but there was no hint of triumph or mockery in the other man's gaze.

'Not all of us have that privilege. How do you know Blake's on the move?'

Vaganov eyed him for a moment longer, then twisted the laptop on his desk so the screen was visible. 'She said she was not going to take public transport, but she is now going too fast to be still on foot.'

Byron felt his eyebrows climb. 'You've put a tracker on her?'

'I may be many things, Mr Byron, but foolhardy is not one of them. No, Blake put a tracker on herself.'

'So where is she?'

'At present, in traffic, heading for the Embankment.'

'What's the range on the tracker?' Byron slipped his feet back into his shoes, then stood. 'And how long will the battery last?'

'Calm yourself. It's a passive tracking disc. Not ideal, but we had to... improvise. As long as she is near a Bluetooth-enabled device, the disc will upload its GPS location to the cloud, from where I can access it.'

'And you can do this from anywhere?'

'Indeed.'

'Then I would strongly suggest that we waste no more time.'

Vaganov opened his mouth to protest, but Byron forestalled him.

'We'll take my car, shall we?'

FIFTY-NINE

Blake sat in darkness in the back of the Kinfolk van. She had her eyes closed, trying to feel their direction of travel by the way the van rolled.

She was propped against the front bulkhead. This made it more difficult, as she was facing backwards, and the turns were reversed. Sitting right at the back of the load bay, against the rear doors, might have made things easier.

But then she would not have been able to overhear snatches of whatever conversation Paarth was having on his mobile phone.

Or his side of them, anyway.

The first of these had been perfunctory – little more than him reporting in that he'd 'got her' and was 'en route'. She would have preferred him to have been more specific about their destination, but since she had no way to communicate that information, it was academic. She might also have preferred him to be more specific about what they intended to do with her once they arrived. But that was fairly academic, too.

Legally, he should have been using a hands-free kit while he was driving, but that seemed the least of the laws he was prepared to break. She hoped he didn't get pulled over for it, though, because then she would have no excuse for not kicking up a stink.

Which would not fit in with her plans at all.

Not when she had gone to all this trouble to be picked up in the first place. And – she hoped – taken to wherever they took the people who proved an inconvenience to them.

People like Shannon.

And Kensy.

Traffic was heavy, if the van's stop-start motion was anything to go by, so it was difficult to judge how far they went. She'd once been told that the average speed of a vehicle in London was somewhere between seven and eight miles an hour. It was almost quicker to walk.

But maybe twenty minutes into the journey, she heard Paarth's phone ring, and pressed her ear to the bulkhead.

'They've *what*? When?'

Whatever news he'd just been given had shocked him, if the fact he was almost shouting was any guide. Blake hoped he continued to do so.

'What do you want me to do...? *Still*...? Yes, but it is not *you* who is taking the risk... And what about the girl?'

Blake held her breath, but all that did was make the blood pound in her ears.

'Both of them?' Paarth demanded then, disbelief and anger stark in his voice. 'But—'

Whoever was at the other end of the call clearly cut his protests short, but did not silence him for long.

'This is not *my* mess... If you're so determined to clean house, then perhaps you should go out there and see to it your-self.' He gave a harsh bark of laughter that contained little mirth. 'Yes, I do... Now get off the phone. They could be tracking us right now.'

He swore. Blake could not make out the words, but didn't

need to in order to understand their meaning, or the frustration behind them.

Maybe even a trace of fear.

It was that last emotion that made her scalp prickle. Because she knew, when people were frightened, when they felt backed into a corner, that's when things tended to get really nasty.

SIXTY

THE WESTWAY

It was a long time since Byron had last taken a pursuit driving course, but he had not forgotten the skills. As he bullied through traffic on the Westway, heading into the city, some small part of him was even a little gratified to see Lex Vaganov clutch at his armrest.

Byron would be the first to admit, however, that having the blue strobes behind the front grille of the Mercedes, and the siren under the bonnet, did make other drivers scramble to get out of his way.

Even so, it was taking too long to get on Blake's trail, and he couldn't help but wish she and Vaganov had coordinated things better.

Or that you'd told me what you had planned, dammit!

He would have tried to talk her out of it, of course. Which was probably why she'd kept him out of the loop.

'How did they know where to find her?' he asked suddenly. 'Kinfolk, I mean. How could you be sure they'd pick her up so quickly?'

Vaganov glanced up from the tracking app on his smartphone.

'Because I reported her to them,' he said, as if it were obvious. 'There's a feature on the homeless app for listing people who are missing and deemed vulnerable. Someone had uploaded her details and description.'

Byron felt his eyebrows climb. He skirted a black cab that had pulled up, seemingly at random, to drop off a fare, narrowly missing the cyclist who swerved around it.

'This is the same app that's accessible to some mystery third party?'

'Nice to know you were paying attention.'

'For heaven's sake – so you've no idea who's grabbed Blake, or what they might want with her?'

Vaganov eyed him with tolerance. 'As far as we know, there are only two alternatives – Kinfolk, or the police.'

'As far as we know.'

'If it was the cops, they would have headed for Limehouse. That's where the investigation is based, after all.' He held up his phone, the tracker app open. 'They are not headed that way.'

Byron was silent for a minute.

Then he said in a deadly quiet tone: 'If it *is* Kinfolk, how did they know to go after Blake? Surely, as far as they're concerned, she's simply one of many who escaped from that house in Bow.'

Vaganov said nothing.

'*Isn't* she?' Byron insisted. 'Or do they know different...?'

Vaganov sighed. 'She needed to... set things in motion,' he admitted, 'so I persuaded Caz to contact Kinfolk and... sell her out.'

'Caz...?' Byron repeated.

'Caz is the reason Tristram Shelseley admitted to killing Shannon Clifford, even though he was not remotely responsible. Until Blake got her out, Kinfolk were holding her to ensure his... cooperation.'

'Oh, for—! When were either of you planning to tell me any of this?'

'I am telling you now.'

'Yes – too late!'

Vaganov twisted in his seat, fixed Byron with a stony stare. 'Too late for what?'

Byron blew out an annoyed huff of breath. 'As soon as you called me – when I was on the way over to the warehouse – I called this in. By now, Diarmuid Mackie may well be under arrest.'

Vaganov's brows came down. 'If he decides to rid himself of loose ends...'

'Yes, I'm aware of that – *now*.'

Vaganov swore abruptly, eyes fixed on the screen of his smartphone.

'What is it?' Byron demanded.

'The signal – it has stopped transmitting.'

'What does that mean? I thought you said this tracking disc didn't transmit anything anyway.'

'It doesn't,' Vaganov said bleakly. 'But it means the nearest phone has been switched off.'

'And that—?'

'*That*, my friend, means that we do not know where they are taking Blake, and we now have no way of following her.'

The further into the journey, the smoother their progress, Blake realised. They must be driving out of London. She'd lost any sense of direction, but reason told her they were heading east. It was the quickest way out of the city.

And, besides, Shannon had been arrested at a retail park in Canning Town, where – according to Byron – a Kinfolk van had been seen. If they had a dump site or some other means of body disposal out east, that would make sense.

I should have asked Lex to dig into other property owned by Kinfolk.

She hoped he might have done so anyway, even without her prompting. She also hoped he was still able to follow the tracking disc tucked into her sock. Paarth hadn't made or received any more phone calls after that last one. She wasn't sure if the nearest mobile had to be in use for the tracker to access the cloud, as Lex had mentioned.

Next time I do this, I want the full James Bond escape kit in the sole of my shoe!

She clung to the thought that there would be a next time.

Although no daylight found its way inside the van, she

recalled from her first encounter with Kinfolk that there had been some kind of interior lighting. She got to her feet, bracing against the roof to steady herself, and groped blindly until she discovered a central dome light. After a moment's fumbling, she clicked it on.

The LED was surprisingly effective. But it illuminated a space that had been stripped of its usual storage boxes containing essentials the charity usually distributed on the streets. Only the empty framework remained. Blake surveyed it, disappointed.

The van took a sharp left-hand corner and she stumbled, almost falling. Something slid along the top of the frame at one side and clattered onto the floor near the rear doors.

Blake followed the noise, hopeful they'd overlooked something that might be useful to her.

What she found was a plastic clipboard with a checklist of the usual contents of the van. The clipboard itself looked too flimsy to be used as a weapon, but it did have a steel-case ballpoint pen stuck into the clip at the top. As she flipped through the pages, she discovered a couple of large paperclips, too.

Not exactly an exploding watch, or a portable jet pack, but better than nothing.

She tucked the pen inside her waistband, and the paperclips into the cups of her bra, where she hoped they might be mistaken for part of the underwiring – if Paarth checked that closely.

Blake had never got that kind of over-handsy vibe from him, though. If anything, he seemed to prefer not to have any contact with the women or girls. Maybe he cultivated that cold, rather aloof air to add to his general menace.

But Diarmuid Mackie, on the other hand, made her far more wary. She gave a shudder. She could definitely see him taking more interest in her underwear than was good for anyone.

Abruptly, the van swung to the right and stopped. Blake had grown used to the sudden turns, jerky acceleration and braking – that was the aggressive way people drove in London. But the difference this time was the door slammed as Paarth got out, leaving the engine running. She heard the rattle of a chain and then a gate being dragged open across rough ground.

So where are we? Building site? Landfill…?

Neither option filled her with glee. She quickly turned off the dome light and settled into a corner, although she stayed on her feet. They bumped along what felt like a rutted track before finally coming to a halt. The engine note died away.

The first thing Blake heard then was the long, mournful bray of a donkey.

Despite herself, she grinned in surprise.

'Well, I wasn't expecting *that*.'

A moment later, the van's side door opened and slid back. She noted the way Paarth jerked it across and stepped back quickly, as if expecting her to come out fighting. When she didn't move immediately, he glowered at her.

'Out.'

Blake did as ordered without protest, unable to tell if that pleased or disappointed him. She took her time about it, though, as if she was stiff from the confinement. It gave her the chance to do a fast skim of her surroundings.

They were at what might have been a riding stables. Wooden buildings with a five-barred gate into a central yard. A slightly run-down look and a definite smell of manure. She glanced up. There were no tall buildings anywhere to be seen. Seagulls circled, high overhead.

'Where are we?'

Paarth made no reply, just gripped her upper arm and marched her towards the gate. They passed through into a yard. Not entirely a stables, Blake saw. More like… a petting zoo?

At the far end of the yard, through a gap between the buildings, she saw a large steel-framed barn and other, older outbuildings in red-brick, past which was the corner of a paddock with goats in it.

No, not a petting zoo. An urban farm.

Paarth unlocked a stout door and led her into an office, then along the corridor beyond, not giving her a chance to look about her. He hustled her to a door near the end and pushed it open.

Inside was a storeroom, lined with empty racking. Dim light filtered down from a couple of narrow windows, right at the top of one wall. Too narrow to squeeze through, even if they didn't have security bars fitted.

Paarth shoved her inside, so roughly that she stumbled and almost fell.

'Stay there and don't kick up a fuss.'

And, to make sure she complied, he reached round the door to the inside handle, and wrenched. It snapped off in his fist.

'What are you going to do with me?'

He frowned. 'That's up to the boss. Just... don't make things any worse for yourself than they already are, all right?'

If Blake hadn't known better, she might have thought that was a plea.

She listened to his footsteps fading and turned a slow circle. A slither of movement caught her eye, down near a corner of the racking. Blake's first thought was rats. It would not have been her first encounter.

But, as her eyes adjusted, she realised it was a woman, crouched as if expecting a blow.

She took a step forwards. The woman raised her head with a wide-eyed gasp.

Blake blinked in surprise.

'Adhiti? What on earth are *you* doing here?'

SIXTY-TWO

LIMEHOUSE POLICE STATION

There was no doubt that Diarmuid Mackie was shaken. Byron, watching him on the monitor, saw beyond the urbane exterior to the frightened man beneath.

Mackie sat at the scarred table in the interview suite at Limehouse Police Station, legs negligently crossed as if on his old chat show sofa rather than about to undergo interrogation. Alongside him, Mackie's high-priced brief was making all the expected objections and veiled threats with the air of a grandee actor hamming his way through a Shakespearean soliloquy. It was a toss-up which of the two men was wearing the more expensive suit.

On the other side of the table, unimpressed, sat Commander Shamshi Daud. Byron would have preferred to be conducting the interview, or at least occupying the second chair, although he hadn't been relegated to that role after making detective inspector. Instead, he had to settle for a link to the tablet in front of Daud, and a seat in the observation room. Once, he'd had the authority to question just about anyone. He wondered when he would learn to accept that loss.

By rights, Daud was too senior to be conducting interviews,

but she had pulled rank and seemed to relish the opportunity. Byron had seen the expressions that flitted across Mackie's face when Daud walked in. Disbelief followed by affront and barely concealed condescension, taking her at less than face value. Byron had no doubts Daud noted his reaction, too, although she gave no sign. She would make him pay for that mistake when she was ready.

If he was honest, Byron was glad of the distraction. The knowledge that they'd lost Blake made his chest tighten and his hands itch. Whoever picked her up in Trafalgar Square had then shut down their phone, severing the tracker's link with the cloud. A phone call from Daud to tell him that Mackie had been brought in for questioning had him heading for Limehouse instead.

'Call me when you find her,' he'd instructed Vaganov, handing over his car keys at the kerb outside.

Vaganov had the sense – for once – not to test him with smart comebacks. He'd simply nodded, and driven away.

Mackie's legal representation – one of the named partners of a firm whose reputation for criminal defence had many a senior investigating officer groaning – arrived with a speed which would, no doubt, be reflected in the size of the bill. On the monitor, Byron could see the man was finally running out of bluster. Even Mackie had heard enough. He rode over his brief's voice with the ease of a man who came up on the club circuit, dealing with hecklers by simply not letting them get a word in.

'At what point in the proceedings would *somebody* have the courtesy to tell me why we're all here?'

He smiled into the silence that followed, his trademark grin.

It hit Daud's stony expression and bounced off. 'We'll get to that, Mr Mackie... in due course,' she said, ominous.

Before he could argue – if he'd been about to – the door to the interview room opened and Hari Desai stepped through, carrying a bulging folder. Byron would not have put it past Daud to have made him pad it out with any old junk, just to cause alarm.

Daud went through the formalities, then sat back in her chair and regarded the man opposite with a level gaze.

'Mr Mackie, it has come to our attention that a group of people who were under the supposed care of your charity, Kinfolk, were being held, against their will, in a property in Bow. What can you tell us about that?'

'Held against their will, you say? Which people are those, then? And what property, exactly?'

'The group are all members of the homeless community. They were locked into a house on Arnold Road.'

The brief began to protest immediately. But as Daud spoke, Desai produced printed-out images. He fanned them out on the table in front of Mackie like a croupier dealing blackjack.

The cameras inside the interview room were angled to catch all the occupants. Byron couldn't see much detail of the pictures, but he could guess their content. Lex Vaganov had been careful to record the locks and bolts on the outside of the rooms, and the cramped, overcrowded conditions. From experience, Byron knew that in the stark light of photo flash, they would look even seedier.

He watched Mackie's reaction. The man had a better grip on himself now. His face showed just the right amount of puzzlement and disbelief.

'Shocking,' he murmured after a moment. 'But I'm not sure what any of this has to do with Kinfolk.'

Desai produced another sheet from the file, without being asked. Byron heard the satisfaction in Daud's voice when she next spoke. She always had liked working with people who could anticipate.

'For the record, DS Desai has just shown Mr Mackie a copy

of the title document for the property in question. It is registered in the name of the Kinfolk Charitable Foundation.'

Mackie leaned forwards as he scanned the sheet, frowning.
'I'm not personally aware of this place, but it's possible that we
do own it,' he allowed. 'I have a feller who deals with all that
kind of thing—'

'What "kind of thing" would that be, exactly, Mr Mackie?'

'With investments – property, in particular,' he said easily.
'I'm sure I don't need to tell you that renting in London is an
expensive business. It makes financial sense for us to buy the
odd building, if it comes along at the right price, and use it to
house the homeless. We gain an appreciating asset, and they
gain a roof over their heads. It's a win-win.'

'If you're also making money out of your tenants, I'm sure
it is.'

'Ah, now, now, we don't charge them a penny in rent. Not a
penny. If they were able to rent somewhere themselves, do you
think they'd be on the streets? Of course not. But nobody will
give them a chance, so they come to us, and we give them somewhere to lay their heads where they're not going to be moved on
in the middle of the night.'

'Commendable,' Daud said. Her tone suggested she thought
it anything but. 'If they're so fortunate to have a bed for the
night, why did you feel the need to lock them in... like a prison?'

'Well now, some of these poor unfortunates have problems
– with mental health, or with addiction – and who can blame
them for that, with everything they've been through? But to
keep everyone safe, we have to ensure nobody goes walkabout,
and intrudes on the privacy and safety of anyone else.'

'So, it's for their own good?'

He spread his hands. 'There you have it. Exactly.'

'Mr Mackie, quite apart from the safety implications in the
event of a fire—'

'Ah, but there's a caretaker on site twenty-four hours a day.'

'Caretaker, or warden?' Byron murmured aloud.

'Quite apart from that,' Daud continued, 'I am given to understand that – while you may claim these people are not charged rent – they are being forced to work sixty or more hours a week for their bed and board.'

'We are trying to reintegrate the poor souls into society. Not everyone on the streets is willing or able to work, but some are. They've slipped through the cracks, as it were, fallen on hard times, or had a run of bad luck. They want a helping hand to get back on their feet, not charity.'

'And your "charity" provides that helping hand?'

Daud's voice held scepticism, but Mackie leaned forwards in his chair, for all the world like a man sincere in his convictions.

'We do, and proud of it we are, too. Anyone who works, they get paid. And we help them navigate the bureaucracy of the benefits system, so they get what's due to them.'

'Funny, because nobody who was in that house had any money on them, nor do any of them appear to have a bank account.' She paused, watching him frown. 'Would you care to shed any light on what happens to these benefits, and wages?'

'I wouldn't expect someone like you to understand—'

'Someone like me?'

The brief made to intervene, but Mackie held up a hand to stay him.

'Yes, someone like you. Someone with a decent job, a respected position, a house, a car,' Mackie said. 'The only way we could give our service users immediate access to their money would be in cash. Do you know how long they'd be keeping hold of it, if they were on the street?'

'Not all of them are addicts, Mr Mackie.'

He gave a dismissive flick of his wrist. 'I'm not talking about them pouring it down their throats, or up their noses, or injecting it into their veins. I'm talking about them having the living bejesus kicked out of them for their last few coins. The only reason we hold their money is that it would be taken from them on the first night if we didn't, and they'd be lucky not to get a blade between the ribs for their trouble.'

'So, once again, it's for their own good?'

Mackie gave a snort and slumped back in his chair. 'Oh, and it's a terrible dark view you have of humanity.'

The brief cleared his throat, and inquired in a silky voice how many of the homeless had made a formal complaint.

'None of them... *yet*.'

'In that case, as my client is not under arrest, we will be leaving now. And if I might offer some friendly advice, Commander Daud, please have your facts in order before issuing any further... *invitations* of this nature, or I will recommend Mr Mackie brings a suit for police harassment.'

Daud's face showed no expression. She let both men stand before she said, 'Just one last thing before you go, Mr Mackie.'

Mackie paused.

'Well, strictly speaking, it's actually more than one... Several young women who recently came into the care of Kinfolk have... disappeared,' she went on. 'One of them was later found, beaten to death. Two others are still missing. I'm sure a man as... philanthropically inclined as you are, sir, should be only too eager to offer us every assistance in establishing the whereabouts of these vulnerable women.' Daud delivered this veiled threat in a tone bordering on bland.

Nevertheless, Mackie glanced at his brief and, with obvious reluctance, retook his seat. 'Is this something to do with the young woman you were looking for when you took away half our records?' he asked.

'Tess Parkin, yes. She was last seen alive at Kinfolk.'

Desai silently pulled out a picture from his folder. Byron could see enough to identify it as Tess's driving licence photo.

The shot Desai laid alongside it was from the crime scene, and not nearly so pretty.

On the monitor, Byron saw Mackie still, then lean a fraction closer before he caught himself and stiffened, his face twisting.

But Byron had caught that first, instinctive desire to look closer.

A man admiring his own handiwork, perhaps?

'You can't possibly think anyone connected with my charity would do something like... like *that* to the poor girl...'

'Well, somebody did, Mr Mackie,' Daud pointed out. 'We now have evidence that, shortly before she died, Ms Parkin was working in a commercial kitchen. Where was that?'

'And why do you think I would know?'

Daud gave a tired sigh. 'OK, Mr Mackie. Let's put our cards on the table, shall we? We have statements from witnesses who worked alongside Ms Parkin in a dark kitchen in East London on the night she was killed. A dark kitchen to which she was transported by one of *your* staff, in one of *your* vans. That same night, we have statements that another worker at the same location – an underage girl called Kensy Young – was injured in an accident. An accident that does not appear to have been reported. Ms Young has since disappeared.'

'I—'

'Not only that, but we now have evidence to link that kitchen with another woman, Shannon Clifford, who died after a blow to the head, received some hours before her demise. She was last seen in the vicinity of one of your vans, on a retail park in Canning Town.'

'Circumstantial!' the brief yelped.

Daud silenced him with a glare she could have used to torch open a safe. 'We are also investigating the whereabouts of two other people last seen at your charity or one of its properties. One is a young man, Ryan Nowak, known as Spider, who was picked up by one of your vans outside this very police station.'

'Really, Commander, I must protest—'

'The second is a young woman called Blake Claremont. We've just received CCTV footage of her getting into yet another of your vehicles in Trafalgar Square, after her whereabouts was reported on a homeless app, which, it appears, someone accessed from the IP address of a computer at Kinfolk's premises. Would you care to comment, sir?'

Mackie opened his mouth, floundered for a moment and closed it again. He threw a slightly pleading look at his brief, who raised a warning hand.

'I need a few moments alone with my client,' the man said smoothly.

'Of course.' Daud reeled off the time the interview was suspended and gathered her folders.

Desai left with her and the monitors went blank.

Byron met the two of them in the corridor, far enough from the interview room not to allow eavesdropping on either side.

'I have to hand it to Vaganov,' Daud said. 'I mean, we'll need to get sworn statements from the developers of the homeless app, and the witnesses, if we want any of this to stand up in court, but it's certainly got that smarmy bugger on the back foot.'

SIXTY-THREE

BOROUGH HIGH STREET, SOUTHWARK

Jemma Weeks hovered nervously just inside the main entrance of one of the high street banks, a stone's throw from Borough Underground Station, south of the river. She was only too aware that she was off her patch and out of her depth. Not to mention that she was about to stretch a friendship to breaking point – and possibly beyond.

'Can I help you, Officer?' one of the staff asked. A sharp young man in a sharper suit.

Not expecting such a quick response to her arrival, Weeks was forced to abandon her second thoughts. 'Er, yes, please. I'd like a word with the manager.'

'Well, I'm a team leader, if I can be of assistance?'

Weeks blinked at him. He looked about twelve. She thought the standing joke was that people thought policemen looked younger all the time, rather than bank managers. Or even *team leaders*.

'I'm sorry, sir. It's the manager I really need to speak to. Ms Youlgreave, I understand?'

He looked crestfallen, but coded her through to the back office and asked her to wait. A few minutes later, she was shown into a suspiciously tidy office where a woman in an equally sharp suit sat behind the desk. She looked up, nodding a dismissal to her minion.

'Thank you, Simon.'

Still, he lingered. 'Can I bring you any tea? Coffee?'

'No. Thank you,' the manager said firmly. She waited until he'd closed the door behind him before pulling a face. 'Honestly. He's not a bad kid, but he's just so *keen*.'

'Hiya, Mags,' Weeks said, taking a seat opposite the desk. 'Regretting chucking in Hendon yet?'

The woman grinned, spreading her arms. 'What d'you think?'

'Hm. I'd say not. You've certainly shot up the financial career ladder, that's for sure.'

'I've been lucky,' Mags agreed. 'And I can do you a cracking rate of interest on a loan or a mortgage, if you're looking?'

'I'm a few years off even thinking about that, I'm afraid.'

'So... it's lovely to see you, Jemma, but I get the feeling you haven't dropped by to reminisce. Is this an official visit? Should I be concerned?'

Weeks grimaced. 'No. Not really...'

'Oh, why do I not like the sound of that. Go on, then. What do you need?'

'It's awkward. You see, a colleague of mine banks with you—'

'Which you know because...?'

'I've seen his cash card.'

'Ah, OK. Go on.' The smile had disappeared, as had the happy-go-lucky graduate she'd roomed with while they were both police cadets, replaced by the formidable Ms Youlgreave, Branch Manager on the fast track.

Weeks took a deep breath. 'He told me he's got himself into... financial difficulties. His father was ill for a while before he died. Greg said he needed specialised care, and he got himself into a hole with credit cards, and was turned down for a loan. And now... well, I *really* need to know if that was true.'

Mags Youlgreave sat back and pursed her lips. 'So, just to be clear, what you're asking me to do is break just about every code of conduct and confidentiality in banking, yes?'

Weeks felt the punch of nerves in her chest. She gave a faint nod.

'You're asking me to provide you with totally unauthorised information that – should it become known – would get both of us fired? And, quite possibly, subject to prosecution?'

Weeks jerked to her feet. 'I know, I'm sorry. I shouldn't have—'

'What's he done?' she asked, waving Weeks back into her seat.

'What?'

'This guy you're asking about.' Her expression still offered no clues.

'Well, possibly gone to a loan shark and—'

'No, I mean what's he done to *you*, personally, that you're prepared to dig the dirt like this?'

Weeks felt her shoulders slump. 'A couple of months ago, we arrested a woman for drunk and disorderly – or so it seemed,' she admitted in a flat voice. 'Only, after she was released, she died from some kind of brain haemorrhage. I told the bloke from the IOPC that neither of us hit her over the head – and we didn't! But Greg dropped me in it.'

'Nice to know who your friends are,' Youlgreave muttered, which seemed double-edged, under the circumstances.

Weeks swallowed. 'And, now, I suspect he's mixed up in something... something else. But if I report him, I *know* he'll twist it and say it's just me trying to get my own back, and...' She threw her hands up, defeated. 'You know what it's like, Mags – the old boy network. I thought all that was long gone, but it's not. It's really not. And I don't know what else to *do*.'

The other woman regarded her silently for a moment, then pulled her computer keyboard closer and began tapping furiously.

Weeks's heart leapt, fearing an official, written complaint was being drafted before her eyes. She stood, suddenly desperate to escape, but Youlgreave again stopped her in her tracks with a raised hand.

'Sit!' she commanded, as you would a disobedient dog.

Weeks dropped.

Before she could plead for clemency, Youlgreave said, 'What's his name, this shining example of chivalrous manhood?'

Weeks reeled off the details.

More clattering of keys followed. Then the other woman sat back with eyebrows raised.

'Did you say his father needed specialist care?'

Weeks nodded. 'That's what he told me.'

'Hm.' She rose, straightened her jacket. 'I'm just going to get Simon to rustle up that tea, after all,' she said. 'Fancy a cuppa?'

'Er, yeah. OK. Thanks.'

Youlgreave stepped round the desk, pausing by Weeks's chair. 'While I'm gone, for *at least* five minutes, you absolutely must not scroll through the confidential information on Mr McCoubrey that's currently displayed on my computer monitor... is that clear enough for you?'

And with that, she left the office, closing the door behind her.

SIXTY-FOUR

LIMEHOUSE POLICE STATION

'My client is prepared to continue with this... interview –
against my professional advice, I might add,' the brief said. He
sniffed. 'I would like it noted that he is doing so of his own voli-
tion and we will, of course, expect anything said here to be
regarded in that light—'

'He talks, we listen. Then *we* decide in what "light" to
regard it,' Daud said flatly.

The brief fluffed up his feathers, but Mackie put a hand on
the man's arm.

'It's all right,' he murmured. 'They'll not find what they're
after from me. There's nothing to find.'

Byron, back in the observation suite watching the monitor,
thought he detected just a hint of threat in Mackie's tone. Or
was it a warning? He shifted uneasily in his seat, wondered if
Vaganov had picked up any trace of Blake's trail. The only thing
reassuring him, at that moment, was the fact that Diarmuid
Mackie was not out there, free to do with her as he liked. Then
he considered the other Kinfolk man, Paarth Sharma. He hoped
that whatever Daud and Desai were going to get out of Mackie,
they got it quickly.

'Shannon came to us as a volunteer, not to use our services,' Mackie was saying. 'Lovely woman. Helped out in the office at first, so she worked closely under me.'

Byron wondered if he was being deliberately provocative, or if he really was blind to the nuances of what he was saying.

'At first?' Daud asked.

'After a little while, she asked if she could move over to working with my wife in the kitchens instead. I agreed, of course, although I was sorry to see her go. She had a great deal of promise... as an administrator.'

'Did she say why she wanted the move?'

Mackie frowned. 'Not as I recall. I did ask, but she wouldn't say.'

'Was there anything about working with you that might have made her... uncomfortable?'

Mackie's face was a professional mask. He allowed one eyebrow to rise slightly. 'I'm not sure I know what you're getting at there.'

'Of course. We can always come back to that later,' Daud said with apparent cheerfulness. 'Who else might Shannon have interacted with in the kitchens at Kinfolk? Besides your wife, that is.'

'Well, any number of our chefs or other volunteers. Or our service users, come to that. And Paarth, of course. Shannon went out on the vans – with the mobile soup kitchen, or handing out sleeping bags and tents and what have you. She was well-liked by everyone.'

'Not everyone, Mr Mackie, clearly. After all, somebody killed her.'

'Yes, but what isn't *clear* to me, is why you seem to think that person is connected to my charity.'

Daud sat back in her chair. It was all the signal Desai needed to begin spreading a sheaf of photographs on the table between them.

'For the record, DS Desai is showing Mr Mackie a series of time-stamped images, taken from CCTV recordings, which show Shannon Clifford heading on foot in the direction of Kinfolk's premises, earlier on the day of her arrest.' Daud paused. 'There is no footage of her leaving again by the same route.'

Mackie looked at her sharply, his eyes narrowing. 'I know what you're trying to do here. A woman dies after she's manhandled by the police, and you're looking for anyone else to take the blame!'

'Forensic evidence tells us Ms Clifford's injuries could well have been sustained at Kinfolk, Mr Mackie. I wouldn't be doing my job if I didn't cover all the bases,' Daud said. 'Did you see her that day? Speak to her?'

'You can't honestly expect a man with my client's responsibilities to recall something so inconsequential that happened so many weeks ago,' the brief protested.

'It's precisely because Mr Mackie has such calls on his time that he *should* be able to account for his whereabouts on any particular day,' Daud countered. 'Sir?'

Mackie sighed. He pulled a smartphone out of his inside pocket and tapped at the screen. 'According to my calendar, I did go to Kinfolk that morning,' he admitted. 'I was the toast-master at an awards luncheon that day, but I recall I'd made some last-minute alterations to my speech, and our printer at home wasn't working. My wife had gone in earlier to supervise the day's meals. I went straight to the office to print out my speech.'

Funny how well he does *remember*, Byron thought. *Or he's just afraid of being caught out, now he knows we've been through the CCTV from the surrounding area – or rather, Vaganov has.*

'Who else would have been in that day?'

'Well, besides my wife, there was Paarth, obviously, and

River. But our other full-time chef was off sick. So I would have thought that Adhiti would have been only too happy to have an extra pair of hands...'

He stopped speaking slowly, as if something odd about that only just occurred to him, or he was aware he might have said too much. If it was indeed an error on his part, Daud pounced on it.

'Why do you put it like that, sir? You mean that your wife *wasn't* happy to see Ms Clifford?'

Mackie was silent for a moment longer, his internal struggle playing out on his features. Byron had spent many years on the other side of the table from suspects and witnesses. It surprised him now that he couldn't be certain which category Mackie fell into.

'I heard raised voices – shouting. An argument,' Mackie said then, with every show of reluctance.

'Did you go to see what it was about?'

'Not at once, no...'

Daud's eyebrows went up. 'Really? An argument and shouting, in a place where – as you've already stated, sir – you have people who might be on drugs, or drink, and your wife was present, and you didn't investigate?'

Mackie flushed. 'I was distracted, with my speech. Besides,' he added stiffly, 'I'm used to my wife.'

'Meaning?'

'She is a creative woman. That kind of highly strung personality, I've found, comes with a certain temperament. If I went running every time I heard her shouting... well now, I'd never get anything done.'

'So you weren't curious at all, about what might have been going on?'

'Ah, now I didn't say that. Of course, when I was finished with the printer and what-have-you, I looked in on the kitchen.

Adhiti was there alone, taking out her frustration on a big lump of beef, I remember.'

'And how did she explain what you'd heard?'

'Now I come to think of it, she did mention that Shannon had been in to see her,' he allowed, frowning. 'My wife said Shannon told her she wouldn't be working as a volunteer any longer, that she'd better things to do with her time, and she was rude about it. Adhiti took exception to her tone, and they'd got to quarrelling, as women do – oh, with respect.'

It was strange, Byron thought, how often that phrase was offered without the respect it implied.

Daud responded with a bland smile. 'And where did she claim Shannon had gone?'

'Well, she didn't. I'm afraid I assumed the woman had left the same way she arrived.' He shook his head, seemingly in sorrow.

'Whereas we already know Shannon didn't, in fact, leave on foot.'

His sigh was regretful. 'Then I can only assume that Adhiti had Paarth take the woman somewhere.'

'You think he would do that? Even if Shannon was, perhaps, injured?'

'Unfortunately, yes, I believe he would. You see, the man is devoted to my wife.'

SIXTY-FIVE

LOCATION UNKNOWN

'Paarth brought me here and locked me in,' Adhiti said, her voice trembling. 'On Diarmuid's orders.'

'Mr Mackie?' Blake forced shock into her voice. 'But... why?'

'Paarth would do anything for my husband – he's devoted to him.'

They were sitting on the floor of the storeroom, in the dim light. Blake had her back against the wall opposite Adhiti. The woman was one of the most stylish Blake had ever met. Despite her present circumstances, there was still something polished about her. Even if the kurta tunic and narrow trousers she wore were creased and stained, and the matching silk scarf hung limply.

'I don't understand...' Blake said.

'Because the police came to take Diarmuid away – to "help with their inquiries," they said.' Adhiti gave a bitter laugh. 'He did not want them to do the same with me, because he is afraid of what I might tell them about him. So...'

'Inquiries into what?'

'I... I do not know, exactly, but he will not want me speaking with them until he has instructed me precisely on what he wants me to say.'

'And Paarth would just... go along with that, no question?'

'He has very *traditional* views about the role of women,' Adhiti said. 'And my husband... he is a monster.'

Blake thought of the women who were dead or missing. 'Yes. He is.'

'This does not surprise you?'

Blake shrugged. 'You learn to trust your instincts pretty fast, on the street. And he likes to... get in your space. Too close all the time.'

Adhiti shivered. 'Of course – it makes it harder to see the fists coming.'

Blake didn't try to hide her surprise. 'He *hits* you?'

Adhiti nodded. 'Never anywhere it will show. When I first came to this country, he assumed that having a wife from India meant I would be meek, obedient – easy to control. Sadly, for him, that is not my nature.'

Just for a moment, Blake saw a flash of contempt on the woman's face. Her smile was both proud and sorrowful.

'So, why stay with him, if he treats you so bad?'

'I ask myself the same question. But, I hope that by staying, at least I might... stop him doing this to anyone else.' She stopped abruptly, biting her lip.

'What do you mean, Adhiti?' Blake asked carefully. 'What is it that he's done?'

For a moment she thought that the other woman might clam up, but after a few moments Adhiti said, 'There was a volunteer who used to help out in the office, but my husband made it so that she couldn't bear to be near him any longer. She asked me if she could help me in the kitchens instead, and of course – knowing what he was like – I said yes. One day when we were working alone, I made her tell me what Diarmuid had done. She did, eventually. She said he took such delight in forcing her to do... things. Things he also demands that I... Terrible things. And then—' She shook her head. 'He is an evil man.'

'What happened – to the volunteer?'

'We didn't know that he was at the shelter that day, I swear to you! He was supposed to be giving some speech in the City. But he overheard us and came storming into the dining hall. I have never seen him in such a rage. He... he hit her. She fell down and did not get up again.' Adhiti had her arms wrapped around her body now, and was rocking back and forth. 'When I tried to help her, he grabbed me, shouted for Paarth, and locked me in the walk-in freezer. I thought I would die in there! And when they eventually let me out, she had gone...'

As the woman talked, Blake felt a cold trickle at the back of her neck. She didn't need to ask the name of the volunteer, or her ultimate fate.

After all, she'd seen Shannon's post-mortem exam report.

What she needed to do, instead, was find some way to get these new developments to Lex.

And Byron.

'I don't even know where we are,' she admitted. 'Somewhere out of London, I think, but...'

'This is the urban farm we sponsor,' Adhiti said. 'It's on the Thames estuary beyond Galleon's Reach at Beckton – out to the east. Rather remote.' She shivered. 'They could do anything with us here...'

Blake rose, dusting off her hands. She offered one to Adhiti, helping her to her feet.

'Well then, I don't think we should hang around to find out, do you?'

SIXTY-SIX

LIMEHOUSE POLICE STATION

'Tell us about Tess Parkin,' Daud said.

'What about her?' Mackie asked.

'Everything you know.'

Mackie glanced at his brief, leaned closer. The brief whispered in Mackie's ear behind his cupped hand, like schoolboys in class.

'She did indeed come to Kinfolk,' Mackie said as he straightened in his seat.

'Huh. Big of him to admit it,' Goodwin said as he entered the surveillance room. 'Seeing as you saw her there yourself.' He took the chair alongside Byron, bringing with him a tobacco waft that cigarette smokers never seemed aware of.

Byron said nothing. Over the monitor, Mackie was still speaking.

'She was battered and bruised, and frightened half out of her wits, poor girl. Her feller, she said, was controlling and abusive, and she'd finally run from him. Went to a friend's place first, but he found her there – threatened the woman and her child. She came to us as a last resort.'

'Did she say who he was, this man?'

Alongside him, Byron was aware of Goodwin's sudden stillness. Was he about to be handed the solution to his murder
case?

But Mackie said, 'Not to me, she didn't.'

'You think she told someone else?'

Mackie hesitated. 'Tess spoke to my wife a fair bit, and *may*
have confided in her. I did ask Adhiti, but she refused to break
the woman's confidence.' Something like annoyance flitted
through his face. 'You'd have to ask her for yourself.'

'We've been trying to locate your wife, Mr Mackie, but
nobody at Kinfolk seems to know her whereabouts. Her phone
is switched off.'

'Is that so? Well, she's her own woman, is Adhiti. She's free
to come and go as she pleases. And I'm sure all of us need the
occasional break from technology.'

Goodwin muttered under his breath. 'You'd think the damn
man would keep better track of his wife.'

Daud raised an eyebrow, as if hearing both comments and
not thinking much of either. 'Don't you find it strange that she's
chosen to isolate herself from all contact, just at the time her
husband is taken in for police questioning?'

'Hardly "taken in" now. You're implying—'

'I'm implying nothing, Mr Mackie,' Daud said. 'You may
infer what you like.'

'Please, Commander,' the brief interrupted tetchily, 'let's
not split hairs.'

'All right. How long was Ms Parkin in the supposed care of
Kinfolk before she was murdered?'

The brief began to splutter, but Mackie held up a hand.

'A few days,' he said. 'And, yes, we failed her, right enough.
But if your man Byron hadn't come nosing around, maybe she
would have stayed where we could keep an eye on her.'

'Oh?' Daud injected a host of meanings into the single
word.

'He spooked her. River took her to one of our rooming houses, where we felt she'd be safer, but she wasn't one to sit twiddling her thumbs and doing nothing, oh no. Tess wanted to work – to earn her keep.'

'What kind of "work" would that be?'

'Now, now, don't go getting those kinds of ideas in your head,' Mackie said with a flash of that trademark smile. 'She'd had some experience in food preparation, she said. I have an interest in a couple of... off-site kitchens – only natural, what with my wife's professional profile – and Tess was helping out at one of those.'

'It would seem, from examination of the clothing found with Ms Parkin's body, that she had been working in a kitchen environment on the night she was murdered.'

Another glance was exchanged between Mackie and his brief. The man gave a faint nod, even if his jaw was clenched tight.

Mackie sighed. 'From what I'm given to understand, some-body managed to turn off the power – accidentally, I'm sure – and in the confusion another girl who was helping out there—'

'Working there, you mean?'

'All right, yes. Anyway, she was injured. Unfortunate, but these things happen, don't they?'

'Do they?'

Mackie had the grace to look a little flustered. 'Well, I wasn't there myself. Paarth assured me he did his best to take care of everything, but – what with all that confusion and the dark... Well, when it was all over, they found Tess had... disap-peared. Paarth said he assumed she'd been frightened by all the goings-on. He searched for her, of course, but the next we heard of her was when your lads turned up at the shelter with a warrant.'

He'd missed a few steps, Byron considered, and glossed over a few others, but his story more or less fitted the facts. Well enough to cast doubts, anyway. Particularly for a man with Mackie's connections.

'Looked for her, did he? Found her, too, would be my guess,' Goodwin muttered. 'Found her and taught her a lesson about not running away. Maybe we should be taking a much closer look at Paarth Sharma...'

'You seem to place a lot of trust in Mr Sharma,' Daud said.

'Well, of course. He's my right-hand man at Kinfolk, and he oversees the off-site kitchens. I've always found him very trust-worthy, although some people might be wary about working with family.'

Daud frowned. 'You mean your wife?'

'Well, not just that, although that can have issues of its own. Paarth is also my brother-in-law, so—'

'Excuse me a moment – are you saying that Paarth Sharma is Adhiti Chatterjee's brother?'

Alongside Daud, Hari Desai's role in the proceedings had been a silent one thus far, so his sudden question caught everyone by surprise.

'Yes, of course,' Mackie said. 'They came over from India together. You mean you didn't know?'

'We can't get out,' Adhiti said, despair in her voice. 'Neither of us could fit through that window, and as for the door...' She gestured to the snapped-off handle.

Blake smiled at her. She untucked her T-shirt and rummaged under it for the paperclips she'd hidden inside her bra.

'What are you doing?'

'Trick a mate taught me, years ago,' Blake said. 'Good job this door opens inwards – wouldn't work otherwise.'

She unfolded both clips into a half-moon, joining them with a couple of small hooks in the middle. Then she threaded the extended wire into the gap between door and jamb, curving it behind the tongue of the latch and out again. She wound the loose ends around her fingers. A couple of sharp tugs against the rounded side of the tongue made it retract enough to pop the door free.

Blake stepped out cautiously into the corridor. They had heard the van drive off, but that didn't mean the place was empty.

The corridor had a fire exit at the far end, operated by a

central push-bar. She checked for alarm contacts around the frame, then clicked it open and left it on the latch. You never knew when you might need an escape route.

When she turned back, Adhiti was watching her

'You are not as you first appear,' the woman said, reproachful. 'Who are you really, Blake?'

Blake shrugged. 'Oh, I'm nobody,' she said, heading back towards the front of the building.

Adhiti hurried after her. 'Of course you are somebody,' she insisted. 'What I mean is, sweetie, why are you here? What have you come for? There is a... purpose to this, I can tell.'

Blake paused.

Adhiti had told her that Mackie had been taken in for questioning. More likely about the charity's exploitation of the homeless than anything to do with Shannon's death. But still, once they started digging, it might come out.

And if it didn't? Well, there was always Lex's way of dealing with things.

In which case, the less Mackie's wife knew about Blake's involvement, the better.

So she said, 'I'm looking for a girl called Kensy.'

'Kensy? I think I remember her... very young – if it's the one I'm thinking of.'

'Do you know what happened to her? I heard there was an accident, at one of the kitchens. I was told Paarth took her away.'

'Really? I know nothing of this. And you can't always take someone's word—'

'The person who told me was there at the time.'

'Ah, poor child.' Adhiti's face grew grave. 'Then perhaps one of the hospitals...?'

Blake shook her head. 'I've checked with all the ones within reach that still have a working emergency department. Nothing.'

'Well... I'm sure she would have been taken care of.'

Yeah, that's what I'm afraid of.

'Is someone helping you look for her?' Adhiti pressed. 'Surely you cannot search everywhere on your own.'

Again, Blake chose caution. 'Just me.'

'Ah. But what is she, this girl, to you? Why are you looking for her?'

'Because I made a promise to a friend.'

She moved on. Blake got the feeling this part of the building was used only by the farm staff. At least, she hoped that was the case. The interior was in need of paint, and the chairs had their foam stuffing exposed through grubby fabric. Everywhere smelled vaguely of animals, hay and manure.

A quick scan of the room revealed no landline phone. One wall held a wipe-board with volunteer rotas, reminders about vet visits, deliveries, and a feed chart for the various animals, listed by name. She skimmed over them while Adhiti stayed by the doorway, as if afraid to enter. Blake could only guess at the breeds by what they were given to eat. Two names at the bottom, she noted – Will and Doris – were to have 'nothing until further notice'.

'Who are Will and Doris, do you know?'

Adhiti shook her head, frowning. 'I hardly ever come here. Not well enough to know the animals by name. I'm sorry.'

'OK,' Blake said.

Something tickled at the back of her mind. She looked over her shoulder at Adhiti, standing probably three or four metres away, looked back at the wipe-board. Then thought of the store-room, going over the layout again in her mind.

'Blake? What is it? What's wrong?'

She turned to face the other woman and sighed. 'A couple of things, to be honest,' she said. 'There are volunteers on this board too. One of them's called Elsie, so a Doris wouldn't be unusual. How did you know Will and Doris were animals, not people?'

'Well, I-I... must have remembered – from my last visit.'

Blake nodded. 'OK, I'll buy that. But what I can't buy is the fact that Paarth only snapped off the interior handle *after* he put me into the storeroom with you. There's no lock on the door, so up until that point, you were free to leave anytime you wanted to.'

She paused, watching for a reaction.

Adhiti said nothing.

'So, my real question,' Blake continued, 'if you're so afraid of Paarth, and your husband, is why didn't you flee while you had the chance?'

'There is no *way* that Paarth Sharma is Adhiti Chatterjee's brother,' Desai said. 'He just... can't be.'

'I'm sorry, but why is that relevant?' Daud asked. 'The clock's ticking on how long we can hang onto Mackie for questioning before that brief starts ringing folk higher up the food chain than any of us – who are, no doubt his golfing buddies – and—'

'And Blake is missing,' Byron cut in.

'Quite,' Daud said.

They were in the observation suite, with cameras and microphones to the interview room firmly switched off while Mackie's legal adviser dispensed further pearls of wisdom to his client.

'Wait a minute,' Goodwin said. 'Is this the same Blake who was last seen arguing with Tess at the shelter? She's—'

Byron opened his mouth, but before he could speak, Daud said firmly, 'She's undercover. One of ours.'

'What? Why would you have an undercover operative inside Kinfolk?'

'At the moment, that's need to know,' Daud said, without

adding, *And you don't need to.* Anxious to head off that line of questioning, Byron glanced at Hari Desai. 'Why were you so surprised when Mackie said they were siblings?'

Desai gave a half shrug, and shifted his feet. If Byron didn't know better, he might think the young detective was embarrassed.

'Because... well, it's a caste thing. I mean, I know that's all very non-politically correct these days, but you still can't help *noticing*, you know?'

'How?'

'The easiest way to describe it is...' Desai's voice trailed off. He cleared his throat. 'OK, supposing you met an English aristocrat in the street, without knowing who they were? Even if they were wearing their old gardening clothes, there would just be a certain something about them that you'd recognise as upper class.'

'Not necessarily,' Daud objected. 'Not everyone would.'

'With respect, ma'am, I'm not talking about everyone. You would, I'd judge – and Mr Byron certainly would. It's not as simple as their accent, but it's the air they have about them, the way they carry themselves, the shape of their bones... I'm sorry, I'm not explaining this very well. But... Brahmin, Kshatriya, Shudra, and certainly Dalit – you just *know*.'

'Accents can be learned,' Daud said. 'And mannerisms can be mimicked.'

'Yeah, they can, but not often so flawlessly that another aristocrat would be fooled by them,' Desai said, and there was no mistaking his embarrassment this time. 'Not for long.'

'I realise that asking is not the done thing,' Byron said carefully, 'but can I take it that you yourself are Brahmin?'

'I'm a second-generation Londoner, sir, but the side of my family still in India is wealthy and... highly regarded, yes,' he said stiffly. 'When I went to uni, my parents hoped I'd stay on in academia. Me becoming a copper was not their first choice.' He gave a wry smile. 'They wouldn't tell my relatives what I was doing until I made detective.'

Daud glanced at Byron, amusement in her eyes. 'Oh yeah, he's posh all right.'

'And... I would have bet anything you like that Adhiti Chatterjee was Brahmin, too.'

'Ah.' Byron understood now the reason for Desai's unease at the turn the conversation had taken. He was embarrassed at having been taken in. 'So, to which caste did you assume Paarth Sharma belonged?'

'Well, you have to understand that the system of four varnas – social classes – has been around in India for several thousand years. It may no longer be as rigidly adhered to in the big cities, but in more rural areas, your varna is assigned at birth and, more or less, that's that. It's nothing to do with wealth so much as position. And Dalits are considered so impure by some that they're not allowed to drink the same water, or walk the same streets as other varnas, let alone speak to them. Mahatma Gandhi spent much of his life campaigning for equality for those he called "Harijans" – children of God.'

'We don't hold you personally responsible, Hari,' Byron said gently.

Desai flashed another quick smile. 'When I first met Sharma, I thought he was Shudra at best,' he admitted. 'They tend to be labourers or servants for the other varnas. But, there was something about him – like he was hiding something, or ashamed of something. So, I suspected he might actually have been Dalit.'

'Has anyone carried out a thorough background check on either of them?' Byron asked.

'Not as far as I'm aware,' Daud said. 'I would have thought – with her profile as a celebrity chef – if there was any dirt to be found, the tabloids would have dug it up by now.'

'That depends how motivated they were,' Byron said. 'Hari, you might want to—'

His suggestion was interrupted by a knock on the door to the observation suite. It opened and one of the detectives Byron recalled from the incident room stuck his head through the gap.

''Scuse me, Sarge,' he said, looking at Desai, 'but the software developer for the homeless app has just got back to us. He said Kinfolk were involved in beta testing the original version of the app, and nobody realised they still had administrator access. He's now blocked them from the system.'

'Thanks, Steve,' Desai said. 'Nice to know they've finally bolted the stable door – even if the horse is long gone.'

The detective nodded and ducked out again.

'So, whenever anyone reported the location of someone on the streets, Mackie knew about it,' Goodwin said with satisfaction. 'That's another nail in his coffin.'

'It's circumstantial,' Daud said. 'He's not the only one with the password to the computer at the shelter.'

'Speaking of which, I'll start that deep dive into Chatterjee and Sharma's backgrounds, if I may, ma'am?' Desai said. He shook his head. 'I still can't believe those two are brother and sister...'

As he went out, he almost collided with a uniformed figure who'd been hovering at the door, just about to knock.

'Weeks? What are you doing lurking out there?' Goodwin said sharply. 'Where have you been hiding all morning? I'm still waiting for that house-to-house report. And we could do with more bodies manning the tip line, so hop to it!'

Byron glanced at the constable's face. 'Was there something you needed, Jemma?'

'Yes, sir. Sorry, sir, ma'am. There's a... gentleman in Reception asking for Mr Byron – a Mr Vaganov.'

'Ah. Did he say what he wanted?'

'Well, er...'

'Spit it out,' Daud said dryly. 'Byron hasn't bitten anyone for days.'

'Well, his exact words were, "The tracker's back online, but how long for is anyone's guess, so if he doesn't get his arse out here in the next thirty seconds, I'm going without him," – er, sir.'

SIXTY-NINE

CITY FARM, BECKTON

Adhiti hadn't spoken in response to Blake's accusations. She didn't need to.

Instead, she straightened, shedding her cowed attitude like it was a shawl dropping from her shoulders. Her chin came up. She met Blake's stare with one that dripped arrogance.

'Well, well,' she said, a drawl to her voice. 'You really are a long way from the simpleton you've been playing, aren't you, sweetie?'

Blake said nothing.

Adhiti reached into one of the pockets of her kurta and pulled out a slim smartphone. Without taking her eyes from Blake, she said, 'You heard all that, I trust?' And she slipped the phone away again without waiting for confirmation.

'Why the games?' Blake demanded. 'Why the downtrodden wife act? What were you hoping to gain from it?'

'From *you*, you mean?' Adhiti laughed. 'Exactly what I have done. I needed to know what you were up to, and who you might be working for. I couldn't rule out the possibility it might even be my fool of a husband.'

'Why would I be working for him?'

'Well, if not Diarmuid himself, then perhaps the Party hierarchy – trying to unearth any skeletons in his closet before they provide him with a nice safe seat. After all, the next election is fast approaching.' Her tone turned mocking. 'One more scandal on top of all the others and this government will be laughed right out of office.'

'Is that something you want to prevent, or encourage?' Blake asked. 'Whose side are you on?'

'The same side I've always been on, sweetie – my own.'

The outer door opened and Paarth ducked inside.

Blake was not surprised to see him. He must have driven the van only a short distance – so she would hear it apparently leaving – then returned on foot.

He glowered without speaking.

'So, what do you intend to do with me?'

Adhiti smiled in a way not designed to be reassuring. 'I *could* tell you, I suppose, but why spoil the surprise?'

She glanced at Paarth. He seemed to take that as an instruction, moving forwards to grasp Blake's forearm.

Just for a moment, Blake considered fighting back. Paarth was twice her size, but that might mean he'd always relied on his bulk to act as a deterrent.

She made a show of fear, using it to cover shifting her feet into a stance, gauging his balance. She brought up her other hand as if in pleading, but was poised, ready to strike.

But then Adhiti said, 'On second thoughts, you said you were looking for this girl, Kensy, I believe?'

Blake nodded.

'In that case, sweetie, we'll take you to her.'

SEVENTY

'Do you still have the tracker signal?'

'For the hundredth time, Byron, yes, I still have it,' Vaganov said lightly. 'You fret like an old woman.'

Vaganov had surrendered the wheel to him before they left Limehouse Police Station. Byron had no objections to being driven, but he drew the line when it was his car.

At least it offered something to distract him from worrying about Blake.

Or not, as the case may be.

Traffic across West India Quay, just north of Canary Wharf, was normal for London, which meant it was heavy and aggressive towards any other driver attempting to cut through. Even lights and sirens made no difference. Eventually, Byron switched them off.

He thought of the last occasion Blake had deliberately put herself in danger. He'd known the utter frustration of not being able to reach her fast enough then, too.

As if sensing his thoughts, Vaganov glanced across at him from the passenger seat. 'If you do not trust Blake to take care of herself, you will push her away.'

'Yes, so you've said on a previous occasion. Please excuse me if I am not reassured.' Byron allowed himself a raised eyebrow. 'Although, I got the distinct impression that my pushing her away would be a preferable outcome for you.'

Vaganov regarded him in weighted silence.

Then he said, 'The only thing I want for Blake is what I have always wanted for her – that she finds someone who appreciates her... unique talents. Someone who appreciates, also, that they are a product of her experience – a fundamental part of who she is. Someone who does not try to change any facets of her personality he – or she – finds... inconvenient.'

'I wouldn't dream of manipulating Blake in that way,' Byron said without heat. 'Any partnership – personal or professional – always contains an element of compromise, but too much on either side is a mistake.'

'Even though – had your late wife curbed her instinct to involve herself in every emergency – she might have lived?'

Byron felt his breath catch in his throat, his pulse pound loud in his ears. For a second, his scarred hands tightened around the rim of the steering wheel, and he howled into the void of mind and memory.

Then the brake lights in front of him flicked off. Traffic moved forwards. He followed suit.

'Yes, even then,' he said.

Vaganov watched him a moment longer. Then he asked, 'What did Mackie have to say for himself?'

'About Blake, you mean?'

'Not necessarily. About any of it?'

'He denied all knowledge, as one would expect. Blamed his wife.'

'Well, that would make sense.'

Byron changed lanes, ignoring the blare of a van horn. 'It would?'

'Adhiti Chatterjee is an entirely fictitious creation – that

story she trots out in all those interviews about learning traditional recipes at her grandmother's knee in an idyllic mountain
village...' He shook his head. 'I could not find a trace of it.'

'And you're telling me this only *now*?'

'I'm sorry – did you ask?'

Byron let out a controlled breath. 'Ms Chatterjee clearly
has something to hide. I would have thought that was relevant.'

'We all of us have something to hide, Mr Byron.'

He didn't add, 'even you,' but Byron heard it all the same.

Perhaps it was that which made him respond a little tartly.
'Indeed – some of us more than others.'

'Just as we sometimes feel the need to reinvent ourselves,'
Vaganov went on, as if Byron hadn't spoken. 'It doesn't necessarily imply there is something sinister going on.'

Byron was saved from answering by the ringing of his
mobile.

'It's Doctor Onatade,' he said, glancing at the screen as he
thumbed the steering wheel control to accept the call. 'Hello,
Ayo, we're in the car. What do you have for us?'

A rich laugh emerged from the speakers. 'Ah, so you're not
alone. It's a good job I haven't called to whisper sweet nothings
in your ear, Byron.'

Vaganov raised an eyebrow. 'Oh, please, don't mind me. I
may learn something...'

Dr Onatade laughed again. 'Sorry to disappoint you, but
this is business – the matter we discussed at lunch?'

He heard the question in her voice, and appreciated her
discretion.

'You may speak freely. I very much doubt I have any secrets
from Mr Vaganov.'

'Well, I have identified the possible murder weapon used to
kill Shannon Clifford.' She paused and Byron heard an imaginary drumroll. 'A meat tenderiser, if you please. So, do any of
your suspects have access to a well-equipped kitchen?'

SEVENTY-ONE

CITY FARM, BECKTON

Blake allowed Paarth to bundle her into the back of the van. The cab doors slammed and the engine cranked. She tried not to think what Lex's reaction would be, when he found out she'd let herself be confined again. His response to this, no doubt, would have been to overpower both Paarth and Adhiti and then frighten one or other of them into revealing Kensy's whereabouts.

When it came to loyalty, she judged that threatening violence on Adhiti might persuade Paarth to talk, more readily than the other way around. But Blake calculated the chances of that method working for her were fair at best. Lex intimidated people just by his looming presence. She usually had to prove she was prepared to do whatever it took. Faced with someone as cold-blooded as Adhiti, that was way further than she wanted to go. Not and square her conscience.

Besides, this way was faster. And, if what she'd learned back at Lex's warehouse was anything to go by, Kensy might not have long.

If I'm not too late already...

Blake had just settled against the bulkhead for the journey

when the van rattled to a stop and the engine died away. The side door slid back, hitting its stop with a clatter, and Adhiti appeared in the gap.

'Here? Kensy's here – at the farm?'

Adhiti merely motioned her out with a jerk of her head.

Blake hopped down, eyes everywhere. They had driven along a paved track between paddocks containing rare-breed sheep, cows, or goats, then off onto the grass. In the distance, Blake could see shaggy ponies grazing, with gulls wheeling over what was probably the Thames estuary. She could smell salt on the breeze, even over earthier farmyard odours, and the faint tang of a sewage works, somewhere nearby. To the left were brick outbuildings, clustered around a larger barn with corrugated metal siding.

Paarth led the way to a bolted stable door, its paint long since peeled back to weathered timber. The hinges had dropped, making the bolts shoot back when they finally came free. He dragged the door open. Adhiti shoved her inside.

It took a moment for Blake's eyes to adjust to the dim interior. The stable was open to the main barn, the aperture blocked by a metal gate. Beyond that, she could see another gated doorway at the far side, leading to the outside. The floor of the barn itself was covered in a thick layer of dirty straw. The ammonia from animal urine stung her nose.

Just as it hit Blake that this was not the most secure place to keep her prisoner, she saw movement inside the barn.

She jerked back with a curse as two enormous animals launched themselves at the gate leading into the stable. They were black and tan, with broad chests and huge heads. For a moment, her imagination painted them into giant Rottweilers. Then realisation hit.

'My God,' she murmured. 'They're pigs.'

They moved with such determination, she thought they'd

charge straight through. They stopped short, but clattered against the railings as though they'd like nothing better.

Old stories came back to Blake of mafia gangs using pigs to dispose of bodies. She'd always assumed they were apocryphal, but the predatory desperation of these animals changed her mind.

One was larger than the other, but both bulged with muscle. They were clearly not above domestic abuse, if the torn ears and bitten tails were anything to go by. Suddenly, the note on the board about depriving the unknown Will and Doris of food took on sinister overtones.

Adhiti paid no attention to the pigs. Instead, she pointed to a heap of dirty clothing and plastic bags on the bare concrete floor.

'What is *that* doing still here?' she demanded with a flick of her fingers. 'I told you to get rid of it *days* ago!'

Blake blinked at the venom in her voice.

Then the pile of rags stirred.

'That's why,' Paarth muttered. 'I mean, how could I when... when she's not *dead* yet?'

Blake rushed across, dropping to her knees beside the crumpled figure. A cloud of flies scattered around her. The smell was bad.

'Kensy! Oh, my God... Kensy, can you hear me? Come on, you need to wake up now.'

'Probably better for her if she doesn't,' Adhiti said. She glared at Paarth. 'Those beasts haven't been fed all week. They'll be starving. Get her stripped and into the pen. They'll take care of it, even if you didn't have the balls for the job.'

'How can you even suggest that?' Blake demanded. 'She needs a hospital. Now!' She hardly dared touch the girl. Kensy looked bad and smelled worse. Her skin was grey and clammy, her breathing shallow.

But at least she *was* still breathing.

'What have you *done* to her?'

'Not enough, clearly,' Adhiti said. She sounded annoyed. 'Or she would not still be alive.'

But alive Kensy was. Blake, skimming her gaze over the girl's body, noted the plastic bag wrapped around her obviously broken leg as a makeshift dressing, as well as around her torso, and a torn corner she had used to collect dripping water from the roof.

Blake was filled with a fierce pride, that Kensy – badly injured and left for dead – had defied the expectations of these people.

By surviving.

She ran her fingers gently over the girl's damaged leg. Kensy whimpered. Blake cursed under her breath.

'You claimed your husband was a monster,' she threw over her shoulder. 'Whatever he's done, he's got nothing on you. Call an ambulance, dammit.'

She sensed rather than saw Adhiti edge nearer, hoping it might be guilt that made the woman want to see for herself.

She should have known better.

Blake caught a flash of movement as the ligature looped around her neck from behind and snapped taut. She brought her hands up fast, but not quite fast enough. She just managed to get two fingers between skin and cloth as Adhiti yanked it tight. The sudden pressure made her eyesight pop, her throat slamming shut. The jarring thump between her shoulder blades told her Adhiti had braced knee or foot against her back for extra purchase.

Blake realised the woman was using the silk scarf she wore as a garrotte. But there was a high-tensile feel to it. As it dug deep into her fingertips, she suddenly knew why.

The scarf was reinforced with wire.

On her knees, one hand trapped, she thrashed like a hooked

fish. Behind her, Adhiti was too far away to grab, her grip too strong to break. She grunted with the effort.

'Now get rid of that one,' Adhiti said to Paarth, who hadn't moved. 'By the time you've done that, this will be finished.'

Blake heard the grim satisfaction in the woman's voice. Her vision began to tunnel, starred at the edges, her throat was breaking and her lungs screamed for air.

Paarth, with obvious reluctance, bent over Kensy, grabbing her shoulders.

Kensy moaned, too far gone to scream in pain.

With her free hand, Blake scrabbled for anything she could use as a weapon, a lever. There was nothing around her. She redoubled her efforts, had almost given up hope when her fingers brushed against something.

With a jolt, Blake remembered the pen she'd tucked into her waistband. The one she'd found in the back of the van. She fumbled for it now. It wasn't much, but better than nothing.

Grasping the pen like a dagger, she stabbed backwards, as high as she could reach.

SEVENTY-TWO

CITY FARM, BECKTON

'Kensy! Oh, my God... Kensy, can you hear me? Come on, you need to wake up now.'

Kensy heard the voice calling her name, but it seemed to come from a great distance, muffled as if by fog.

Shannon, it has to be.

The words were almost the same as the last time Kensy heard the dead woman speaking to her, but the voice was different. She knew she recognised it. She simply couldn't remember where from.

She could have sworn she could feel hands on her, too. When she shifted, restless even under their gentle touch, that hurt just as badly. A moan of protest escaped her.

The hands lifted abruptly, as if yanked away. She heard grunts and scuffles, close enough to stir the air around her.

Fearful of the ever-present pigs, Kensy forced her eyes open, slitted against the light. But swirling above and around her were people, rather than pigs, moving rapidly. They might have been dancing.

'They're not dancing, our kid.' Shannon's voice was

suddenly clear in her head. *'They're fighting. And you better hope the right one wins...'*

Fightin'? Fightin' over what?

'Fighting over who, *more like. Who d'you think?'*

Hazy and blurred, Kensy saw a windmilling arm, then the two women – she was almost certain they were women – broke apart. One was shrieking, and then she tumbled backwards, disappearing from view.

The shrieking stopped abruptly.

Another figure reared up, big and dark. Kensy couldn't remember who he was, either – only that she was terribly afraid of him.

He lunged for the woman who remained. They grappled. He towered over her, his hands at her throat, and Kensy's gut hollowed.

'Don't write her off yet. She's a survivor, is that one. Knows more dirty tricks than we've had hot dinners between us, I'd bet.'

Deep down, Kensy knew this was important, but it suddenly seemed not important enough to keep her eyes from closing. Between one long slow blink and the next, the man had let go of the woman. Then he was staggering back, clutching his arm, his thigh, his neck. Bright red liquid pulsed through his fingers.

What's she done to him?

Shannon's voice in her head came through, bubbling with glee. *'She... improvised.'*

The man had half-collapsed over the metal railing now, as if stunned or in shock. Kensy could feel the pigs' agitation, hear them biting and squealing as they barged each other out of the way.

One jumped up, jaws snapping as it made a grab for him. He yelled in response. Shock or pain, Kensy couldn't tell, but it had hold of him and was tugging at its prize.

'One little push, that's all it'll take...' Shannon's voice was a whisper in her ear.

Kensy didn't see what happened next. The woman was up close behind him. And the next moment, the man tumbled over the railing. The pigs momentarily scattered, lumbering back a few paces as he sprawled inside the pen in a jumble of limbs.

The pigs stilled, regarding him.

Then, as one, they charged.

SEVENTY-THREE

CITY FARM, BECKTON

'Turn right here!' Vaganov said.

Byron took the roundabout fast enough to slide the Mercedes into a four-wheel drift, tyres squealing. As their exit came up, he hit the accelerator again and the car shot forwards, through a pair of galvanised palisade gates that were standing open, and along a concrete track. After hitting a couple of bone-jarring potholes, and swerving around a few more, Byron reduced his speed.

Vaganov, who was bracing himself against the grab handle over the door, glanced sideways. 'Thank you,' he said, not without irony. 'Or I would have sent you a bill for new dental work.'

'In that case, don't tempt me to make it worthwhile.'

They reached the main courtyard of buildings. There were no vehicles in sight, and no obvious signs of people. Byron braked to a crawl and both men leaned forwards.

Byron nodded to the smartphone Vaganov held. 'How close will that get you to Blake's actual location?'

'It will lead us right to her. We are not there yet. Go left.'

Byron drove along a paved track that was just wide enough

for one vehicle. They passed various animals in paddocks on either side, who watched their progress like spectators at a sporting event.

'It has to be the barn,' Vaganov said, glancing up from the screen. His voice hardened. 'No vehicle, so where the hell are they?'

Byron pulled up. As soon as the Mercedes's engine switched off, they heard screams from inside the building. Both men threw themselves out and ran for the doorway.

Inside, two huge pigs were fighting over something on the floor of the pen, squealing and grunting as they battled, churning up great mounds of straw. Byron caught flashes of cloth and lumps of...

'My God, is that...?'

Even as he murmured the word aloud, one of the pigs yanked something free from the other and swung towards them with it clenched triumphantly in its jaws.

A hand and arm, Byron realised, severed above the elbow. A watch was still fastened around the wrist.

Because of the pigs' dark colouring, Byron hadn't immediately recognised the blood gleaming around the snout and jaws of both. The cold hard shock of it froze him momentarily to the spot.

It was Vaganov who broke the spell.

'Blake!' he yelled.

He lurched forwards, reaching for the top rail of the gate.

'Don't be a fool, man,' Byron snapped, grabbing his arm. 'They'll make mincemeat of you.'

Vaganov's eyes narrowed. He let go of the railing long enough to reach inside his jacket and bring out a slim baton, similar to those carried by the police. He extended it with a practised flick of his wrist.

Byron let go of his arm. Vaganov nodded, and began to climb over the gate, until another shout made him pause.

'Lex, leave it!'

'Blake! Where are you?'

'Over the far side.' Her voice was rasping, hoarse as if she'd shouted herself raw, but unmistakably Blake. 'You can go around... but hurry!'

Vaganov jumped down on the outside again. Both men broke into a run. Compared to Byron, Vaganov was built like a sprinter, all bulk and power. Still, they were evenly matched for speed.

On the far side of the barn, they spotted the Kinfolk van outside an outbuilding attached to the main structure. The weathered stable door stood ajar. They reached it almost in step. Byron slipped through first, Vaganov hard on his heels.

Blake lay on her back on the mud-spattered floor, limbs entwined with those of Adhiti Chatterjee. Blake had the other woman pinned down with a variation of a classic judo hold. Both her legs were around Adhiti's neck, hooked together at the ankles, while she kept one of her arms totally immobile, bracing it across her body, forcing wrist and elbow into a brutal lock.

At their arrival, Adhiti made a bucking attempt to free herself. She let out a howl of rage that sounded barely human. Blake tightened her grip, half-throttling her. In seconds, Adhiti subsided in a daze.

'I've got *her*,' Blake said. 'Please, look after Kensy. She needs help – right now.' Her voice cracked. 'God alone knows how long she's been here—'

Byron bent over the girl. She was unconscious, filthy and feverish. He could barely discern a pulse – a fact he reported to the emergency services handler who answered his call.

Vaganov rolled Adhiti out of Blake's grip and planted the swearing, spitting woman onto her stomach with one arm twisted behind her and a knee in the small of her back to keep her down.

Blake sat up stiffly. Byron helped her stand. There were

bruises forming around her throat. Her skin was pale, her eyes huge and distant.

Byron kept the phone to his ear but tilted it away from his mouth.

'Who's that in the pen?'

'Paarth.' Blake glanced briefly in the direction of the pigs, still fighting over the bloodied rags strewn around them. She shivered, but her face was expressionless. 'He... fell in.'

Vaganov and Byron both simply stared at her. Blake swallowed, with difficulty. A trickle of blood dripped from her nose and she wiped it away with the back of her hand.

'At least... that's my story, and I'm damn well sticking to it.'

SEVENTY-FOUR

Weeks had been turning things over in her head for most of her shift. But the more she did so, the less sense it made. And the less certain she was of the way forwards.

Deep down, she knew what she *should* do. Of course she did.

Report it – hand off the whole can of worms to a senior officer and have done with it.

But she knew that wouldn't be the end of the matter, not by a long shot.

In fact, it would be only the beginning.

Because as soon as you pointed the finger at another copper, you broke the unwritten rule. It was all very well for the top brass to make a big performance about rooting out corruption and misconduct in the Met. They didn't have to live with the day-to-day consequences. They wouldn't have to walk solo into some nasty situation down a dark alley, not knowing if their promised backup was ever going to materialise.

If you don't support us, you can't expect us to support you.

She'd argued with herself all the way back to Limehouse

nick. When the custody sergeant sent her to deliver Mr Vaganov's message to Byron, she'd been glad of the distraction.

And now, she found herself loitering in another corridor – outside her inspector's office this time – still hesitating.

Gathering her courage in both hands, she approached the door. She stepped quietly, listening. If she really was going to do this, the last thing she wanted was anybody else at the station knowing she'd had a private word with Huw Lloyd.

Who knows what *the gossip-mongers would make of that.*

For a few seconds, all she heard was silence. Then came a burst of laughter from within.

Male laughter.

And something about it made the hairs rise at the back of Weeks's neck.

Without stopping to think, she bolted, heading for the stairs. Before she could reach them, the handle rattled on Lloyd's office door. She froze, turning back in time to see DI Goodwin emerge. He spotted her dithering, and his eyes narrowed.

'What are you doing lurking up here, Constable?' he demanded. 'There's call sheets to be collated, if you've so much time on your hands.'

Inspector Lloyd stuck his head out and scowled at her. 'Weeks! What's this I've been hearing about you being AWOL half the day? That's not going to put the shine back on your career prospects, girl, now is it?'

'Er, no, sir.'

And just when she'd taken a deep breath to ask for maybe a few minutes of Lloyd's time, another figure emerged from behind him.

Greg McCoubrey, looking more relaxed than a man in his position had any right to be.

Unless...

Weeks's brain went into hyperdrive. A thousand different

scenarios exploded inside her head, scattering in all directions. They led to a thousand different possible outcomes.

None of them seemed to end well for her.

'Well then?' Lloyd said, bullish. 'What can I do for you?'

'Er, nothing, sir,' Weeks mumbled.

She fled.

SEVENTY-FIVE

Byron sat at the breakfast bar, drinking his first coffee of the day. He was reading the transcript of Diarmuid Mackie's statement regarding Shannon Clifford. And he was trying not to think about the woman asleep in the guest room downstairs. In particular, he was studiously avoiding any examination of the strange warmth in his chest that came from simply having her in his home.

In preparation for another day of officialdom, he had donned white shirt, suit trousers and highly polished black shoes. His jacket and tie lay over the back of the sofa. He read in silence. No radio or TV news, no music. It allowed him to fully absorb the weight of information before him.

Beyond the wall of glass, the sun glistened on the wet slate and slabs of the roof terrace. It had rained overnight, but the day looked set to be bright and mild.

'Good morning.'

He glanced up. Blake was at the top of the stairs leading into the living area from the bedrooms, her hair freshly washed and still damp. He had again provided the robe from her last visit. She wore it now. He wondered when he would stop noticing, and remembering. She seemed almost hesitant, as if unsure of her reception.

He recognised the need to clear his throat before he spoke. 'Good morning. I trust you slept?' He avoided asking if she'd slept *well* when he knew that was doubtful.

'Some. Do I smell coffee?'

'Take a seat, I'll pour you a cup.'

She took the stool diagonally opposite, resting her elbows on the countertop. The loose fit of the robe left the bruises on her arms and around her neck starkly visible. She seemed either unaware or unfazed by them.

'How do you feel?' he asked, placing a mug in front of her and sliding back onto his seat.

She didn't answer until she'd taken her first sip, closing her eyes with a groan that made his toes curl.

'Better now. And better still for a comfortable bed and a hot shower. I... appreciate it.'

'Happy to oblige.'

By the time they had been allowed to leave the scene at Beckton, it was getting dark. Vaganov had called for a car and slipped away earlier, at Blake's insistence. Byron felt the man should stay, give a statement, but a phone call from Daud overruled him. No doubt she had her reasons for wanting to keep Vaganov's involvement unofficial, even if she wasn't sharing.

They were an unlikely combination, whichever way Byron squared it. But he had to admit that Vaganov's absence raised fewer questions than his presence would have done.

'Any news?' Blake asked now.

'Too early for much, I'm afraid. Forensics have a lot of ground to cover in that pen.'

She gave a shiver. 'Don't they just.'

'You were lucky, Blake. What was to stop Paarth knocking you over the head as soon as he picked you up? By the time we arrived, he could have been halfway through feeding you to those pigs.'

She put her mug down, a little sharply. 'I'm well aware of that, thank you *very* much. And Lex also made his feelings perfectly clear on the subject. I'll just have to try to be better prepared next time.'

'What "next time"?'

Blake's gaze, meeting his, bordered on defiant. 'I got the job done, Byron. I found Kensy while she was still alive. That's all that matters.'

'Is it?' He shook his head. 'You took such risks...'

'Risks that were mine to take. I have no one to answer to.'

'Blake, that's not the case. You have to answer to all those who... care about you.'

The ones who would be left behind to deal with the consequences.

'Maybe so, but that still doesn't give anyone the right to veto my actions.'

'You may think that – you may even believe it,' he said carefully. 'But I've delivered enough devastating news to next of kin over the years to disagree. One untimely death has an outward ripple effect on so many other lives.'

Byron expected some glib comeback. Instead, she eyed him steadily.

'How did you bear it?'

Not the question he was expecting. He took a deep breath, and said, 'By knowing I would do my damnedest to find those responsible. To... provide justice.'

'That would depend on your definition of justice, I suppose.'

He regarded her for a moment. 'Tell me... did Paarth really *fall* into the pen with those pigs?'

'Are you sure you want to ask that question?'

'Yes,' he said. Then: 'I'm just not absolutely sure I want you to answer.'

'Quite the dilemma.' She lifted her mug again, partially hiding a smile. 'Let me know when you reach a decision.'

He rested his elbows on the countertop and leaned closer. Watched her pupils dilate and caught the hitch in her breathing.

'I have spent my entire career not shying away from the truth,' he murmured. 'What bothers me most, Blake, is that – when it comes to you – for the first time I might not want to know.'

'Well then,' she managed. 'You better tell me when you reach a decision on that, too.'

'I—'

Whatever response he'd been about to make was cut short by the buzzer from the main door below. Byron settled for passing her a look which said this conversation was not over. He pulled out his smartphone and accessed the doorbell camera. It showed Daud waiting on his doorstep. As the camera activated, she gave him a small finger wave. He released the door without comment.

Shortly afterwards, Daud appeared at the top of the steps leading from street level, not in the least out of breath. She paused momentarily in the doorway, regarding the pair of them at the breakfast bar.

'My, my. Isn't this cosy?'

Byron hoped that, although tension between them was obvious, the reason behind it was less so.

'Isn't it?' Blake agreed. 'Normally I'm not allowed on the furniture.'

'I don't suppose I could borrow him for a private word, could I?'

Byron would have protested, but Blake shrugged and got to her feet. 'I need to get moving anyway – Lex is taking me over to see Kensy.' She glanced at Byron. 'If that offer of clothing is still open, I'll take you up on it. I think the hospital will take a dim view if I turn up still stinking of farmyard.'

'Of course. Help yourself to whatever you need.'

She gathered the robe closer, saluted them both with her coffee, and disappeared down the stairs.

There followed a stretched silence, then Daud murmured, 'I hope you know what you're doing, Byron.'

'So do I.' He rose. 'Coffee?'

'I better not. Been out at Beckton all night. I'm on my way home to catch a few hours' kip. Any more caffeine and I'll be mainlining Night Nurse just to get my eyelids shut. But I thought you'd like an update.'

He gestured her into a seat. She took Blake's vacated stool.

'So?'

'The forensics people have made a preliminary search of the pigpen and managed to recover most of the late Mr Sharma, as well as parts of at least one other body.' She pulled a face. 'I doubt it will end there.'

'What about the pigs?'

'Well, they've been read their rights, but are so far refusing to squeal.'

He recognised the gallows humour for what it was – the copper's natural defence mechanism.

'I meant will it be necessary to euthanise them in order to recover... evidence?'

'Not my call to make, although I imagine if they simply let nature take its course, they'll recover it eventually. Anyway, we called in a specialist vet to get them sedated and moved. That breed can be aggressive at the best of times, but she reckons they must have been starved for days to behave as they did.'

'Poor beasts.'

'You have to wonder, though, if they had such a convenient

method of body disposal, why dump Tess Parkin in the river? It seems so... careless.'

'Unless they wanted her to be found – some sort of warning to the others, perhaps?'

'That might explain the severity of the beating,' Daud agreed. 'Or one of them panicked, or was interrupted, and dumped the body at the first opportunity.'

'You're assuming, of course, that the same person was responsible for the deaths of both Shannon and Tess.'

Daud's eyebrows went up. 'But the two women crossed paths – and they both fell foul of Kinfolk, one way or another. You really think we're looking at two killers?'

'If it were my investigation, I'd be keeping an open mind at this stage.'

She shrugged. 'Well, we'll know more once they get Adhiti into interview later. You'll want to observe, I assume?'

'I wouldn't miss it. If Mackie was telling the truth about his wife attacking Shannon Clifford, that would let constables Weeks and McCoubrey off the hook.'

'It would rather, wouldn't it?' Daud said. She yawned widely.

'Are you going to be all right driving home?'

'Don't worry – I have a young Lewis Hamilton wannabe from Traffic waiting downstairs to chauffeur me. One of the perks of rank.'

'In that case, go home, Shamshi. Go to bed. We can continue this later.'

She allowed him to shepherd her towards the doorway.

'Oh, I almost forgot – young Hari Desai's instincts about Chatterjee and Sharma turned out to be spot on,' Daud contin-ued. 'The Indian authorities were forthcoming, shall we say. It would seem that when they moved to the UK, she totally rein-vented herself.'

'Isn't that the main reason most people emigrate – for a

better life?' Byron nudged her again, checked she was steady on the stairs.

'Yeah, but most people don't change their name – not to mention their face – to leave behind that kind of a criminal record.'

'Seriously?'

'They'll know more once they start questioning her later this morning. I'll grab some shut-eye and a shower and be back at Limehouse for that. But, yes, everything from murder downwards. Or should that be upwards?' She flapped a hand. 'To be honest, I'm too tired to tell.'

'Home! Bed!'

She paused on the stairs long enough to glance back with a weary smile. 'We got him, though, didn't we? Regardless of who actually did the dirty deeds, Diarmuid Mackie's political ambitions are well and truly kiboshed.' Daud stifled another yawn behind her hand. 'So, congratulations all round, and our work here is done.'

Byron waited until she was all the way down, well out of earshot, before he murmured, 'Not yet, it isn't...'

SEVENTY-SIX

ROYAL LONDON HOSPITAL, WHITECHAPEL ROAD

Kensy woke from a nightmare. Surging up into brightness and confusion, with the smell of pig still ripe in her nostrils.

For a few seconds, the strangeness of her surroundings made her writhe in panic. Then, as the memory of her shattered leg flooded in, she froze, expecting the pain to follow.

It didn't come.

'Are you all right? Do you need me to call someone?'

The voice – female, youngish – was familiar but she couldn't place it. She snapped open her eyes to find someone leaning over her. A bright square of light behind the woman's head threw her face into shadow. Kensy shrank back in reflex.

'Kensy, it's OK, it's me – Blake. Do you remember?'

Blake? What's she doing here? And where is here, anyway?

The fear loosened its grip, allowing more detail to seep in around the edges. She was lying in bed in a room that was all shades of white and beige and pale grey, with a tiled ceiling and polished floor. The bed had a frame on both sides to stop her falling – or climbing – out of it, even if she had the energy. There was something attached to her arm, something else clipped loosely to the end of her finger, wires to pads stuck to her shoulder and chest. She could hear muted voices and bustle in the background.

Antiseptic replaced the smell of pigs.

A hospital, then. I'm in hospital...

Relief had her slumping back into the pillows. Instant tears welled. She put her head back, bit her lip and stared at the ceiling as she willed them not to fall. They fell anyway, trickling from the outer corners of her eyes and down towards her ears, so hot they scalded.

It was almost too stuffy to breathe. She was burning up despite the cool blast from an electric fan near the bed.

'Here,' Blake said, offering her tissues from a box on the bedside cabinet.

Kensy grabbed a handful, nodding a thank you but not meeting her eyes.

As she scrubbed at her sweating face, she glanced towards the bottom of the bed. The blankets were raised up, like they were draped over a framework to keep them away from her feet.

'My leg! I can't feel my leg! Did they...? Is it...?' She couldn't quite bring herself to say the word 'amputation'.

Wordlessly, Blake stood up. She lifted the blankets at the bottom of the bed, folded them back. Kensy craned her neck and found herself staring down at two feet, toes on both pointing upwards, like they were supposed to.

That's where normal ended, though. There were three or four circular rings of flat metal around her left leg from knee to ankle. From the rings came wires and stays and pins that held the whole thing in position, with her calf at the centre.

'What...?'

'It's an external fixator,' Blake said. 'Your leg was really badly broken, so they pinned it, but you needed skin grafts as well, where... well, where the bones were sticking out, so they couldn't put it in the usual plaster cast.'

Kensy stared at the contraption, horrified as much as fascinated.

'Those pins and wires and stuff don't really go right *into* my leg, though, do they?' she ventured, although part of her already knew the answer.

Blake nodded. 'It's the only way they could hold everything in place on the inside, and still deal with the grafts at the same time,' she said. 'But hey, think of the Brownie points you'll score for this. Motorcycle racers often ask for an ex-fix because you heal faster. Plus, it's seriously cool.'

'Unlike these dork socks,' Kensy complained, hiding her relief. 'Definitely *not* cool.'

Her feet were covered in toeless socks. The kind old ladies wore to stop them getting swollen ankles, or blood clots, or something. She tried wriggling her toes. The ones on her left foot felt numb, and only moved a fraction, but at least they moved.

Kensy let out a pent-up breath. 'Thank you,' she managed.

'They tell me a whole team of surgeons worked all night on you.'

Blake draped the blankets back over their framework again. She looked the same but different. It took Kensy a moment to realise it was because she was clean and tidy – her hair brushed 'til it shone. And she was wearing good clothes. A pair of trousers that looked like they'd been bought new, and to fit *her*, rather than whoever donated them. Her shirt might be a man's, but it was clean and even *ironed*.

'Was it you who came and... found me?' Kensy asked. 'Where...?'

'You were on a city farm, out near Galleon's Reach – Beckton. What do you remember?'

'Not much, to be honest.' Her voice was raspy, but it was a relief to be able to talk to someone who was really there. 'One minute I was at the kitchen site, and the next thing they'd taken me to that place.' Despite the temperature, she shivered.

'By "they" I assume you meant Paarth – and Adhiti?'

'She was in on it, too, was she? I thought *he* might be – her old man, I mean. I always got that funny vibe from Mr Mackie, but I never saw either of them there – where they took me. But Paarth turned up – after.' She gave a bitter laugh that came out more like a sob. 'I thought he'd come to finish me off...'

'You were lucky,' Blake said, squeezing her hand. 'And clever. If you hadn't wrapped up those burns, and your leg – and that was brilliant by the way – or managed to catch some water like you did, well...'

She smiled, and Kensy found herself smiling back. It felt like a long time since she had last done so.

She eased back into the pillows. Patches of skin all over her body felt scraped and raw. The skin over her ribs was stretched so tight she feared it might split apart at any moment. She was suddenly overwhelmed by heat and exhaustion, and relief.

'Why do they keep it so hot in here?'

'It's not that warm, actually, but you have a fever. The leg's infected, and they've had to give you quite a bit of blood, as well as a massive dose of antibiotics.'

There was an IV stand next to the bed. The clear tube from it disappeared beneath the bedclothes and Kensy was reminded of the dull ache in her arm where, no doubt, the needle went in. She tried not to think about that. She'd always hated needles. Maybe that was part of the reason her tongue felt glued to the roof of her mouth and she could hardly swallow. Blake gave her one of the ice cubes the nurses had left. It formed a cold pebble in her mouth.

'What're you doin' here, Blake?' she asked when the ice had melted. 'I mean, what are you *really* doin' here?'

Blake didn't answer right away, just looked to the side, her face sad and serious.

'I ran away when I was just a kid – a bit older than you,' she said. 'For a long time, when I was on the streets, Shannon looked after me.'

'What – *my* Shannon?'

'Yes. She came to my rescue when I was in a tight spot and kind of took me under her wing, taught me how to get by. I'm guessing she did the same for you.'

'Yeah.' Kensy swallowed. 'She was always the first to stand up for you, if you was gettin' bullied, or taken advantage of, and that.'

This time, her difficulty speaking had little to do with a dry mouth. The thought of never seeing Shannon again, never sitting in her kitchen drinking a mug of hot sweet tea, never being able to ask her advice, or have a hug...

Kensy sniffed, hard. Her fingers curled into fists against the bedclothes. 'I can't believe she went back to the drink, and got herself nicked. She *knew* they wouldn't let me stay with her, if she fell off the wagon...' Her voice trailed off, ashamed at her selfishness.

'She didn't, Kensy,' Blake said quietly. 'Shannon wasn't drunk when she was arrested – she was already dying.'

'But... it was the cops! They beat her up when they arrested her, just like they did us when they raided that place on the Mile End Road.'

'She died from a blow to the head, but not right away. Byron got an expert to look again at the post-mortem reports and she reckoned that Shannon was assaulted well before her arrest. She had a bleed on the brain that made it seem as though she was drunk.'

Kensy felt the realisation of all that meant gradually settle on top of her, getting heavier, pressing down. Her face scrunched up with tears she could no longer hold back. She sobbed, which made her ribs bite back, and that had her weeping all the more.

Blake said nothing, just let her cry, handing her tissues from the box and holding her hand until she was through the worst of it. Eventually, she could breathe again.

'So... who? Who actually...?'

'Who killed her? Well, they've narrowed down the time frame, and tracked her movements, and... it was while she was at Kinfolk earlier that day. It rather seems as though it was Adhiti or Paarth.'

'I just don't understand why. I mean, Shannon volunteered for Kinfolk. I always thought they was...'

I thought they was on our side. That they was the good guys.

She couldn't quite read the look in Blake's eyes, but she caught the sympathy there as the young woman shook her head.

'Shannon found out Kinfolk was exploiting people like you, stealing the benefits that were due to you, making you work long hours in dangerous conditions... Well, you know all about that, I guess. What actually happened?'

Kensy told her about the lights going out, and the fire, and falling, and waking up at the farm. She left out the bit about talking to Shannon's ghost – that part she wasn't ready to share with anyone.

'The police found some old mobiles at the farm – including yours, and one they think might have belonged to your mate Spider.'

Kensy fiddled with the used tissues in her lap and nodded sadly. 'I hadn't seen him since... well, since he told Paarth he'd go to the newspapers about what they was doin'. Anyone who went against that Kinfolk lot had a nasty habit of disappearin', y'know?'

'Kensy, while you were at Kinfolk, or the dark kitchen, did you meet a woman called Tess Parkin?'

'Yeah. Well, I think so – I never knew Tess's last name. She was at the kitchen, the night of the fire and that. Really jumpy, she was – thought she saw someone watchin' her.'

'Did she say who that might be?'

Kensy frowned, then shook her head, carefully. 'No, just that she didn't want no one findin' out where she was.' She held up her hand with the cut finger – now sporting a new dressing of its own, she noticed. 'I cut me'self, and she sorted it. I asked her if she was a nurse. She said no, but she'd stayed with an old flatmate in Neasden, Viv, who was. Said as how she s'posed some of it had rubbed off. If she hadn't helped me then – given me the scissors and tape and stuff – I would have been in deep lumber later. So, if you see Tess, would you tell her thank you, from me?'

But when she glanced up and caught the expression on Blake's face, she stilled. 'What? What've I missed?'

SEVENTY-SEVEN

NEASDEN LANE, NEASDEN

Blake sat in a bus shelter on Neasden Lane.

She was not waiting for a bus.

Nor was she reading, despite the open paperback on her knee. She wasn't listening to music, either, although she nodded her head in time to the non-existent beat from silent earbuds.

Instead, she was watching the entrance to a house just across the road, a little further down. A three-storey Victorian mid-terrace that had been divided into flats. The cluster of wheelie bins jostling for space around the front door gave her an idea of how many.

A woman trudged into view, leaning into a pushchair that dangled with bulging shopping bags. She wore a bright yellow padded jacket against the cold, and skinny leggings. The pushchair was the type where the child faced the parent rather than the direction of travel, so Blake couldn't judge the kid's age. As she neared, Blake realised that the woman herself was younger than she'd first thought. She just moved like an old lady with bad feet.

Blake brought her phone out of her pocket and thumbed

open the photo of her target, surreptitiously comparing it to the
woman who approached.

Once she'd given Lex the gist of her conversation with
Kensy in hospital, it hadn't taken him long to point her in this
direction.

'And we have a winner...'

She closed the book, stuffing it into her bag, and peeled out
the earbuds as she crossed the road. By the time the woman was
struggling to manoeuvre the laden pushchair past the bins and
up the front step, Blake was only a few steps behind her.

'Oh, here, let me help you. Shall I get the door?'

The woman looked up, startled. She hesitated. Only for a
second, while her eyes darted over Blake. She'd dressed to
blend, in jeans and trainers – nothing too official or threatening.

'You sure it's no trouble?' The woman's tone was dubious.

'Of course. I'll grab the shopping, if you can manage the
pushchair? Gosh, these bags weigh a ton – you must've been
stocking up. Upstairs, is it?'

The woman had wiry red hair pulled back from a face
devoid of makeup. There was a scattering of freckles across her
nose and cheeks. Without the tiredness, the tension, Blake
considered, she would have been pretty.

But when she bumped the pushchair up the worn staircase
– carefully, moving backwards one step at a time – and the baby
waved her arms and giggled like she was on a fairground ride, a
smile managed to break through.

'She's enjoying herself,' Blake said.

The woman glanced at her sharply. 'You from the social?'

'Why would I be?'

'Look, like I told the last busybody who came round, that
bloke was nothing to do with me, or the baby – he was looking
for the friend I had staying. Wasn't my fault he tore the
place up—'

'I'm not from social services, Viv,' Blake said. 'But I *am* here to see you.'

Viv's first instinct was to flee. Blake saw it in her suddenly dilated eyes, the way her pale skin flushed, and the death grip she had around the pushchair's handle.

'Oh God.' Her voice was a croak. 'You're not with the filth, are you? 'Cause, if *he* finds out I've talked to you—'

Blake shook her head. 'Definitely not.'

Viv's shoulders slumped. 'Should've known better, though,' she muttered. 'Random strangers never just offer to help. Not unless they're after something.'

'Who's "he", Viv?'

'I don't know. I *don't*!' she added, catching Blake's expression. 'All I know is that he's a right nasty piece of work.'

A door opened further along the landing. A small, white-haired old lady shuffled out half a step, craning her neck. She wore a nylon housecoat and fluffy slippers.

'I thought I heard voices. Is everything all right, dear?'

'Yes, thank you, Mrs P!'

Viv's singsong response was accompanied by a smile from which insincerity didn't ooze – it gushed.

'Only, after that last time... Well, you can't be too careful these days, can you?'

'We've been shopping,' Blake said brightly, brandishing the shopping bags. 'Disposable nappies. Want to see?'

The old woman opened and closed her mouth a couple of times, then she sidled back inside and shut the door smartly behind her.

'Wow, that's the quickest I've ever got away from her.' Viv giggled, much as the baby had done, and the fight went out of her. 'I don't know who you are, but you can come again.' She shouldered open the door to her flat and gestured Blake inside. 'The nosy old bat heard us talking in the hallway all right, but can't hear her own TV unless she's got the volume maxed out,' she said, backing the pushchair into the living room. 'She was the one grassed me up to social services before, I'd lay money on it.'

She set the brake and shoved a dummy into the baby's mouth. Then she turned, hands on hips. 'So, come on then – if you're not a cop, and you're not from child safeguarding, or whatever they're calling it this week, who are you, and what *do* you want?'

Even in the ill-fitting tracksuit provided while her clothes underwent examination by the forensics team, Adhiti Chatterjee contrived to look poised and elegant. She had angled her chair slightly so that she faced both Goodwin and Desai across the interview-room table. One arm rested negligently along the seat back. Alongside her, the young female solicitor – albeit from the same prestigious firm as Mackie's brief – seemed strangely outmatched.

Watching from the observation suite, Byron reflected one would never guess that Adhiti had spent half the night in the Casualty department of the nearest hospital, handcuffed to a constable while she waited to have the stab wound to her leg treated. And then been transported back to Limehouse, where she went through the inevitable processes following an arrest.

If she was feeling the lack of sleep, it did not show. Neither did any emotion regarding the death of her brother.

'If she was any cooler about this,' Daud remarked, as the detectives went through the preliminaries, 'they'd be risking frostbite in there.'

'You have to admire her composure, if nothing else,' Byron said.

'Twenty quid says she dumps all the blame onto Sharma.'

Byron shook his head. 'I wouldn't be so sure, if I were you.'

Daud threw him a questioning glance, but said nothing.

In the interview room, Goodwin was running through events at the farm.

'We've had a very detailed statement from Blake Claremont,' he said, tapping the iPad in front of him.

'An unstable homeless person who has already shown herself to be a thief, and whose mental capacity we *will* be calling into question,' the brief said quickly. 'Not to mention that she attacked my client with an offensive weapon—'

'According to Ms Claremont – not to mention an independent witness – your client was attempting to strangle her at the time,' Goodwin countered, 'with a fairly unique scarf. Our forensics people have been taking a close look at that and getting very excited, I can tell you.'

The brief flushed, floundered, and fell silent.

Goodwin stared at her for a beat longer, then slid his gaze back to Adhiti.

'It seems you knew exactly where your brother had taken Kensy Young, after she was badly injured at one of your dark kitchens, and yet you were apparently surprised to see her there. Why was that?'

The brief opened her mouth again, but Adhiti held up a peremptory hand.

'Because he was supposed to have got rid of the girl *days* ago,' she said, as though it should have been obvious.

Byron saw the pained look on the solicitor's face, but she didn't interrupt.

'Why hadn't he done so?'

'Because he's weak – always has been.' Adhiti's expression

held contempt. 'He was squeamish, even as a boy. Could not bear to kill anything, even to put it out of its misery.'

Goodwin couldn't hide his disbelief. 'You mean he was happy enough to chop up the bodies and feed them to those pigs, but not to finish them off if they weren't quite dead yet?'

'Is he *trying* to make the woman clam up?' Daud demanded, fidgeting with irritation.

Byron raised an eyebrow. 'He may well be employing some strategy we're not privy to.'

'He may well be a blithering idiot.'

'One who's nevertheless reached the rank of DI?'

'One who's been promoted to the level of his own incompetence, more like,' she shot back. 'Now stop distracting me and pay attention.'

'Yes, ma'am.'

In the interview room, Desai was laying out a set of photographs.

'We've identified the weapon that caused Shannon Clifford's fatal head wound as a meat tenderiser,' Goodwin was saying. 'All such items have been collected from your kitchen at home and at the shelter. Likely to find a match, are we?'

'You tell me, sweetie – you seem to have it all worked out.'

The DI ignored her mocking tone. 'What we don't know is *why* you killed her.'

'Why? Because she was threatening to expose us. "Exploitation" she called it. I call it making people earn their keep instead of expecting a free hand-out.'

The brief winced.

Adhiti ignored her. 'Nobody was there offering food, and clothing, and a warm, dry, *safe* space to sleep when *my* family was thrown onto the streets.'

Goodwin consulted the report Byron knew had been sent by the Indian authorities. 'I thought an uncle took you in after your father died?'

'"Died"!' She almost spat the word. 'He was beaten to death for some imagined slight – for not paying enough respect to a man of higher standing. And my "uncle" saw the opportunity for free labourers. My mother was sick, but he put her to work in the fields with my sisters. The goats my brothers tended were treated better than we were. They were considered more valuable.'

'What about you?'

'I was fourteen. He had a different use for me.' Her chin lifted. 'And when I fought him, marked him, he sold me to a man old enough to be my grandfather.'

Desai spoke for the first time, voice careful. 'This was the man you killed?'

'The first, yes. Then I ran before his family could exact their revenge.'

'That was when you joined a gang of local bandits?'

She laughed. 'You make it sound like a choice, Detective Sergeant. I had no choices – only least worst options. When they captured me, it was join them or die. They gave me to their leader. When I had learned all I could from him, I killed him while he slept and took control of his men.'

'Just like that?' Goodwin commented.

Adhiti ghosted a smile. 'They all knew they had to sleep sometime.'

Daud gave a low whistle. 'That is one scary lady.'

'It's all about control, isn't it?' Byron said. 'She went from having none at all to wielding it over others. That's what this is all about.'

'I did what I had to,' Adhiti was saying now. 'But eventually they betrayed me, as I knew they must. I had already made my plans to get out.'

'Take the money and run?' Goodwin suggested.

'The timing was... unfortunate.'

'You went to prison,' Desai said. 'That must have been no picnic.'

'But there was a public outcry,' Goodwin put in. 'You became the poster child for female oppression. Got you a commuted sentence, didn't it? Then an official pardon.'

'They recognised that I was a victim of circumstance,' she agreed. 'I was able to retrieve the money I'd hidden, and went to find my family. I returned to the village of my uncle. They told me there had been a cholera outbreak. Only Paarth remained.'

'So you changed your name, your face, came over here, and started again,' Goodwin said. 'Quite a transformation.'

'It was.' Again, she gave that faint Mona Lisa smile. 'And do you know what was one of the most gratifying things?' She inclined her head in the direction of Desai. 'To have a man like your sergeant there – someone from a *good* family – bowing and scraping to someone like *me*, who was born the lowest of the low.'

'Shame your brother wasn't so convincing,' Desai said without heat. 'When Mackie finally told us the relationship between the two of you, the game was up.'

She shrugged. 'Paarth served a purpose. As did my fool of a husband.'

'How involved was Mackie in the less... savoury side of your charity?'

'Little more than a figurehead. He didn't have the brains for anything else.' She pursed her lips, almost a pout. 'It would have been useful to have him in government. But, just at the point when I was finally about to manoeuvre the useless man into a position where he might obtain some real authority and influence, Shannon tried to put a spoke in the wheel.'

'If politics are so important to you, why didn't you stand for parliament yourself?'

'Oh no, I don't think so.'

'No,' Byron murmured. 'Far better to be behind the scenes – the power *behind* the throne.'

Daud flicked her eyes towards him briefly. 'All the power without the scrutiny. She would have revelled in that.'

'But you already had wealth – status, celebrity,' Goodwin was saying. 'Wasn't that enough?'

She laughed. 'Oh, sweetie. When you come from nothing, whatever you get is never enough.'

'Where did Tess Parkin come into all this?' Desai put in. 'What was she threatening to take away, or prevent you from getting, that she had to die, too?'

But Adhiti was shaking her head. 'Not guilty,' she said firmly. 'I have done many things, Sergeant, but killing that woman was not among them.'

SEVENTY-NINE

NEASDEN LANE, NEASDEN

Slouched in the front passenger seat of the Bentley Flying Spur, Blake watched the procession of shops and flats roll past beyond the tinted glass, muffled and at a distance.

Behind the wheel was Lex Vaganov, looking utterly relaxed. But then, Blake rarely saw him appear any other way. With the exception, perhaps, of the previous day at the farm. That was as close as he'd come to losing his cool.

In the rear seat, jaw tense enough to crack her teeth, was Viv. She sat bolt upright, as if trying not to mark the magnolia hide upholstery, nervously jiggling the baby on her lap. Even the child had been awed into silence by her surroundings.

With hindsight, Blake wished she'd been more insistent that Lex pick a different mode of transport. He had enough to choose from. But he'd been confident that Viv would take the outrageously expensive car as a sign they had the resources to protect her and her child. And initially, she'd seemed reassured, but now she was clearly having second thoughts. To the point where Blake had avoided contacting Byron to bring him up to speed. She had the feeling that to do so within Viv's earshot might just send the woman into a panic.

Lex, on the other hand, was used to people giving him their word and keeping it. Mostly, they were too afraid of his reputation to do otherwise. He took advantage of a red traffic light to glance across at her.

'Make the call.'

Blake resisted the urge to check behind her as she slid the mobile out of her pocket. She hit speed-dial before Viv had a chance to object.

Byron answered within a couple of rings. 'Hello, Blake.' He spoke quietly. There was little background noise.

Indoors, then. Still at Limehouse, at a guess.

'Hi,' she said. 'How's it going?'

'Adhiti has admitted – on the record – to killing your friend Shannon.'

'Ah.' She felt a long tense breath leave her. 'That's... good to know. Thank you.'

'But she denies having anything to do with Tess's death.'

'And you believe her.'

'Strangely enough, I do. At this stage, I don't see what she has to gain by lying.'

'Well, in that case you may be interested to know I spoke to Kensy about anything Tess said to her that might help. Apparently, she'd mentioned a former flatmate in Neasden. Tess stayed there when she first ran.'

'Did she? That *is* interesting. Any chance your friend Vaganov might be able to...?'

'Already done.'

'Of course.' Was that a hint of derision in his dry tone? 'And did Tess say anything to this flatmate about the abusive boyfriend?'

'Oh yes. In fact, the toerag came round and tore her place apart, looking for Tess.'

'So she knows who he is?'

'Well, she does and she doesn't.'

'Thank you, that's a very coherent statement,' he said mildly.

The lights changed and the Bentley wuffled forwards, negotiating potholes with disdain.

'She doesn't know his name,' Blake went on, ignoring him, 'but she says she would recognise him if she saw him again.'

'Too right, I would. I'd know that ugly mug anywhere,' Viv muttered from the back seat. 'But—'

'*But*,' Blake added, 'currently, there's absolutely no way on earth she's prepared to stand up in court and positively identify this man – her words, not mine.'

'Why such vehemence?'

'Why do you think?'

'Ah... he's a police officer, isn't he?'

'Yup.'

'I feared as much. And you definitely can't persuade her to make a positive ID?'

'Unofficially? Possibly. But officially? Not a chance. Although, you're welcome to try,' Blake said cheerfully. 'Otherwise, we're going to have to go about this another way. Any suggestions?'

EIGHTY

LIMEHOUSE POLICE STATION

Jemma Weeks was coming towards the end of a shift that had seemed to drag on forever.

The one bright spot, as far as she was concerned, was that at least she hadn't had to endure Greg McCoubrey's company. Well, not much of the time, anyway. She'd mostly been stuck doing drone work, manning the phones, inputting reports and statements. Still, it was exciting to be involved in a murder enquiry, however peripherally. And when DS Desai announced to the incident room that Adhiti Chatterjee had admitted outright to the murder of Shannon Clifford – among others – Weeks was aware of a weight finally lifted.

She'd been itching to sneak into the observation suite to see it for herself, but the IOPC man, Byron, had staked a claim, along with the high-flying Scotland Yard commander who'd been sent to interview Diarmuid Mackie. The firmly closed door had not invited interruption.

But at least now Byron would know for sure that she and McCoubrey weren't guilty of causing Shannon's death. Maybe that would mean he'd no longer haunt the corridors at Limehouse.

But then she thought of her visit to the bank, and McCoubrey's own admissions.

Maybe we haven't seen the last of the IOPC, after all.

She was taking a quick tea break when a fellow PC sought her out with another summons to Inspector Lloyd's office. She mentally crossed her fingers that there was no ominous reason for it this time. Nevertheless, she climbed the stairs with apprehension in the pit of her stomach.

Her mouth was dry as she knocked and entered. McCoubrey was already inside. He stood braced, feet apart, arms folded across his chest, an aggressive tilt to his head. He caught her eye, but quickly looked away.

Perhaps the reason for his stance was the presence of that same intimidating commander Weeks had met the day before. She sat in one of Inspector Lloyd's visitor chairs, swung away from the desk to take in the room at large.

Leaning against a filing cabinet to the side of McCoubrey was DI Goodwin, hands in his trouser pockets. He didn't glance at Weeks as she came in.

With the inspector as well, the room was crowded.

'Um, you wanted to see me, sir?'

'Come in, Weeks. Don't dither, girl,' Lloyd said sharply. 'And don't look so timid. It's good news – for the pair of you.'

'Sir?'

'DI Goodwin was just explaining to Greg here that Adhiti Chatterjee has confirmed striking the fatal blow to Shannon Clifford, well before you two went anywhere near her.'

Although Weeks already knew this, hearing it officially took some of the tension out of her shoulders. 'That... is good news, sir. Thank you.'

Goodwin turned. 'She admitted to hitting Shannon with a meat tenderiser – so hard that, believing she was dead, the late Mr Sharma doused her in booze and loaded up the "body" to dispose of it in what we gather was their *usual* manner.'

'The pigs?' Weeks asked faintly.

'The pigs,' Goodwin agreed with a grimace.

Lloyd sat back in his chair behind the desk, lacing his fingers across his stomach, and smiled in satisfaction. 'So, as far as your Mr Byron is concerned, Commander, it's case closed and we should soon have him out of our hair, eh?'

'About time. He's been hanging around here like a bad smell,' McCoubrey said. 'Oh – no offence, ma'am.'

'Never fear, Constable McCoubrey – I took that remark entirely in the spirit in which it was intended.'

McCoubrey scowled, while Weeks hid a smile.

Oh, nicely done. I must remember that one.

'Excuse me for asking, sir,' she said, 'but what about Tess Parkin? Has Ms Chatterjee confessed to her killing as well?'

'No, she hasn't,' Lloyd said. 'More's the pity.' His eyes flicked in Goodwin's direction.

'Oh, she'll crack. I have every confidence,' Goodwin said quickly. 'She's too full of herself not to. I just need to keep working on her.'

But all the tension Weeks had thought gone was suddenly back with a vengeance.

'Considering how forthcoming she's been on her other... activities, I can't say I share your confidence,' Daud remarked. 'Which is why I'll be pursuing a different line of inquiry.'

Goodwin's face darkened. 'With all due respect, ma'am, this *is* still my case.'

'And I have no intention of taking anything away from you, Detective Inspector.' She paused, smiled. 'Not until it becomes *absolutely* necessary.'

EIGHTY-ONE

JUST OFF AINGER ROAD, PRIMROSE HILL

By the time Blake returned to Primrose Hill, it was late. She used the code Byron had given her to open the front door, slipping off her trainers in the hallway and carrying them upstairs.

The lights in the stairwell were movement sensitive. They came on ahead and went off behind her as she climbed. There was something a little eerie about it, as if the house itself was watching her.

The door to the living area was open. When she stepped through, she found only one row of under-cabinet lighting left on in the kitchen. The rest of the room was in darkness, except what bled through the glass wall leading from the roof terrace.

Blake moved to the kitchen, noting the empty bottle of wine on the breakfast bar. A glass stood next to it, with a half-moon of dark plum lipstick on the rim. Her stride hitched, just for a moment, then she shook it off.

If Byron has a woman – women, even – it's nothing to do with me.

But even as the thought formed, she recognised the lie for what it was.

From one of the upper cupboards, she took down a glass

and filled it from the water dispenser built into the fridge door. She stood leaning on the breakfast bar while she drank, feeling the chill of the icy liquid all the way down to her stomach.

'You look as though you needed that.'

The voice came quietly out of the darkness, making her start. A shadow detached itself from the others, rose and solidified into the outline of Byron. He came forwards, bare feet silent on the wood floor. He still wore part of the suit she'd seen him in that morning, but with shirtsleeves rolled back, open-collared and tieless.

One hand was hidden in his trouser pocket, which she took to be force of habit. In his other was a wine glass with the last dregs of red in the bottom.

'I'm sorry. I didn't mean to startle you.'

'I didn't realise you were still up,' she said. 'Why were you sitting here in the dark?'

'Sometimes I like the dark. It *can* be... soothing.'

She heard the slight emphasis and wondered if he'd intended to give away so much by it. Perhaps that was the wine talking.

'In that case, do you mind if I join you for a while? I think I need to decompress before I call it a night.'

As she refilled the tumbler, he slid his empty glass across the breakfast bar towards her.

'Would you mind filling that for me? Shamshi Daud dropped in earlier and I made the mistake of trying to keep pace with her in Malbec. Always an error of judgement on my part.'

Blake poured, following him back to the sofa. After the briefest hesitation, she sat alongside rather than opposite, their elbows only inches apart. When he reached across in the gloom towards one of the table lamps, she dared put a hand on his arm.

'You don't need to on my account. I'm happy to sit in the dark.'

With you.

She felt his doubts under her fingertips. But, after a moment, he settled back into the cushions.

The silence swished and swirled between them.

'How did things go in Neasden?' he asked then.

'OK – eventually. Lex arranged somewhere safe for Viv and the baby to stay tonight, but getting her to trust us enough to go took some doing. She's scared – didn't want me to leave her.'

She'd found Viv rather over-clingy, if she was honest, but it felt unkind to say so. Not every parent turned into a tiger to protect their young, as she knew to her cost.

'I suppose that's only to be expected,' Byron said. 'And Kensy?'

'She's remarkable, considering everything she's gone through. Just to have survived at all is quite something.'

'How bad are her injuries?'

'Worse than they should have been. If Paarth had taken her straight to a hospital...' She shrugged. 'They're still worried about the possibility of sepsis, and she's going to need more grafts.'

'She's lucky – if that's the right word – that the man was less ruthless than his sister.'

'I've given Kensy an open invitation up to Claremont, when they release her. She'll need someone to look after her while her treatment's ongoing. And Caz is there already – a friendly face.'

'Caz? I thought she was the one who betrayed you to Kinfolk?'

'She did exactly as I asked her to. Otherwise, as I've said before, I wouldn't have been picked up so fast, and Kensy might not have made it. Besides,' she added quickly, sensing he was about to reproach her again, 'until we've got a solid line on your bent copper, we need as few other... distractions as possible here.'

'In that case, perhaps you should join them,' he said, his tone dry. 'Because I'm afraid I find *you* a constant distraction.'

His candour surprised her, but she remembered the empty bottle. Maybe not so much of a surprise, then. She took another swallow of icy water and put down her glass on the side table next to the sofa.

'Do you know who it is?' she asked, taking a chance on the Malbec loosening his tongue. 'This bent copper, I mean.'

'Oh, I have my suspicions, but proving them is another matter entirely.' He sighed. 'If I had—'

She caught his free hand, mid-gesture, turning it over so his scarred palm was uppermost. He froze, but didn't pull away.

Slowly, she traced his scars, her touch careful, reading the thickened tissue like braille. He seemed to be holding his breath.

She kept her eyes on what she was doing, afraid to look at his face – for what she might not see there.

'In palmistry, many lines crisscrossing the palm are called Obstacle Lines,' she said. 'They indicate a person of strong intellect – one who travels with influence.'

When he would have pulled away, she resisted. On impulse, she leaned down and placed a kiss in the cup of his palm.

'If I flinch at the sight of your scars, it's not because they repel me,' she said. 'It's because when I see them I'm reminded of what you must have suffered.'

When she released his hand, he let his fingers curl closed over the spot she'd kissed, as if to preserve it.

'Blake, I—'

The entry buzzer sounded, loud in the darkness. Byron tensed. The moment between them vanished with the abruptness of a slammed door.

'Are you expecting anyone?'

He shook his head, already on his feet and moving towards the security camera. Blake followed, looking over his shoulder at the screen.

Whoever stood outside wore a hoodie and baseball cap, both pulled well forwards to cover the face. Their hands were concealed inside the hoodie pockets. It was impossible to tell gender, never mind identity.

'You could always just ignore it,' she suggested, 'and perhaps they'll go away?'

'I could but... we both know that way madness lies.'

She nodded, stuffed her feet back into her trainers and laced them.

'What are you doing?' he asked.

'Stall them for a couple of minutes, would you? Just long enough for me to box them in.'

'Box them in...? What—?' he began. 'Blake, there isn't a back door to this place.'

But she was already heading for the wall of glass leading out onto the roof terrace.

'Yes, there is – it's just the garden path that's tricky.'

EIGHTY-TWO

JUST OFF AINGER ROAD, PRIMROSE HILL

Shortly after Blake disappeared out onto the roof terrace, Byron started down the stairs, moving slowly.

Part of him was giving Blake time to... do whatever it was she had in mind. And part of him had no real desire to find out the identity of the mysterious figure at his front door anyway.

He wasn't sure, being honest with himself, which of the two ideas scared him more.

The movement sensors clicked the stair lights on ahead and off behind him. He hoped that was enough to make his unknown caller wait.

Or not...

When he finally reached the front door, he checked the security screen again. They were still outside, hunched close to the door as if trying to stay hidden from the street.

But as he watched, his unknown caller was yanked backwards and whirled away as if on a wire. He fumbled with the locks, apprehension forgotten. By the time he got outside, Blake had the figure face down on the pavement with one arm twisted up behind their back.

He thought of the three storeys between the roof terrace and the street.

How on earth...?

'Let her go,' he said quietly, recognising their captive in the light spilling from the doorway. 'I don't think Constable Weeks poses any threat to my safety.'

Blake nodded and released the woman, stepping back.

Byron leaned down to help Weeks to her feet. Her baseball cap had come adrift. She looked dazed and more than a little shaken.

'You better come in,' he said. 'Blake—'

But when he looked up, she had melted into the darkness and gone.

Frowning, he led Weeks into the house, took a final glance up and down the street, then shut the door behind them.

Weeks stood shivering in the hallway.

'I'm sorry about that,' he said. 'I am – perhaps understand-ably – warier than most of unexpected late-night visitors.'

'I-I know – and I'm s-sorry – but I didn't know what else to do!'

'OK, Jemma, why don't you take a moment, take a breath, and tell me why you're here? I'm sure your inspector has told you by now about Adhiti Chatterjee's confession regarding Shannon Clifford, so you must be aware that you and PC McCoubrey are no longer under investigation.'

'No, it's about Tess – Tess Parkin. I think... It's just... I have this horrible feeling that Greg McCoubrey might have killed her!'

EIGHTY-THREE

THE MARINA, LIMEHOUSE BASIN

'Are you clear on what you need to do?' Commander Daud asked. 'If not, now's the time to say so.'

'Yes, ma'am,' Weeks said. 'That is – I think I'm clear, ma'am.'

She was in the front passenger seat of Byron's Mercedes, dressed in civvies, with Daud in the back. It was the morning after her unsettling visit to Byron's home in Primrose Hill. How did a copper afford a place like that? Maybe he'd got some kind of big compensation payout. Not that he didn't deserve it, what with all he'd gone through.

Weeks still wasn't quite sure who had jumped her outside Byron's place. Whoever it was, she never got a good look at them – they didn't follow when she was led inside. She could only assume that Byron had permanent bodyguards assigned. And who'd want to live like that?

'Relax, Jemma, I'm sure you'll be fine,' he said now. 'We're very impressed with the initiative you've shown over this whole thing.'

'Yes, when you're ready to move out of uniform, let me know,' Daud added. She grinned. 'Although if you could try to avoid coming up on IOPC radar again in the meantime, that would be good.'

Weeks flushed. 'Yes, ma'am.'

'Speaking of which, you *do* have your baton, don't you?'

The flush deepened. 'Er, well, I thought if anyone *does* come after us...' She wondered if she ought to mention she had cuffs and PAVA pepper spray in her bag, too.

'Good,' Daud said. 'Don't be afraid to use it.'

Byron flicked her a pained look in the rear-view mirror. 'Just... be judicious.'

'Bollocks,' Daud said. 'This is a bent copper we're talking about. One who might well have beaten a woman to death. If you have to protect yourself and the witness, do what you need to.'

Byron sighed, but said nothing.

'Yes, ma'am,' Weeks said again.

* * *

She had laid it all out for Byron last night, and again for Commander Daud earlier this morning. About her suspicions over Greg's behaviour after her visit to the old Russian guy in the flat overlooking Clemence Street. And then his admission when she'd collared him at the gym.

'So, McCoubrey admitted to you that he burgled Kinfolk's office himself, then was conveniently first on scene?' Daud asked, not hiding her disbelief.

'To slow down Tess's identification, yes.'

'Her place had been thoroughly wiped,' Byron put in. 'The delay would have given them time.'

'And McCoubrey did all this at the behest of some apparently unknown individual who, so he claims, was holding his marker from a loan shark?'

'That's what he told me, ma'am.'

'But we only have his word for it that there's any such person. McCoubrey himself could be the abusive partner Tess was so afraid of – with very good reason, as it turned out.'

'I don't think so, but he could well have been working for whoever was.' Weeks hesitated. 'The clincher was when I went to Greg's bank.'

'Go on.'

'Well, ma'am, it seems he paid off his debt at the end of last year. Instead, someone's now paying *him* every month, in cash, which he foolishly pays into his current account.'

'So where's that money coming from?'

Weeks glanced at Byron, received a slight nod. 'He *might* have been going to the house on Clemence Street to collect, not deliver.'

'Achieving what, exactly?'

'Culpability? It shifts Greg from being a victim to a co-conspirator.'

'And if he's been sticking the money straight into his bank, he's too dumb to recognise that fact.' Daud's gaze flicked to Byron. 'You have an inkling who might be pulling McCoubrey's strings, don't you?'

'Perhaps,' he allowed. 'But, either way, we need to lure him into the open before anyone else ends up dead in the river.'

'And I'm sure you have a plan to do just that.' Daud sat back with a smile. 'Oh, this I have to hear.'

'Apparently, Tess had a friend she went to for shelter when she first ran from the boyfriend,' Byron said, ignoring her response. 'But she had to move on when he came looking for her, and smashed the place up.'

'So this friend can identify him?'

'She *can*, yes. Whether she *will* is another matter. Viv has a young child, and he really put the frighteners on her. She's gone into hiding.'

'But you know where to find her?'

He nodded, added almost with reluctance, 'And if we let an address be known around Limehouse Station...'

'He would be mad not to consider the possibility of a trap.'

'Oh, I quite agree,' Byron said. 'But this woman's evidence could mean life in prison for murder. What choice does he have?'

* * *

Byron pulled the Mercedes into a marked bay at the edge of the marina at Limehouse Basin. The three of them got out into steady drizzle.

The flotilla of boats moored to the pontoons were still battened down for the winter. Limehouse Basin was separated from the tidal waters of the Thames by lock gates, so the water level stayed constant. There were disadvantages to that, of course, the obvious one being the layer of green sludge coating the surface. In places it looked solid enough to walk on.

'None too appetising, is it?' Daud murmured, following Weeks's gaze. 'Don't think I'd go for a dip, if I were you.'

'I wasn't planning on it, ma'am. Apparently, you run the risk of catching leptospirosis.'

'What's *that* when it's at home?'

'Some nasty bacterial disease that can make your liver and kidneys pack up, I believe, ma'am,' she said. 'I read about it in *Time Out*.'

'Sounds a laugh a minute.'

Weeks glanced at Byron. His face was expressionless.

Another vehicle nosed onto the parking area. A huge Bentley. It glided into a nearby space, shrinking Byron's Mercedes to the size of a shopping trolley by comparison.

Weeks saw two people inside. The man behind the wheel scowled at them through the glass. He had a haircut too short to grab hold of in a fight. Weeks was suddenly glad of the armoury in her handbag.

In the passenger seat was a slight woman with red hair. She sat hunched low, hoodie pulled up to avoid being recognised.

Perhaps you should have chosen a less showy form of transport, then...

The scowling man climbed out with an umbrella, went round to shelter the woman as she got out, too. Her clothes, in contrast to his, were cheap, her trainers scuffed and stained.

'Jemma, this is our witness, Viv,' Daud said. 'You'll be looking after her.'

'Of course,' Weeks said, smiling at the woman.

Viv made no response. She kept her head ducked, staying close to the big man. And not simply, Weeks judged, to be out of the rain.

'I do hope you know what you're doing, Byron,' the man said, his voice silky with threat.

Byron ignored his tone. 'Shall we?'

Daud nodded. 'Thank you, Mr Vaganov. We'll take it from here.'

The marina development was surrounded by apartment buildings. Flats with Juliet balconies overlooking the water. The man, Vaganov, walked them to the entrance of one building, keeping the umbrella over Viv, then turned on his heel without a word.

The lift was crowded with the four of them, all trying to avoid eye contact while standing inches apart. As soon as they got out on the fourth floor, she saw a constable on duty outside one of the flats – not someone she knew from Limehouse. He straightened at the sight of Daud.

'Anything suspicious so far, Ronnie?' she asked.

'All quiet, ma'am.'

'Good. Stay sharp.'

Inside, Weeks was surprised to find the flat was well-appointed, even stylish.

'Is this a safe house?' she asked.

Daud grinned. 'No – AirBnB.'

'How long do I have to stay here?' Viv asked in a whiny voice. 'I miss my kid.'

Daud exchanged a glance with Byron. 'We'll have a full set of mugshots assembled later today,' she said. 'As soon as the identification's been made, it's all over.'

'And I won't have to see *him* for real?'

'We hope not.'

Viv's answering sniff spoke volumes.

EIGHTY-FOUR

BRANCH ROAD, LIMEHOUSE

Sitting in the back of an unmarked surveillance van nearby, Byron and Daud had spent several hours listening-in on the desultory conversation between Weeks and their witness.

Weeks did her best to draw Viv into conversation about her child, but that made the woman sulky and defensive. She would only say that her baby was being properly looked after, and there was no need to get the social involved again.

The TV proved no distraction. She channel-hopped through game shows, property renovation programmes, daytime soaps, and old movies, without settling on anything for more than a minute or two.

Weeks tried to be cheerful, offering constant cups of tea, including to Ronnie outside the door. But the morning dragged towards midday.

'Did Viv tell Blake anything else about this bent copper?' Daud asked. 'Is it *just* McCoubrey we're looking at, or is anyone else involved do you think?'

But before Byron could answer, a shrieking siren came through from the flat.

'What the hell is that?' Daud demanded. 'Fire alarm?'

Byron nodded, already dialling Weeks's mobile. It rang unheard at the other end amid the clamour of the siren.

Through the surveillance microphone, they could hear Viv's voice, filled with panic: 'Jemma! What's going on?'

Weeks: 'I'm sure it's OK. I'll get Ronnie to go and see.'

There was a pause, then Weeks again: 'Ronnie's gone. Look, you stay here.'

Viv: 'What? Why? Where are you off to?'

Weeks: 'Just to make sure this is a false alarm.'

Viv: 'And if it's not, you're gonna walk back into a burning building to get me, are you? Yeah, right. If *you're* going, I'm coming with you.'

'Don't do it, Jemma,' Daud muttered under her breath.

But after a moment's hesitation, Weeks said: 'All right, but keep behind me.'

'Dammit. Can't you reach her?'

Byron shook his head.

He was already on his feet. 'Where's the backup team?'

'Five minutes out.'

He glanced at his watch. 'If we hurry, we're less than two minutes away.'

She jerked open the side door, throwing him a quick grin as she jumped out. 'In that case, Byron, do try to keep up.'

EIGHTY-FIVE

THE MARINA, LIMEHOUSE BASIN

Weeks opened the door of the flat and checked both ways before leading Viv out. The other woman had her hood up and her head ducked again.

A few other apartment doors were open. People milled about, unsure how seriously to take this.

'Does the alarm often go off for no reason?' Weeks asked a woman across the hall, shouting to be heard.

The woman shook her head. 'I've been here five years and this is a first.'

'In that case, I'd suggest vacating immediately.'

'Aw, really? I've just got off nights!'

'And take the stairs,' Weeks added.

She could see that someone had already ignored this basic advice. The display above the lift doors was slowly counting up as it rose. She hurried Viv towards the staircase.

There were few people making their way down. Either most of the residents were out during the day, or were in denial. Nobody seemed in a hurry.

As they reached the second floor, the door burst open and the uniformed figure of Inspector Lloyd appeared.

'Weeks! This way!'

'Sir? What are you doing here?'

'You didn't think Daud could commandeer one of my people without running it by me first, did you?' he demanded, stepping back to hold the door. 'Look lively, girl! There's a fire exit at the end there, and we've a car waiting to get the witness to safety.'

Weeks checked on Viv, still sticking to her like glue. Still with her head down.

But as they moved out of the stairwell, some primitive part of Weeks's brain lit up with a siren to match the fire alarm.

Frowning, she glanced back.

Time slowed.

She saw Lloyd, letting the stairwell door swing shut and falling into step close behind them.

The empty corridor, with the apartment doors all firmly closed.

Leaving the only way out the fire exit at the far end.

The door was ajar. It began to open from the outside.

She drew level with the lift doors. The mechanism chimed as the lift returned from its upward journey. The fire safety system finally cut in, locking the car. The doors parted.

Slumped in a corner, bleeding from a head wound, was the uniformed constable from outside the flat.

'Ronnie!'

She halted. With a growl, Lloyd gave both women a brutal shove in the back, forcing them on.

The fire exit was fully open now.

Greg McCoubrey filled the gap.

As they neared, Lloyd gave her another violent push, sending her stumbling almost into Greg's arms.

'Get rid of her,' Lloyd told him. 'I'll take care of this one!'

But as he grabbed Viv's upper arm, her head reared up for the first time. The hood fell back to reveal her face.

'What the—?'

Even as his question formed, Viv snapped her head forwards. By luck or judgement, the timing was perfect.

Her forehead cracked into the bridge of Lloyd's nose. Even over the fire alarm, Weeks heard the crunch of broken cartilage. Blood spattered the front of his tunic.

He released his captive with a roar.

Weeks yelled, '*RUN!*' and threw herself onto McCoubrey.

Viv didn't need to be told twice. In a second, she was out of the fire exit and thundering down the metal stairs.

Lloyd, streaming blood and curses, charged after her.

McCoubrey gave a grunt and shot his elbow into Weeks's face. It glanced off her cheekbone. Stars exploded in her vision as she staggered back.

By the time she'd gathered herself, he was halfway down the fire escape. She bounded after him, reaching into her bag. As she hit the paved area at the bottom, she brought out the baton. With a downward flick of her wrist, it sprang open and locked.

The fire door had closed behind them, muffling the alarm. McCoubrey heard the distinctive noise of the baton. He froze for a beat, then turned back.

'Really, Jem? Thought you'd lost your nerve about using one of those,' he mocked. 'I mean, look what happened last time. Hit someone in the wrong place again and you'll definitely go down for it.'

'We both know I didn't kill Shannon,' Weeks said. 'And *I'm* not the one who should be worried about going down.'

He brought his hands up into a boxer's stance and lunged forwards. She dodged a right cross that should have flattened her and thwacked the baton into the side of his knee.

McCoubrey winced, swung again.

Weeks hit him again. Same spot. Harder this time. Like she meant it.

Not holding back.

The joint gave way. He dropped.

Ignoring his yells, Weeks kept him pinned with a boot on his kneecap while she wrestled the cuffs onto his left arm. 'Your trainer was right, Greg – you really don't move your feet enough, do you?'

Baring his teeth, he tried launching another punch.

She twisted the solid central bar of the cuffs, driving the steel bracelet into the delicate bones and nerves of his wrist, forcing his compliance.

She snapped the other side of the cuffs onto the handrail of the fire escape, then used the cuffs from McCoubrey's belt to shackle his right arm further along, leaving him at full stretch.

'If you can reach your keys *and* unlock yourself, good luck to you,' she threw over her shoulder.

Weeks ran towards the front of the building and the marina. Without the fire alarm in her ears, she suddenly heard her phone buzzing in her bag. Daud's voice, sounding frantic.

'Weeks! What the hell is going on?'

'They jumped us,' she managed, breathing harder now.

She rounded a corner. Two figures were struggling near the looped chains marking the edge of the quay.

'He's got Viv – by the dockside!'

Lloyd had managed to get both hands around Viv's throat. Weeks could tell by the set of his arms the effort he was putting into throttling her.

A surge of adrenaline gave her more speed. But she just knew she wouldn't reach them in time.

Then Viv threw one arm over the top of Lloyd's and spun towards him, like a dance. Her momentum broke his grip. Now she was the one who had hold of him, pinning his hands, trapping him within range. She swept an elbow up and back, twice, into the side of his jaw. Weeks saw his head jerk sideways.

Then he was falling.

It was a good three metres from the quay to the water below. Inspector Lloyd cannonballed beneath the slime and was instantly engulfed.

He had not yet resurfaced when Weeks arrived, panting, alongside Viv.

She became aware of pounding feet. Byron and Daud, followed by half a dozen uniformed officers.

'Who is it?' Daud demanded, gesturing towards the water just as Lloyd reappeared, gasping and spluttering.

'Huw Lloyd,' Weeks said, breathing almost normally again. 'McCoubrey was with him. And Ronnie is injured.'

Daud took charge, issuing orders, bringing in ambulances and reinforcements.

Byron touched Viv's arm. 'Are you all right?'

'I think so,' she said ruefully, touching her throat. 'Why do they always try to strangle you? That's twice in a week.'

Weeks blinked. The woman's voice and manner had altered. More refined, confident. Almost as if...

'You're not Viv, are you?' she said accusingly.

The woman smiled, held out a hand. 'Blake. Sorry for being a pain. Part of the act.'

Weeks glanced at Byron, trying not to sound offended. 'Didn't you trust me, sir?'

'It wasn't a question of trust,' Byron said. 'You're not an experienced undercover officer. Not knowing we'd played a substitute Viv was one less thing for you to worry about.'

'And I promised her she wouldn't be at risk,' Blake said. 'It was the only way she'd agree to identify Tess's abusive boyfriend.'

'Which she's now done,' Daud said as she rejoined them.

Weeks glanced down at her erstwhile inspector, clinging to one of the floating pontoons and retching up filthy water.

'Mind you,' Blake remarked, 'I think he's done a pretty good job of identifying himself.'

EPILOGUE

CLAREMONT, DERBYSHIRE

Six weeks later

Blake waited until Byron's Mercedes had pulled up on the gravel forecourt at Claremont before she opened the front door and stepped out to greet him.

She was aware that it was the first time she'd done so as owner/occupier of her family home, rather than interloper/suspect. It... changed things, somehow. She wondered if Byron felt the same way.

He was already out of the car as she emerged, going round to open the door for his passenger.

Kensy climbed out awkwardly, her broken leg still encased in a bulky framework of metal pins, plates and wires. There had been multiple surgeries to effect a repair. Not to mention numerous skin grafts and treatments to deal with her burns.

But her smile of thanks became a big grin when she caught sight of Blake, and she allowed herself to be hugged – carefully – and made a fuss of.

Virginia appeared. Blake's... stepmother. She still couldn't get used to thinking of the icy blonde as anything other than the second wife of her late and unlamented father.

Even if Virginia had thawed a little these days.

But she was friendly enough towards Kensy, ushering her inside. Virginia's daughter from her first marriage, Lily, was around the same age as Kensy. She'd been bouncing with anticipation about meeting her, but was now playing it graciously cool.

While Kensy was ushered into the kitchen with the promise of sugar and fizz, Blake took Byron around the side of the house to the rear terrace. Wicker furniture had been set out on the flags, four chairs and a sofa, arranged around a low table. It was the middle of May but felt like high summer. A tray of tea, complete with a plate of sandwiches, stood waiting for them.

'It's good of you to offer Kensy a home while she recuperates,' Byron said, taking the sofa.

Blake shrugged. 'She feels like Shannon's kid, so what else was I going to do?' she said. 'Besides, Virginia's the responsible adult. It's her name on the foster care paperwork.'

'Nevertheless...'

She poured tea from the pot – real leaves, through a strainer. The housekeeper was pushing the boat out. She'd even cut the crusts off the bread.

'I take it Caz didn't stay?' Byron asked.

'She was anxious to get back to London.' Blake handed over his cup and saucer. 'Speaking of which, what news?' She could make small talk with the best of them, when she had to. This was not one of those times.

'The CPS is happy with the case against Adhiti regarding Shannon's death. The rest of it – the misuse of the app, the running of a modern-day workhouse – is complicated enough that it could take months, if not years, to come to court.'

'And what about Laurel and Hardy?'

'The IOPC proper have taken over the misconduct aspects of the case, and Daud's team is handling Tess's murder, so it's all rather out of my hands, I'm afraid.'

Blake couldn't help but glance at his hands as he spoke. He stilled, as if remembering her palm reading – and what came after. Was that what caused the teacup he was holding to wobble, a little tea to slop over into the saucer? He emptied it back into the cup, mopped up with his napkin.

If she didn't know better, she might almost believe he was... flustered.

Ah well, in for a penny...

'I wanted to thank you,' she said. 'For trusting me enough to let me play the part – Viv. The whole thing.'

He inclined his head. 'You're welcome, although I don't think Mr Vaganov has forgiven me yet.'

'That's all right. He hasn't quite forgiven me, either.'

Byron set down his cup and leaned towards her, intent. 'But, Blake, next time, I would be grateful if you would trust *me* enough to tell me what you're planning, before you get in quite so deep. I'm talking about the whole homeless masquerade.'

'Well, it's a step forwards if you accept that there will *be* a next time.' She smiled, mirrored his pose. 'Especially after it took you six months to even *try* getting in touch after we first met.'

He took a breath. 'As I said before, I really wasn't at all certain that you—'

But she reached out and took his face in her hands, cutting off whatever reasoning he'd been about to voice.

'Byron.'

'Yes?' Was that a hint of amusement lurking in those mossy brown eyes?

'Two things,' she said softly. 'Firstly – don't you dare leave it so long this time.'

She felt his face shift into a smile under her fingertips, even if his voice was grave. 'Yes, ma'am. And secondly?'

'Shut up and kiss me.'

A LETTER FROM ZOË

Dear Reader,

Thank you so much for choosing to join me in Blake and Byron's world in *The Girl in the Dark*. Although it's a standalone story, this is the second book in a series following the partnership between former con artist and former copper. If you enjoyed this novel and want to keep up to date with future instalments, just sign up at the following link. Your email address will never be shared and you can unsubscribe at any time.

www.bookouture.com/zoe-sharp

Setting this book among London's homeless population was an idea that grabbed me from the start. As I was writing this book, the UK cost of living crisis was really beginning to bite, with more and more ordinary people facing the possibility of losing the roof over their heads. And when you fall from the bottom rung of the ladder, it's a long way down.

Blake spent a large part of her youth living rough, and has not forgotten the hard lessons learned there. At the time, it seemed to her a better option than remaining under the controlling hand of her father. I wanted to leave the question open at the start of this story – what would make her go back onto the streets?

I do not believe homelessness is – as a former Home Secretary suggested – a 'lifestyle choice', but a last-resort position of constant discomfort, hunger and fear.

As for Byron, I wanted him to be a different sort of copper. Giving him the role of special investigator with the Independent Office for Police Conduct seemed a particularly prescient move. Public trust in the police has reached an all-time low, according to His Majesty's Chief Inspector of Constabulary. Every day seemed to bring another news item on police misconduct, corruption, or abuse of power.

Interwoven with these themes in my story is the central thread of the relationship between Blake and Byron. Both have traumatic pasts to overcome. Both are taking tentative steps towards one another. I'm as interested as my readers to see where they end up.

I do hope that you've enjoyed *The Girl in the Dark* and, if so, that you might leave a brief review. Just a few heartfelt sentences can make such a difference, and help new readers discover one of my books for the first time – be that Blake and Byron, the award-winning Charlie Fox series, the Lakes crime thrillers, standalones, or short stories.

I always love hearing from my readers. You can get in touch via my website, on my Facebook page, through Twitter/X, Instagram, or Goodreads.

Thank you again. I always think that a satisfied reader is a writer's best friend.

Zoë

KEEP IN TOUCH WITH ZOË

www.zoesharp.com

facebook.com/ZoeSharpAuthor
x.com/AuthorZoeSharp
instagram.com/authorzoesharp
goodreads.com/authorzoesharp

ACKNOWLEDGEMENTS

Angela Melling
Ayo Onatade
Brian Price
Celine Kelly
Charlie Lane
Chaz Lockett
Claire Rushbrook
Derek Harrison
Elizabeth Cook
Fran Renwick
Gill Lockett
Hannah Snetsinger
Jane Eastgate
Jess Readett
Jill Harrison
John Lawton
Lauren Finger
Lewis Hancock
Mandy Kullar
Nick Lockett
Noelle Holten
Peta Nightingale
Rhianna Louise
Ruth Tross
Sally Wall

Samantha Norman
Sarah Hardy
Sue Lord

PUBLISHING TEAM

Turning a manuscript into a book requires the efforts of many people. The publishing team at Bookouture would like to acknowledge everyone who contributed to this publication.

Commercial
Lauren Morrissette
Jil Thielen
Imogen Allport

Data and analysis
Mark Alder
Mohamed Bussuri

Cover design
Blacksheep

Editorial
Rhianna Louise
Nadia Michael

Copyeditor
Jane Eastgate

Proofreader
Claire Rushbrook

Marketing
Alex Crow
Melanie Price
Occy Carr
Cíara Rosney

Operations and distribution
Marina Valles
Stephanie Straub

Production
Hannah Snetsinger
Mandy Kullar
Jen Shannon

Publicity
Kim Nash
Noelle Holten
Myrto Kalavrezou
Jess Readett
Sarah Hardy

Rights and contracts
Peta Nightingale
Richard King
Saidah Graham

Milton Keynes UK
Ingram Content Group UK Ltd.
UKHW030952140324
439440UK00004B/165